79

Heaven-High
and
Hell-Deep

a novel by
Peggy Poe Stern

Moody Valley
Boone, North Carolina

Published by
Moody Valley
475 Church Hollow Road
Boone, N.C. 28607
moodyvalley@skybest.com

Cover painting by Peggy Poe Stern

Library of Congress Control Number: 2003115093

ISBN: 1-59513-055-1

Printed by Moody Valley

Printed in the United States of America

September 2006

Praise for the book, "Heaven-High and Hell-Deep"

"A good story with lots of local color. Laine is an interesting character with guts and temperament---we know her."

Nora Pervical author of
"Weathers of the Heart".

"Wow! As I read the manuscript, I could hear your voice telling the story. Practice reading out loud. When this book goes to print, you'll be giving a lot of readings."

Bill Kaiser,
President of the
High Country Writers

"You have great detail and believable characters."

Marian Coe, author of
"Eve's Mountain",
"Key to a Cottage" and
"Legacy".

"You're a good story teller. I'm hooked."

Maggie Bishop, author of
"Appalachian Paradise" and
"Emeralds in the snow".

"This is great! Your descriptions are so good. I love the story. I like the fact it is based on true life."

Joyce Blanton, Treasurer
High Country Writers

"I love this!!! Great Characters---very believable. I get so mad at Momma and Susie---makes me want to 'fight'! I'll buy this book as soon as it comes out!"

Jessica Pisano

"Great, great job on this!"

Stacie Kurtz

"Great! Your good use of vernaculars to tell the story reminds me of Mark Twain. This is excellent work. You're one of the top writers. Keep it going!"

Travis Roland

"Great! Really superior stuff."

Clete Jones

"It is unique and wonderful. Has very much the same flavor as "Gap Creek", by Robert Morgan and that's not bad."

B.J. Foster, author of
"Bayou Shadows"

"It is wonderful! Some of the description is the best I have ever read. Great sentences."

Lila Hopkins, author of
"Weave Me a Song",
"Talking Turkey and Eating Crow", and her upcoming novel, "The Golden Chord".

"This is awesome. It is so genuine that I feel like I'm there. The pacing and action and dialogue are dead-on. I'm really enjoying this. Keep it up!

Bruce Grooms

"Great Story. Perfect dialogue."

Mat Turner

Peggy Poe Stern's story of Laine in Heaven High and Hell Deep cost me a night's sleep. I could not put the book down. Laine is a young Scarlet O'Hara with soul. Her grit, her curiosity and her jaw-set determination honors the memory of every woman who ever baked a "pone" of cornbread here in the mountains.

> Grace Wakeman,
> Journalist and mother who
> knows what it takes to bake
> a "pone" of cornbread

Indelible characters – each and everyone. Compelling story with descriptions that put me in every scene. I couldn't put it down.

> Ree Strawser, author of
> "Long Gauge Dress"

"I really enjoyed reading this and didn't want to put it down. Laine is a superb heroine."

> Jan Luquire

"Great lines! Very powerful and true! Wow! This is REALLY good. All of it rings true of the mountain people. I know you've lived this."

> Rick Boyer, author of
> "Billingsgate Shoal",
> "The Man Who Whispered",
> "Daisy Ducks", and many
> other novels including
> The Doc Adams novels.

To David,

A man of fortitude,
A man of determination,
A man of courage,
A man of silence,
A father and a friend,
A perfect husband.

To Tonda, Marla, Trampas, Brandon, Amanda and Caleb. My six wonderful and encouraging children.

To Megan, Jessica, Michelle, Ashley, Alexis, Jacob and Mathew. The pride of a grandmother.

To Thomas Alexander, the first great-grandson.

To Lois, Glen, Shirley and Rick. My mother, father, sister and brother.

Special thanks to:

Terry Kay, author of 'Dances With The White Dog', whom told me "all words are the same. It's how you use them that will make the difference."

Dianne Graham, an instructor and friend that encouraged and gave help over and beyond.

The High Country Writers group in Boone, N.C. They stand beside you and lift you up when you fall.

Bruce Grooms who never gave up on me.

John Patrick McAfee who gave the right advice at the right time.

Rick Boyer, writer, instructor and friend.

Catherine Bare, Joyce Blanton, Danielle Bussome, Carolyn Howser, Lila Hopkins, Carole King, Joanne Nelson, Ree Strawser, Grace Wakeman, and Sharon King who suffered through reading and correcting drafts.

Jane Y. Wilson the best writer and friend a person could have.

Karen Hall, Executive Producer of 'Judging Amy,' who told me I am a talented writer and not wasting my time.

Chris Walker who read the manuscript and used the words "very good, excellent actually."

And Thank you God, I finally got one finished.

Chapter 1

I squatted in the garden picking half-runner beans. Twenty-two quarts, a full run, was boiling nicely in the copper canner over the open fire. Dad had laid up three walls of rock making a canning pit the right size to place the canner on top of metal bars. Dad taught me how to build a hot fire and keep wood fed in it for three hours for each canning. That way the heat could be kept out of the house. Dad said that was the way his own Momma had done it.

I had eighteen quarts of broke beans sitting on the porch and needed four more quarts for the second run. The August sun was shining down hot, making me feel grumpy and overworked. I grumbled to myself that Momma and Susie could have helped some, but Momma claimed to be having one of her spells.

Susie was tending to Momma and watching Joey in the cool shade inside the house while I'm stuck in the sun toiling over a hot fire.

Susie was older and bigger than me but that doesn't make any never mind when it came to work. I got more than my share. Susie had it easy. Momma claimed Susie took back after her and was sickly. I never saw anything sickly about Susie. I saw spoiled and petted but not sickly. I saw long slender hands and long fingers with filed nails, hair blonde as Momma's and creamy white skin without a hint of the sun's hated tan. Momma said tan face and hands were a sign of poor white trash. If that was true, there weren't many women in our mountain hollow that weren't poor white trash, me included.

Joey was my sweet little brother, the much-adored male child in the family. Joey was spoilt worse than Susie. He was only three years old and as fat as a pat of butter with pink cheeks and chubby legs that could run like a blue streak.

I saw his little face, all crunched up and red the day he was born. "He's ugly," Susie had said. But to me, he was the most beautiful thing I had ever laid my eyes on. To this day, Dad reminded me he was not a baby doll for me to cuddle.

I stood, picked up my hamper of beans, rested it on my hip and started out the row when I heard Joey cry. It brought a cold knot to my chest. Then I heard Susie scream.

"No! Joey! Laine, help!"

I dropped my hamper and took off at a run. I jumped rows of beans and knocked over a stake of tomatoes then jumped the garden fence. I felt my skirt catch on wire and rip, but I didn't slow down. I rounded the corner of the house and pure terror put extra speed in my legs. Joey was rolling on the ground in front of the bee gums. Bees covered his body as thick as maggots working rancid meat. I could see bees covering Joey's little head and others swarming around his body.

There seemed to be miles between Joey and me as his cries tore at my soul. My heart was near bursting knowing what was happening to Joey.

I leaped the creek and clawed up the bank on my hands and knees. I grabbed his writhing body up off the ground and tumbled backward toward the creek. I half jumped and half fell into the shallow water.

His chubby hands were trying to rake the bees off his head and face. I pushed Joey in the water face and all. I grabbed handfuls of sand and dirt and scrubbed at the bees still clinging to him. Honeybees lit on my arms and doubled up their bodies as they stung. I felt them stinging my back and tangling in my hair but I paid them no mind.

Suddenly, Dad grabbed the back of my dress and lifted me out of the water with one hand while grabbing Joey with the other.

"Get to the house and outta them clothes. They're full of bees!"

Susie stood on the porch screaming. Momma leaned against the door with one hand on her heart and the other over her mouth. They were frozen to the spot as they watched.

They parted to let us inside, watching as Dad laid Joey on the floor and ripped off his clothes, mashing any bees he came to.

"Hush, hush," Dad's voice tried to soothe Joey. "I've got you now. They won't hurt you no more."

I stripped out of my clothes as I hurried into the adjoining bedroom, trying to mash the bees in my hair with the material of my dress. My entire body was burning from stings, but I tried to pay the pain no mind. I pulled my only other dress on and rushed back to Dad and Joey. Fear was exploding in my chest. I had seen hundreds of bees covering my brother and knew what that many bees could do.

Dad had Joey's body stripped naked and laid out on the linoleum rolling him from side to side looking for bees. His plump little body looked like fire-coals had burned him.

"He'll need doctorin bad," Dad said, as I kneeled on the floor.

Joey's face was starting to swell something awful. His cries turned into sobs as Dad gently raked at some of the dirt I had rubbed in Joey's blonde hair.

I heard Momma collapse on the couch and whimper louder than Joey. She sounded like an animal wild with fear and keening out of control. Momma was as white as clabbered milk. Her keening took on a higher pitch. I looked at Susie, wide-eyed and breathless, slumped on the floor beside Momma. Tears ran down Susie's cheeks. All either of them had to do was look at Joey's swelling head to know he was bad off.

"I'll have to go fetch the doctor." There was desperation in Dad's softly spoken words. "I'll ride the mule to make it faster."

"Take Joey with you," Susie sobbed.

Dad looked at Joey and shook his head slow.

"The ride would hurt him more'n it would help." He turned toward me. "Laine, go piss in a pan. Dip rags in it and lay them on the stings. Ammonia helps draw out the pain of stings some."

Dad stood as I gathered Joey in my arms. "I'll send Granny Mable to help," he said.

Dad's body was jerking as he went out the front door. A honeybee, hunched up and stinging, was on the back of his neck, but he didn't seem to feel it.

"Bring me the pot," I told Susie as I carried Joey to Momma's bedroom and laid him down on her bed.

His head was almost twice its normal size, and his face no longer looked human. Skin had swollen over his eye sockets until only the tips of his eyelashes could be seen. His lips had turned inside out and his mouth was open as he struggled to breathe. Joey's fingers had swollen to the size of pickling cucumbers.

Susie came to me, clutching the chamber pot to her chest. She stared at Joey.

"It weren't my fault," she moaned. " I didn't know he had snuck outta the house till I heard him cry."

"Nobody's blamin you." I grabbed the pot from her hands and set it down on the floor. I jerked up my dress and squatted over the pot, and listened to the trickle of piss.

"You're actually gonna put that on him?"

"Dad said it would help him, and I'll do anything to ease the pain he's sufferin."

Susie put her hands to her eyes and ran back to Momma. I looked through the bedroom door at them huddled together on the sofa. They could cling to each other and do what they could to help ease their sorrow. I didn't have time to give them any comfort. I was going to save Joey.

"Please God," I prayed. "Help me ease his pain. Help me keep him alive!"

"He's dyin," I heard Momma moan. "My boy's dyin. Oh God! I can't live and bear it. Why couldn't it have been anybody but my little Joey? My baby boy! My precious baby boy!"

I ripped up the skirt of my discarded, torn dress and dipped it in the pot, squeezed it lightly, then placed the strips on Joey until I had his entire head, face and body covered. I tried to wrap his hands, but he flung them as though he were still fighting the bees. I lifted the chamber pot onto the edge of the bed and stuck his little hands into what was left of the piss.

I heard Momma get up off the couch and drag her stumbling feet to the bedroom. She came up behind me and looked down on Joey.

"You've wrapped him in rags!" she sniffed.

Dad said to. I'm trying to draw some of the pain out."

"Onions. Lightly cooked onions are good at drawin out poisons," she whispered through trembling lips.

Then go cook some! Why didn't you jump off the porch and help him? I wanted to say. Instead I said, "Sit with him until I cut up onions and cook them."

"I can't bear to look on my baby." Tears ran down her cheeks. "I'm nigh onto passin out now."

She turned and rushed back to the couch. I heard the broken words of Susie as she tried to soothe Momma. I wanted to yell at them to cut up the onions and bring me Dad's chewing tobacco. Any fool knew tobacco was good for stings. I also knew all the crying and squalling in the world would not help Joey. I propped pillows on each side of Joey's twisting body to keep him from rolling off the bed and ran to the kitchen. I sliced onions, skin and all, into a frying pan then carried the pan out to my canning fire. I put several more pieces of wood in the fire and held the pan over the heat until the onions cooked clear. I took the pan back to the bedroom.

His face was starting to get a tinge of blue and there was a rattling sound as he tried to breathe. Joey's feet and hands hardly moved. I put the pan on the floor and turned Joey into different positions trying to make him breathe easier. Nothing helped.

"Susie!" I yelled. "Come here! Help me raise him up."

Momma's cries became louder as Susie left her. We lifted Joey into a sitting position, but he continued his struggle for breath through grotesque lips. His tongue, twice its normal size, stuck out of his mouth.

"Bring me a spoon," I told Susie. "He's choking on his tongue."

She brought the spoon. I tried to press his tongue down as Susie held onto Joey, but it did no good. His breathing was labored and shallow, turning his skin bluer by the minute.

"Do something, Laine," Susie demanded.

"Lay him flat."

We laid him flat on his back and I climbed on the bed beside him. I put my mouth over his and tried to force my breath in his mouth. I pinched his nose closed and tried again. It seemed to help a little so I continued to force my breath into his mouth.

I don't know how long I tried to breathe for Joey. It could have been only a few minutes or it could have been an hour before I felt a hand on my back.

"Stop, child," a gentle voice said. "You can't do no more now."

I raised my head and looked at the face of Granny Mable. She lived alone in a small house down the road next to the mill. She served as mid-wife and passed out whatever medicine she could to people in need. Dad had sent her.

"Help Joey! He can't breathe," I said as I grabbed the hand that touched my back.

"I know child. Come now. Come on into the front room. There's no more abody can do."

"No!" I screamed at her and flung away her hand I had been gripping. "I'll breathe for him." I pressed my mouth on Joey's again and tried to breathe harder into him. I wouldn't give up! I wouldn't let him die! He was my brother!

"It's no use child. He's done passed over. Your breathin won't help him. Nothing can help now. It's done too late."

I heard her words but I had no intention of listening to them. I was strong and I was determined, and I would not let Joey die!

"Laine, stop this. Your pa'll be back soon with Doc Robinson."

I wouldn't stop.

Granny Mable sighed, knelt down beside the bed and began to pray.

I tried to breathe for Joey until I was beyond exhaustion. Finally, I collapsed on the bed, drew Joey to my breast and cried. I heard Granny Mable get up and go into the front room, leaving me alone with Joey.

Once Dad and the doctor arrived, I left Joey with them and went outside. I took the cans of beans out of the canner and sat them on the grass. I put more split firewood on the fire, and filled my eighteen cans of beans with water and screwed on the lids. My canning would be four quarts shy of a full run.

The doctor walked out of the house to where I was.

"Elaine?" Doc Robinson called my name.

He was old and white and wrinkled. He had such a sad smile on his face. I felt sorry for him as he came closer to me and reached out his hand to cup my chin. He lifted my face and observed me closely.

"You got a lot of stings," he told me gently.

"I'm all right." I turned away from his hand.

He nodded but did not seem to believe my words as he looked at the canning of beans. "You're helping your Momma finish the canning?"

"I do the cannin, Momma don't."

He took a deep breath of air and looked along the little creek where the garden was.

"Where were you when Joey got in the bees?"

I told him, and wished he would go away and leave me alone. He didn't get here in time to save Joey, and I didn't want him hanging around now after it was too late.

"Who was watching the boy?"

"Susie, I reckon. Momma was having another of her spells and couldn't help with the beans or Joey."

"How come you got to the boy before any of the others? Where was your father?"

I gave him a look I hoped told him what I was thinking. I didn't like him referring to my baby brother as 'the boy'.

It was time for him to leave. I wanted to be alone with my hurting, but I answered him anyway.

"I'm quicker," I told him. "Dad was patchin the wagon at the barn." Anger was beginning to burn in me hot as the fire under my canner.

"How old are you?" he persisted.

"Fourteen." I looked at his wrinkled face. "How old are you?"

"Older than I thought I would ever get."

"Joey won't get that old," I told him and gritted my teeth together.

One gray eyebrow lifted and the sad smile faded until his face sagged. "I couldn't have saved Joey if I had been here when he got stung. A full-grown man couldn't survive the number of stings he got. To be honest with you, Elaine, I'm concerned about the stings you got. You're a small boned girl and you're not carrying much weight on your body."

"I didn't get enough to hurt me none. You can't help me no more'n you can help Joey."

He looked at my face for several moments, then he looked at the beans sitting on the grass and the ones I had just put on to cook. He looked at the fire I had filled with logs to burn long and split wood to burn hot.

"I gave your mother and sister something to calm them down a bit. I had in mind you might need something, too."

I looked him in the eyes, hard. "I don't reckon you've got a thing in that black bag of yourn that would help me."

He studied my face again then said, "Somebody has to do the canning." Turned and walked away leaving me standing near enough the fire to feel the heat burning on the back of my legs.

Susie came out the kitchen door and moved slowly across the porch. She stopped and clutched the porch post.

"Laine, bring Momma in some cold spring water."

I watched her turn and walk awkwardly back into the house. The doctor's medicine was working on her.

When I carried Momma her glass of water, she was asleep on one end of the sofa and Susie was asleep on the other end. Dad was sitting on the bed beside Joey's dead body. His head hung down and his hands were over his face. His shoulders trembled. I knew he was crying without making one single sound. I drank the water.

The neighbors came to help with the death of Joey. Some folks didn't even know us but heard about the awful way Joey died. When old people die, it seems a matter of course, but when a three-year-old boy is stung to death by honeybees, it's worth gathering together and talking about. Nobody in their right mind would want to miss seeing what that poor baby looked like after that many honeybees stung him to death.

A lot of the women came walking on foot, others by wagon load, to help out. Several of them took the task of scrubbing the entire house clean. They washed floors, and walls, and ceilings. They had the windows shining and the lace curtains washed, starched, stretched on a nail rack, dried and rehung. The Warm Morning cook stove had been rubbed until the enamel glowed, and the front room heating stove had been polished with stove black. There wasn't a towel or sheet in the house that escaped being washed and put back in its proper place. Even the bedclothes had been washed and aired.

The men built a small coffin and dug a small grave. They brought jugs of moonshine and hid them in the hayloft for Dad. "A bit of numbin," they said. Dad helped build the coffin and dig the grave. Then he stood in silence and watched the bee gums. I figured he might bust them up but he never did, just watched them.

After the cleaning was done, the women had the men bring the coffin in the front room. They washed Joey from head to foot and combed his blonde curls about his face until he was prettier than any girl even though the swelling hadn't gone away completely. Somebody brought an almost new suit of clothes and put it on Joey, then laid him in the coffin on a blue blanket.

Once fixing Joey was done, the women began bringing in food. They had everything from deer meat to foods I had never seen before. There was food filling the entire kitchen. I kept thinking how much Joey would have liked to eat all those sweet pies and cakes. He sure did love pies, but he would never eat another bite. The very thought made me head for the back door, but Momma's trembling voice stopped me.

"Laine honey, come on in here a minute," she moaned in a weak voice.

I got plumb shaky when Momma called me honey. It wasn't natural coming from Momma. I took unwilling steps from the kitchen to where Momma sat on the sagging couch beside the preacher. She dabbed at her eyes with the damp handkerchief she had twisted into a hard knot in her hand. She sniffed a time or two, shook the handkerchief out, and then blew her nose into the handkerchief.

"Laine, honey, fix the preacher some fresh coffee and cut him a big piece of that cherry pie. No need for him to go hungry while we make the…the… arrangements."

New tears flowed from Momma's eyes. She dabbed and sniffed.

"Won't you have a bite with me, Mrs. Elder?" the preacher asked as he reached out his hand and patted Momma on her shoulder in a comforting gesture.

"No," Momma moaned feebly. "I've not been able to put a bite of food in my mouth since...since..."

"It's all right," the preacher soothed. "We understand."

"You can bring Susie some, Laine." Momma gave her eyes a final dab and made a visible effort to control her tears. "She's suffering so bad."

Susie was sitting hunched up in a chair trying not to look at Joey's coffin or the preacher. She mostly stared at her hands and shifted her feet back and forth. Momma insisted earlier that Susie stay beside her while she and the preacher made Joey's final arrangements. All I wanted to do was slip out of the house and get away.

I left the front room and put a fresh pot of coffee on the stove to perk. I stuck stove wood in the firebox to perk the coffee fast. Good coffee needs to perk slow.

When I carried the two saucers of pie into the front room, Momma was bent over Joey. Her fingers touched his little face in a slow, longing manner.

"Oh Lord! I can't see him put in the ground tomorrow. I have to keep him with me a while longer. Oh, dear God! Such a dark hole! I just can't live and bear it!"

"It's best to let him go," the preacher said as he put his arm around her shoulder. "His spirit has left this world and gone to the next one. Let his body go too. He's settin on the right-hand side of God right now. He's shoutin with joy and singin with the angels. He's playin in streets gold."

"No! Not tomorrow. Not tomorrow," Momma cried.

The preacher tugged on Momma in an effort to get her back to the couch. I saw her body go rigid. Momma had no intention of being moved away from the little coffin where her precious baby boy lay. The preacher had no intention of letting her stay beside her baby.

I walked over to them and held out the saucer of pie toward the preacher.

"Here," I said. "Take this and I'll get your coffee."

He looked at me and took the saucer of pie. I went to Susie and handed her the other saucer. The preacher left Momma crying at the coffin and went to sit on the couch to eat his pie. I took him coffee. He sat the saucer of half-eaten pie in his lap, took the coffee, and grabbed my hand. His voice took on a sorrowful, cajoling tone.

"You know you have to help your Momma get through this. You've got to make her see that God's will's been done. He had a reason for takin that baby. God always knows what's best."

I looked into his eyes and felt my lips draw back from my teeth. "If God let them bees kill Joey, I'll never bend a knee to that son of a bitch."

I saw unbelieving shock on the preacher's face as I turned and walked out of the room and out the kitchen door.

God having a reason for bees killing a baby. Joey playing in streets of gold. My ass!

I did the things that had to be done. Then I climbed the high hill and sat on the knob under a hickory tree and watched the moon rise in the sky. By this time tomorrow, my sweet little brother would be six feet under ground, unless Momma had her way.

I could see our house down in the valley. People had started coming for Joey's wake. I knew Momma would want me to help out, but I just couldn't make myself do it. I thought of serving food and washing dishes while folks talked, prayed and cried. No, I couldn't do it, not right yet.

I curled up on the ground and listened to the calls of katydids and whippoorwills as night came on. The night air smelled sweet as the gentle wind blew over my body.

When I opened my eyes, it was morning. The sky was beginning to light up and birds were starting to sing. I stood up and stretched myself free of stiffness. I brushed the leaves off my clothes and headed down the hill toward home.

Women were cooking breakfast while the men were doing up the work. There wasn't much left for me to do, so I wasted no time getting back outside. I went into the wood shed, sat down on a pile of wood and just sat there until I got hungry enough to go inside and hunt some food.

The women were moving about in a hushed way, their faces tired and drawn from the night's vigil of respecting the dead.

One woman lifted her apron and dabbed at her eyes as she looked around the kitchen door into the bedroom where Momma was still sleeping.

"Poor Mert. I'm glad she took some of the medicine the doctor left her."

"I can understand her grief. It would rip my heart out to see dirt shoveled over my baby."

"Lord! How she'll live and stand it is more'n I know. It's more'n a mother was meant to bear up under. It was a blessin the doctor left medicine to make her sleep."

"She'll have to put her trust in God, knowin it's meant to be," another woman said.

"God's will, not mine, be done."

"That baby has to be buried today. Things rot quick in the hot part of August."

"Hush. It'd make her worse thinkin of her baby rotting."

"It'll happen. They'll have to keep her doped up till after the funeral."

"Dear Lord in heaven! Let's pray she'll come to herself and let that baby be buried without a fuss."

Several women wiped their eyes with apron tails.

I stuck my head through the door and saw Susie sleeping on the couch. I grabbed two biscuits and two slices of fried ham off the table, and I took out the door. I'd hide out till they were all gone if I could.

Chapter 2

After Joey's funeral, things went down hill. Momma took to her bed with determination while Susie carried her plates of food and begged her to get up. Momma ate but refused to get out of bed. She lay there dabbing at her eyes with a hanky. When I came around, she looked at me with strange eyes. Eyes that glared and accused.

Women from church came to visit her almost every day and brought her teas and tempting things to eat. They cosseted her like she was a child in need of comfort.

The preacher stopped by often to talk to her.

"God had his reason for takin that baby. You know he's gone to a better place than here on this earth. He'll never suffer again. There's no bees in heaven." I heard the preacher telling Momma as I peeped into the front room.

"Oh Lord!" Momma moaned and clutched both hands in her hair. "I aim to die and go be with him!"

"Now sister Mert. There's no need takin on like this. You've got to believe in God's wisdom." I heard him say as I carried in stove wood to build a fire and start supper. I laid the firewood on the stove and went back out the door.

The preacher could yak on about the wisdom of God, but I had no intention of listening. The preacher said God had a reason to take Joey. Bullshit! Joey died because Susie let him get in the bee gums.

Preachers opened their mouths and let whatever flow out that sounded good at the time. He didn't know where Joey

15

had gone. Heaven? Hell? Just what did the preacher know that God kept secret from other folks?

I crossed the dirt road to the barn. I could hide there until the preacher left.

Dad was sitting in the corncrib with a bent, dirty, peck bucket between his knees. His big hands held an ear of corn and his thumbs shelled grains into the bucket. I'd never seen Dad doing that before.

"I come to feed the chickens," I told Dad.

"Thought I'd shell you up some corn to last a day or two," Dad said.

Dad's face looked a little red. I figured he'd been into that numbin medicine the men had hid in the loft. I didn't blame him none. I might crawl up there in the loft and try a swallow of that stuff myself if I didn't have so much work to get done. I suspected I'd fall down after a mouthful of liquor and break a leg. I'd seen it stagger Dad before.

"Guess I'll have to take milk and eggs to the store to sell soon," Dad said.

I heard the dread in his voice. He hadn't been off the place since Joey died. I knew he dreaded facing people. Reckon Dad never did take much towards words and sympathy. He once told me that sympathy was something that came out of folk's mouths to make them feel better when they were actually thinking, 'Thank God it happened to them instead of me.'

"I'm gettin several dozen eggs a day, and Eula likes em to be fresh. I can take em in," I offered, but I didn't want to.

I would have to hitch the mule to the wagon. That confounded mule was the meanest beast alive. He tried to bite me whenever he got close unless I had a stick in my hand. I broke the hoe handle over his nose for biting me once. I still had tooth marks on my shoulder, a lighter shade than my skin.

"I'll go tomorrow mornin." Dad watched his own thumb move on the corncob. "You can go with me."

"Well."

I went to feed the chickens. There wasn't one time every three months I went with Dad to the store. I didn't think I wanted to go this time, but I would.

I crawled out of bed the next morning at four-thirty instead of five o'clock. I had to get the work done up early if I was going in with Dad. It took me two hours to milk six cows and get the milk strained and in the springhouse.

The store bought nearly all the butter, buttermilk, and sweet milk, and took all the eggs the hens laid. The store bought hams, but mostly folks about bought our live pigs. I never got any money from things sold. Momma put it all toward living. She always wanted me to add another milk cow, more chickens, or extra sow to raise pigs from.

Dad didn't have time to help much with livestock. He hired out to work at the sawmill. He would go back soon.

I might have managed more stock in the summer time. When school was in, I had a hard time getting everything done before leaving for school. I loved going to school and didn't want to miss. My teacher told me a little learning could go a long ways.

Dad told me once to ignore Mamma's wants and complaints as much as I could. He said Momma had ways and wants just a little different than some folks.

I stopped on the back porch before I got my milk buckets off the pegs and looked around. The morning air was soft with a bit of cold. It wouldn't be long till frost.

The maple trees were showing a little color.

Joey would have liked to see the pretty colored leaves instead of rotting in the ground.

Bitterness burned in me at Susie letting him get killed.

I gave my buckets a swing and stepped off the porch into the crisp blackness of morning.

The cows were lying together on the sheltered side of the barn chewing their cud. They glanced toward me as though I was nothing but a bird or rat.

The cows were all good milkers. I had two Holstein, two Guernseys and two Jerseys. One of the Jerseys was my pet. I had raised her on a bottle because her momma got milk fever and died.

Dad butchered her momma. I canned her. Dad said, "Waste not want not."

Dad said if I could keep the calf alive, I could have her as my own. I named her Pet. She had her first calf in the spring. She was mine, but it didn't do me any good. Momma still got the money for the calf, milk and butter. Somehow it just didn't seem right in my mind.

I went where Pet lay and kicked her with my bare toe. She slowly rose up, hind feet first, and started toward the barn. I stood in the spot where her body heat was left in the ground.

I stood there, warming my toes, watching the dawn break. Slowly, light squeezed out of the darkness and painted my world with pastel colors. Trees showed light green along the broken down fence line. The drooping barn turned silver. The sky became light blue with feathery clouds hanging low.

My heart ached with the beauty.

It also ached with anger as I stood there watching daylight take away the darkness. Momma and Susie ought to be out here helping me instead of lying in the warm bed asleep. They expected me to do all the work then cook for them. Well, this morning I wouldn't do it. I'd give Dad a biscuit with jelly on it. They could starve for all I cared.

I watched Pet go over to the Holstein cow, lay her chin across her back and mount her. The Holstein sidestepped from under her and tried to mount Pet. Bullshit! Just what I needed today, a bullin cow wanting to be bred.

I hung my buckets on nails in the barn hall and carried the mule some corn before I started milking. He would be through eating when Dad came to hitch him to the wagon.

I was stripping my last cow when Dad came into the barn.

"You're milkin early," he said in his gentle voice.

"Yeah, figured we ought to start early. Pet's bullin. I'll take her over the hill when we get back."

Dad went to the stall and looked in at the mule.

"I been thinkin it hain't right for you to be leadin cows to the bull. Don't hardly seem a fittin thing for a girl to do."

It was a good thing my milk bucket was sitting on the ground between my knees, if I had been standing up with it in my hand, I'd probably have dropped it right there in the dirt. I had been taking the cows to the bull for the past three years. What had come over Dad?

It wasn't a hard thing for me to do. I tied a rope around the cow's neck and took off. Sometimes I dragged the cow and sometimes the cow dragged me. The older cows seemed to know where I was taking them and hurried. Cows only stood for the bull a few hours. I had to be fast or I would have to wait until they bulled again. I figured some things needed to be gotten done and over with in a hurry.

Pete Jones had a fine Jersey bull in a field next to ours. If I took down two rails on the fence, the bull would jump the other two. I didn't figure we owed anything for the service if the bull jumped into Dad's field to breed our cows.

Most of the time I had a little trouble getting the bull back over the fence, but I managed.

Since Dad never asked me how I got the cows bred, why was he bringing it up now? Had to be Joey dying and the preacher coming by.

Religion stuff.

I wouldn't pay Dad any mind. I finished stripping my cow dry and stood up with my bucket.

"I'll get this strained then feed the hogs. I think that old black sow is fixin to drop pigs. She's all pooched out, and her teats are hangin down."

"You didn't let the boar with her did you?" Dad got the harness for the mule off the wall. "Don't like em to have pigs this late in the fall of the year."

"Remember that old boar busted the fence down and got with em?"

"Better fix her a place then."

I saw dad look up toward the loft and knew what he was thinking about. That liquor was calling him even before he had a bite of breakfast in his belly. I went out of the barn knowing Dad would be up in the loft as soon as the door closed.

The sun was well up in the sky by the time we got to the store. Dad had swallowed too much liquor and the mule knew it. Dad was not in good control. He let that darned mule act up all the way. I wanted to get off the wagon and take a stick to the mule and Dad both, but I didn't say a word. If it had been in the middle of the day, the butter would have melted but mornings were cool enough. So, I stayed quiet and we finally got there.

The store was a large building. It was built square with a front porch and half a dozen steps from the ground to the porch. The store had been painted white a long time past. The steps and porch had never been painted.

Mrs. Eula's husband died a few years back from a bad heart and left her with the store and two sons. The last time I came to the store with Dad, I saw her younger boy looking me over. His body made me think of a bowl of dough before it had been rolled out to make biscuits. I didn't look back.

Mrs. Eula was beside herself when she saw us. She bustled about like a guinea hen in her excitement and let her loose, false teeth snap up and down as she talked. Reckon she had folks wanting milk, butter, and eggs right bad if she was this excited to see us. I knew Mrs. Eula didn't want to miss a chance to make a copper.

"God bless you," she said to Dad. "I hope your sorrow's easin some. If there's 'ary thing I can do to help, let me know."

I thought about saying she could add another copper or two to what she paid us, but I didn't. I stood beside Dad and watched him down his head and look at his worn boots like he just didn't know how to handle sympathy.

"Thank ye, Ma'am," he mumbled.

It was then I noticed a man standing in the shadows at the back of the store. He was watching Dad and me real close. My eyes met his and I looked away, but not before I had a good look at him. He was a fine looking man, but old enough to have a wife and a house full of younguns.

He wore a new hat pulled low over brown hair. His face was tanned like all mountain men, and his eyes were a grass green. I'd never seen eyes that color. I looked back at him for a closer look. This time he grinned and touched the brim of his hat with one finger. I nodded my head but did not grin back.

He was a big raw-boned man that appeared strong enough to carry our mule by himself. He was right good looking. Then I changed my opinion to mighty good-looking. I turned my back on him and watched Mrs. Eula count out money into Dad's hand. Momma must not have given him orders to buy stuff for he didn't get a thing.

"Be sure to come back the end of the week," Mrs. Eula was saying. "Folks missed your fresh produce."

And you missed the money. I thought but didn't say anything. Dad nodded his head and mumbled, then turned around and walked out of the store.

Dad was a tall man with a slender build that walked hunched over. I noticed his shoulders seemed to stoop more than normal, and his head was hanging lower. I wanted to put my arm around him.

"Ouch!" I said to myself. I stubbed my toe on one of the porch planks and felt a splinter stick in. I sat down right there in front of the door to pick it out.

"Who's that?" The deep voice of the man asked Mrs. Eula.

"That's Wesley Elder and his least girl, Elaine. You've heard about him I'm sure. It was his boy that got stung to death by honeybees some days back."

"Yeah, I do recall hearing that. How old is she?"

"The girl? Around fifteen I guess. He's lucky he's got her. Never was a harder workin girl. If the rest of the family worked like her, they'd be the richest folks in a hundred miles. I tell you, it'll be a lucky young man what marries her."

"They live far from here?"

"Not far unless you're draggin a broken down wagon with a mule too old to stand up. They sell pigs and cured hams and about anything else the old man and girl can grow. The girl mainly does the work. The old man ball hoots timber at the sawmill."

I eased off the porch and got in the wagon with Dad. I'd never heard anybody speak about me before, and I didn't know what to make of it. I had always thought I did a lot of work around the house, but I never figured anyone else thought that too. For the first time ever I looked at our wagon and tried to see it like other people might.

I saw the wagon was worn and split with age. Parts of the planks had worn away with use and been replaced with odd sized pieces of wood nailed on crooked. The wheels wobbled and bounced about enough to churn butter. A body could hear the creaks and groans of the wagon a long time before we arrived.

"Dad, is our mule old?"

"Pretty old."

"How old?"

"Don't rightly know. Got him when your Maw and I were first married. Mules live to get old and mean," Dad said gently as he looked at the hind end of the mule.

"He's mean cause he's old?"

"Old and smart," Dad said as he pushed his cap back on his head. The liquor was wearing off and he looked the worse for it. "Mule steps in a hole once, he'll never do it twice. He remembers that hole. Horse will step in it over and over again. Just won't learn."

We rode on in silence beneath the warm sun for a while. Dad never said a word and the mule was behaving.

We passed two houses. I looked them over carefully.

One belonged to Abraham Miller. It set way back from the road on a rise overlooking a portion of his farm. It was such a pretty, comfortable looking place I couldn't help but stare at it as we drove by.

I wondered what it would be like to live there?

In my mind I saw soft, feather tick beds with store bought white sheets with somebody hired to bring me breakfast while I lay in bed. My hands were white and soft from lack of work and my face was milk white and pretty.

Made me think of Susie.

I turned my eyes from the white house with a feeling of dislike. I didn't want to lie in bed and be petted. I was strong and I was healthy. A body wasn't meant to set on their hind end and do nothing all day long.

Reckon I wasn't intended to live in a fancy white house. Reckon I'd always be Wesley Elder's least girl, the one that worked hard.

The second house I saw made anger boil in my gut. I wanted to stop the wagon, run up to that place and shake the living daylights out of somebody. That house wasn't near as good as our barn and slightly better than the hog pen.

Trash was cast all over the dirt packed yard. Chickens were scratching everywhere among piles of rags and rusted tin.

A young girl, near about ten years old, was sitting on what was supposed to be a porch but was more like warped planks laid next to each other. Her face was dirty and her blonde hair was a patchy mess of tangles. Her head hung down as though like she was crying. An old woman came out of the house and grabbed the girl by the arm. She yanked her to her feet, shaking her by her slender arm, then dragged her into the house.

"Some folks don't know no better'n that," Dad said. "Them's the Munsons, you know. No proper raisin."

I knew of the Munsons all right. Every kid around had heard, "Don't act like that or folks'll think you're a Munson."

It wasn't like we didn't pass those two houses every time we went to the store. I wanted to put them out of my mind and not think about them again. Instead, I questioned Dad.

"Dad? What makes the difference in the Millers and the Munsons?"

Dad was silent for a few minutes as he pushed his cap further back on his head and thought. I watched his lips twitch to the side and the wrinkles come to his forehead which told me he was in deep thought.

"I've wondered that very same question over and over in my head. I reckon there's more reasons than one. I've heard the Munsons were well-off folks back before my great granddaddy's time."

I watched him take a deep breath like he was going to tell me a long tale.

"They say it came from marryin up with a crazy woman. Heard one of the Munson men married up with a woman what didn't have the brains of a chicken. They said she was as pretty as a picture. She had milk white skin and yellar hair. Her eyes were as blue as the July sky. From the first time that Munson man sat eyes on her, he had to have her. There weren't nothing nobody could do about it. He married her. They had a whole bunch of children, every one of them as crazy as their momma. Why, they was so crazy no body with any mind at all would marry one of em. So, they married up with each other. Seems they went down hill from there."

He shook his head and gave a long look at the Munson place before we went around the bend out of sight.

"Folks around here won't have much to do with em. Nobody wants to marry one. That leaves em breedin with each other like a pack of dogs. "

I was surprised at what Dad said. He'd never talked to me about such a thing before.

"Folks and the church tried to help em out ever since I can remember, but there's no help. Reckon time will take care of em one way or another."

"Dad, what makes the Millers have what they have?"

"Lots of hard work and education. I always wanted me an education."

I gave Dad a close look. I'd never heard him say a thing like that before.

"Went to school long enough to read and write, then my Daddy died. I was the oldest of eleven kids. Had to help feed and raise the lot."

A sad look came to his face.

"Didn't think of a life of my own until they all left home and my momma died."

For the first time I realized he was a lot older than Momma. I just thought he naturally walked bent over and moved slow, but it wasn't natural at all. He was an old man. The hair under his cap was gray with age, not white in color.

"How old were you when you married Momma?"

"Let's see now. I reckon I was about forty-two years old, and your Momma was fifteen at the time."

Twenty-seven years! Dad was twenty-seven years older than Momma. Maybe that was why Dad was quiet and let Momma boss him around all the time. Dad was just too old to make her mind him.

"Maybe a Miller should marry a Munson."

Dad shook his head. "Don't hardly work that way. One good man can't make up for a crazy woman. It'll still run in the blood. Babies might come out crazy just the same. I've heard it takes seven generations of breedin to purify bad blood out of a body."

I was silent for a few minutes while I thought over what Dad had just told me. It made me worry what could happen to people. It made me worry about what could happen to me. "Does Momma have any crazy blood in her?"

Dad lifted his head and chuckled, showing his tobacco stained teeth. His brown eyes danced beneath the brim of his cap. He shook his head, glanced at my face, then back at the mule's rump.

"Oh no-o! Your Momma is as smart as smart ever comes. That mind of her'n works day and night. It's even goin in her sleep, I think. Hain't nobody in this valley what could out think your Momma."

"She won't work," I said the words before I could stop myself, but Dad didn't seem to take offense.

Instead, he lifted his head and roared with laughter. After his bout of laughter, Dad got himself under control and spoke.

"She don't want to."

Chapter 3

It was dinner time when we got home from the store. I went inside to fix us a bite to eat while Dad unhitched the mule and turned him in the field. I looked in the bedroom to see that Momma was sitting up in bed with Susie combing her hair. Momma loved to have somebody comb her hair, and Susie loved to comb it.

The sight irritated me. I thought the least they could have done was built a fire in the cook stove so I could get dinner cooked quicker. I built the fire, then peeled the potatoes, and put them on to cook. I mixed up cornbread and put it in the oven. Then I moved the pot of pinto beans to the hot part of the stove so they could warm up. This was dinner along with plenty of milk, butter, jam, molasses, tomatoes and onions.

After we ate, I took a hemp rope out of the barn and tied it around Pet's neck. I led her out of the pasture and headed off through the woods. I hoped to be back in about three hours. Depending if Pet behaved herself and the bull was in the woods at the top of the hill.

During the heat of the day, the cattle would usually head for the hill in the deep shade of the woods to escape the flies. With luck, they would still be there.

Pet didn't want to go along peaceably. She tried to pull loose from me and go back to the other cows. I finally had to break a switch off a tree and swarp her on the flanks.

After we crossed the creek and started up the hill toward the Billy Field, Pet started to sniff the air and bawl as she got wind of the bull. Her big bovine eyes got bigger and she tried to take off in a run. I yanked on her rope sharp and brought her under control, although she bawled and tried to pull me along faster than I could walk.

I should have seen that fist size rock lying there in plain open sight, but I didn't. My toe hit the rock so hard it rolled out of the ground and sent pain all the way up my leg.

Pet knew I was disadvantaged. She lunged forward and took off at a run. I hung onto the rope long enough for her to pull me down in the dirt and drag me a while. She was almost out of sight when I rolled off my belly and sat up. My best and only dress was covered in dirt and green cow manure where Pet had let fly.

My knees were skinned. Both my hands had rope burns. I stood up and dusted myself off the best I could.

"That damned bullin cow! When I catch up with her I'll whip her every step back to the barn," I said out loud as I took off in a run after her.

Pet made better time than I did. I could hear the bull bellowing to her before I got to the fence. By the time I got there, limping and sweating, the bull had jumped the fence and was riding Pet. I pushed hair out of my eyes with a dirty hand and watched.

"Go for it, you damned bovine!" I said out loud, still put out at being dragged and scraped by an old heifer that couldn't wait.

"Not very pretty language for a young lady," A voice said behind me.

I whirled around to face a man sitting on a log. He had the blackest hair, and looked to be in his twenties. I could see every tooth in his mouth he was grinning so big and wide.

"Who're you?"

"My thought exactly where you are concerned," his grin faded. "Are you hurt badly?"

He looked me up and down. His gaze lingered on my bare foot then came back to my face. He stood up and I was surprised at how tall he was. He had to be over six foot tall. He moved toward me taking his white handkerchief out of his pocket.

"You have blood on your face. If you will grant me the liberty, I would like to wipe the blood and dirt away. You appear to have a worse cut than I originally thought. You could need stitches."

His voice was smooth and deep and his words sounded educated, but I had no idea where he came from. I'd run these woods all my life and had never seen him.

"I'm okay," I said quickly, and put my hand out to stop him coming any closer. He glanced at my hand and I heard his breath catch in his throat. He grasped my hand by the wrist and looked closer at my palm.

"My God!"

I jerked my hand loose and hid both hands in my skirt.

"Rope burn," I said lightly. "My cow got out of the field and I was trying to lead her back home when she pulled me down," I lied. It was a better choice to tell this stranger than the truth.

"I already guessed what happened with the cow. My concern is with you. You look like you were dragged down a gravel road. Couldn't you let go of the rope?"

"I didn't want to let go of the rope. I was tryin to hold her back."

"You intentionally held onto that rope while she was dragging you? You would have to be out of your mind."

"You don't understand plain English do you?" I raised my voice in defiance and met his blue-eyed stare.

He shook his head in slow motion. "I'm afraid you might need medical attention."

I didn't know if he meant for my scrapes or for my holding on to the rope. "Are you tryin to insult me?"

"No Ma'am," he said in all sincerity. "Your face is bleeding. Your entire foot is covered in blood, while the palms of your hands are raw meat. Your dress is all but torn from your body with your hair full of limbs and leaves, not to mention cow manure. I assure you your health is my only concern."

"All I need is a wash and my cow back."

I felt my face redden as I looked at what the cow and bull were doing.

"Please sit down for just a moment until i am assured you're not hurt. Then I'll get my father's bull back across the fence and help you with your cow," he said as he held out his white handkerchief toward me.

Oh my lord, if he was Pete Jones's son, I had been stealing services from his dad's bull for three years, and now I was caught.

No. I'd told him the cow had run away from me. He didn't know what I'd done.

I reached out and took his handkerchief and absently scrubbed my face. I was surprised at the blood and dirt on the handkerchief. "Why have I never laid eyes on you?" I managed to say.

"I live away from here, just visiting my folks and these woods."

I knew Pete Jones had grown children, but I didn't know how many.

"I'm sorry about your bull and all," I hoped I sounded meek. "I'll fix your fence. Honest I will."

He looked surprised. "I wouldn't think of you fixing the fence. It's my father's job to maintain his fences. Please, will you just sit down for a few minutes? Once you've gotten your breath back, I'll help you home with your wayward cow."

I took a few steps to the log he had been sitting on and sank down.

"Now, that's better," he said gently, and took his handkerchief out of my hand and began to wipe my face.

No one had ever touched me in the gentle way he was doing. His face was close mine, and I could feel his breath on my cheek. One of his fingers lifted my chin and his eyes searched every inch of my face until his eyes met mine then stopped.

My breath caught.

"I hope that cut on your cheek doesn't leave a scar. You're much too pretty to have scars."

A look came over his face that I didn't like at all. He moistened his lips with his tongue. His fingers caressed the side of my cheek in a way that sent chills over me.

How dare him, I thought. How dare him touch me. I tried not to grit my teeth as I spoke.

"You've got about as much bullshit in you as I've got cow shit on me!" I knocked his hand away, seeing surprise on his face. I ignored it.

"What?"

"You heard me. You'll not be foolin around with me in these woods. I don't care if it is your dad's bull. I'm takin my cow home and you won't be followin me either. You try and I'll bash you between the eyes with a rock bigger than I fell over!"

I jumped up and ran toward Pet and the bull. I grabbed the rope hanging around her neck and gave her a yank. She balked for an instant then began to follow me.

The bull followed right behind the cow.

I stopped, grabbed up a rock and hit the bull on the head with it. I saw Pete Jones' son take a few steps toward me, a puzzled look on his face. The puzzled look vanished and a shit eatin grin appeared.

He chucked as he picked up a good size limb and got between the bull and me. He expertly forced the bull toward the fence as I went out of sight with my cow.

I stopped at the creek near the house and washed up as best I could, not wanting anybody seeing me all dirty and bloody. I would have to mend my Sunday dress as best I could tonight after I fixed supper and got all the work done. Tomorrow I would be making me an everyday dress from a feed sack.

I turned Pet loose and went to the hog pen to fix a place for the sow to farrow. If she was going to have a litter, maybe it would be soon. That way they might live through the winter.

I washed up on the back porch real good before I started supper. I found an old dress that had once belonged to Susie and put it on while I mended and washed my Sunday dress. It wasn't nearly in as bad a condition as I feared.

That night when we were sitting at the table eating, Dad looked at my hands and face. He didn't say a word to me. It was a silent meal. Momma had decided she didn't feel well enough to sit up at the table. Susie told Dad that Momma was a knot of nerves all day long. Susie ate in the bedroom with Momma.

I got up at five o'clock the next morning as usual and was surprised to find a fire burning warm in the stove and coffee perking. I stood there for a minute and smelled the coffee. Too bad the drinking of it could not come close to the wonderful smell of it perking in the early morning air.

Dad came in the door with an arm load of wood. "I'll be going back to the sawmill."

Those were his only words as he dumped the load in the wood box. I put some lard in the skillet to melt and began mixing up a batch of biscuits. A man needed a hearty breakfast to work at saw milling. I packed him his lunch.

Maybe he was getting over Joey some. I wondered if he was too old, and Momma too sick with her spells, to have another youngun.

After I had finished the morning chores, I started a fire outside and filled my canner full of water then went to the garden and picked a bushel of tomatoes to can. I had scalded the tomatoes and was peeling their skin off when someone spoke.

"Morning Miss."

I looked up to see the man at Mrs. Eula's store. His green eyes sparkled at my surprise. I had not heard him come around to the back of the house and was taken almost speechless at seeing him beside me. I didn't think a snake could have moved as silent.

"Good morning."

I felt my breath quicken in my chest. What was he doing here with Dad gone and all? How was I supposed to talk to a man? What could he want?

"Hope I'm not disturbing you," he said politely.

He looked all about the place as though he was going to buy it. He looked at the garden, the patch of field corn for the livestock, the sorghum cane, and the small stack of hay I'd stomped around the pole. He looked at the canning jars I had washed and set on the back porch, then at the tomatoes I had scalded and the ones still in the hamper. He looked at the back of our unpainted house where two narrow windows showed curtains the neighbors had washed and stretched when Joey died. Then his eyes came to rest on me.

"Dad's not home."

I felt like squirming while he looked me over. I was wearing a worn out dress of Susie's and I hadn't even bothered to comb my hair. It hung loose and tangled about my head. Tomatoes covered my apron and hands. I looked a mess while this stranger was standing before me looking as though he was dressed for church.

"It was your dad I came to see," he said. "Heard he sells hams."

"Yeah, but we don't have any now. It'll be after hog killin before we do," I told him as I looked into his green eyes. Something about him made me feel a little jumpy.

"Would you have any grown hogs for sale by chance?"

"We don't sell grown hogs, only pigs in the summer."

He squatted down beside me on the grass and looked me in the face. He lifted his hand and touched my cut cheek with firm fingers.

"Somebody hit you?" he asked me calmly as though me getting hit might be an every day occurrence that warranted little concern on his part.

"I was leadin the cow when she pulled me down," I told him and wondered just who did he think would hit me?

He let his finger rest for a brief second on my chin. I recalled Pete Jones' son touching my face. The feel of this man's fingers did not seem as personal as the fingers of Pete Jones' son.

"How old are you, by the way?"

"Fifteen, almost."

"Fifteen," he seemed to be thinking about that word. "A lot of girls get married by that age. Do you have some young man hiding out behind the barn?"

Color came to my cheeks. His words made me think of Jones and breeding the cow. I ignored the question.

He frowned. "Don't your momma can?"

I shook my head. "Momma's sickly."

"Who built your outdoor canning pit?"

"Dad. It gets too hot in the kitchen. It's better outside."

"Most things are, Elaine. I can call you Elaine can't I?"

"Most folks call me Laine. Eula calls me by my rightful name."

"You milk, churn, raise hogs and chickens and do what else I wonder?"

"I do whatever needs to be done."

He reached down as bold as you please and picked up both of my hands. He looked at the backs and then at the palms. His thumb rubbed my calluses then he inspected the rope burns.

"Rope burn. Where the cow pulled me down," I told him a little nervously, but I did not move my hands from his.

He turned my hands over and kissed the back of my left hand. I gasped, but I didn't take my hand out of his, and he didn't let go.

"It's not often a man finds a girl that looks like you and can work like hell too," he grinned. "Sweet girl, don't you be marrying nobody before I get back to buy some hams." He kissed the palm of my hand, stood up, bowed to me, then left as quietly as he came.

It was dark when Dad came home from the sawmill. He was leading a young, red bull up the road with a rope made up of several strands of twisted twine. I could not believe my eyes. The last thing in this world we needed was another mouth for me to feed.

"Did you buy that thing?" I asked none too kindly.

"Borrowed him from Abraham Miller. I'll graze him for a couple of months for his services. Abe raised him as a pet. He's as gentle as gentle ever comes. Abe said he was just like a dog."

"Dad, I've only got one cow left to breed and we don't have much grass left."

Winter was coming on and I sure didn't want to feed a bull. It would push me to have enough feed for our stock. Another animal was not what I needed unless he came with a haystack and a shock of corn.

"We'll manage. It hain't fittin for a girl to be goin across the hill," Dad turned his back on me and let the bull in with the cows.

I wanted to say it was just as fittin now as it had been for the past three years.

I watched Dad go into the barn and I expected into the loft. I went to get chop for the hogs. I was getting low on chop, which is ground corn, cob, husk and all. I had to ask Dad to take corn to the mill. Maybe, I had enough corn to do another month. It would be late October before the field corn would be ready to shuck.

I came around the corner of the barn with the empty slop buckets as Dad came out of the barn. He didn't seem nearly as tired as he had a short time before. Been in the loft nipping on that jug for certain. I reckon that liquor had the power of fortification.

"You're runnin late tonight, hain't you?" Dad asked.

"I canned tomatoes." Mention of the tomatoes made me remember the man at Eula's store.

"A man showed up here today."

Dad stopped in his tracks and turned toward me. There was a frown between his eyes, and a troubled look came on his face.

"Know him?" Dad asked.

"It was that man at Eula's store. He wanted to buy hams or grown hogs."

Dad slowly nodded his head. "Grown hogs, maybe, but any fool would know hams hain't for sell until after hog killin time."

"That's what I told him, and he said he would be back."

Dad's frown deepened and he looked toward the house where Susie had just lit the lamp in Momma's bedroom.

"Did he see Susie?"

Now what kind of question was that for Dad to ask?

"He didn't see nobody but me."

Dad's gaze shot from the house back to me.

"He saw you at Eula's store, too. What exactly did he say to you? He's not from around these parts."

I felt uneasiness in Dad. He must think the man was coming by to look at Susie. Susie was the right age to get married, and nobody could deny she was good-looking.

I remembered the stranger kissing my hand.

"He said for me not to marry until he came back to buy hams."

Chapter 4

The day after the man came to buy hogs, Dad came home from the sawmill, and I followed him inside. The house was empty. Dad went into every room looking for Momma and Susie just like he might have overlooked them.

"Where can they be?" I asked Dad.

Dad pushed his cap back on his head as though he were thinking long and hard, and for a few moments I though he wasn't going to answer me.

"The graveyard," Dad said in a whisper.

He took out of the house with his long legs taking strides just short of a run. I was running and still couldn't keep up with him. He crossed the yard, jumped the creek and climbed the hill that took him to the graveyard. I couldn't understand why Dad was in such a tizzy. It seemed like a normal thing for Momma to visit the grave of her dead baby. I could see Momma sitting beside Joey's grave saying a prayer and shedding tears. That wasn't reason enough for Dad to be acting like the world would come to an end if he didn't get to Momma fast.

When we got to the graveyard, I didn't believe what I saw. Momma had Dad's shovel and had almost dug Joey's coffin out of the ground. The metal was clanging against wood as she dug furiously. Momma was covered in dirt and her dress was torn in several places. Tears mixed with dirt had made streaks down her cheeks, while her eyes were flashing angrily.

She appeared possessed of super-human strength. I thought all the demons in hell couldn't stop Momma from digging that coffin the rest of the way out.

"My God, Mert!" Dad said as he jumped the fence and went to her. "What're you doin?"

He reached out to her and she swung at him with the shovel. Dad barely managed to dodge her strike.

"He don't want to be in there!" She yelled at Dad. "It's dark and cold. I aim to get him out. I told you I didn't want him buried in the ground!"

Dad stood there with his mouth open and his eyes wide. He seemed to be wondering what to do next.

Momma went back to digging.

I saw a movement near a Chinquapin bush at the fence. Susie was crouching there and crying so hard her whole body shook with sobs. I went over to her and kneeled down as I put my arm around her wanting to give her comfort. She slapped my arm away.

"D-d-do-n't tou--ch me! It--it's your –fa-fault!"

I stood up and moved back from her. What did she mean it was my fault? I wasn't in the house when she and Momma left for the graveyard. And I had been canning beans when Joey died. She was the one supposed to be watching Joey. I took several more steps backward then turned my back on her. I jumped over the fence and stood on the outside of the graveyard as I watched Dad grapple Momma for the shovel. I saw one of her swings connect with Dad's shin. A painful yell escaped Dad along with a string of cuss words he didn't use often. He made a leap for Momma. Both of them fell into the dirt and they wrestled about with Momma screaming to the top of her lungs. Finally, Dad won the battle and pinned her arms behind her back while he sat on her legs with her face in the dirt.

"Get the shovel, Laine!" He hollered without taking his eyes off Momma.

I climbed back over the fence and cautiously retrieved the shovel that was lying near Momma.

She was whining like an angry animal. Her teeth were bared in a snarl while the side of her face was pressed in the fresh dirt.

Dad managed to get to his feet while holding Momma, and lifted her up out of the dirt. When Momma tried to get loose, Dad tightened up on her arms until the pain made her stop fighting.

"Open the gate," Dad yelled to me through gritted teeth.

I wasted no time opening the gate then getting out of the way as Dad dragged her through it. Momma looked at me like she wanted to tear me to pieces.

"You—," she yelled at me, but Dad gave her a silencing jerk and said, "Shovel all that dirt back on Joey's grave, Laine."

I stood there watching Dad drag Momma off the hill. She fought him every step of the way. Susie scuttled after them attempting to hide behind every clump of weeds she could find.

I started shoveling dirt back on the grave, wondering just what Momma would've done when she dug her baby up and found him stinking rotten?

When I got back to the house, Momma and Susie both were lying in the same bed asleep. Dad was sitting on the couch with his head in his hands looking whipped. He lifted his head and looked up at me.

"I gave them both some of the stuff the doctor left to make them sleep. She just needs a little time to get over things. She'll be all right."

I knew his words were more to convince himself than me.

"Why did she try to dig him up? You know he'd have to be rotten by now."

I saw Dad wince at my words but he answered me.

"Susie said Mert had a dream about him being cold and afraid of the dark. In her dream you were holding him in his coffin and wouldn't let him out."

"I didn't do anything!" I insisted.

"I know. She's just off in her head a little right now. You know how she loved that boy of her'n. She'll be fine in a day or two. You better go get the work done while I watch them," he rubbed his hand over his face and looked toward the bedroom. "Guess Dr. Robinson knew what he was doin when he slipped me more medicine."

That night I found it hard to fall asleep. I'm not sure Dad slept at all. I heard him moving around most all night long as he went to the bedroom to check on Momma and Susie. I didn't hear a sound but snoring from them.

When Momma woke up, I expected her rage to continue, but she was happy and smiling. The first thing she did when she came into the kitchen was reach out and pat Dad's cheek.

"Wesley dear, you're gonna have to take things easier. You look worn to a frazzle. Let Laine do the work around here. It won't hurt her none."

She turned from Dad to where I was fixing breakfast at the cook stove.

"Laine, honey, I hope you're fixin those delicious biscuits and gravy you make along with scrambled eggs and sausage. I'm feelin hungry this mornin." Her words were as sweet as sugar, but there was nothing sweet in her eyes as she looked at me.

She lifted her hand and puffed her hair back from her face in a primping manner.

"I really must have Susie brush my hair for me. Poor baby, I hope she's awake by now," she started to leave the kitchen then turned back to me. "See if there's some of the good cherry preserves in the can house. My little Susie just loves that stuff."

Dad and I both were silent as we watched her leave the kitchen in a frisky walk like a girl might have if she were trying to flirt a little, a walk that wasn't like Momma's at all.

"Scares the hell outta me," Dad said below his breath as though saying the words out loud might help.

I poured Dad a cup of coffee and he drank half of it down scalding hot. He didn't blink an eye.

"I'll get the preserves outta the can house while you finish cookin," Dad said, stood up and left the kitchen carrying his coffee cup and pushing his cap back further on his head. I noticed he was favoring the leg Momma had hit with the shovel.

When he came back with the preserves, I made him sit down at the table and pull up his britches leg. The skin on his shin had been barked from his knee down to the top of his boot. It looked raw, painful and bruised on both sides of the skinned shin. I took a bottle of alcohol down from the shelf and poured some on his leg.

"I ought to put a bandage on that," I told him.

"Naw, it'll be all right. I've barked my shins worse."

Momma came into the kitchen right then and saw me kneeling down doctoring Dad's leg. The smile on her face faded as she looked from me to Dad, then her eyes came back to rest on me. If looks could damn, I'd be in hell right now stoking the fire.

"Just what do you think you're doin?" she demanded..

"Pourin alcohol on Dad's leg," I told her in a not to pleasant tone.

She reached down and jerked up Dad's britches leg until she could see his shin.

"Why Wesley dear, how in this world did you do a thing like that to your leg?"

"That's where you hit me with the shovel," Dad said to her and reached down and covered his shin with his britches.

"Now you know good and well I never done such a thing," Momma said primly as she turned her back on him. "Bring mine and Susie's breakfast to the bedroom, Laine. We're not feeling well."

"Changed her tune in a hurry," I said to Dad as he watched her disappear through the bedroom door.

"She does that," Dad kind of sighed. " Dish up a plate for em and I'll take it to em. Go get your outside work done. I'll look after things in here."

For the rest of the day I could hear Momma's whining voice calling Dad back to her every time he left the bedroom. She needed water. She needed her pillow fluffed. She needed her chamber pot because she was feeling too feeble to walk all the way to the toilet.

That night I was in a sound sleep when the sound of Dad's footsteps running through the house woke me. I jumped up and followed him outside. Momma was on the bank with a long pole in her hands. She was pushing the bee gums over and rolling them into the creek.

"Mert, honey," Dad said soothingly to her as he reached her side. "Lay your pole down, darlin girl and we'll go back inside the nice warm house. You need to be in your bed. It's cold out here. The dew is fallin."

"Killin bees," Momma mumbled. "Killin bees."

And she poked at the gums again knocking the third gum over. I saw its shadow go down the bank and land in the creek with a splashing thud.

"Put your pole down, little girl. It's time to go inside now. Susie needs you. She needs you bad!"

Momma stopped poking at the bees and lifted her head as though she was listening for the sound of Susie.

"I don't hear her cryin."

"She'll wake up and be afraid if you're not with her," Dads voice was cajoling as he reached out and touched her arm. "That's it darlin. Let me help you over that slick grass. Don't want my girl slidin into the creek and gettin wet. The nights are gettin cold. Won't be long until the timber changes. You always did like it when the timber changed. All those pretty colors. Remember you allus said you wanted a dress with all the colors of the leaves in it? Now where do you reckon we can find you a dress like that? Suppose Eula could order you one?"

"You'll get me one?" Momma sounded like a petted child as she let Dad take the pole from her hands and guide her back toward the house. "You'll really ask Eula to order me a fancy dress like that?" Momma chuckled softly. "Every woman in the valley would turn green with jealousy."

"Yes they would," Dad eased the kitchen door open and guided her inside as though one wrong move would make her break like a dropped egg. "Next time I go to Eula's I'll ask about the dress. Now, you just slip back in bed with Susie before she wakes up."

"Okay. But do be quiet. We don't want little Susie to wake up. She's such a nervous little thing. She's not strong, you know. She's just like me."

A short time later Dad came out of the bedroom acting as nervous as Momma claimed Susie was. He clasped his hands together, wrung them around each other and run both hands through his hair.

"Laine," He whispered. "Go out and see if you can get the bee gums back in their rightful place while it's still dark and the bees won't come out much. We can't afford to lose our supply of honey. I'll not be able to leave Mert for a while. She's sleeping but Lord knows when she'll wake back up."

"What went wrong with her?" I wanted to know. The graveyard and now this. I wondered how she would blame this on me.

"There's nothing wrong with her. It's just her way of relieving her hurtin at losing Joey. She'll be fine. You just get the bee gums back in place."

I didn't want to tackle a job as difficult and dangerous as moving gums full of bees by myself. I had never seen it done before, but I knew it would be a job for a man with a net hat, padded gloves, and a smoker I had seen Dad use to rob bees of their honey. I lit a candle and went down into the can house and searched until I found Dad's smoker. It looked something like a coffee pot with a side pump much like a handle and a spout where the smoke puffed out when the handle was pumped. I found a rag, lit it from the candle, and stuck it inside the pot. I puffed each gum full of smoke to addle the bees. Then I went to getting the gums back as best I could.

It took me half the night to get the gums up the bank into their place. I had stings from angry, mashed bees. My hands and arms hurt me the rest of the night. They were swollen and burning the next morning, but I had to cook breakfast and do the work anyway. There wasn't a soul to pet me like Dad was petting Momma and Susie.

Dad carried food to them and helped Momma feed herself. Susie managed to feed her own self as she gave Momma worried looks. After they were full, Dad tucked both of them under the covers and sat down in a straight-backed chair in the corner of the room.

"You won't leave if I go to sleep?" Momma whined.

"I'll stay here," Dad promised.

"You won't slip off to that sawmill?"

"Not today," Dad said tiredly. "Not today."

I almost had the kitchen clean when I felt Dad's hand on my shoulder.

"Be quiet and don't wake em while I go outside to the toilet," Dad whispered near my ear.

I nodded and stopped making any noise. There was only the click of the kitchen door as Dad went outside. I eased to the door of the bedroom on bare feet and cautiously put my eye to the crack Dad had left open. I knew he hadn't closed the door completely so the sound of a closing door wouldn't wake them. I saw Momma open one eye and peek around the room to see if Dad was there. When she decided he was gone, she lifted her head, looked at the still sleeping Susie and jumped out of bed. She rushed to the window and watched Dad go into the toilet.

She left the window and went to the tiny mirror sitting atop the dresser and observed herself closely. She gave the mirror her most pretty smiling look then gave it a sickly pitiful look. She fluffed her hair up with her hands then rubbed her hair as flat about her head as she could. She stepped back from the mirror and rubbed her hands over her breasts to her waist then over her hips. She twirled around the room back to the window in time to see Dad come out of the toilet. She danced herself over to the bed, smiled lightly, eased back in bed and closed her eyes. I slipped to the kitchen and started washing dishes as Dad opened the door and came in.

I went to Dad and put my lips close his ear and whispered so low I hoped Momma couldn't catch any sound. "She's only pretending to be asleep. I saw her get up and watch you out the window. When she saw you comin back, she jumped in bed and closed her eyes like she was still asleep."

I didn't know why I couldn't tell Dad about rubbing herself and dancing.

"You sure?" Dad whispered.

I nodded. "I peeped through the crack you left in the bedroom door."

"Don't let her know you saw her," he frowned. "I gave her enough of that medicine to knock a horse out. She must have slipped it all to Susie when I wasn't lookin."

He poured himself a cup of coffee without bothering to be overly quiet, and went back to the bedroom and put his eye to the crack in the door before he went inside. I knew he was checking to see how good a look I could get of Momma and the bedroom. He left the door wide open, crossed the room and took his seat in the chair. I saw him watching Momma closely as I looked through the bedroom door.

I went outside to do up the work.

I don't know if Dad told Momma I had seen her or not. But every time she looked at me she had an angry, sullen look on her face. Her hands twitched and moved like she wanted to slap me.

It was after dark that night before Susie woke up. Dad carried supper to Susie and helped her feed herself, but he didn't help Momma with her food. I heard him ask Susie if she wanted him to help her walk outside to the toilet. Momma told Dad Susie could use her chamber pot.

I thought Dad should throw that thing in the creek and let them both go to the toilet like normal people, but Dad didn't object. He set the pot out from under the bed for Susie and left the room to give her some privacy.

I looked at Dad and opened my mouth to let him know what I thought, but he shook his head and motioned for silence. I hushed my mouth and said nothing. He could do whatever he thought best for them regardless of how strange I thought they were acting.

That night Dad made Susie sleep with me and he slept in bed beside Momma.

Chapter 5

The house was silent except for Momma and Dad both snoring in their bedroom. Susie was asleep beside me with her arms thrown out and her legs bent away from her body. She took up more room than a girl her size should. There were times when I dreamed of sleeping in a soft bed all by myself. In the summer I got tired of feeling her heat and in the winter I got tired of fighting for the cover. Right now I had to get up and use the pot or go outside in the cold. I chose the cold. It seemed degrading for somebody my age to be squatting on a chamber pot. Besides, it was under Momma's bed where it had become a permanent fixture during the past week. Momma declared she no longer had the strength to walk all the way to the toilet. I questioned that myself, but it wasn't my place to say anything. I did take a stand and refuse to empty the it for her. I firmly believed in the person using the pot, emptying it. Susie emptied it for her when Dad wasn't there for I wasn't about to.

I got out of bed and walked barefoot onto the back porch trying not to make a sound. Dad had to get up early for work, and I didn't want to wake him because I had drunk too much milk before I crawled in bed. Dad had finally gone back to the sawmill after Momma had started to act some better.

I silently closed the back door and stood there waiting for my eyes to adjust. I breathed in deep of the cool night air. It filled my lungs and contented my soul. The silence surrounded me until my heart swelled with delight. The moon had risen over the treetops as big and yellow as a crock of butter. Harvest moon, I thought as I looked about the earth around me. The moon was so bright I could see every detail of the beautiful, silent earth. It could almost be daylight except the world was in black and white instead of color.

It was then I saw a movement in the garden. It must be some kind of animal, a coon probably, eating vegetables. I was considering going back inside and waking Dad up to get his shotgun when I saw it move again. I blinked, closed my eyes then opened them wide. There in my tomato patch was a thin, pale figure. She had a ripe tomato in her hand, and was eating it like she hadn't seen a bite of food in some time. She grabbed another and ate it just as fast, then grabbed several more tomatoes, put them in the skirt of her dress, slipped through the fence and was gone into the woods.

I felt a knot inside my chest as I realized the poor little Munson girl was starving.

I stood on the porch a long time before I went to the side of the house and peed in the shadows. I wondered if that little girl ever slipped outside in the night because she drank too much milk?

By the time Dad got up the next morning, I had baked twice the amount of biscuits. I made gravy out of a can of sausage and scrambled a big pan of eggs. Apples were baking in the oven along with the biscuits. None of my family would be hungry today.

"You expectin company?" Dad ask me with a frown on his face.

I told Dad what I had seen the night before. His frown deepened.

"You thinkin about leavin what we don't eat in the garden tonight?" he asked me with a look of disapproval on his face.

"I want to make sure my family has plenty to eat. I think the little girl was starvin."

Dad looked at me and was silent for a while before he spoke.

"Like I told you. Church tried to help them. Folks here about tried to help them. Both gave it up. Givin somebody food keeps them from bein hungry for a short while. If they learned how to grow their own food, they might never be hungry. You can't help somebody what won't help themselves," Dad told me firmly.

"Dad, how do you teach a little girl to grow food?"

Dad looked puzzled "You know the Munsons always growed a garden. Even if they didn't, the Millers garden is closer to them than ours. Why would a child come this far to steal a tomato?" his puzzlement turned into concern. "Laine, don't you go messin around anywhere near them Munsons. Don't mean to bad-mouth folks, but them Munsons hain't fit for decent folks to be near, especially children."

I watched the way Dad downed his head and looked away from me. That was the worst I had ever heard him talk about people, and his actions showed me he didn't want to this time. He was telling me something he thought I needed to know.

The morning sky had turned a rosy red with daylight by the time I got to the barn to start milking. Just like all the other mornings, that darned red bull was standing by the barn door determined to block my way inside. He knew I gave the cows ears of corn and he wanted his share, which I denied him. He liked to shake his head and paw the ground and do his best to butt me. Once he butted me against the barn.

This morning he was not in a good mood. He took his stand against the door and no matter how I yelled and kicked at him he would not move out of the way. I had to go through the cuttin room door then back out into the hall, then climb into the loft for the pitchfork. An ill-tempered bull was going to required a little persuading.

A couple of sharp jabs and he stopped trying to burst through the door and let the milk cows pass by him.

By the time milking was over, I felt like I fought with the bull more than I milked.

I had to fight this red bull twice a day. I only had to take the cow through the woods once a year.

I turned the chickens out of the hen house and shelled a few ears of corn before I went to feed the hogs. Dad had made two wooden troughs out of ten-foot slabs of wood. Water swelled the slabs enough to hold liquid fairly well. I dumped the contents of the slop bucket from the house into the trough then filled the bucket up with water and stirred in chop. It took six buckets full to feed the hogs we had. That didn't include the garden scraps I threw in to them.

I didn't see the black sow. I would check on her just as soon as I fed the boar hog. He was kept in a separate lot from the sows. That way we had some control of when the sows farrowed.

That black sow was pushing out a pig when I got to her.

I went against Dad's orders and got in with her. Dad told me repeatedly that sows could be mean, and boar hog could be vicious. Our's weren't.

I bent down in the hay and counted five pink pigs wiggling to suck. The sow leaned over and began to clean up number six. It was then I saw a spot of pink pushed into the corner by itself. I picked up the pig and found it icy cold. I put my fingers on its little chest and detected a faint heartbeat. It was alive, but just barely. I cupped it in my hands and rushed to the house. If I worked on it some, I might get it warmed and breathing enough to live.

I dumped all the hot water from the tea kettle into the wash pan and dipped the pig in. The water wasn't very hot but it might do the trick.

It was then Susie came into the kitchen.

"What are you doin with that nasty pig in the house?" she demanded as though it was her kitchen and I was an intruder.

"What do you think I'm doin? Cooking it for dinner?"

"Don't get smart with me, Laine Elder!" She reached for the tea kettle and found it empty. She turned on me in unrighteous fury.

"You've used up all Momma's hot water! You build a fire in the stove this minute and heat her some more!"

I stopped massaging the pig in the water and looked up at her. She had her chin lifted like a queen as she sneered down her nose at me.

This didn't set well with me.

"Unless both your arms and one leg is broke, don't be tellin me to build a fire in the stove. You do it for yourself."

"How dare you talk to me like that? Momma needs hot water and you used it all," she yelled as she turned on me and shook her fist in my face.

I took the pig out of the water, wrapped it in a kitchen towel and held its body next to mine. I felt it twitch.

"There's your hot water. If you want it, use it," I lifted my chin and looked down my nose at her, mimicking the tone of voice she had used with me.

Her hand flew out and slapped me across the face.

I didn't know I moved until I felt my fist make contact with her nose. She gave a shriek then a strangled sound as I dropped the pig and clasped her throat with both my hands.

I rammed her head against the plank wall of the kitchen so hard the plates rattled in the cupboard.

Susie slid down the wall as she tried to scratch my face with her sharp fingernails. I added my body weight to make her land hard on her tailbone. Anger consumed me until a killing rage burned in me. I wanted to pound Susie into the floor. I loosened one hand from her throat and slapped her across the face with the same force I used when I broke the hoe handle over the mule's nose.

Momma grabbed me by the hair and back of my dress. She lifted me off Susie and flung me in the floor with a force as strong as any man. Momma, who claimed to be too weak to live, was towering over me with fury contorting her face.

"How dare you hit my little girl?" Momma yelled. "You ever touch her again and I'll kill you with my bare hands! You killed my Joey. I won't let you hurt my baby girl. You worthless piece of trash. You no account excuse for a human being. You don't deserve to live. You're the cause of all the problems around here!"

Momma's eyes blazed at me. Her lips pulled back to show her teeth and gums. Bits of slobber foamed at the corners of her mouth. I prepared myself to fight her and Susie both. Suddenly, she turned from me and looked at Susie lying in the floor with her hand cupped over her bleeding nose.

"Momma's poor baby," she crooned to Susie and seemed to forget me, and her anger.

She bent over and dabbed at the blood from Susie's nose with the tail of her nightgown. Susie whined just like Joey used to whine.

Momma slipped her arms beneath Susie, lifted her up as though she weighed no more than the pig. She didn't bother to look back at me as she carried Susie into her bedroom and lay her down on the bed, still crooning to Susie.

I shivered and could not figure out why. It didn't seem right that a woman too weak to walk to the toilet would be able lift and carry a hundred and twenty pound Susie as though she was a paper sack.

I got up off the floor still watching Momma and Susie through the bedroom door. Momma lifted her own nightgown over her head, wadded it up in her hand and wiped all traces of blood from Susie's nose and face.

"Momma's sweet baby. Momma's precious," Momma mumbled as she crawled up on the bed and lay down beside Susie. She pressed Susie's face against her naked breast.

Susie nuzzled against the soft flesh and sobbed as Momma rocked her back and forth. She rubbed her hand over Momma's body when Momma began kissing her hair and face. Susie's sobs faded as she moved her face over Momma's breast.

Momma lifted her eyes and saw me. I felt sick. Like I was witnessing something horrible. I turned away and picked up the little pig, rewrapped it in the towel and took the pig outside to find a warm spot of sunlight. I rubbed life back into the pig as I talked to myself.

I wouldn't pay any attention to what I saw.

Momma was so upset she just forgot she had taken her nightgown off.

Momma was just having another spell.

Momma accused me of killing Joey. Susie should have looked after Joey.

Susie was strange.

Momma was strange.

I was seeing things.

What had I seen? What were they doing?

I had a notion to walk off, leave them and all the work behind.

My stomach felt like throwing up.

I held the living pig in my arms as I walked up the garden path that ran along the creek branch. The sun was coming out warm, taking away what was left of the morning chill. The cold nights had brought out the red of the leaves. Gold and yellow were coming on fast. Soon the trees would be bare skeletons of themselves, and the snow would be deep. I shivered at the thought. I would have to get me some warm clothes and shoes. My old shoes were worn and too small for me, but I had them and my shabby winter coat stored in the attic. I would need them if I couldn't come up with better.

I went to the plate and pint jar I left in the garden last night. Both were still there, but empty. The little Munson girl had eaten. I told myself I should be thankful for what I had. I could be like the little girl, ragged with no food and little hope.

I stayed outside the rest of the day. I didn't want to see Momma and Susie again or think about what they were doing. Nor did I attempt to can anymore of the garden vegetables, although I knew I should. Any night now there would be a killing frost and nothing would be left for me to can. Waste not want not, I told myself, but anger and disgust took priority over good sense.

I sat down in the middle of the garden and cried.

I waited on Dad to come home, knowing I had to tell him what happened before Momma did. I would tell him the truth, except for the part about Momma and Susie on the bed. How could I tell something like that?

It was getting dark and Dad still hadn't come home, so I just started out walking down the road to meet him. I hadn't gone half a mile when he came around the bend. I could see his slow walk and downed head in the lingering twilight. He saw me and stopped still in his tracks.

"What's wrong?" he asked quickly in a voice that trembled with his fear.

"Susie and I got in a fight."

I saw relief come over Dad even in the fading light. His lips twitched with the grin he tried to hide.

"What was the fight about?" he asked me and began his slow walk homeward. I matched my steps with his.

"The black sow had pigs this mornin. One was nearly froze to death, so I took it to the house and poured water out of the tea kettle into the wash pan. I remembered you tellin me to put a froze animal in warm water to thaw it out and warm it up."

He nodded his head in approval.

"Susie came in the kitchen and got mad cause I used all the hot water. She demanded I start a fire and heat some more water right that minute. I was busy with the pig, so I told her she could do it herself. Then, I took the pig out of the water and told her there was the hot water. She could use it if she wanted to."

" then.....?" Dad encouraged me to continue.

"She slapped me across the face."

Dad's eyebrows lifted. He could not hide his grin this time. "Is she still alive?"

"Momma pulled me off her."

We had been walking up the road toward the house as we talked, but my last words stopped Dad still.

"Your Momma pulled you off Susie?"

"She pulled me off the top of Susie and threw me down in the floor harder than you could. She said she would kill me if I hurt her baby girl. She said it was my fault that Joey died, then she picked Susie up in her arms and carried her to bed." I told Dad as fast as I could get the words out.

I wanted to tell him the rest, but I couldn't.

I saw the color drain out of Dad's face even though it was dark. He seemed to stagger and I feared he was going to sit down in the middle of the road. He got himself under control.

"Your Momma dragged Susie to the bedroom?"

"No. She picked her up off the floor like she was a baby and carried her to the bed."

"Did it strain her?"

"She carried her as easy as I did the pig."

Dad began to walk on and I could hear him breathing hard. I thought he might say something about Joey. Surely he knew I wasn't the one that let Joey get in the bees. I didn't know what I should say to him, so I just walked beside him until he spoke again.

"Is that all that happened?"

I looked at a pothole in the road, the weeds on the bank and the faint light in the sky, anywhere but at Dad.

"Tell me, Laine."

I couldn't. "I went outside," I finally managed to say.

"I see. Did you fix em any dinner?"

"No."

"Have you been back in the house?"

I shook my head then realized he might not be able to see me in the dark.

"No."

Dad was silent again.

"Did the pig live?" he finally asked.

"Yeah."

"That's good."

Dad's steps grew slower as we got near the house. He stopped in front of the barn and looked at the light in the bedroom window. One of them had lit the lamp.

"Laine," Dad said gently. "You check on the animals and I'll go in. When I have a light on in the kitchen and a hot fire goin come on in and fix supper. Hear?"

"I hear."

I watched Dad go toward the house with reluctant steps.

It was nearly an hour later when Dad lit the lamp and had a fire going. I sighed into the dark night air and went into the house. Dad sat at the table with his knife in his hands and a stick of pine wood. He was shaving off long curls into the wood box.

"I thought you might need some shavings to start a fire with."

I knew that wasn't why he was cutting shavings. He had to have his hands busy in hopes his mind would work. His cap was pushed way back, and I wondered what Momma and Susie told him, but I didn't ask.

I cooked supper and put it on the table. Dad took up two plates full of food and carried them into the bedroom. I heard Susie mumbling something about the food not being fit to eat and then I heard Momma moan pitiful like.

"It's fit to eat," Dad said in his calm voice.

I thought about going in there and telling them I hadn't put rat poison in the food, yet.

Dad carried two glasses of milk to them before he came back to the table to eat his own food. He looked as worn and tired now as he did when Joey died. I wanted to say something to him about the way Momma and Susie acted, but I didn't know what words to use. How did I tell him I though Momma and Susie both had lost their minds?

We ate in silence until neither of us could force another bite down. Finally, Dad pushed his chair back from the table.

"When you wash up, you might carry a pint of milk and the leftover bread out to the garden," he said in a low voice.

That night Dad slept on the sofa and I slept in the bed alone. Momma and Susie were together.

The next morning Dad took their breakfast to them before he ate his own. When he started to leave for the sawmill he hesitated and turned to me as though he were having an afterthought.

"When you get the work done, hitch up the mule and make a trip to the store. Eula would be mighty glad to have an early delivery."

Dad didn't have to say anymore. I knew he didn't want me around the house with Momma and Susie.

"Reckon I can do that," I told him, although I dreaded fooling with the mule.

Dad left for the sawmill with a look of concern still on his face.

The bull behaved himself and the mule wasn't acting up, so things weren't as bad as they could have been. I had every thing I had to sell on the wagon and moved on down the road at a good pace. I let the mule have his head and he went along like he was happy to be going somewhere.

When I walked into the store alone, Eula threw up her hands and her mouth opened so wide her upper teeth fell down on her lower lip. She used her tongue to wiggled them back in place.

"Elaine, child, what are you doin here without your pa?"

I tried to give her a calm smile. "Dad said for me to bring the stuff in today."

"By yourself? Where is he? He ain't sick is he?"

"He went to the sawmill early. He's been workin mighty hard lately. He don't get home till after dark."

Eula nodded her head and looked at my homemade feed sack dress and bare feet as she walked out from behind the counter.

"How is your mother?" she asked me and her eyes narrowed as she bit her jaws together until her teeth didn't pop up and down.

"About the same."

"Last I heard, she had taken to her bed with grief. Has she started getting about any?"

I knew Eula loved to gossip and anything I told her the entire hollow would know about before night fall. She never asked such personal things when Dad was here. I guess she thought I wouldn't know she was gossiping, being I was still young.

"Not much," I said as non-committal as I could.

"Did your Momma sew that dress for you while she was in bed?"

I didn't much like the way Eula asked that, but I let it slide. Sometimes you just had to overlook old women that thought it was their God-given right to know everything that went on.

"I'm capable of sewing my own things," I told her and knew my voice had lifted in defiance.

"Yes," she agreed. "I do believe you are the most capable girl I've ever come across. Your Dad has enough sense to know that too."

I frowned for I didn't understand what she meant by that remark.

"I'll help you carry your stuff inside the store," she offered.

"I can manage."

"You manage better'n any youngun ought to have to, but I'll help anyway. Then you can help me carry it to the spring house," she added.

I thought that was fair enough on both our sides.

When we were through and I was standing at the counter waiting to be paid, Eula rushed to the back of the store. She came back with a dusty bolt of rose-colored material and a pair of dusty brown shoes.

"Now, I don't want you to take me wrong in any way child. I was cleanin out the store yesterday. You see, I have new stuff comin in for winter, and I wanted room to put it. I found this old bolt of cloth and these shoes back under the horse blankets. The cloth is stained in places but there might be some good abody could get out of it, and those shoes, well... somebody might be able to get into them if they have small feet. I would be right glad if you would take them out of my way."

I started to refuse her at first, and then I thought of all the milk, eggs, and butter we had carried to the store. I heard folks say she never paid the going price for anything, but they sold to her because she was closer than anywhere else. I thought she probably owed us a lot more than a half ruined bolt of cloth and mashed shoes.

"Well," I said. "If you want me to."

"I want you to." She popped her teeth up and down a few times. She seemed to be studying on whether to say something else or not. She must have made up her mind.

"I know you're still young and all, but all young girls study about things. I wonder if you've ever thought about finding yourself a fine young man and marryin him? You could have a good, fine life if you married the right young man to take care of you."

"I'm not hardly fifteen yet," was all that I could think of saying.

I had an idea she had her doughboy son in mind as the fine young man, and he wasn't in my mind at all.

"Sometimes a young girl can have a better life married than she can livin at home," she said encouragingly, like I was a little kid that needed persuading.

"That might be true enough," I answered as I tied the money in a rag I used for a handkerchief.

It was the first time I ever had money in my possession, but I knew it wouldn't last long. The money would go to Momma as soon as I got home. I wondered if Momma would send Susie out to get the money from me? I knew she would be anxious for it. I turned away from Eula and started out the door.

"Elaine," Eula said quickly. "You come back as often as you can with or without your Dad. I'll take your stuff twice a week if you'll bring it in. I'll be doing more cleanin and clearin out in the back. If I find more stuff I need to get rid of, I'll save it for you."

"Yes ma'am," I said politely and hurried on out the front door to where the mule was tied to a tree limb. He looked like he was getting ornery, and I dreaded the drive back home.

The mule seemed to know he was headed toward home and the barn. I guess he knew I would give him a couple ears of corn once we got there for he went on at a reasonable pace. I stopped once next to a nice grassy spot on the side of the road and let him graze for a few minutes while I got behind a bush. I had left around seven o'clock that morning and it was now noon. The bouncing of the wagon made me need to stop and pee. I guess I could have used Eula's toilet, but I didn't want to. There was something about looking down into somebody else's crap that didn't settle too well with me. I would take a bush any day, even if I had to use grass to dry off with instead of a piece of catalogue.

I passed Abraham Miller's place without seeing a soul out and about.

Being it was dinner time, I suspected everybody might be inside eating. I didn't see anybody at the Munson place either. I hoped they had food to eat that didn't come out of my garden, not that I would begrudge a hungry body food from my garden. I just didn't want them to take what I didn't offer.

Suddenly the old mule stopped in his tracks, lifted his head and gave out a loud bray. I slapped the lines on his rump but he still didn't go. Instead, he seemed to be staring up the road as though he could see something around the bend. I listened and heard the sound of hooves on the clay of the dusty road.

A man riding a fancy sorrel saddle horse came around the bend. He was dressed fine with a fancy black hat pulled low on his head. His saddlebags were bulging and a satchel was tied behind his saddle. It took me a moment or two before I recognized the man.

It was Pete Jones's son. Of all the people I never wanted to see again, he was one. He stopped beside my broken down wagon nailed together with uneven planks.

"Hello again," he tipped his hat in a gentlemanly manner. "I'm glad to see you are in one piece and your wounds are healed from your cow driving days."

He would have to remind me of that embarrassment. I wanted to click up the mule and ride on as though I hadn't seen him.

"Good day to you, Mr. Jones," I said in my best school learned manner. "It's a fine day to be out ridin." I looked at his saddlebags and satchel. "Or, are you travelin?"

He lifted his brows and looked down at me like he thought my greeting was funny then he spoke civilly.

"Traveling, I dare say. My visit with my parents has ended today. By the way my name is Jonas. What is yours?"

I frowned up at him. "Jonas? I thought it was Jones."

"You're right. I'm Jonas Jones. To this day I think my mother was suffering from the pain of childbirth when she named me."

I had to grin at that even though I didn't want to. To be named Jonas Jones was as bad as being named Millie Miller or Lue Lewis.

"Please don't tell me your name is Mary Leary," he spoke as though he had read my mind.

"Not Mary Leary today. I'm Laine Elder."

"Hello Laine Elder," he bowed to me from the back of his horse. "I'm pleased to meet you. Maybe we will meet again sometime when I return to visit my parents."

"Maybe."

I looked at him hard and saw he had that shit eating grin on his face. I got the feeling he was making fun of me somehow, and I didn't like it.

The old mule began to stomp and give the prancing horse side-glances like he was tired of the hold up.

Jonas noticed the mule's impatience, touched the brim of his hat with his finger and rode off on his high stepping horse. I clicked my mule up and went on home. Jonas Jones stayed in my mind every step of the way. We had met twice and neither time seemed proper. It left me feeling like I had an itch that needed to be scratched. I just didn't know where the itch was located.

☙

Dad came out of the barn when I pulled the wagon up. I hadn't expected to see him because he had gone to the sawmill early that morning, and it wasn't much past mid-day now.

"You sick?" I asked him.

"No."

I thought he looked sick. His eyes seemed to have sunk into his head and his face had taken on a shade of pasty gray. He had that worried look on his face he sometimes got when he didn't know what to do next. He seemed old and bent.

"I'll take the money in to your Momma."

Dad held out his hand to me before I could even climb down from the wagon. He looked toward the house and I saw Momma's bedroom curtain move. I knew Momma and Susie had seen me leave that morning and must have been pitching a fit in fear I would try to keep some of the money.

I pulled the rag out of my pocket and handed it to Dad without a word, although I was thinking a lot. Momma must have thought I would buy something while I was at

Eula's store. I recalled the stained, pink cloth and mashed shoes and decided I better hide them in the barn for the time being.

Eula's words came back to me. 'Sometimes a young girl can have a better life married than she can livin at home.'

I didn't unhook the mule. Instead, I tied him to a tree limb and hurried toward the house by the side way. I ran through golden rod and blackberry briars to make sure none of them saw me sneak up to Momma's bedroom window. I got there in time to hear Momma say, "The money ain't all here. She kept part of it. The sneakin thief!"

"Now Mertie," Dad said softly. "Every copper is there. I know what she took to the store and you saw me count the money. Laine never kept one single copper."

"You lie for her!" Momma's voice was sharp and accusing. "You're just a worthless piece of old meat taking up space. If you was any kind of man, you'd do somethin about her."

"What would you have me do?" Dad's voice sounded tired and defeated. I knew his head would be hung and his eyes would be looking at his feet, while his face would show his helplessness. I wondered what had happened to that backbone men were supposed to have? I never once heard him stand up to Momma. Instead, he tried to console and calm her down.

" You could whip her until she got some sense. You allow her to beat on little Susie and defy me. She runs around here like she owns this place and you don't even care."

She sounded like she had been abused and mistreated in the worst kind of way, and it was all Dad's fault. Her voice shook as though she were about to cry with her misery.

"Why don't you get some rest now?" Dad said, and I heard his footsteps walk out of the bedroom.

I slipped away from the window and went back to unhitch the mule with a feeling inside me that I was trying to turn into anger.

The mule was feeling mean. I left him tied up when he thought I should have turned him loose. The first thing he did was try to bite me. He got enough of the skin on my arm to leave a blood blister. I hit him over the head with my fist. All I did was hurt my hand and get kicked at by the mule. He missed me and tried to make up for it by stepping on my bare foot. But I was wise to that trick of his, and moved my foot quicker than he moved his. I grabbed a stick I kept by the barn and the mule calmed right down. He walked through the gate like a perfect angel.

I went back to the house for my milk buckets and met Granny Mable in the front yard. She was carrying a brown paper poke in her arms.

Chapter 6

🕊

"Evenin Laine," Granny Mable nodded her head toward me. Her eyes searched my face for what seemed like a full minute. I felt as though she had entered my brain and searched out my secrets.

"I came to see your momma. I heard she's not doin too good."

"She's all right."

"Losin a child takes part of a person's heart right out of their chest. I don't reckon there's a thing that will ever put it back. It don't make any difference if there's a dozen children alive and a dozen more to come, that piece of heart is never replaced.

"Yes," I said. "I can see that."

"Patience and understanding's a thing we all have to develop in ourselves," Granny Mable looked toward the house. "I brought some tea for your momma what might help her some. It contains herbs with unnatural powers. Soothes the raging beast within. You might try some."

"I don't care for tea," I told her as I crossed the yard to the back door. Granny Mable walked at my side.

"Your dad never cared for tea either. It's an acquired taste," she smiled at me gently. Her eyes were soft with understanding. "You're your father's child, Elaine Elder. Not one fiber of you was handed down from your Momma, unless it'd be that hot temper of yours. Temper is like a fire. It's a mighty fine tool to have if it's contained and used properly. If it gets out of control, disaster occurs."

68

I made no comment to her as I opened the back door and let Granny Mable go inside in front of me. I got the milk buckets off the wall. Granny Mable patted my shoulder, turned her back on me and went to find Momma.

When I got to the barn, the confounded red bull was pawing the ground and snorting. The last cow, the big Holstein, was bullin. She was riding around on the other five cows and putting up a fight against the bull. She wasn't quite ready to breed, and she wouldn't settle down until she was ready and it was over and done with.

I had added aggravation all because Dad brought in that red bull.

I laid my arms on the top rail of the gap and stood there looking at the mayhem. For one red copper I would leave the bunch of them unmilked. I knew I wouldn't get one red copper, and if I didn't milk them, Momma wouldn't get one red copper either.

I left the gap and went in through the cuttin room door and climbed in the loft to get the pitchfork. I would need persuasion to get the bull and cows separated long enough to milk.

I opened the door and stuck my head out to see if I could let a cow in and saw Dad standing not three feet in front of the door. He had his back to me and was watching the bull and cows. He turned at the sound of me opening the door.

"You wanta help me get em in?" I asked Dad.

"Can if you want me to."

"I want you to. That old bull is mean as a stripped snake. He gives me a fit every time he thinks I'm not watching,"

Dad gave me a funny look and frowned. "Why, that bull hain't mean. He's nothing but a pet. Abraham raised him. It's natural for him to be a little excited since the cow's bullin."

"He's a little excited when they're not bullin, too. I have to keep the pitchfork handy or at least a keen hickory to

switch his ears with. He don't like to have his ears
switched."

Dad looked at me for a minute. "You switch his ears?"

"When he tries to get in the barn instead of lettin me get
the cows in. He tries to fight me all the time, but I know
how to handle him. That nose of his is a tender spot, and he
can't stand havin his ears poked with the pitchfork any
more than he can a keen hickory."

"I reckon not," Dad said as the red bull came to the barn
door.

He knew I would be putting out feed to milk the cows
with and he was ready to go after it. I pointed my pitchfork
at him to head him off.

"You don't need that, Laine. You're afraid of him for no
reason. He's as gentle as a kitten," Dad scolded me gently.
"See. I'll show you."

Dad took a few steps away from me to the bull, reached
out his hand and began to scratch the bull between his
horns. The bull lowered his head, moved it from side to
side in what looked like pure enjoyment. He then moved
his head up and down against Dads scratching fingers.

"See that? He just wants his ole head scratched and a
little pettin."

"He might be wantin pettin from you, but he wants to
fight with me," I told Dad warningly. "I don't trust that red
bull as far as I can pick him up and throw him. You'd better
not either."

Dad chuckled at me. "I never thought you'd be afraid of
a pet bull."

"It's not that I'm afraid of him. I just don't trust him. I
have to milk with that son-of-a-gun twice a day. I know
what he can do."

Dad shook his head and grinned like I was being a silly
girl. He opened his mouth to say something but only an
'uhhh' came out. The bull's big curly head was against the

pit of Dad's stomach as he lifted Dad's feet off the ground. He made a mad rush forward, taking Dad flying through the air. Dad grabbed a stubby horn in each hand. His legs moved in rapid motion as though he was running in the air. Dad hung on until the bull decided it was time to butt Dad into the ground. He lowered his head and slammed Dad against the ground with a force that knocked the breath out of him.

Dad should have been glad I had the pitchfork in my hand and was young and quick as a racer black snake. I had the sharp tines of the pitchfork in the side of the bull's neck about the time Dad hit the ground. He gave Dad one firm butt then whirled on me. I jabbed a tine into his soft nose.

The bull bellowed and shook his head. He pawed up dirt with one front foot, then the other.

"Haa!" I yelled. "Haa! Get back!" I swarped a tender ear with the tines, then swarped the other ear. The bull backed up a step, looked at the pitchfork and considered another attack.

I jabbed his nose.

The bull snorted, turned around and walked away as though nothing had happened.

Dad was on his feet with his eyes wide and his mouth hanging open. He rushed to me in a bent position and grabbed the pitchfork out of my hands.

"My God!" he said breathing hard, "Get in tha' barn quick! He's dangerous!"

My mouth must have hung open too, when Dad said that. The bull had already walked away. I had driven him back much like I had done a dozen times before.

"He'll behave for a while now. He don't like the pitchfork, especially on his ears." I said.

Dad didn't seem to hear me as he grabbed my arm and dragged me into the barn hall.

"Did he hurt you?" I asked Dad after he had slammed the door shut.

Dad took a couple of deep breaths. "No. Reckon not. Damned bull coulda killed me."

"Why, he's just a pet," I said.

"He's a damned mean pet!" Dad rubbed his stomach. "Has he acted that way before?"

"He tries to get me just about every day, but I won't let him. He respects the pitchfork."

Dad looked at me like I was crazy. "You're tellin me he tries to fight you?"

I reckon Dad was either hard of hearing or never listened to what I told him.

"Since the day you brought him home. He slammed me against the barn door once."

"You're saying that you, a hundred pound girl, has been fighting with a seven hundred pound bull?"

"I've been whippin the piss outta him almost every day."

Dad was silent for a full two minutes before he spoke.

"I'll go by Abraham Millers tomorrow. He can come up here and help get that bull back home. It's a wonder he hain't killed you long before now."

I thought about telling Dad it was him the bull nearly killed. But, I didn't say a thing for the cow would be bred by tomorrow and the bull would be gone.

Dad stood guard with the pitchfork while I did up the work that night, and then again the next morning, then he headed down the road to get Abraham Miller.

I was lying in the barn loft in the hay waiting on Dad and Abraham Miller when they showed up. I wanted to see what would happen when they tried to tie a rope around that bull's neck, and I knew Dad would run me back to the house if he saw me. Dad always ran me to the house when men came around the barn.

Years had put a lot of weight on Abraham Miller and taken hair away from his shinny round head. I'd seen more hair in squirrel gravy than he had, but there was a jolly way about him. I watched him and wondered about the education he had that made him better off than most folks. If I ever got a chance, I'd ask him what education had taught him. Right now I wanted to see how his education helped him handle his pet bull.

"That bull don't look mean to me," Abraham said to Dad.

"I didn't think he had a mean bone in him, till he danged near killed me."

"Say that girl of yours saved you?" Abraham asked with a big grin on his face.

"She shore did. I'd been a goner if it weren't for her. He had me on the ground with his head in my belly with those stub horns pokin when she took the pitchfork to him."

"I've heard that girl is something else," Abraham said. "The way Eula talks about her, you'd think she could walk on water."

Abraham leaned against the barn and looked at the cows and bull lying in the barnyard chewing their cuds.

"That little gal is the one that does the milking isn't she? Hasn't the bull bothered her?"

"She said he slammed her against the barn once but she whupped the piss outta him. I'd put my money on that gal of mine if she was fightin a grizzly bear." Dad spat at the base of a fence post and reared back. "Reminds me of my own momma, that girl of mine."

"I know you're telling the truth. There's not a man alive would say a little girl beat a bull off him unless she did it," Abraham's chuckled. "Reckon we'll have to get her to help us get him back home?"

"I told her she was to stay away from that bull," Dad said. "I lost one youngun to bees. I don't want to lose another to a bull."

Abraham hung his round head and looked at his feet. "I knew he would butt a little, but I thought it was all playful like. I'd never let you bring him here if I'd known he'd go beyond playful. I'm just glad he never hurt her or you."

"No harm's been done yet."

Abraham pushed his cap onto the very back of his bald head and scratched his shiny dome. "Let's get a bucket of corn and put a couple of ropes on him. Between the two of us we may be able to get him back home without any problem."

They didn't have any trouble getting him to eat the corn and getting the ropes around his neck, but that was as far as they were getting. The bull liked where he was and didn't want to leave the cows.

"I guess I'll have to get the pitchfork," Dad said and dropped the end of his rope. "Laine said he respected it."

"Hurry back. I don't want him to think I'm you. You might not be able to whip the piss outta him like your girl did." Abraham chuckled again and I wondered if he would be chuckling by the time he got that confounded bull home.

It was nearly dark when Dad came up the road with his feet dragging and two ropes dangling in his hands. He had never looked quite that tired when he came home from the sawmill.

"Did you have any trouble?" I asked him.

A faint grin touched Dad's lips.

"You know, a fat man rolls when he falls down."

Chapter 7

How peaceful it was milking without that red bull. It was like the bull had never been there to disturb the peace of the barnyard. The cows came in the barn one at a time, and I milked them without a fight. When I let the last cow out the door, I didn't close it immediately. Instead, I stood there a minute and breathed in the sweet air. I was glad that red bull was gone. Funny though, I missed him.

I heard the noise before I ever got to the house. Momma was having another of her spells. Her voice was sharp and screeching. Chill bumps raised the hair on my arms, as I went to the back door and stopped to listen, not knowing if I should go inside with the milk or not.

The door flew open, and Susie came running out. Her arm hit mine but she didn't slow down. She made a beeline for the woodshed, opened the door and slammed it shut behind her. She had never done that before when Momma pitched fits. I followed Susie to the wood shed.

The door groaned as I cautiously opened it. My eyes adjusted to the dim light until I saw Susie crouched in a corner almost hidden by stacks of wood. I saw from where I stood that she was shaking all over. Her face was buried on her knees and her arms were clasped over her head. It was a pitiful sight.

I went over to her and placed my hand on top of her arms.

"It's all right," I said. "It'll be over in a little while."

I felt her stiffen. She unclasped her arms and knocked my hand away. Her head lifted. Her face was wet and puffy. Her eyes were wild with fright.

"It's you," she said between clinched teeth. "You're the cause of all this! I wish you were dead instead of Joey!"

I felt like I had been too hot and then dropped into cold water.

"Why?"

"You've taken over!" She raised her hands into the air, her fingers grabbing. They were slender hands with slender fingers, soft hands clutching for something that wasn't there.

Taken over? How in this world had I taken anything over? I didn't have time to take anything over. All I ever did was work!

"You're crazy!" I said.

Susie became obsessed with rage. Her body shook. Her eyes looked the size of Banty hen eggs. Her gaze went to a stick of wood on the pile. I knew she wanted to pick up that stick of wood and hit me with it. Good sense and memory came to her. She was bigger than me, but I was meaner. She could pick up a stick of stove wood. So could I.

"I hate you, and Momma does too," she finally spat out at me.

I let it slide over me like water in a pipe.

"You deserve each other," I couldn't stop myself from saying. "Get up outta that dirt and go back to Momma. Crawl in her bed and feed on each other! I don't care!"

"You're vicious!"

I looked down on her in disgust. Her soft hands clutched each other as she gathered her feet beneath her and stood up. She gave me one last glaring look, then ran out of the wood shed back to the house. Momma was still pitching a fit.

Dad came out the door and leaned against it. His cap was pushed way back on his head letting gray hair stick out in strange directions.

"Damn, hell, and tarnation," he said. "Son of a blue-assed bitch. She'll kill me yet!"

I wanted to slip back into the woodshed and not let Dad know I had heard him, but if I moved, he would see my movement. I stood still. Dad looked up and saw me anyway. He walked over to me not seeming to care that I had heard him.

"Go to Granny Mable's. Tell her your Momma needs something strong enough to calm her and make her sleep."

I took off without saying a word to Dad. I knew where Granny Mable lived but I had never really been there, just passed near her place when I was picking berries. I took a short cut by crawling under fences and wading through creeks. I heard her dog bark before I came in sight of the house. Granny Mable met me on the path.

"What is it, child?" she asked in her comforting voice.

"Momma. Dad said she needs something to calm her and make her sleep."

She sighed and put her arm around my shoulder with the lightest of touch. She guided me along the path toward the house. My nose picked up a variety of fragrances from the many plants she had growing along the path and around her house."

"Things smell good," I said.

She nodded her head. "I've been digging roots. Have to be outta the ground before it freezes."

I had the feeling she was pleased I smelled her roots.

"Come in, child and set yourself down while I gather you some things."

She led me into the front room and sat me down in a chair. The room was dark and had only a few pieces of furniture, but I felt contented. She left me and went off into the kitchen. She came right back carrying a mug in her hand.

"Drink this. You'll like it. It's sweet sassafras."

I gave it a cautious sip and sure enough, I liked it. I drank the entire cup while I waited on her to gather stuff for Momma. She came back with two little bottles topped with corks. She held them out in front of me, and I saw they contained dark liquids.

"Child, this is strong stuff. Give it to your daddy and tell him to let her have two spoonfuls twice times a day, but no more. She ought to quieten down and sleep. That's all it will do for her though."

I stood up and reached for the bottles. She pulled them back.

"I'll put them in a poke for you. That way you won't drop and break em."

She pulled a brown paper bag out of her apron pocket and dropped the bottles inside and rolled them up, but she didn't hand them to me.

"I don't know how Dad pays you for this," I said.

"Why, child, I never charge folks. I just want to help if I can."

She looked at me so hard I felt like squirming. It seemed like she wanted to say something to me and was waiting to see if I was listening.

"If you want to learn more about herbs, you could come here each day and I'd show you what I know. You could even spend the night if you wanted."

I thought it over in my mind and decided I would like that, the learning about herbs. It would feel strange to spend a night at Granny Mable's. She was somewhere between a doctor and a witch.

"I'd like it, but it's winter soon. I hope to go to school some."

She nodded. "School's good. I want you to know you can come here and learn about herbs, or you can come just because you want to."

She handed me the bag and I left. Her black dog came up to me wagging its tail, but it eyed me suspiciously and sniffed at my legs. I scratched him behind the ears and his suspicion faded. He followed me where the end of the path met the woods then stood there watching me leave. I looked back at him and thought he looked a little lonely standing there all by himself.

It was beginning to get dark in the woods, and the shadows were deep and quiet. A north wind was rising in the sky, blowing cold through the tops of the trees. Leaves drifted down. Some touched me lightly. In a couple of weeks these woods would consist of gray bareness until the snows came.

A pheasant flew up in front of my feet and put my heart in my throat. I didn't know why a darned pheasant waited until you almost stepped on it before it took flight. Reckon they just wanted to put the fear-of-God in a body. I went on, hurrying my steps. It was starting to get dark. The earth seemed to become silent and settle in for the night. The day birds were hushed and the night birds weren't out yet. All I could hear were Katydids calling, but they wouldn't be calling much longer. They would be frozen.

I fought sadness trying to sneak into me. I longed to fly away with the birds, or hole up in a cave and sleep like a bear. Even a groundhog had enough sense to bury itself warm and deep under a tree root. Me? I had no other choice but to stay right here on top of this earth and suffer the cold. I sighed and forced my mind away from winter.

I left the woods and waded the same creeks and crawled through the same fences. It was good and dark by the time I got home. I smelled wood smoke and knew Dad had a fire going. I hadn't expected him to have supper cooked, but he did.

He took the bottles from my cold hands. "Food's still warm. Eat yourself some before you wash up the dishes," he said and went into Momma's bedroom.

I ate looking at three dirty plates sitting on the table waiting for me to wash. I filled another plate and carried it to the garden to find Dad had already left a full plate of food there for the Munson girl.

For the next four days Momma and Susie slept a lot and the house was peaceful, but Dad didn't go back to the sawmill. He stayed real close to the house and always seemed to be listening for sounds from the bedroom.

"Strip those molasses cane and get things ready to boil em off. It's almost past time," Dad told me.

Usually, Dad helped me with the molasses, but this time he didn't. It took me almost a solid week to strip the cane of leaves and seedpods then clean the mill, troughs and tubs all by myself. Dad hitched up the mule and I walked him around and around in circles until all the cane was mashed. The mule and I were exhausted.

At least Dad helped me boil the molasses off and keep wood in the fire. He even traded off with me on stirring and skimming the green castings from the top of the boiling molasses.

Momma and Susie never came outside.

"Is Momma doin better?" I asked, licking the spoon.

Dad frowned. "She'll do better soon. She needs a little more time than I thought. Havin Susie by her side helps a lot, but it's been hard on your sister. She's frail. Takes back after your Momma. You need to understand that, Laine. Susie's not like you. You and me can get knocked down, crawl away, and come up to fight another day. Your Momma and Susie are like dandelion fluff. A strong wind would blow them clear to kingdom come."

I didn't say anything back to Daddy, but I wanted to. How on God's green earth did he think Momma and Susie were frail? I felt like bending a knee to God in thanks on making me like Dad instead of Momma.

"Hadn't Susie ought to sleep in her own bed and you with Momma?" I wanted to know because Dad had been sleeping on the sofa for the entire week that I had been making molasses. I was glad Susie wasn't in bed with me. I was bone tired by the time I hit the sack. Without Susie, I got to rest better. Still, it wasn't right, her sleeping with Momma and Daddy not.

Dad downed his head and kicked a log closer to the fire. "Soon," he mumbled. "Soon."

"It hain't..."

"Soon," he repeated and walked away.

Chapter 8

🕊

I woke up feeling I had to hurry. Everything was happening too fast and getting out of control. Over the past week a fear had settled in the pit of my stomach. I felt something awful was going to happen. Dad was worn and haggard. He watched Momma and Susie like a hawk, avoided looking me in the eyes, and thought of excuses to keep me out of the house.

I didn't know what to think about Momma. Her anger and hatred seemed to grow each day while she lay in bed. She complained from the time she woke up in the morning until she fell asleep at night. Susie stayed in the bedroom right by her side, if not in bed with her. I could hear her alternately complaining, and then consoling Momma.

I was in the house washing cans for vegetable soup. Light frost came during the night and a killin frost would be tonight. This was my last chance at canning our food, except for canning the hog meat we would kill come Thanksgiving.

Susie came from the bedroom to the kitchen door and stopped, staring at me like I was in her space. I saw hatred flashing in her eyes. If she had the ability to eliminate me from the face of the earth, she would have done so.

"What're you doin in here?" Susie demanded in a petted voice I had heard her use with Momma.

I deliberately looked down at my soapy hands in the dishpan of water. Then I looked at the cans I already washed and had sitting on the table.

"I'm playing the guitar," I told her sweetly.

"You're so smart aren't you?" She gave me a triumphant look. "You're not allowed in here any way. Dad promised you wouldn't be in the house after breakfast was over."

I stopped washing cans and looked at her. "What?"

"You can't be in Momma's house except to clean and cook our meals. Dad said so."

Dad came rushing out of Momma's bedroom after hearing Susie's words.

"Susie." He placed a trembling hand on her arm. "Your Momma needs you."

Susie gave me a triumphant look and left the room. She had done what she intended to do. She let me know Dad sided with her and Momma.

Dad downed his head and left the kitchen. I followed him outside. I caught up with him before he got out of the yard.

"Is what she said true? I'm not allowed in the house unless I'm waitin on them?"

Dad kept walking toward the barn, acting like he wasn't going to answer me. His hands gripped into fists and his eyes looked at his boots. He didn't stop until he got inside the barn hall. Finally, he leaned against the wall like he no longer had strength to stand.

"Laine, understand. Your momma's drove me crazy. I can't find a minute's peace. I keep hopin time'll heal her, but it ain't done no good. I'm wonderin if it will. There's got to be something bad wrong with her. I don't know what. "

I agreed with Dad. There was something wrong with Momma and Susie both. Sick in the head. But what was wrong with Dad? Did old rocks crack and turn into sand?

"You told em I was only allowed in the house long enough to wait on em?"

"And to sleep," he said with downcast eyes and a shameful face.

"Why?" I asked fighting tears. "Why are you turnin against me for them?"

Dad's head sunk between his shoulders, and his back rounded and bent until he looked stooped and dejected, but he spoke to me.

"I married your Momma for better or worse. I took her on to care for her, and I'm bound by God and law to do it until the dirt is shoveled in on my grave." He shook his head and scrunched up his face like his next words were hurting him. "I'd give my own life for you, Laine, just like I would have my little Joey. But it won't come to that, not with you. You're of my own seed. You're made to endure the hardships of life and survive. All you need is a chance, a better one than you'll get living here. I'm bound and determined you get it. Until that chance comes along, you'll just have to abide with whatever decisions I make."

"But Dad…"

"Don't you back-talk me girl, and don't give me none of your sassy mouth."

I turned my back on Dad and walked out the door. I took the path through the woods to the top of the hill and sat down under a White Pine tree in the soft needles. I felt the chilling winds and listened to its moaning through the pines. It moaned and so did I.

I didn't leave the hill until twilight settled in the valley below, and shadows were deep in the woods. Pitch dark wasn't far away. Tonight I would not do the work nor would I cook supper. I would go to the garden, like the little Munson girl, and eat my food raw.

I thought of Granny Mable. I could go to her. Helpless. Dejected. Head hanging like a beat dog. I could not go back inside the house where I was no longer wanted by Dad.

My world was full of darkness by the time I reached home. The cows were standing around the barn waiting to be milked. Grunting hogs, murmuring chickens, a hungry mule wanted my care.

I choked down tears that threatened as I slipped in the cuttin room door. I breathed in the sweet smell of chop, corn and animals. I wanted the familiar smell of the barn to soothe the pain that was tearing me apart before I left for Granny Mable's.

"You took long enough. I've been waiting some time."

I jumped about a foot at the sound of a man's voice. I saw the outline of him sitting on a sack of chop.

"What th' devil?" I managed to say when I got some breath back.

"I didn't mean to scare you. Your pa said I could wait in here for you. He didn't invite me in the house. I guess he had his own reason not to."

He spoke to me in a tone of voice that made me think of a man trying to calm a skittish horse. Which I guess was fitting since he had nearly scared the life out of me. It was the man from Eula's store, the one that came to buy hams and hogs. It wasn't hog killing time yet.

"Why're you here?"

"I brought another wagon load of winter supplies to Eula. I traffic and trade. That's how I earn my living. Why don't you sit down on something? I have a need to talk to you."

He continued to sound like a horse calmer, and I knew he wanted to persuade me of something he feared I might not go for. So, I sat down on a sack of feed wondering what more I would have to endure today?

"Talk then," I said.

He began to talk. A man's voice in the dark.

"I unloaded Eula's stuff and knew I couldn't leave without seeing you again." His voice became a soft whisper. "I planned to wait until I came after hams, but I was too close to turn around and leave."

His voice lowered to a tender persuasive tone. I couldn't imagine what this man was leading up to. I knew of no reason why he wanted to talk to me unless he wanted to buy animals. If that was the case, he would have talked to Dad not me. I might be the one to take care of the animals, but Dad had the final word in what happened to them.

"I've already spoken to your pa."

That was it. He wanted the animals, but why would Dad have him wait and talk to me?

"Your pa gave his consent for us to marry," he said the words as though it was a simple matter. It wasn't a romantic proposal of love and devotion. It wasn't a proposal at all. I opened my mouth but nothing came out. I tried again.

"I don't know your name," I managed to say as I felt my chest constrict. There was a pain in me that started at my toes and went to the roots of my hair. Dad had come up with a solution to his problem. I could either marry this stranger, go to Granny Mable, or I could join the little Munson girl and sleep in barns and steal food from people. Great choices I had been given by the man I thought would love me regardless.

"My name is Rafford Johnson. You can call me Rafe for short."

I swallowed a couple of times.

"You're a man. Why would you want to marry me? I'm not really old enough to marry a grown man."

He chuckled. "I want to marry you because I am a grown man. You are young, healthy and hard working. That's reason enough."

"It hardly seems like reason enough to me." He was talking about our marriage as though it held no more consequence than the buying of Dad's hog.

"If you want me to give you reason enough to marry me, all you have to do is get off that sack of feed and come here. You'll have reason enough in about five minutes." His words were spoken so softly I did not feel them as a threat, nor did I have any inclination to go to him.

"That's not what I meant. Marriage is forever. It don't seem right to marry a man when I didn't even know his name five minutes ago," I tried to explain.

"I know your name, Laine. I've known it for some time now. You'll make a good wife. I own a house and land. It's a far sight better than this."

He didn't know how right he was. I had nothing here. Dad turned against me. I felt unwanted tears slide down my cheeks. I thought of Granny Mable. Could I go to her? Maybe Rafe was my best choice, my only choice.

"How do you go about a marriage?"

"Your pa will ride with us to the preacher's house and everything will be taken care of nice and legal."

"That's all it takes?"

"That's all it will take. The preacher marries a lot of people on the spot. He doesn't need any advance notice. Preachers have a box full of the proper documents."

I thought of the pink material Eula had given me. I could make a wedding dress out of it and wear the brown shoes. I had tried the shoes on, and they fit well enough. I might be able to get the dress made tomorrow.

"When do you want to do this?" I figured he would need some time to prepare things.

He stood up. "I've got my wagon behind the barn. You can wait in it while I go get your pa."

"Now!" I shouted. "You mean we'll get married now?"

"Did you have a long courtship in mind? Do you want me to court you like a tom cat after a sow cat?"

"No!"

"Then what is your objection to now?"

"We don't know each other yet. I ought to know you before I marry you."

"You'll have plenty of time to know me. We've already been over that knowing thing. Do you want to go to the wagon on your own, or do you want me to take you as I go get your pa?"

"I can find the wagon by myself." I hoped I didn't sound as defeated as I felt.

I hurried into the barn loft where I had hid my bolt of pink material and my shoes. I put the shoes on and tucked the bolt under my arm. A thought entered my mind. I went to the hay in the corner of the barn where I uncovered Dad's jug of numbin liquor. I lay my bolt down and picked up the jug. I turned the jug up to my mouth and let the liquid touch my lips. My tongue tasted it, expecting fire. I was surprised. It was just like water. "Here's to ya, Dad." I thought as I took a quick swallow. Pure fire reached my throat. Coughing shook me as I tried to breath. Tears ran down my cheeks while I gasped for air. I would surely die on the spot and welcomed the death. My insides were on fire. My ears were buzzing.

Minutes later, the coughing was over, and I had my bolt of cloth under my arm and was climbing on the wagon seat. I heard the footsteps of Dad and Rafe. They weren't talking.

Dad didn't look at me as he got on the wagon. I looked at him through the darkness, long and hard. He made me think of a dog that had been severely whipped, and I felt the same way. Rafe Johnson was the only one in good spirits. He whistled a tune as we traveled the dark dusty road in a good wagon.

We got out of the wagon and plodded, single file, to the preacher's door. Rafe knocked loud and impatient. The preacher opened the door after the third knock. Surprise flickered over his face as he saw the three of us standing there.

"Brother Elder," he said. "What can I do for you?"

Dad didn't get a chance to answer. Rafe beat him to it.

"We've come to get married."

The preacher hesitated for an instant and looked around Rafe at me. "Come in," he finally said and opened the door wider.

The room was warm and comfortable. It had a wood stove burning in the middle of the room with a sofa that didn't sag facing it. I heard the sound of his wife in the kitchen banging pots and pans. The sound gave small comfort.

"You have given Elaine your permission to marry this man?" the preacher asked Dad in his Sunday voice.

"Yes. She has my permission." Dad refused to meet the preacher's gaze.

"Well," said the preacher. "Girls do marry young now-a-days." He looked at Rafe. "What's your name? Don't know you." "My name is Rafford Johnson, and I'm not from around here."

"Rafford Johnson." The preacher said the name as though he tasted the words. "At least you're old enough to marry." The preacher sounded relieved as he looked at my stomach. His expression said he was thinking I had gotten what was deserved after talking to him the way I did at Joey's death.

"Maw!" he hollered. "Come on out here. We've got another marriage to conduct."

I repeated what the preacher told me to, and that made me married to Rafford Johnson. He owned me like a bought sow.

I didn't feel like a married woman as we rode the wagon over the bumpy road. I had the papers in my hand signed and witnessed. I was Mrs. Rafford Johnson. Elaine Johnson. I said the name over in my mind and looked at the man beside me. I thought he looked pleased even in the dark. I didn't bother to look at Dad.

Dad gave me away to please Momma and Susie.

Rafe stopped the wagon in front of our barn. No. In front of Dad's barn.

"Once we get the stock loaded I'll be on my way," Rafe said to Dad.

"What stock? On the way where?" I couldn't help but ask.

"I'll be taking you all the way to Kentucky. It'll be a long time before you come back here. If you want to take anything with you. You'd better get it now."

The finality of what he said hit me. Kentucky? Long time? What did I have to take with me to start a new life? All the food I had canned came to my mind. I knew I could never haul glass jars without breaking them, but I could take potatoes, onions and apples. I wanted to take some of my garden seeds. I didn't expect Rafe to have any. I jumped off the wagon and ran to the can house. I lit the candle I kept in the can house and divided the seeds in half. I took three sacks of potatoes, one sack of onions, and two sacks of apples. I left plenty for them, although I felt I should have taken half. I added some candles and matches and looked about for what I might need as a married woman. I picked up a dented pan that had gotten into the can house, and looked at the jars of molasses. I wanted a couple of those.

I thought about going in the house to get my Sunday dress and the old coat and socks I had stored from last winter. I didn't. I wouldn't be able to stand the look of triumph on Momma's and Susie's face.

When I got my first load dragged to the road, I couldn't believe what I saw on the wagon in crates. There was the black sow with her entire litter of pigs, a chicken coop with half a dozen hens and a rooster. Pet was tied to the back of the wagon. I felt my heart soften toward Rafe. He wasn't leaving behind everything I loved. I would be taking part of home with me. Rafe loaded my produce along with four sacks of corn and two sacks of chop.

Dad looked at the loaded wagon, but he didn't look at me. "You might as well load up a grown hog if you've got the room. She'll need meat this winter, and I'll be pushed at hog killin without her."

Rafe didn't argue. He picked out the best hog to take with us. Once we were loaded Rafe looked at me.

"You best put your coat on. It gets cold at night."

"I'll be all right," I said as I crawled onto the wagon.

Dad took off the jacket he had worn for years and wrapped it around my shoulders. "Have a good life," he said as his hand squeezed my arm. He turned from me and hurried to the house.

I fought tears.

Rafe clicked the team of horses up and we started off down the road in pitch-black darkness. Soon the moon would be up, and the horses could see better.

We didn't get out of the valley when Rafe pulled the horses off the road into a little clearing. Rafe got off the wagon and came around to my side. He reached up and lifted me down. Surely he wasn't going to stop for the night? It was dark and the traveling was slow, but the horses would be fine if Rafe let them pick their way.

"You're not stoppin are you?" I asked as he took my arm and led me a little ways from the wagon.

"For a few minutes," he said as his hands felt down the front of my dress.

It dawned on me what Rafe had in mind. "No." I said. "Not here. Not like this."

"Yes. Right here, like this."

Chapter 9

We had been driving since daylight over what Rafe called a road, but it looked more like a goat path climbing upward through the woods. It was obvious it had not been used in a long time. There was barely room for the wagon between the large trees. Saplings had grown up in the road and scraped the bottom of Rafe's wagon. I was relieved the wagon was in much better condition than Dad's. The saplings would have torn out the bottom of Dad's wagon. They only made the riding bumpier in Rafe's.

Sometimes we came upon a rock or a tree limb so big Rafe would have to get off the wagon and move it out of the way. Other times Rafe would wait for me to jump off the wagon and move them.

The sun was high in the sky when Rafe stopped the wagon and got off the seat. I noticed the broadness of his shoulders, and the thickness of his chest. He looked strong, like a well-fed bull stretching after a rest. I wanted to feel proud of my husband, but try as I might, I could not muster up the feeling. I consoled my troubled mind by assuring myself it would come with time; after all, I didn't know this man yet.

"There's a creek down that way." He pointed down the bank. "Fetch some water. Roast some potatoes."

I didn't like the way he said that. It sounded as though he thought no more of me than he did the horses pulling the wagon. I was his wife. A wife should have a special place with her husband. But then he didn't know me either.

I thought about setting things straight with him right away when it came to giving me orders, but I decided not to do that. I would give us time to get used to one another first.

"Won't the animals need water?" I asked him.

"Water them if you want to," he told me as he stalked off in the woods.

I decided nature was calling him as badly as it was calling me. I found a secluded spot down near the creek and relieved myself before I did anything else. Then, I got my dented old pan out of the wagon and dipped it full of water, dreading how many pans full it would take to water all the animals.

I got one of the matches and had a fire started by the time Rafe got back to the wagon. I put the potatoes in the fire to roast before I started watering the animals. I had milk from the cow and four eggs the hens laid. I could feed Rafe a meal.

Rafe grinned down at me with a mocking expression on his face. "You use matches to start a fire?

I smiled at him the way I thought a new wife should. "I do."

"I expected you to rub sticks together to get a fire from the way Eula talked about you."

"Really?"

Rafe squatted down in front of me and looked me over from head to toe, as though he were finding out things about me by looking.

"How do you like being my wife?"

I looked into his green eyes, lifted my hand and touched his cheek and felt the coarseness of beard and the firmness of jaw. Rafe Johnson was a fine looking man.

"I don't rightly know yet," I told him truthfully.

Up until this moment, I had hated every minute I was with him. Maybe it was fear settling in my gut, for I had imagined him taking me to a place in Kentucky worse than the Munson's. All the preparations I had done for winter were left behind with Dad, Momma and Susie.

"You don't know?" His eyes narrowed.

I rubbed my finger lightly over his bottom lip. It was smooth, soft.

"The breedin part hurt more'n I ever knowed it would," I admitted and let my hand fall and my eyes drop from his. "It still throbs."

"First time's always like that. From now on it won't hurt." He looked me in the eyes and said harshly. "You ever spread for a man other than me, I'll kill you."

Shock silenced me. Anger mixed with fear came next.

"Rafe?" I tried to keep my voice from shaking as I spoke. "We are goin to have a good life? We won't fight and hate each other?"

Rafe spit into the fire. "So long as you do what you're supposed to," he said as he stood up and went to the wagon.

I had trouble keeping my hands from trembling as I put sticks in the fire. I would do my best to love and respect this man. I would.

I had half the animals watered when Rafe came around the wagon and grabbed my wrist. His eyes narrowed and his mouth tightened. "When will the potatoes be cooked?"

"Another fifteen minutes or so."

His fingers tighten on my wrist. He pulled me a step or two away from the wagon, and ran his tongue over his lips.

"Lie down."

I didn't move.

Rafe stepped forward and spraddled his legs until I stood against his belly. I felt the bulge at his crotch with repulsion. He took my hand and placed it on the bulge.

"Feel that?" His eyebrow lifted. "It won't hurt this time. Lie down," he ordered again, and I did.

He lied.

We drove the wagon through the woods for two more days with nothing to eat but warm milk, eggs, apples, and potatoes. It felt to me like we were wandering around in circles. When we crossed the creek it was always the same fullness of water. I didn't understand why the creek never got narrower or broader as most creeks do. The vegetation was always the same and the animals were getting tired and losing weight. The horses appeared to be as bewildered as I was. They shook their heads and rattled their harnesses as they tried to go in a different direction than Rafe had them go.

We needed to leave the woods long enough to find grass for the horses and cow to eat. I had been feeding them my meager supply of corn, but I didn't want to use it all up on our trip to Kentucky. I turned to Rafe and asked a question.

"What kind of place do you live in?"

"It's plenty good enough for the likes of you," he said.

In the three days we had been married I learned Rafe had an unreasonable temper and could not take anything that sounded like criticism, but I tried to ignore it.

"Do you have a supply of corn and potatoes and such to plant in the spring, or must I save what we have in the wagon?"

"I can trade on them when the time comes. It don't mean you can be wasteful. I won't have a spoiled wife on my hands."

He was as hateful as Dad's old mule. I longed for a hoe handle. "Rafe? You do want me as your wife don't you? No body forced you to marry me or anything?"

Rafe turned his head and looked at me. I thought I saw his handsome face soften a little.

"Nobody forced me to marry you, Laine."

The very fact that he had said my name made me want to laugh with joy. It was the first time since our wedding.

"As I told you before, I married you because you are young, healthy, and work hard. You should be worth the aggravation a wife puts a man through." A flicker of a grin eased the harshness of his words. "You're even getting used to the breeding part."

Another lie. I looked at him hard not knowing if he was serious or trying to poke fun at me. I hadn't noticed any humor in him up to now so I took him as being serious.

"I'll try to do what you want if you'll show me how."

Rafe Johnson laughed.

I remembered seeing him in Eula's store and thinking him the best looking man I had ever seen. At this moment I thought it again.

"You're the handsomest man I've ever set eyes on," I blurted out impulsively. "I never thought a man like you would want to marry me."

His face took on a different look, as though he had been contented in some way.

"You don't want to run back to Eula's pudgy son? Eula wanted you for him, you know."

"I didn't want her doughboy."

"He was well off. A house, store, land and a bank full of money." Rafe looked straight ahead as he spoke.

"All that might be okay if he didn't go along with it. Fancy livin hain't worth much if you're in misery."

"You're saying you'd rather live in a shack with a man you like, than in a fancy place with someone you don't like?"

I thought of the shack that Rafe was surely taking me to and hid a shudder. Dad's house wasn't much but it was warm, and we had plenty of food. I guess I could do the same with Rafe. We would make do.

I looked at him for a time then slid across the rough, wooden seat until I was against him. I carefully touched his arm with the tip of my finger.

"I'd take a man over possessions any day of the week," I said with as much conviction as I could manage.

Rafe grinned then hit a rock with the wagon wheel that jarred every tooth in my mouth.

"Kentucky sure must be a far piece," I said wearily. "I don't know how you stand to travel this far often? Every bone in my body hurts from all the bumping and jarring."

"It's not much further. We should be there by dark."

His words brought the first relief I had felt in three days. Any kind of shack would be better than an open wagon, in a cold woods, with nothing but Dad's old coat to keep me warm.

It wasn't an hour later that Rafe drove the wagon out of the deep woods onto a road that looked a little more like a road. There were two ruts with grass growing in the middle although we were still in trees and laurel bushes.

The horses and cow tried to grab mouthfuls of the tough grass as they walked. I felt a difference in the air. It was getting colder and we seemed to be climbing higher as we traveled. Many of the colorful leaves had fallen to the ground and crunched under our wheels. The red of the Oak, the gold of the Maple, and the brown of the Beech trees created a fairyland of beauty around us. The wind blew the leaves from their limbs and let them swirl over the ground. All it would take was one good rain and the trees would be bare, but right now our surroundings were so pretty I wanted to stop the wagon and roll in the leaves like Joey might have done. We rounded a curve in the road and a house came into view.

Emotion flickered in my chest and a feeling of contentment came over me. It was like I was looking at a much-loved place that now needed some maintenance.

Frost- bit weeds of Spanish needle and Pigweed were towering in healthy growth. The yard had several huge oak trees shading the house, and the road we were on continued around back of he house and out of sight.

Kentucky sure had one nice house, at least. It was a huge house with many large windows and doors. There were two porches on the front supported with big round posts and little white picket fences on both the porches. There were five long, half circle steps leading from the ground to the first porch. It had to be at least fifteen feet across the porch to the front double doors. Never in my life had I seen a porch that big. The porch on top of that porch was the same in size.

There were little bushes growing in front of the house and climbing vines at the corners. I counted four chimneys and wondered how much firewood it would take to keep that big house warm in winter. I forced my eyes to leave the house and look at the outbuildings. I could see several small buildings and a tremendously big barn surrounded by wooden fences that separated meadows of lush green grass. The grass was so tall it fell over and showed signs of light frostburn.

I wondered why there were no animals in the meadows to graze the grass down. I turned my head and listened. There wasn't the sound of chickens cackling or the bawl of a cow. There wasn't even the bark of a dog. The pretty old place seemed deserted. There wasn't any smoke rising from either chimney. There should not be such lack of life on a farm like this. If old folks lived here, they could still have a dog and a few chickens running about. I turned to Rafe wanting to ask questions as he drove the wagon off the road and stopped in front of the barn. I knew he must be stopping to rest the horse and feed the animals before we went on. I hoped no one would mind our intruding.

"How much further do we have to go?" I asked Rafe.

He gave me a triumphant look. "We're here," he said proudly. "This is my place. You can find somewhere to put the animals before you fix supper." He tossed me the reins and climbed off the wagon and headed toward the house.

After some of my shock wore off, I got off the wagon and led my cow to the pasture with the least amount of grass in it. I knew she would be hungry and didn't want her to eat enough green stuff to bloat her especially after the grass was frostbit. I would let her eat until I found a place to put the chickens, then I would put her in the barn before I found a place for the hogs. I put the horses directly into a stall where I gave them corn and water. Tomorrow I would let them graze a little at a time. They would have to cool down and rest up before they had much grass to eat. A horse could founder in a heartbeat.

I carried two pigs at a time to a barn stall until I had them all inside. Then I got a bucket with some corn in it and led the sow to the pigs. The shoat Dad had given us was so tired and poorly fed it followed me with ease.

I dragged the sacks of potatoes off the wagon and stored them in the barn hall. I didn't want to take a chance on frost chilling them during the night. I left the wagon where it sat in front of the barn. I would find where it was kept when morning came.

Right now, I was so bone weary all I wanted was a soft warm bed to sleep in. My three days of misery were over and the shock of Rafe owning this wonderful place had me in a state of disbelief.

I feared if I closed my eyes and opened them again, all would be gone.

I crossed the yard to the door Rafe had unlocked and entered. It was a single door on the right hand side of the impressive double doors and led directly into the kitchen.

Pleasure and repulsion hit me at the same time. There was a large table in the center of the big room with six chairs pushed under the table. A green enamel cook stove sat near the back wall in the center of white painted cabinets that could have held every item Momma owned including cans in the can house. Waist high counters run the length of the cabinets, which delighted me.

What didn't delight me was the mess! There wasn't one spot as big as the palm of my hand not covered with molded pots, pans, and dishes. It looked like an army had eaten then left the remains where they had fallen. I could see one reason Rafe wanted a wife that would work. There was enough work in this room to keep three people busy for a week.

Rafe came into the kitchen through a closed door that led from another part of the house. I found myself wanting to ask him if he had suffered broken arms for an extended period of time. I knew I would be wise to hold my tongue.

"I guess I need to know where the wood shed and spring house is," I said with as much enthusiasm as I could manage. "A person could live in a kitchen as grand as this. I can hardly wait to see the rest of the house," I smiled up at Rafe and did not add that it would take a lifetime to clean if the rest of the house looked like the kitchen.

Rafe pointed to another closed door with a look of pleasure on his face. "Open that door and see what you find."

I opened the door and caught my breath. Right there in the house itself was the springhouse. The room was about eight by ten foot in size with shelves on three walls and a concrete trough on the other. Water was running from a pipe on one end filling the trough, and running out of an overflow pipe on the other end.

I could not believe my eyes. I would live in a house with running water inside.

There would be no tromping through deep snow this winter to fetch and tote water, milk and butter from the springhouse. I could even keep the eggs fresh and cool on the shelves. I wouldn't have to put them in a crock in the water unless I wanted to. I noticed there were dozens and dozens of tins and crocks setting on the shelves collecting dust and cobwebs. I would see what they contained later.

"Oh my," I managed to say as I turned in a circle and stared.

Rafe smiled. "I thought a woman might like this, even if they weren't the lazy type."

"Oh Rafe! I've never seen the likes in my life. I never dreamed of such."

Rafe was clearly pleased with my reaction.

"There's a wood shed built up against the back side of the house nice and convenient like. All you have to do is step off the back porch and get wood. Your little toes won't hardly touch snow this winter," He said a bit sarcastically.

"Why, this place is a mansion! Rafe, are you rich?"

Rafe's entire face brightened, and for the first time I felt a spark of the feelings toward him I had wanted to feel. He looked like a happy man instead of the brooding one I had been with the past three days.

"Did you think I would be a no-good trashy white man begging for his next bite of food?" His broad chest seemed to puff out and his chin lifted to an arrogant angle. "I'm a man of means. One to be reckoned with, I might add. I get respect wherever I go."

I had to admit I was surprised. It was true he cut a fine figure, but there was something else about Rafe that I couldn't place my finger on. It was something that made me afraid.

"Were you raised here? Are your parents dead?" I asked, but knew I had made a mistake by the change in Rafe.

His green eyes grew cold while he looked at me. I saw his hands clinch into fists. I moved quickly to Rafe and slipped my arms around his waist. I smiled and tried to sound like a loving wife.

"You've done mighty fine. Especially to be as young as you are. I can't believe I was lucky enough for you to marry me. I'm sure you could've had any number of pretty girls."

Some of the coldness in Rafe's eyes faded and I knew one of the secrets to living with him would be to make him feel good about himself. I guess some men just needed to be bragged on.

I was surprised when he answered my questions.

"I was raised a long ways from here in a rocky Kentucky hollar. My folks died when I was just a boy. They never had a pot to piss in their entire life. They left me to survive the best way I could, " his eyes narrowed for a few moments then brightened again. "I earned this place all by myself. My folks didn't hand it down to me on a silver platter. Show some respect for the fine conditions I've put you in by fixing me a decent meal."

Rafe turned and disappeared into another room. It was nearly dark inside and I looked about for an oil lamp, but didn't see one. It would be impossible to find where they were kept any time soon in this mess. I gave up on the lamps, lit a candle and hurried out to find the woodshed while there was still some light.

As Rafe had said, I found a nice woodshed in need of having a loose door hinge repaired. The only problem was I couldn't see any wood and it wasn't because of the darkness. The woodshed Rafe had been so proud of was empty except for wood chips scattered over the floor where someone had split wood in the past. I gathered what I could of the chips in my arms and consoled myself by thinking the chips would make good kindling. There might be limbs on the ground beneath the oak trees I could gather to cook supper with. I would certainly find more on the hill in back of the house. Woods always had fallen limbs.

Fortunately for me, no one had picked up limbs from the yard in some time. I found plenty enough sticks to cook supper and enough to cook breakfast with the next morning.

I apologized to Rafe for serving him the same meal of eggs and potatoes we had eaten for three days. At least we had boiled potatoes and fried eggs on real plates with one of the candles from home lit to see with.

"I'll fix you a better meal tomorrow after I find where everything is," I promised as we ate. "I couldn't find where the oil lamps were stored. You may have to show me."

"You'll find things as you clean," he told me. "What you can't find, make a list and I'll see what I can get on my next trip."

I wanted to ask when his next trip would be and to where, but I remained silent as to that.

"I got all the animals put in the barn stalls. I should be able to milk even in the dark. I haven't been through the house yet," I told him. " You might ought to tell me where I'll be sleepin or show me."

"You'll be sleeping in my bed. You'll be welcome to share it as long as you don't snore or keep me awake. I'm a busy man. I need to sleep good at night." He sounded like the hardest working man that ever lived. "It's the first door on the right after you walk up the stairs," he added.

I hadn't gotten a chance to see beyond the kitchen. When I got back to the house from milking, Rafe had taken the candle to the bedroom and had blown it out long before I got there. Leaving me unable to see anything about the house. I had to feel my way up stairs and find the first door to the right. Rafe's snoring helped me find the right room. Only part of me was disappointed to find him sound asleep instead of waiting up on me. The other part was glad he was asleep and didn't wake up when I got in bed. I wouldn't have to endure the breeding tonight.

Rafe slept in bed a lot like Susie. He took up his room in the middle and left me hanging on the edge, but I had to admit the bed was comfortable although it smelled musty and the covers were tangled.

I suspected Rafe didn't clean kitchens, cut firewood or make up beds.

I opened my eyes the next morning with the first light. Energy had returned to me with rest. I wanted to see the house in which I was to live. I eased out of bed and tiptoed from the room.

Rafe slept on.

All I could make out in the bedroom was dark shadows that showed the bedroom in a worse mess than the kitchen.

The hall was floored in wood, smooth beneath my bare feet, with a rug running down the center of the long hall. The walls appeared to be narrow beadwood boards and looked mighty fine in the dim light. A rug covered the stair steps. The handrail felt like polished silk beneath my hand. As soon as daylight came I would come back to the stairs and see what the place looked like. Right now I wanted to build a fire in the cook stove to take away the chill from the early morning air.

Kentucky was definitely colder than home.

Stepping onto the back porch, I breathed deep of the cold air. My rooster crowed from the direction of the barn. I looked into the dawning sky and said my thanks to God for letting me be lucky enough to marry Rafford Johnson and him having a place like this one. Abraham Miller's place couldn't compare to this. I wished Momma and Susie could know what a fine house and land this was.

They would be so jealous of me!

I had a hot fire going and hot water in the water closet by the time the kitchen was light enough for me to see. I washed the pots and pans I hadn't gotten washed last night and cleaned out a cabinet to put them in.

Whoever purchased the cookware and dishes certainly knew quality and bought it. Even I knew it was quality and I had never come in contact with it before. I washed dishes that were heavy and felt like everyday ware along with thin lightweight dishes with pink roses on a pure white background trimmed in gold. I carefully put these dishes away by themselves. I would only use them on Sunday and special occasions. The heavy dishes I put within easy reach.

There were several quart jars of salt and pepper in the back corner of a lower cabinet, and a twenty-pound sack of flour and one of corn meal, with the tops still sewn together, in a little closet. These were store-bought stuff, not ground at the local mill.

There was a bucket, dented and worn, that was surely used as a mop bucket and two shiny buckets covered in dust that could have been milk buckets. I would wash up one and use it for that very purpose. Right now I used the two buckets to carry water from the wonderful springhouse and refilled the water closet attached to the wood stove. It would take a lot of hot water before the kitchen was clean. I just wished I could find some kind of soap to use and decided to search in the tins and crocks on the shelves in the springhouse.

I wanted to dance with joy when I pried the lid off one of the tins and found it contained hog lard. Rafe must have bought it on one of his trips since I saw no signs of hogs around the farm. I pried off another lid and found more lard. I left the other tins unopened for the time being and took one of the smaller crocks off the shelf. I untied the white string and removed the circle of oilcloth used to cover the crock. It contained dried leaves from some kind of plant. I took a pinch of the leaves in my fingers and rubbed it beneath my nose. Mint. The crock contained dried mint leaves. I guess somebody had saved it for making mint tea, but it had been there for a while. The leaves didn't have a lot of strength left in them but appeared to still be usable.

Another crock contained bottles of flavoring. There was vanilla, lemon, orange, black walnut and rum flavoring in small bottles. There was even a pint jar filled with cinnamon sticks and sealed with a zinc lid. Another crock had small jars filled with dark liquid and closed with corks. There were pieces of white tape on the jars written on in pencil. Cold, fever, congestion, swelling, constipation, gout, sore throat, cough, headache, and liver were written on the tape. I guess this was Rafe's medicine supply. It didn't look like store bought stuff. He must have gotten it from somebody like Granny Mable.

I put off looking in the rest of the tins and crocks until later. I had better take my newfound milk bucket to the barn.

I went through the side yard and stared at the out buildings and fenced lots. I had never seen anything so fine in my life. The barn had been painted red some time ago and the tin roof was painted black.

I opened the barn door by lifting a plank out of a slot that had been designed for the purpose of keeping a barn door closed tight and secure in all kinds of weather. A hardheaded mule would have problems figuring out how to open this barn door.

I thought of Dad and his old mule and felt a stab of pain. I forced the thought out of my mind as I went into the barn. There was the smell of a musty, unused barn being penetrated by the warm smells of my animals. Soon I would have life back on Rafe's farm.

I found a shelf on the wall just inside the door. It was there for the milk buckets, just like in Dad's barn. I set my bucket on it and walked down the hallway. There were twelve stalls, six on each side. I had only filled four stalls. Rafe could trade on more cows and I could earn money for myself just like I had earned for Momma. I hoped it wasn't too far to a store. Three days to Eula's was too far for me to travel often. I wondered how often Rafe did his traveling. Maybe he could take my produce with him. I opened a door and discovered it was the cuttin room. To my surprise it was nearly full of sacks containing chop, oats and shelled corn that looked perfectly good. Rafe must have had animals here not too long ago. I guess he kept some feed for the ones he traded on.

I hoped he didn't get any notion of selling my animals. I had no intention of letting any of them go. A farm like this could support twenty times more animals than I had.

I saw stair steps along the side of the wall leading from the cuttin room to the loft. I took them and found another pleasant surprise. Hay. Over half the loft was stacked to the rafters. I sniffed the air for the sweet smell of fresh hay and found it lacking. It wasn't this year's hay for the light had turned it yellow. Still it was usable, and I was mighty happy. There was hay and grain for the animals. How did I ever get so lucky?

I fed everything real fast and milked in a hurry. I would see to things better after I fed my husband breakfast. Unfortunately, the chickens hadn't laid eggs this early and the cow gave only a fraction of milk I usually got. She would pick back up in a few days of eating the grass and being fed well. The trip to Kentucky hadn't been an easy one on the animals.

The smell of breakfast cooking brought Rafe to the kitchen. He looked puffy eyed and grouchy.

"Good mornin," I said and rushed to him and placed a kiss on his cheek. I wanted to show him how happy I was to be his wife and have the good fortune of hay and grain to go along with everything else.

He gave me a long sour look. "You've seen the rest of the house," he mumbled.

"Not yet," I gave his arm a squeeze. "What I've seen so far is mighty impressive," I admitted.

Rafe sank down at the table without returning my kiss or commenting about the clean kitchen.

"How about a cup of coffee?"

"I'm sorry Rafe. I've not been able to find any coffee yet. I'll perk it for you if you'll tell me where it is."

"You should have brought some from home."

"You don't have any here?"

Rafe frowned. "I reckon you wanted everything laid out on a silver platter for you? You ought to be thrilled with this place after what you've been used to."

Rafe's words surprised me, not to mention the tone of his voice. I wanted to say something harsh back to him. Instead, I pretended to be the good wife and spoke sweetly as I could manage.

"I'm thrilled with this place, and I'm thrilled to have you. I just couldn't find coffee, but I made you biscuits and gravy."

"I hope it's fit to eat," he said as he rubbed his hand over his face.

I noticed he had not washed all the dirt off his hands from our three-day trip and considered, only for a moment, of dipping up a wash pan of warm water for him. I needed a good wash myself and would do that very thing sometime today.

"I'll cook food anyway you want me to if you'll tell me how you like it," I said sweetly but my sweet feeling had started to fade fast.

He ate two full plates of food and drank all the milk without saying one word about my cooking being fit to eat or not. I didn't ask if he liked it. When he had finished, he pushed himself back from the table and stood up.

"I eat dinner at twelve. That should give you time to get this place cleaned up."

I saw him leave the house a few minutes later with a gun over his shoulder. He was headed toward the woods, and I wondered what kind of game he was after? I wouldn't mind having a turkey to eat, but common sense told me not to hold my breath waiting for Rafe to kill one.

I put a couple sticks of wood in the stove to keep the water hot and went into the little hall where the stairs were. I opened the door next to the stairs and entered the living room. I looked about me then hurried to the two large windows and drew the curtains open until I could see the room better.

I had never seen such fine things before. Not even in a Sears and Roebuck catalogue. The curtains I had just pulled back were made of a rose colored lace with a lighter shade of rose material lining them. There was a darker rose-colored fringe decorating the edges of the curtains on the sides and top.

The sofa was a deep red color and as soft as a kitten when I rubbed my hand over it. It had walnut wood carved with flowers, birds and fruit on the curved, arched back; with eagle heads carved in the arm rests. The legs were carved like a birds claw clamped onto a round ball of glass. There were two red chairs to match and a short glass table sitting in front of the sofa.

I couldn't believe my eyes. There was a tiny vase sitting in the center of the glass table with dried up pansies in it. No way in my mind could I see Rafe ever putting them there. Where could they have come from? I pushed it from my mind and continued to look around. A rug I had never seen the likes of was lying on the floor beneath the sofa and chairs. It felt like inch long velvet underneath my bare feet. It had all the colors I had ever dreamed of in it, including the rose pink in the curtains and the matching red of the sofa and chairs. There were lamps of colored glass with fringe surrounding candles that were too pretty to ever light and burn. There was a rock fireplace that took up half the wall with bookshelves on both sides taking up the other half. There were even real books filling the shelves. Fancy carved tables and dressers were against the walls along with long mirrors in carved frames.

I saw myself reflected in one of the dirty mirrors and stopped and stared. I had never seen myself from my feet to my head in a mirror before. I looked like a full-grown woman with long dark hair wearing a shabby dress that barely covered my slender body. I forgot about my reflection and wanted to wash the dirty mirror.

It would do my soul good just to clean this room. I went back into the hall to look at the rug on the stairs. It was a rich wine color with shades of pink, rose and blues. I got down on my knees and looked at the little brass headed tacks that held the rug to the steps.

I stood and rubbed my hand over the polished oak of the handrail. It felt the same as it did that morning – smooth silk. I slowly went up the stairs one step at a time looking at the pictures on the wall. One picture was of mountains and trees surrounding a lake. The picture was so beautiful I almost thought I was there. Another picture in a gold frame was of pastel flowers that picked up the colors in the rug. The walls were of bead board polished and golden with age.

The floor of the upstairs hall was the same fine oak of the living room and downstairs hall. I pushed the door open to the bedroom Rafe and I had slept in. There was so much trash and clothes scattered about I couldn't tell much except I thought it would be really nice once I got it cleaned.

I pulled the cover back from the bed and looked at what were once white sheets. They looked like someone had

jumped up and down on them with dirty shoes. I tossed the
cover on the littered floor and stripped off the sheets and
pillowcases. If I hurried, I could have them washed and
dried before bedtime that night. I hoped I could get the
sheets washed in time to start cleaning the bedroom before
I had to cook dinner.

I found two washtubs hanging on the wood shed wall
and felt like dancing. I was sure there was everything a
person could want hidden somewhere in this house.

I would find every treasure, one piece at a time.

Later I could go over the house and the farm with a fine-
toothed comb. Right now, I filled both tubs with warm
water and placed the sheets in one to soak. I wished again
for soap.

Surely a fancy house like this had soap somewhere.
Momma kept soap in the kitchen, but a house like this
might have a washroom. I started walking through the
downstairs of the house, opening doors.

There was the kitchen, the living room, and a dining
room with fancy table and chairs and a lace tablecloth.

I opened another door and found a room with a piano in
the center of it. I knew what a piano was. I had seen them
in books, but this was my first real one. I went to it,
cautiously lifted the lid and touched a key. I poked nearly
every key before I could make myself stop.

On the far side of this room a door opened into a
bedroom not as large as the one Rafe slept in. This room
was neat as a pin except for the layer of dust. The bed was
narrow with an iron head and footboard painted white. Next
to the window was a door cracked slightly open, which led
onto the side porch of the house. I had a feeling that no one
ever slept in this room and wondered why the door was
open.

Leaving the bedroom by the open door, I walked
through the yard to the back of the house finding another

door near the woodshed. I opened the door and heard the hinges squeak in rusty protest. I was looking into a small storage room containing a variety of supplies and tools. My eyes came to rest on a five-gallon glass jar with a large lid. In the jar, to my delight, was soap. At least two dozen square bars of soap. I laughed out loud. I knew this place had everything a body could want.

I unscrewed the lid and took out a couple of bars and rushed back to my tub of sheets. I could now wash and clean big time. Getting the sheets as clean as possible, I dumped them into the rinse water, rung them out with my hands and carried them to the clothesline strung between posts in the back yard. There were even clothespins on the line. The pale sunlight and cool winds would dry them.

After I had the sheets hung up, I started wondering what I could fix for dinner.

I looked off into the distance and saw apple trees at the edge of the woods. If I had time after dinner, I would gather as many apples as I could and find a place to store them for winter use. I found myself longing for canning jars to can the apples in. Surely I would be able to find some if I looked hard enough. I already found quart cans filled with salt and pepper. There had to be more cans somewhere.

On the way back from the barn I picked up sticks of wood for the cook stove. I would have to find a lot of wood to last all winter. There was probably a lot of dead fall in the woods. I wondered if Rafe would be any good at cutting wood? Somehow I didn't think he would be good at anything pertaining to hard physical work although he had a fit, hard body. Surely he had to do some sort of hard work to have the muscles he had. He was strong. He was handsome. He had a beautiful house and farm that hadn't been handed down to him from his parents. How long had he owned this place? Who had he bought it from? Oh Rafe, I wondered how was it I was getting more comfort from the house and land than I was getting from him? Why did he always seem so grouchy and unhappy? Was I doing something wrong? Surely there was something I could do to make Rafe happy especially when I wanted to so badly. I didn't want to be a wife like Momma had been. One that thought only of herself and her own needs.

I quickened my steps. It wasn't long until I had to start cooking dinner, and I wanted to take that bath I had promised myself. I dipped some more hot water from the water closet and poured it into one of the washtubs, took my feed-sack dress off and stepped in with determination. I scrubbed my hair and body with the soap I had found then rinsed myself off with the milk bucket full of water. The soap had a lot of lye in it from the way it smelled, and wished I had some bubby roses to mash on my body so I could smell good, thinking Rafe would like a sweet-smelling wife. I put my feed-sack dress back on and ran my fingers through my long hair in an attempt to get the tangles out. I should have brought a comb from home, too. I forgot about myself. I had to start dinner for my husband.

I could make some corn bread and some onion soup and bake him some potatoes nice and golden brown along with stewed apples and maybe even an apple pie. I was glad I had slipped a couple of jars of molasses in the potato sacks. I was afraid I couldn't haul glass jars in the wagon without breaking, but I took a chance on the molasses. I thought the potatoes would protect a jar or two. It had. Now I had sweet for special occasions.

It was long past mid-day and Rafe had not come home. I worried about him and keeping his food warm without ruining its taste. I wanted this meal to be something special. Finally, I pushed all the food to the back of the stove and went upstairs to clean the bedroom. I had gotten good and started when I heard the kitchen door slam.

I rushed down the stairs with a smile on my face. My husband was home at last. I wanted him to feel like the most important person in the state of Kentucky. After all, he was my very own husband.

There was no smile on Rafe's face. He was sour and looked ill tempered. Maybe it was because he hadn't killed anything; at least I didn't see him carrying anything. I crossed the kitchen and put both my arms around his waist and turned my lips up to kiss him. He turned his cheek away and looked irritated.

"Kissie, kissie." He sneered and pushed my arms away.

Fine! I thought. If he didn't want me to kiss him, I wouldn't. I was only trying to be the kind of wife I thought I should be; one that was loving and kind and showed affection.

"You're late," I said as I turned away from him.

Rafe looked at me hard. "I won't have a woman telling me when I'm late and when I'm not."

I ignored his remark as best I could. I was puzzled though. Why was Rafe Johnson such a moody man? It seemed to me Rafe had everything a man could want. He was young and healthy with uncommon good looks. He had a house that was nothing short of a mansion, and a farm on top of a mountain that appeared to be rich and fertile. He had barns and outbuildings like none I had ever laid eyes on. He now had a young, healthy wife that was willing to work and try to love him. What was wrong with him?

I took up the food in the pretty, pink flowered bowls because I wanted this meal to be special, and set them in front of him on the table. He spooned out the food onto his plate and began to eat before I could even sit down. I reckon he was hungry after hunting in the woods all morning.

"Did you have any luck?" I asked.

I had gotten tired of the silence. The least my husband could do was talk to me. How was I to know how to make him happy if he wouldn't talk?

"What do you mean by luck?"

"Did you kill anything when you went huntin?"

"I wasn't trying to kill anything. I was enjoying some peace and quiet."

I took that as telling me I talked too much. I let him eat in peace and quiet. When he had almost cleared his plate, I got up and cut him a big piece of warm apple pie and placed it in front of him along with a little cup of cream. He looked at the cream like he didn't know what it was for. I didn't say a word as I took the cream and poured it on my pie. He looked at my pie as I ate, but he didn't put cream on his.

After he finished eating his pie and I still hadn't said anything, he looked at me.

"You're pouting. I hate a woman that pouts."

"I'm not poutin," I told him, but I was. "I was lettin you eat in peace and quiet."

He grinned. "I'm going to take a nap while you clean this filthy kitchen."

I didn't like his remark for I had cleaned on the kitchen. His grin made me wonder if he was trying to aggravate me or if he was serious.

He got up and left the room without saying anything more to me. I felt like crying. Why could I not make my husband happy? What was I doing wrong?

I cleaned the kitchen from dinner then went outside.

I breathed deep of the clean mountain air. The sun was warm on my skin. The wind was so still only an occasional leaf floated down to the ground. For a few moments, I let the thought of Dad enter my mind and wondered what was going on back home? I wondered if they missed me and wished I were still there? I hoped they did. My life back home seemed so far away, and my life here didn't seem real. When it did become real, I wondered if it would be paradise or a nightmare.

I heard one of the horses kick the barn wall and went to let them and the cow out to graze a little more. I stood near the fenced pasture and watched the pair of sorrel horses move about. They were a perfectly matched pair of fine workhorses. I wondered where Rafe had found them? Being the trader he said he was, I reckon it could have been anywhere. I thought about the trafficing and trading he said he did for a living. It surely must pay good for him to have a place like this. It would take Dad several lifetimes to earn enough money to buy this place.

I left the fence and wandered around behind the barn. I didn't want to think about Dad and the life I was forced to leave behind. I would never get over the hurt of being thrown out. I felt like Dad had given me to Rafe, a man he knew nothing about, just to satisfy Momma.

I heard the sound of water near several hemlock trees. It was just a little stream, a spring branch running out of a large rock cropping on the hill behind the house. I dipped my fingers in the water and found it icy cold. I was pleased. A good farm had to have good water.

I lifted my head and saw a fence surrounding a patch of land with dried weeds over knee-high that had been killed by frost. It looked like a garden and I went over to investigate.

It was a garden! It had a garden gate. I opened the gate and walked in. It was much larger than my garden back home. There were still signs of vegetables growing. I saw carrot and beet tops not killed by frost. There were dried-up bean vines beneath the weeds with pods still hanging on them. I picked a pod and found dried up beans that were still usable. I pulled up a long carrot, then another. I saw the tips of purple beets sticking out of the cracked earth.

They were big but still good. I saw a row of cabbage with some of the heads beginning to crack. Near them were several long rows of mounded up dirt. Potatoes, I thought with delight and rushed to a mound and kicked it with my bare foot. My toe hit potatoes. I looked around in total confusion. It looked like nothing had been harvested from the garden. Who would plant a garden, care for it halfway, and then leave it?

I knew for certain Rafe did not plant the garden. He didn't even know it existed or he would have told me so when I asked about supplies. I sat down in the dirt and dropped my head in my hands. I remembered the dried pansies in the fancy living room. Last year's hay was in the barn loft, but not this fall's hay. Rafe didn't seem to know there was hay or grain in the barn. Someone had been here in the spring, somebody besides Rafe. What had happened to that person?

My first instinct was to rush into the house and ask Rafe. My second instinct was not to ask Rafe at all and give him a chance to tell me.

I lifted my head from my hands and got up from the dirt. Since there was a garden, there was probably a can house somewhere. I would search until I found it. I wanted to see what was inside the can house I could use for food this winter. The potatoes would store. The carrots and cabbage, not split, would store for a little while. Again, I assured myself, this place had everything.

I went to every outbuilding, including the toilet in an attempt to find the can house. I walked the edge of the woods behind the house where the hill started to climb steep. Can houses could be dug into steep banks. Dirt was a good insulator. There was nothing.

I checked the bed sheets for dryness as I passed them on my search. I was relieved. They would be dry before bedtime. I wondered if Rafe was sleeping on the bare mattress. He probably had his boots on. A sudden fear ran though my blood. I shivered from the top of my head to the bottom of my feet. What if Rafe was going to be like Momma? What if he took to bed and was too danged lazy to do an hour's worth of work?

"I'll take him out in the woods and shoot him," I said out loud and felt better for it. I knew men weren't lazy like that.

I looked up at the side of the house, at the many windows. I would have plenty of time to wash every window, clean every room in the lovely old house. A warm feeling flowed over me. I would love this place, if not Rafe.

I saw a movement at one of the upstairs windows. It wasn't the room Rafe and I had slept in last night and I was cleaning today. I had looked out that window and it was on the other side of the house. At least Rafe had chosen another room to take a nap in and wasn't getting the mattress any dirtier than it already was.

I went to the barn to let the horses and cow back in their stalls, pulled an arm-load of grass and threw it to the black sow and pigs. The pigs were growing fine and should have no problem surviving winter in a warm barn with plenty of food.

"Cute aren't they?" A voice said near my ear.

I whirled around to face Rafe.

"You nearly scared the life outta me," I told him.

He could still sneak up on me as silent as a snake. Just like he did that day when I was canning tomatoes. He grinned down at me, and I felt a flicker of admiration at his good looks. He no longer seemed to be in an ill-tempered mood as he was before his nap. His eyes were shining and his face was uplifted in humor.

"What's my little wife doing?" He asked sweetly and pushed a strand of hair from my face. I was so shocked I didn't have a word to say. He frowned.

"I noticed you washed your hair. You'll probably find brushes and combs around this place somewhere. There's got to be clothes too. There was an old man and woman lived here when I bought the place. Let them live here until they died not too long ago, so anything you find is yours."

I hadn't known how upset I was until relief hit me. Rafe just answered my confusion.

"When did they die?"

Some of his new-found joy faded from his face at my question.

"Not sure of the exact dates since I was away on business. Man went before the woman. She passed on back in the late summer sometime."

I put my arms around Rafe's waist and gave him a quick hug. I reckoned I must jump to conclusions too quick. Rafe had let the old folks live here after he purchased the place. The old woman started the garden before she died.

"Rafe, I looked everywhere but I couldn't find a can house."

He shrugged his shoulders as though a can house was of no importance.

"Use the spring house. It doesn't freeze in there."

As I looked at Rafe, I saw a look come into his eyes I was beginning to recognize. He took me by the arm and led me into the barn and up the stairs to the hayloft.

"Rafe. Hay can be awful scratchy. It can have thistles and even briars in it. Beds are much nicer."

"I'll be on the bottom," he laughed as I shook my head.

Chapter 10

I woke up to the cold of the mountain air and put Dad's jacket on along with the brown shoes before I went downstairs and built a fire in the cook stove. Dad's smell was in the jacket causing a sadness to rise up in me. I heard of being homesick, but I had no intention of letting it get a hold on me as I reminded myself that I had no home to go to. I assured myself Rafford Johnson had given me my very own home. There would not be mother's angry eyes watching every move I made, nor Susie, nor my Dad.

I walked through the hall discovering quickly why a big house had so many doors. Every room had to be closed off to keep heat in that room. In winter, I could only live in the room that was heated. The other rooms would remain closed up until spring. Dad's house only had four rooms. The cook stove and the front room heater kept the house warm. In a house this size, it would take a person full time just to feed the fire if the entire house was used.

I heard Rafe stumbling about upstairs. He came down and sat at the table waiting for me to put his food before him. He looked grouchy, and it wasn't because he didn't get enough sleep. I knew he slept sound as a rock at night, and snored like a fattened hog. I fed him then broached the subject that had been worrying my mind.

"It will take a lot of wood to heat the house this winter. I reckon we better hitch up the horses and go start cuttin some."

Rafe looked at me like I was crazy. He turned up his glass and finished off what milk was left. He stood up, stretched himself and scratched his full stomach. His face had a thoughtful look to it for a few moments before he spoke.

"You'll have to make do until I get back. I've stayed home with my little wife longer than I should have. Folks gonna be mighty upset if I've not delivered their supplies before winter sets in."

His words sat me square between two emotions. Aggravation was first. There was work that needed to be done, and I needed his help to do it. I was surprised to feel the second emotion. Relief! I was actually glad at the thought of not having Rafe around.

"What about firewood?"

Rafe shrugged broad shoulders. "There's enough deadfall to do you until I get back. Snow don't set in for another two, three weeks. There'll be lots of deadfall then. The snow and ice breaks all kinds of limbs out of the trees."

I must have looked at him like he was crazy. Did he expect us to heat a house on deadfall alone? Dad and I sawed slabs from the sawmill every weekend for months to get enough wood to last us. This house in Kentucky was high on the mountain and Dad's place was in the valley. The wind had a way of blowing over the top of Dad's house, while this house was situated right on the crest where the full blast of the winds would hit it. It would take more wood than Dad and I cut to keep the kitchen warm.

Rafe turned his back on me and went out the door. I grabbed the dishrag and threw it at the closed door. It hit the wood and slid down to the floor limp and useless. Throwing it was an act that accomplished nothing. It didn't even make me feel better.

An hour later Rafe was gone. I stood at the window, with the rose curtains, and watched him drive away. He didn't come to the house to tell me bye, where he was going, or when he would be back. He hitched up the team and drove down the little road we had driven up a few days before. He had no food and no change of clothes with him. He just left.   He's just checking to see if the horses will be frisky, I told myself. He'll be back to get his things. A man didn't go on a trip with nothing.

I went to the storage room on the side of the woodshed and opened the door. When I had found the soap, I had seen a hamper with hemp sacks in it. Next to them in the corner was a good selection of tools. There were hoes, shovels, an ax, and several other items. I took the hamper, sacks and all, along with a hoe and shovel and headed for the garden. I wanted the vegetables dug before a freeze hit. I knew the freeze wasn't long off. I could feel it in the air.

I dug potatoes and carrots and temporarily put them in the barn hall so the sun wouldn't turn them green. I would bring them to the house after I cooked the noon meal. I didn't want Rafe to come back and find me with no food fixed. Even though deep inside, I knew Rafe would not be back for a while. Frisky horses wouldn't keep a man gone half a day. He had left for certain and hadn't even bothered to say scat to me. I consoled myself by thinking Rafe was a man used to living alone. He'd never had a wife to tell where he went and when he would be back. He would learn in time.

By that evening I was feeling right proud of myself. I had every hamper and sack I could find filled and sitting on the back porch. While I was picking up the apples, I found black walnut trees and gathered the nuts the squirrels hadn't gotten. My hands were stained brown from pinching off their hulls. Several of the hulls I had chopped up fine and put them in the hog food. Dad always said the juice from walnut hulls killed worms. Which puzzled me since there were always maggots in some of the hulls. But then, a maggot would eat anything but a red-hot fire coal.

I scrubbed all the stain that would come off my hands and bare feet before I went up stairs. I didn't want to touch anything with my stained hands. Nor did I want to walk on the lovely rugs with dirty feet. I had to find some quilts to cover up the potatoes and vegetables. I didn't want a freeze to come during the night and ruin them, and I didn't want them in the springhouse yet. I was afraid the springhouse would be too wet for them to keep good. I wasn't sure how to solve my problem, but by tomorrow I would think of something. Right now I had to find quilts.

I let my hand slide over the stair rail and my feet scoot on the rug. Oh, the pleasure I got out of the feel. I had a smile on my face as I opened the bedroom door across from Rafe's bedroom, and mine. It was a lovely room. Not at all trashed like Rafe's had been. The first thing I saw was the burl walnut headboard of the bed. It had to be six feet tall with its top curved and delicately carved in wings that had me thinking of graceful birds. There was a dresser, a chest, and a washstand all in the same burl walnut. It was elegant yet had a masculine feel to it. I thought the old man must have had this room. I opened drawers and found men's clothes neatly folded. I took out a shirt and shook it out. The collar was threadbare and the elbows had been worn through and patched with a similar material. A shiver went over me, and I felt like I was trespassing into something that didn't belong to me. I folded the shirt carefully and put it back in the drawer feeling that the old man's clothes had more claim to the house than I did. I found no extra quilts in the room and I didn't want to take them off the bed. I left the room undisturbed, and went to the second door on the left.

This room had a much plainer bed and dresser, but it had a small, orange velvet love seat sitting in front of the window. Such a pretty little thing. The bed and dresser was made of cedar and the shade of the wood was faded and softened by age. The window had cream curtains with orange-fringed tiebacks, which matched the love seat and picked up the color of the wood. A cream, hand-knotted rug lay on the floor. I opened the drawers of the dresser and found them filled with sheets and pillowcases. Some were fancy with hand embroidery and crocheted lace. Others were plain and for everyday use. I thought of Susie. She would have given her eyeteeth for the fancy ones. I found no quilts and no clothes.

I crossed the hall and opened the door to the room adjacent Rafe's. My breath caught in my throat. Not one thing in this room was in place. Dresser drawers had been pulled out and dumped in the floor and left there. A vanity was covered in clothes with what looked like face powder dumped on them. Perfume bottles were scattered on the floor along with brushes, combs and hand mirrors. I wondered if Rafe liked perfume.

Bedclothes were on the floor and the mattress and springs were off the bed frame. The double doors of a large armoire were wide open with clothes halfway on hangers and others lying in a heap. I saw coats and jackets and sweaters. I made my way to the armoire and picked up a piece of clothing. It was a woman's dress. I picked up another and another. There were at least two dozen dresses lying in the pile. They ranged from everyday cotton to soft silk.

I began to hang them back on hangers. They must have belonged to the woman that died not too long ago. The question was who would ransack her room like this? My mind told me it had to be Rafe. He had to be looking for something, but what? Money? If someone had broken into the house and did this, they would have also gone through the other rooms, unless they found what they wanted here. I felt fear go through me like ice. I was alone in a strange house and in a strange land. I didn't know if there were any people between here and Dad's. I hadn't seen anyone, or even a house while we traveled. I would be sure to lock all the doors as soon as I milked. I wouldn't want someone slipping up on me while I slept.

I clutched a silk dress in my hands and went to the window to look out. This was the window I had seen movement at yesterday. Rafe must have been doing this instead of taking a nap. But why make such a mess of it? I rubbed the material of the dress against my cheek. Rafe had said I could have anything I found. I reckon I now had plenty of clothes and a hairbrush and comb. I left the window and hung clothes up.

I found every day shoes and fancy Sunday high-heeled shoes. I found a thick-soled pair of leather ones that laced up the front and looked a lot like a man's shoe. These must have been for the old woman to wear in the cold of winter. Although they appeared to have been worn a lot, they were well cared for with several coats of wax on them. I slipped them on my feet and found them about three sizes too big. I was glad. A thick pair of wool socks would take up the room and keep my feet warm. My hands touched wool coats and sweaters the likes of which I had never seen before. I couldn't stop myself from thinking of Momma and Susie. If only they knew... all this because they didn't want me.

As I straightened up, my mind tried to make sense of the messed up room. The only thing that made any kind of sense to me was that Rafe had been looking for money. Could the old folks have left money hidden? Did he find it? Was that why he left?

The fear I had felt earlier faded slightly. Maybe I didn't have to be afraid of invaders in the house, but I would still lock the doors. I took the bedclothes from the room, dragged them downstairs, and put them over the potatoes and vegetables even though the blanket, quilt and sheets were of fine quality. I might as well use them since I wanted to wash them tomorrow. If I had to clean the bedroom, I might as well do a good job, starting with clean sheets.

I did up the evening work as fast as I could manage. I didn't linger with the animals as I usually did. I wanted to make sure I had plenty of daylight to check out all the rooms in the house, and make sure every door was locked. I had carried in an arm load of sticks to brace the windows so no one could push them open. After I had locked all doors and braced all windows, I went up the stairs laughing at myself. I wasn't really fool enough to think no one could get in when glass broke so easily.

I went to the end of the upstairs hall and opened the door that led out onto the porch. I walked over the wood floor to the railings that reminded me of a picket fence and rested my hands on the rail. There in front of me was Rafford Johnson's farm. My cow was grazing in the pasture next to the big barn. I could hear a hog grunt and the clucking sounds the chickens made as they settled on the roost for the night. A faint wind was blowing up the valley and whining off the bare limbs of the trees. The colored leaves lying in piles on the ground were turning brown in the twilight of evening. The world before me was peaceful and I was entirely alone. I stood there and watched the shadows darken until they faded completely away. Night had come silent and cold. It was time for me to go inside. There was a bed waiting for me without my husband lying in it wanting his comfort. I was pleased.

I woke to the light of dawn and stretched out in the empty bed. I pulled the cover to my chin against the cold and lay there watching the room grow lighter. For the first time in over four years I didn't have to get up and fix breakfast for someone. I didn't even have to get up unless I wanted to. I wanted to, but not right then. I would lie where I was until I could see every object in the room. Then I would go into the old woman's room and find myself warm clothes to put on and a pair of her everyday shoes. I smiled to myself, for the first time in my life I had everything I ever wanted, except Dad, and I wouldn't think about him right now.

I reckon there's something about not having to do something that makes you want to do it. I got up and went to the window and looked out. The sky was beginning to turn pink over the tree line of the furthest mountain. A heavy frost was glistening on the earth. Morning had come, and the world was good.

I picked the shabbiest, most worn clothes I could find in the old woman's room and put them on. If there had been two of me, the clothes might have fit. I didn't care. I could always take them up when I got time. Right now they were the warmest clothes I had ever worn. The sweater felt like a blanket, and the dress came down to the tops of my shoes. I had found socks in the bottom drawer of the armoire and put them on. I hummed a happy tune as I went down the stairs and built a fire in the cook stove. I would need a lot of hot water to clean everything I was going to clean today. Since I had a fire built, I baked a couple of biscuits and stewed an apple. The only thing I lacked was butter for my biscuits. But that was all right for in a few days I would have enough cream saved up to churn butter.

After the work was done up, I decided it was time to tackle finding a place to store the vegetables. There wasn't a room in the house that wouldn't freeze at night unless it

was the wonderful springhouse. Rafe said it didn't freeze
and I hoped he was right. I opened the door in the kitchen
and went into the damp, cold of the springhouse. I looked
at the room with an eye toward storing potatoes.

The window that let the light in wasn't a good thing. I
could hang a quilt from the inside and nail another quilt and
some boards on the outside. I could leave the kitchen door
open or use a candle or lamp when I wanted light. The
other problem would be the dampness. The floor I was
standing on was wet, but the shelves against the wall where
the crocks and tins were stored were only damp. I might be
able to move everything from the wall adjacent the kitchen
and build up a floor of planks and store the potatoes on
that.

I closed the kitchen door and began to move the crocks
from behind the door to the other shelves. I looked in each
crock with fascination. I found crocks of paraffin waiting to
be melted down and used and small crocks of paraffin with
wicks in the center for candles. I found crocks full of shoe
polish, brown and black. I found rancid hog lard I though
the old man must have saved to rub on his boots to make
them repel water, or the old woman could make lye soap
from the lard. I found tin jugs of turpentine and kerosene,
and one jug of liquor. It lacked less than a cup being full.
The old folks must have used it for medicine instead of a
beverage.

At least a dozen round tins were in a wicker basket and
contained some of the worst smelling salves I had ever
smelled. There was one red salve that wasn't too bad, and a
black salve that smelled like coal tar. One of the tins could
have cleared a stopped up nose twenty feet away. I had
heard tell of polecat salve and thought this might be it. It
stunk so bad a person would claim to be cured rather than
rub it on. I put the basket in a far corner. I wondered if Rafe
ever caome down with the croup? If he did, I had the cure.

I found a five-gallon crock of kraut and another of pickled corn. The brine could have taken hair off a hogs back. I carefully dragged them to the far wall being careful not to spill any. When Rafe got home, I would have him help me empty them.

Finally I had the shelves cleared and wondered if I might be able to pull the planks off to use as my wooden floor. I gave one of the middle shelves a hard pull and was surprised to see the wall move. I pulled again. Right before my eyes a section of the shelves swung open. They were fastened onto a door that looked exactly like a part of the wall. I opened it as wide as I could and looked inside. There were stairs leading down under the house. I laughed out loud. I bet I had found the can house. I got one of the paraffin candles and took it into the kitchen. I got a splinter of wood from the wood box and stuck it in the fire and lit the candle. It didn't give off much light, but it was enough.

I stepped carefully on the stairs and found them sturdy. They were not going to crumble beneath my feet and let me fall into a dark hole. They were well built like the rest of the house, sturdy and strong.

The smell of damp earth and mold rose up to meet me. I recognized the smell of old apples and shriveled potatoes before the candlelight fell on them. I wanted to dance a jig when I saw shelf after shelf of cans. There were green beans, beets, pickles, squash, tomatoes, peas, pears, and applesauce, blueberries, blackberries, strawberries and pints of jams, jelly and preserves. There was even a shelf of half-gallon jars filled with grape juice. I wouldn't go hungry this winter. The old folks had been busy.

I held up my candle and tried to see about me. The cellar was about seven foot high and fifteen by twenty feet in size. The floor was dirt, but the walls were laid up of rock and mortar. Shelves were built along two walls and bins were built along the other two with the stairs running from the springhouse to the front of the bins. I found Irish potatoes, sweet potatoes, winter squash, apples, onions, cabbage and carrots in the bins. All were shriveled, rotten, or sprouted. I wondered if any of them might grow if I saved them until spring? The cabbage, squash, apples and carrots needed throwing out. Especially the cabbage.

I took my time walking around the room and looking at everything. I saw a shiny flash on the shelf and looked closer. My candle was reflecting on a quart can full of coins. I picked up the can and saw it contained silver dollars. I had never seen this much money in my life! Could this have been what Rafe was looking for? I carried the can up the steps into the springhouse. I would pour the money out onto the kitchen table and count it.

When I entered the kitchen my heart went into my throat. There in the middle of the kitchen stood a man.

"Well, well," he grinned and looked me over from head to toe. His eyes came to rest on the jar I held against me. "What have we here?"

An expression came over his face that said he knew more than I knew.

"Who're you?" I managed to ask.

He was tall and bony but looked to be strong. His clothes, hands, and face had a dirty blackness to them as though dirt had been ground in for a long time. His face seemed to be oozing oily blackness. Tobacco juice ran down the corners of his grinning mouth as he leered at me with satisfaction.

"Don't matter who I am. Hit's you that's in a pile of trouble." His words were spoken with confidence and cocky bragging.

"Get outta my house!"

He pushed a sweat-stained cap back on his head with his dirty hand and laughed in my face. I smelled liquor along with tobacco.

"Ain't your house, you purty little piece. Where's Boise? Did you slip in while she's out in the wood somewhere? She wouldn't let the likes of you in here knowingly. Too jealous of her man," he sniggered like a school kid with a secret.

"Get out!" I demanded and took a step backward.

"Don't reckon a thief can order me outta Boise's house." His lips parted and showed a mouth half full of snaggled, brown teeth.

I thought of the tore up bedroom and feared this man might have done it. I was afraid he had seen Rafe's wagon and horses were gone and thought he could come back and find what he was after.

"You better get outta here before Rafe gets back," I threatened and hoped he would be fool enough to believe Rafe would be back soon.

"So you claim to know Rafford? Reckon you probably do at that."

"I'm his wife, and you better get out!"

Mocking laughter poured out of his mouth as he took a step toward me. His laughter faded into a leering grin.

"I'd say ole Rafford would give Boise and half the farm fur a wife like you, but you hain't his wife. I know that fur certain. With your looks you could warm a man's bed on a mighty cold night. You ain't a bit hoss-faced, and those tits of yourn's stickin straight out beggin fur a man. It's only fittin I take a tad a you fur myself. Rafford Johnson han't entitled to hit all. He's done got more'n he deserves. That sneaky son-of-a-bitch."

I felt anger run over me at what he said, and I wanted to bash him over the ugly head with the can I was holding.

"You filthy talkin piece of trash! Get out of here or I'll kill you with my bare hands."

Before I had time to react, his hand snaked out and grabbed hold of my breast. A flame of repulsion shot through me. I jumped backward away from his hand, but he didn't let go. His hand tightened sending a sharp stab of pain through me, his other hand grabbed for me. He caught the neck of my dress and ripped it down the front, causing me to drop the can I was holding. I heard it roll across the floor. I hit his arm with my fist in an attempt to make him turn loose. He didn't. I clawed his face with my other hand feeling my fingernails dig into flesh. He turned loose of my breast and bellowed with pain and rage as he rubbed his face with his dirty hand. He looked at his palm as though he couldn't believe the blood he was seeing on it. He bellowed like an angry bull and lunged for me. I dodged and landed against the stove feeling the handle of the cast iron skillet poking against my side. I grabbed it with my right hand and swung with all the power I had in me.

I heard the crack as it hit his forehead. He dropped to the floor like I'd pole axed him. Blood squirted over his face and spread to the floor. I leaned over him and looked at the deep gash running across his entire forehead. The gash appeared to open wider as the blood flowed. His body twitched and his legs and arms jerked a few time before his eyes rolled back into his head then slowly closed and he lay still.

My Lord! I'd killed him!

What was I going to do? There was a dead man lying at my feet bleeding on the linoleum. I couldn't stand him bleeding all over my clean floor. I dropped my skillet and grabbed his skinny leg up by the dirty boot. I dragged him out of the kitchen, across the porch, down the steps into the yard. I turned him loose and his head rolled sideways as his arms flopped out. His leg lay where I dropped it. The other one was straight with his toe pointed out. His mouth hung open, and I saw a wad of brown tobacco as big as a hen egg. Brown spit was mixing with blood and trickling onto the grass.

I reached up and touched my cheeks with both hands. They were dry. I wasn't crying and screaming my head off like a mad woman. I was looking down on a man I had just killed and feeling little more than astonishment. My mind couldn't take in that a man could be killed that easily, but dead he surely was.

I reminded myself the man had attacked me, and I had hit him with a frying pan in self-defense. It didn't help me at all for he was still dead. I didn't know what to do about it. A tremor ran through my body and I felt icy cold. I tried to make my mind think, but all I could do was look down at the bloody face. I didn't know where he had come from or what he intended to do here unless it was robbery. I knew what he wanted to do to me.

He seemed to have some knowledge of the old folks that once lived here. Boise must have been the old woman jealous of her man. I didn't know where Rafe came into this. All I knew for certain was that I was in a strange land, and I didn't know anybody here and only Rafe knew me, and he was gone.

I would be hung.

A shiver ran over me. I took a deep breath and tried to think. I wondered if the people of Kentucky would believe he attacked me and that I killed him in self-defense? Somehow I didn't think so. What was I to do?

I ran from the dead man to the storage room on the side of the woodshed and grabbed the shovel. I would dig a deep hole in the potato patch and bury him. The potato ground was already dug up and wouldn't look like a grave had been dug. No one would ever have to know what happened. I went to the garden and began to dig a hole feeling mighty glad the ground was soft. I could have the hole dug before nightfall. I wouldn't want to leave a dead man laying in the yard all night long.

I had dug a hole about a foot deep when I heard a noise. I looked up and couldn't believe what I saw. The dead man was sitting on a wagon seat, his head, face and shoulders covered in blood. He was whipping the horses with a switch as he tried to make them run faster. The wagon sounded like it was falling apart as it bumped and bounced down the rough road. A black dust rose from the wagon at every bump it hit.

I stood there watching it go out of sight.

Dread came over me. It wouldn't be long until he was back with the sheriff. I left the hole like it was and took the shovel to the storage room. I would finish storing the vegetables and apples in the cellar along with the can of money I had found, but I wouldn't bother canning any food. There were plenty of cans in the cellar. Besides, I would probably be in jail.

Three days passed without anybody showing up. I scrubbed the house and listened for the sound of the sheriff coming for me. There were times when I thought of facing the sheriff and telling him what happened. At other times, I planned to hide in the cellar.

It was nearing suppertime when I heard the rattling sound of a wagon coming up the rough road. I snuck into the front room and pulled the pink curtain back enough to place my eye in the space and see out. All the plans of action I had come up with the past three days fled from my mind as relief flooded over me. It wasn't the sheriff at all, but Rafe.

I saw that the wagon was loaded high with crates as Rafe pulled the team up in front of the barn and stopped. He threw the reins down on the ground and strode off toward one of the out buildings. He opened the door and looked in. He stood there for a minute, reached up and pushed his hat back on his head and spit toward the door. He cocked his head sideways for a minute then turned around and strode toward the house, leaving the horses hitched to the wagon.

I met him at the kitchen door and threw my arms around his waist and hugged him in a near death grip before he even stepped inside. He took me by the shoulders and moved me back enough to look at my face. The look lasted for a few moments before he spoke.

"What happened?"

"I've missed you."

I did miss him being here when the man showed up. If Rafe had been home, I wouldn't have had to hit the man over the head with the frying pan.

Rafe's lips twitched. "No. I want to know what happened with Zeb?"

"Zeb?"

"Don't play dumb, Laine. The man here three days ago with the coal. I looked in the shed where he had dumped coal."

"His name was Zeb?" I clutched Rafe's arms. "Did he die?" I heard my own voice tremble. Rafe raised his eyebrows.

"No. He's not dead that I know of. They say the Doc put a hundred and thirteen stitches in Zeb's hard head. Some gash he had."

I thought I saw Rafe hide a grin, but then I felt shaky with relief and wasn't sure what I was seeing. At least I hadn't killed that awful man. Rafe had me by the arm and guided me to the kitchen table. He pulled out a chair and sat me down in it.

"Uh huh." Rafe grunted. "Start from the beginning and tell me what happened."

I bit my lip, closed my eyes, then opened them again without looking at Rafe. I didn't want to tell anybody what happened, nor did I want to tell about my new-found can house.

"I was in the spring house fixing a place to put all the potatoes. I came back in here to find a man standing in the middle of the floor. He wanted to know who I was, then laughed when I said I was your wife. He wouldn't leave when I told him to. Reckon he thought I was a whore or something."

I downed my head and felt like crying with shame, but I continued. Rafe had a right to know what happened.

"He said my teats stuck out and he grabbed hold of one. Said it was only fittin he take a tad of me for himself."

I saw the muscles in Rafe's jaws clench. Red started creeping into his face. His eyes glowed. "Then?" he insisted.

"I scratched his face, and he turned loose. It made him mad, and he came after me. I took the fryin pan to him."

Rafe frowned, stepped to the stove and picked up the frying pan.

"This one?"

I nodded and watched him rub his finger over the smooth edge of the pan like he was testing the sharpness of a knife.

"This is the first cast iron skillet I've ever seen with a dent in it," he said then started laughing.

Rafe dropped the pan back on the stove and roared in his mirth. He took his hat off his head, and hit the stove with it as he laughed. He reached in his hind pocket and pulled out his handkerchief and mopped at his eyes. Then bent over and stomped his feet and laughed harder. His laughter was more than I could take.

I started to cry.

It took some time for Rafe's amusement to fade. When it did, he pulled out a chair from the table and sat down. He didn't seem to care that I was crying.

"You know what old Zeb told?" he asked me in a voice calm and cold. "He said a limb struck him across the head on the way back from delivering coal."

I sniffled and tried to stop crying as Rafe said, "Zeb claimed he couldn't remember a thing except being hit by the limb." Rafe lifted his left eyebrow, and the muscle in his jaw twitched. "They said the Doc asked him if he'd seen my new wife? He denied seeing you. Said he couldn't find a soul to pay him for the coal."

All the laughter had gone from Rafe's face as he gazed at me across the table. His green eyes were like marbles of glass.

"It seemed as soon as the Doc finished sewing him up, Zeb got on his coal wagon and drove off. Nobody has seen him since."

"Do you think he died?"

Rafe shook his head. "He's not dead, yet. That's why he left. He knew I'd kill him when I found out what happened. I might have killed you too if you hadn't split his head open then told me about it. I can't stomach a lying woman."

I don't think I was crying anymore.

"Don't look so shocked, my little wife. I'm proud of you."

"It was awful!"

"You won't see him again. He won't settle anywhere in a hundred mile radius. He knows I'll kill him when I see him. No man messes with my wife and lives to tell about it. I'll find him."

The look on Rafe's face sent a new chill over me.

"Fix your hungry husband some supper. Then you can go out and take care of the horses and wagon. I brought you back some things. Made a good deal on em."

Chapter 11

𝒴

The clouds had gathered dark and heavy making twilight come on fast. It took a long time to get the stove hot, cook Rafe's supper and get him fed. I left the dishes on the table. It didn't matter if I washed them now or after dark. Rafe went off through the house as I went outside to see to the team and wagon. I wondered what all he had brought back from his trip. I knew hogs were in the crate. The sound and smell gave that away quick.

I picked the lines up off the ground where Rafe had left the horses ground tied and climbed onto the wagon seat. I drove the team and wagon as close to the pasture gate as I could get it. Rafe had a bushel sack full of stuff sitting on the wagon seat. I thought this might be coffee and other foodstuff. I was glad Rafe hadn't put the sack in the back with the hogs and the crate of chickens I heard squalling. It sounded like there were guineas in the crate along with the chickens. The back of the wagon smelled as though the animals had been in their crates for some time. I took the chicken crate off first and carried it across the yard and turned the chickens and guineas in with the other chickens.

I had moved my chickens from the barn to a wired in run that let the chickens out yet protected them. Sometimes I would let the chickens out of the hen house during the day to catch bugs in the yard, but I always put them up at night and made sure the door was closed tight. Situated on top of the mountain was a sure place for predators.

139

I went back to the wagon and looked into the slatted crates containing the hogs. I could see what looked like a boar hog with tusks longer than my hand. As I peeped in between the slat of the crate, the boar hog dived at me hitting one of his tusks on the wood slats snapping the slat in two. It didn't take me long to realize this was one mean boar hog. No wonder Rafe got him at a good deal. It was what Dad would call a killer boar too old and tough to be good for much except dog meat. How anybody loaded that thing into the crate was a wonder to me. I peeped into the other crate at the sow hog. Her temperament didn't seem much of an improvement over the boar. I now understood why Rafe was letting me unload the wagon. Confound his mangy hide. I hoped that mean boar got a chance to take a bite out of Rafe's hind end. It'd serve him right for leaving me to handle a mean boar hog.

I studied on the problem for a few minutes and looked out over the pastures. There were at least fifty or sixty acres separated into four tracts with six smaller, fenced lots near the barn. There was less than a foot between the four wooden boards of split locust making the fence, with the bottom board being only inches from the ground. Only small pigs could escape. It would hold the two big hogs fine even if they were as mean as old jack himself.

I mixed up a bucket of chop and water.

The first pasture was closer to the road. I would try to get the two mean hogs into the first pasture tonight.

I went to the garden and scraped up my dresstail full of potatoes and carrots I had left lying on the ground that were too damaged to store. I pulled up two heads of cabbage that were split and carried them back to the wagon. I lay potatoes and carrots down on the ground in a trail to the pasture and placed the heads of cabbage inside the pasture. I left the chop and water in the bucket near the cabbage, then went into the barn and brought out the pitchfork.

I got a hammer from the storage shed and climbed on top of the wagon and beat the nails loose that were holding the door on the crate containing the sow. I left one nail holding the door lightly, and then turned to the boar's crate. I knew I was uncrating several hundred pounds of fighting hell, but it had to be done. A hog couldn't live in a crate. When I was down to the last nail, I knocked the sow's door off then the boar's door. I scooted backward off the wagon seat and grabbed the pitchfork. I climbed up on the fence and waited for the hogs to come out of their crates.

The boar snorted and fussed as though he was mad the door was open and wanted to fight the emptiness. He stuck his head out, sniffed the air then hit the ground with a grunt and snort. He shook his head throwing specks of slobber from his mouth, then raised his snout and sniffed the air. The sow came out of her crate right behind him. They must have traveled a long while without being fed judging by the way they went after food. They were eating the trail of vegetables grass and all as they made their way toward the gate. They smelled the cabbage and made for them with determination.

I jumped off the fence and closed the gate. I had the hogs up. I watched as they turned over the bucket of chop in their rush to eat, spilling it on the ground.

I tossed the crate doors onto the wagon, climbed on the seat and drove the wagon around the barn. I unharnessed the horses and put them in a stall. I brought grain and water for them, knowing if I had led them to the creek, they might drink enough of the icy water to colic them. I had an idea Rafe hadn't taken any better care of the horses than he had the hogs.

I got the sack of foodstuff from the wagon and went to the house for the milk buckets.

Rafe was standing on the porch watching me. I started to tell him that most men would lift a finger to help out, but didn't. The thought hit me that the less Rafe did to help, the easier my job would be.

A smirk came to his lips. "I'd heard you were a smart cookie with animals. Reckon I'll have to give it to you. You managed those hogs all right."

I stopped and looked up at him. "You knew those hogs were meaner than the devil and didn't tell me!" I was plumb put out at him. A mean hog could kill you in a very painful way.

"Naw, they're not mean." His smirky grin widened. "Got them from a woman that didn't know how to handle them. Her old man raised the hogs. He died about two months back. Too much work for the old dame."

"How did you get em in a crate?" I asked.

"She had some neighbors come and load them. I bought all she had. I was able to sell all but these two. They're too tough to eat. Figured you could raise pigs. Make my money back that way."

"Looks to me like she should'a given you them two."

"Give me more than that," Rafe grinned and leaned against the porch post with a satisfied look about him.

I hurried on in the house. I had to get my milking done. Dark was on me. I put the sack in the center of the table without opening it. I just hoped Rafe had plenty of coffee in that sack if it would keep him from being grouchy.

Rafe came in the kitchen behind me and slipped his hands around my waist, moving his hands up over my breasts. He pressed his crotch against my butt and rubbed slowly.

"I've got to get the milkin done."

"That old cow can wait. You tend to her twice a day. It's been a while since you've tended to your husband."

"It's dark already," I objected.

"Being it's already dark, it won't matter now will it?"

What Rafe had in mind didn't fill me with delight. It felt more like drudgery, comparable to grubbing a stump.

"It won't take me long to milk, Rafe. After I milk, I won't have to get outta bed."

Rafe frowned and looked displeased. "Sounds to me like you're trying to be lazy. One thing I won't tolerate is a lazy wife. It won't hurt you or that cow of yours to milk after dark.

Rafe took me by the upper arm and led me through the kitchen and up the stairs. He lay me down on the bed and lifted my dress, the one I was wearing that belonged to Boise, the old woman. He unbuckled his belt and let his pants drop to the floor and kicked them off along with his boots. He straddled me.

It would be over in a minute or two.

I lay there wondering what it was about a man that made him like this act so much? Rafe moaned and groaned and slobbered on me. Sometimes I thought about cleaning the house, or the old folks that lived here. Tonight I was thinking about milking in the dark.

Rafe's weight collapsed on top of me for a minute before he rolled off. He grunted, farted, moved his private part sideways with his hand and began to snore. I didn't move until I knew he was sound asleep, then eased out of bed, closed the door quietly behind me and hurried to the kitchen. I put a dipper full of hot water in the wash pan and tried to wash all traces of Rafe from between my legs.

I went out into the cool night air and felt the tingle of cold on my skin. I looked up at the velvet blackness of the night sky and the millions of twinkling stars and felt contentment with the earth and the beauty that surrounded me. I was thankful for the bounty that I had and figured I could live with what Rafe did if it meant I got this place as a trade off.

Rafe was still snoring when I came back up stairs and crawled in bed beside him. He lay smack in the middle of the bed, flat on his back with his arms and legs spread out. There wasn't a whole lot of room left for me, but I would make do.

I looked down on him with the moonlight coming through the window lighting his face in the pale glow. Odd, I thought, how the stranger in Eula's store with his hat shadowing his face looked far more handsome than the same man in my bed.

Rafe slept long and hard the next morning. He got mad when I came up stairs at around eight o'clock to check on him.

"Don't wake me!" he grumbled and turned his back on me. I had no trouble doing as he asked, and left him alone to sleep as long as he liked.

"Laine!" he yelled some time later. "Where in th' hell are my clothes?"

I had carried clean clothes to the bedroom for him to wear. The britches he had worn yesterday smelled like hog manure. I had them soaking in soapy water in the washtub.

I hurried upstairs and opened the bedroom door and pointed toward the britches on the chair next to the bed.

"I'm washing your dirty ones. I'll wash your shirt, too, if you'll take it off."

Rafe looked at me then down at the shirt he was still wearing and started unbuttoning it.

"Hell! If I have to strip naked, you might as well carry me up a washtub and a few buckets of hot water for me to wash in."

I had no intention of lugging that washtub and water up to the bedroom.

"It's too cold up here," I said sweetly. "Come on down to the kitchen where the fire is warm. I'll fix your breakfast then you can wash up where it's comfortable."

He must have liked that idea, being he didn't object. I went back downstairs thinking I was finally learning to be a wife.

I tried to remember if I had ever known Dad to take a bath. He washed his dirty feet in the wash pan before he went to bed and shaved on Sundays, but I couldn't remember a whole body bath.

I had things to do outside while Rafe was in the washtub. I found it an embarrassment to look at a naked man even if I was married to him. God surely didn't have beauty in mind when he made a man's private parts.

Rafe came out on the porch looking mighty pleased with himself after his bath. He looked around until he spotted me at the clothes line hanging up his britches and shirt to dry.

"Laine," he called. "Before you empty that water you ought to crawl in yourself. A man likes a sweet-smelling piece once in a while." He stepped off the porch and headed toward the woods.

I saw he was carrying a gun in his hand. I recalled thinking of the perfume I had wanted to wear for Rafe. I didn't much want to anymore.

Rafe was gone during all the warm part of the day and came back with the coldness of evening carrying one dead, stiff gray squirrel. He tossed it on the kitchen table.

"Wouldn't mind having a little squirrel gravy and biscuits," he told me as he went through the kitchen and up the stairs to the bedroom. He didn't so much as give a glance in my direction much less notice that I had bathed, fixed my hair, put on one of Boise's silk dresses and dabbed perfume behind my ears.

Biscuits and squirrel gravy, my ass!

Chapter 12

Rafe announced at breakfast that it was time for him to go on another trip. He ate his biscuits and squirrel gravy, then stood up and stretched himself.

"You know how to shoot a shotgun?" he asked me right out of the blue.

"I've never shot any kind of gun."

I had seen Dad shoot lots of times. Being I was a girl, Dad didn't think it fitting that I learn to shoot a gun.

Rafe said no more to me as he left the kitchen and went upstairs. As I dipped out hot water from the water closet into the dishpan, I heard Rafe's footsteps coming down the stairs. Most of the time he walked silently, but this morning he seemed to be unusually noisy. He came through the door into the kitchen whistling a happy tune.

"Here. It might be a good idea for you to have this."

I looked over my shoulder and saw he was breaking down a double barrel shotgun. He squinted one eye and looked into both barrels.

"Come out on the porch. I'll show you how this thing works." He whistled a few more notes.

I wiped my hands and followed him outside. He handed me the gun and had me put shells in both barrels.

"I've got enough shells here to last you years, and I expect you to practice shooting while I'm away." I saw him lift his left eyebrow and something like a grin came to his lips. "If you see Zeb, shoot the bastard, and then ask

146

questions later. Leaving you here alone don't settle too good with me," he admitted. "I have no other choice. You have to look after things here, and I have to go."

He put the gun in my hands and lifted his eyebrow again as he did so.

"Put the butt of the gun tight against your shoulder. Shotguns kick. The tighter you press against your shoulder the less kick you get."

I pressed the gun against my shoulder, and looked up at Rafe. He grinned, and I thought I saw a touch of warmth come into his green eyes as he looked down at me.

"Don't look uncertain, my little wife. You're tougher than the average mountain lion, and I want to keep you that way. Lower your head until you can look over the sights with one eye and take aim at the trunk of that oak tree near that knot."

I closed one eye, as I had seen Dad do, and sighted on the knot.

"Don't let your chin rest on the butt like you're doing. It can kick and break your jaw, or split your face. Yes. That's it. Now, squeeze the trigger, don't jerk it."

I gritted my teeth, pressed the butt against my shoulder as hard as I could and squeezed the trigger. The next thing I knew Rafe had me in his arms. Pain was throbbing through my shoulder and my right arm felt numb. The kick of the gun knocked me backward and Rafe had caught me before I hit the porch.

"What th' hell?" Rafe said as he sat me back on my feet and took the gun out of my hands and broke it down and looked it over.

"That's not possible."

"What happened?" I wanted to rub my aching shoulder but had too much pride to do so with Rafe watching me.

"You pulled both triggers at the same time, but then, that's impossible. You had to pull one trigger then the other almost at the same time."

He took two shells out of his pocket and handed them to me. "You load the gun then shoot at the knot again. This time only squeeze one trigger at a time."

The way my shoulder was hurting I wasn't anxious to try again, but I did as Rafe said, under his critical eye. He positioned my hands on the gun, and adjusted the butt against my shoulder.

"Don't tense up like that. Relax. That's better. Hold it like a friend. Gentle but firm like you sometimes hold your husband when you're not feeling self-conscious. No." He chuckled. "You tensed again."

He moved behind me until his body was cupping mine, and placed his arms round me and positioned the gun butt on my shoulder higher up than I had it. He moved my left hand slightly.

"It won't kick as hard this time so don't be afraid, besides you have me as support behind you. Just take a deep breath, hold it, now squeeze."

I did and was surprised that the kick of the gun was different than the first time. It gave me a jolt backward against Rafe's solid body, but didn't move Rafe.

"That's better. Now the other barrel."

I did as Rafe said and fired the gun a second time without any problem. He took the gun from my hands and moved away from me.

"That came easy once you got the hang of it," he grinned down at me as though he was immensely pleased. "I've got an idea you can shoot the ass out of a rat if you took a notion to."

He reached down and pinched hard on my butt. I jerked away. For a moment I could have shot his ass off. The way he ginned, he knew what I was thinking. His grin faded and he told me seriously, "Keep this near you, loaded, and use it if necessary. Don't be afraid to shoot this gun and keep the doors locked, especially at night." His face brightened. "By all means keep that iron skillet handy," he chuckled to himself as he left the porch and went back into the kitchen whistling as he went.

While I was making up the bed, he hitched the horses to the wagon and drove away just like before. He didn't tell me good-bye or take a thing with him. Leaving again without the things I thought he should take on a trip. But, he knew what was best for him, and I felt no desire to look after Rafe.

I left the bedroom and went to stand on the top porch and watched him drive the team of horses and wagon down the bumpy road. I wanted to feel sadness at his leaving, wanted to miss his presence on the farm and sleeping beside me at night. Instead, it seemed like a burden was leaving me.

I stayed on the porch long after the sound of the wagon faded away and listened to the silence. Except for the whining of the wind, there was no sound. The stock and chickens were quiet. Not even the guineas were chattering. I looked up at a sky that was boiling with dark clouds. The wind swirled fallen leaves and moved the tops of the naked trees. They swayed back and forth in slow motion. I could feel damp heaviness in the air I breathed and knew it was here. Winter. It was setting in. I breathed in deeply of the brisk air and felt like I was the only person alive. I was high on a mountain that flattened out in front of the house to acres of pastures before it pitched downward into a never-ending line of trees. Then the land rose to meet the far mountains, blue and misted in the distant horizon. Behind the house was the hill. Tall, steep, wooded. With virgin timber and tangled undergrowth of mountain laurel and ivy. I knew the woods would be full of wildlife, for all woods were alive with animals of one sort or another. Someday I would climb the hill and go over its ridge to find out what was on the other side, but not today. Today I better get back to gathering deadfall for firewood. I knew all too well what it felt like to be cold.

Rafe hadn't helped me with firewood. When I asked him about it, he patted me on the arm, grinned and said the coal Zeb dumped in the coal shed was his contribution. He would have more delivered when that ran out. I wondered about his comment. From what Rafe said, Zeb knew Rafe would kill him if he ever came across him. I didn't think Zeb or anyone else would be delivering coal again.

A crow appeared in the sky and landed in one of the giant oak trees in the yard. It cawed twice then flew into the pasture to see if there was any food left in the hog trough. Good thing that crow could fly, for those two hogs Rafe brought home were vicious as hogs ever came, especially that ugly boar hog. I had to stand on the backside of the fence to pour food into the trough. Once, the boar hog reached through the fence and grabbed the tail of my dress in his mouth ripping out a chunk. He gouged and rooted at that piece of dress like he hated the faintest scent of human and intended to root it into the earth.

As I stood there looking out over the land, loneliness tried to enter my chest, but I pushed it away. It didn't matter that I was completely alone. It didn't matter that there wasn't one single person to say a word to me. I could talk to the animals. I could manage.

I recalled what Rafe had said about Zeb and the doctor that put one hundred thirteen stitches in Zeb's ugly head. The doctor asked Zeb if he had seen Rafe's new wife? Somebody, somewhere, knew I existed and where I was living. I left the upper porch and went downstairs and outside to drag in deadfall.

Days passed, each one getting a little colder. I lost track of the day of the week, the month of the year. Talking to my animals wasn't enough. I longed for the sound of another human voice. Sometimes, when I was near the barn, I would think I heard Dad's voice say, "Laine." I would look up and find myself alone. The Lord only knowing how many miles separated me from Dad. I wondered if he ever thought about me, ever missed me. Momma and Susie probably kept him too busy to think of me, much.

I turned my face toward the wind and looked at the steep hill behind the house. My feet started moving me along. Today I was going to climb the hill all the way to its rocky top.

I did, but it wasn't a short climb, nor an easy one. There were huge trees with fallen limbs among entwined and twisting ivy thickets. Rocks were lying on top of each other. Some boulders were as big as a house and covered in moss and lichen. On the very top of the hill, it flattened out a little then came to a point. Scrub trees grew sparsely in the rocky crags. It was too rough and rocky ground for much to survive. The winds whipped at my clothes, and I shivered as I climbed onto the highest rock outcropping. Before me was a sheer rock face dropping hundreds of feet straight down. My breath caught in my throat as I took in the view before me. I was surely standing on top of the world looking down into valleys. I saw the glitter of the sun reflecting off tin roofs miles away. There were buildings down there, even if they looked no bigger than the head of a pin. That meant I wasn't alone in Kentucky. There were houses and people, so very far away.

The wind swirled around me harshly, and then gentled enough to bring a sound to my ears. It was the sound of barking dogs. Not the sound of a dog on the hunt, or the urgent sound of a treeing dog, but the sound of a hunting dog on a trail. I turned as two dogs came into sight and climbed up onto the rock where I stood. They were red wheaten in color and appeared to have their hackles raised, but they came toward me with wagging tails. I realized they were half-grown pups as they wrapped themselves around my legs, each going in opposite direction. They were tied to a double lead clipped to their collars. I reached down and got hold of their lead chain. They had escaped from their owner with the chain still on them. I wondered how they had managed to travel through the woods without getting tangled up on something.

"Easy baby, easy." I coaxed as they reared up on me. "Down now. Get down."

The dogs obeyed the word down and sat lightly on their haunches, staring up at me with golden eyes. I dropped to my knees and hugged their warm bodies against me. They licked my face and whined as they tried to climb on me again.

"There you are," came a breathless voice.

I looked up to see a young man climbing over the rocks. He was tall and thin as a post. His face was flushed red and covered in red freckles. Beneath his cap, red hair stuck out in tufts. He looked tired and sweaty and out of breath. The first person I had seen, besides Rafe and the no-account Zeb in a long time. The shock of seeing him made me jump and tighten my grip on the dogs.

"Sorry, Ma'am. I didn't mean to startle you. My dogs got loose, and I was trying to catch em."

I stood and saw his brown eyes look me over. Startled was not the right word. He almost scared the life out of me. One encounter with the likes of Zeb was enough.

"Who are you?" I noticed my voice wasn't quite steady.

"Abe Farrow," he said. "I live down in the hollar there."
He pointed toward one of the little specks of shining tin I
had been looking at. "That's my folks' place, but you can't
get here from there. You sure have a good sight from up
here, don't you?"

There was a sparkle in his eyes and his grin was warm.
My fear disappeared as he took the dog's lead from my
hand.

"Sorry, if they scratched you. They're just pups. I was
trainin em to scent a trail when they pulled loose from me.
I've chased em half the morning." He looked at the dogs
with irritated fondness.

"What kind of dogs are they? I've never seen anything
like em."

His face brightened with pleasure, and he seemed to rear
back. "My dogs are Rhodesian Ridgebacks, a rare few here
in these United States. Fine huntin dogs. Brave as sin.
Loyal to the death, and can fight bear, cat, or groundhog. A
Reverend Helm introduced them in 1877 to Rhodesia. I
managed to get me a pair. These are their first pups.
They're called Ridgebacks because of that hair growing
down their back in the wrong direction." He patted their
heads in turn. "I reckon you must be Rafford Johnson's
new wife."

"Yes. How did you know?"

"Ah, folks like to keep track of things." He looked
embarrassed. "I like to come up here and look about. Folks
call this spot here the Pinnacle," he added quickly as he
pointed. "If you go in that direction you go into Pogy and
on into Tennessee. That direction is Whaley and there leads
to Heaton and Elk Park. See that place with the shadow?
That's Dark Ridge. A lot of Rafford's land, right over
there, takes up most all of a place called Nowhere. Down
there is the town of Banners Elk. They say a man named
Banner used to run a herd of Elk down there. One old bull

Elk took a likin to people and escaped at will to roam about people's places. Folks started sayin Oh, that's just Banner's Elk. Funny, hain't it, how places get their names."

"Is that true? About the Elk?"

He grinned. "Naw, sounds good though, don't it? Actually, there are five or six Banner brothers that bought up land. Folks used to call the place Upper Elk. Now, some are starting to call it Banners Elk. My story is better." He grinned as he pointed way off in the distance. "See that far valley? If you squint your eyes just right, you can see a road. That place is called Trade. They say Indian Tribes used to meet in that valley to trade with each other. So it's called Trade Tennessee, and that's the truth. Folks travel that way to get over into Ashe County."

"Ashe County?" I questioned. That was the name of the county I lived in before Rafe took me away. "Is Trade Tennessee near Kentucky?"

He looked at me right hard, then looked back at the distance. "Trade hain't no where near Kentucky that I know of. Kentucky's a far piece from here if you're talkin about the state. Han't never been there myself, don't know as I ever will be. Right over that little hump of a hill is the North Carolina line. You just see a tip of Tennessee. Course Pogy goes into Tennessee. I wondered how Pogy got its name. It is actually spelled Pogia, but folks say Pogy. Been meaning to ask somebody that might know being I hain't had time to think up a thing." He reached out to a scrub huckleberry bush and broke a twig off and stuck it in his mouth. "Ma'am, if you don't mind me saying, you'll have to be careful when you go walkin about. There's some mighty rough country on this mountain a body could get lost in. If you took a sheet of paper and scrunched it up in your hand, that's what the terrain of this mountain would look like. You best go on short walks till you get used to the place. Say, now don't you be afraid none if you hear dogs barkin. There's been a pant'er killin sheep down around Old Fields of Toe. It's called Newland now that it's become its own county, but I like Old Fields of Toe best. I've had my grown dogs on that pant'er's trail a time or two but he's a sneaky devil. Jumped from treetop to treetop and finally lost em. I've got an idea he'll head up on this mountain before long. These rocks make fine cover for a big cat. Come to think of it, you best not be out much at night. Cat travels at night. Does his huntin."

He gave me a nod of his head and stepped off the top rock and was gone as quick as a puff of smoke, dogs and all. Well, the first person I'd met and he was gone before I could ask any questions, and there were a lot running through my mind, especially about Kentucky. The boy said Kentucky was a long ways off and he had never been there. According to Rafe, I was in Kentucky. There was something wrong here, something bad wrong.

I turned and looked down into the valley and wondered how long it would take to walk that distance, where Trade Tennessee turned into North Carolina. I turned away from the sparkle of tin roofs and made my way down the steep hill toward home.

Time moved on, and I saw nobody. Not Abe Farrow and his dogs, not even Rafe. I wondered where Rafe could be and why he had been gone so long. Time was marked by getting up each morning, doing the work, then going to bed at dark. Each day flowed into the next with nothing different but the sound of the wind blowing in the trees at night. Sometimes it moaned like a lonely woman. Sometimes it only whispered.

The snow started to fall in big, downy flakes. It looked like white feathers floating straight down toward the earth.

Within minutes everything was covered in white. The pure, clean white of a first snowfall filled me with wonder as I stood at the edge of the woods and looked about me. The woods were deep with silence. Nothing but the flakes of snow had life. Nothing stirred. Finally, after a lengthy time of standing and watching, the cold penetrated my oversized sweater and made me get busy again.

I picked up a tree limb in each hand and braced them under each arm. I had better double up and drag two limbs instead of one for the snow would soon be too deep for me to drag any firewood. I had to gather as much wood as I could. I didn't know how much snow this mountain got or how long it would last. It could be many weeks or even months before I saw the ground again.

By milking time that evening, the snow was well over the everyday shoes I wore, but I had not stopped long enough to get the high-topped boots the old woman had in her room. I would go do that now, for my feet were wet and my legs cold. The skirt of my dress had dragged the snow until it was frozen halfway up my thighs. My fingers and hands ached from cold, and my hair was matted to my head with frozen snow.

I took time to build a fire before I left the kitchen, feeling hungry for supper. I was cold and the fire would be hot by the time I found myself dry clothes and changed into them. I climbed the stairs barefooted and went into the old woman's room for another everyday dress. Thoughts of her pulled hard on my mind as I entered the room. Somehow, I couldn't see her as being old. She had pretty silk dresses like a young woman might wear on Sunday. I found brushes and combs and hand mirrors that made me think she had her share of vanity. There was lipstick, powder, fingernail polish and face cream all in a drawer along with several bottles of perfume. I took a pretty little bottle of perfume from the dresser top and touched it to my wrists and sniffed it. It was the second time in my life I had ever worn perfume. The first time Rafe hadn't even bothered to smell me. When he came back, I would put on a little for him and see if he would notice better. It beat the odor of lye soap by a long shot.

I stopped my silly thinking of Rafe and perfume and took off the wet dress, still frozen and stiff. I scolded myself for not taking the dress off in the kitchen. That way I wouldn't have to carry it back down stairs. Somehow, it hadn't seemed right for me to walk from the kitchen to the bedroom naked; besides, it was cold. I slipped another of the woman's everyday dresses over my head and pulled it down. I shivered and the dress didn't help much in giving me warmth. Men had the right idea about wearing britches and long sleeved shirts. At least their legs were protected from the snow.

I thought about the snow and britches for a while. I didn't see any reason I couldn't wear britches in this cold like a man wore. It wasn't like anyone would see me, or care if they did.

I left the old woman's room and went across the hall into the room I thought belonged to the old man. This time when I pulled open the drawers, I didn't feel like the clothes had more right to the house than I did. The house was mine now, and the clothes were mine for the taking. Everything belonged to me.

I went through the drawer until I found the most worn shirt of the bunch and laid it on the floor beside me. I opened the second drawer and took out an undershirt, dingy with age and many washings. I opened the next drawer down and found a worn and patched pair of long johns. I took the dress off and put the long johns and undershirt on. I felt their comfort instantly. I put the shirt on and buttoned it up, then rolled the sleeves up several turns. In the bottom drawer, I found several pairs of britches and one faded pair of bibbed-overalls. The sight of them stirred emotions in me. The familiarity of the men back home came to my mind and I wanted to wear these, even though they would be too big. I would roll up the legs and shorten the galluses as far as I could.

I lifted the overalls out of the drawer. Something was inside their folds. I reached beneath the bib and pulled out a thick book bound in fine brown leather. I opened the book and read the words. 'The Diary of: Boise Holloway' I turned another page and saw neatly written words on the lined paper. I flipped through the pages and found all but the last few written on. How many pages and years this diary covered I wondered. I put the diary beside me on the floor and found a pair of wool socks. They came all the way to my knees when I put them on my feet and pulled them up. Next were the overalls and they fit me better than I expected. Mr. Holloway must have been a little fellow. I put the diary back in the drawer beneath the britches. I would read it later when I wasn't in a hurry and there was light enough to read by. The diary might tell me about the old folks that once lived here. Thoughts of them lingered in my mind like a song that wanted to be sung.

I had never before milked in the snow in such comfort. I now know why men dress the way they do. I wondered why women didn't dress the same as men and why women seemed determined to condemn the few women that did. I had heard Momma say "Indecent, the way she tries to dress like a man!" It would be a long time until I put on another dress to wear in cold, snowy, weather unless I just had to, indecent or not.

It was dark by the time I done up the work and came back into the kitchen. I had lingered too long in the barn with the animals. I watched their contentment as they settled in, and found myself wishing I wasn't alone on this cold, snowy night, but I had learned long ago that wishes were a useless thing. I had heard Dad say repeatedly, "If wishes were horses, beggars would ride." I didn't have any right to complain for I was riding a better horse than I knew existed.

I lit one of the paraffin candles even though I hated to waste them on myself. For some reason tonight, I wanted the light. The cold darkness seemed to be closing in on me. Sleep should be what I was doing when dark came, but I didn't want to sleep. I reckon the silence of the snowy night must be making me lonely.

The old woman's diary came to my mind like smoke entering a room. A need to read it ached in my head, and I decided I might as well go upstairs and bring it down to the kitchen. I could read by the candlelight as I waited for my bread to bake.

I carried the candle upstairs and slipped the diary from beneath the britches. I took the diary back to the kitchen, sat down at the table and opened the diary to the first page. I began to read.

I shall never forget this date of June 6, 1910 because Father surprised me today. He sat down at the table to eat dinner and announced that he had quit his job as Dean of the small college in our town. He said he was old and tired of working eighteen hours a day. He wanted to move away to a quiet place where he could enjoy doing the things he had always wanted to do. Like reading his beloved books. Maybe, he said, he would be able to do a little writing of his own. He suspected he had great volumes of informative words to be delivered to mankind.

This may have sounded good in Father's mind, but he didn't fool me. He wanted to move away for my sake. I had become a public disgrace. People talked behind my back, some with pity, others with scorn. My only consolation was that Mother was not alive to endure my downfall. She sat high standards for our family name. My sin would have destroyed her. Some consolation!

Father is carrying through with his plans to leave our quaint Boston town for someplace in the isolated mountains of North Carolina. I thought it was a point of interest the place he is considering moving to is called Beech Mountain. I assume it is because of the tree and not a beach of water.

I do not want to leave the only home I have ever known, but I long to be free of the looks and behind-hands whispers. I hope Father realizes I never intended to bring this down on us. Sometimes things that seem so harmless and natural at the time can turn into a monster that will haunt the rest of your life. I fear I will never be free of this, and because of me, my monster will haunt father.

Father told me that the purchase of the place in North Carolina has gone through. Our home here is up for sale. Father is afraid we will not get a realistic price for a home of this fine quality. People know he longs to sell because of me. I advise him to hold out for a fair price regardless of me. A longer time here cannot harm me any worse than I am harmed already. He assures me he will not be hasty accepting an offer unless it is of reason. The house and land should bring an excellent price being it is the envy of the entire town. Our family estate has been handed down from generation to generation, as was our esteemed name of Holloway, until I disgraced it all.

I lay her diary down on the table and took the bread out of the oven. How had she disgraced it all? I wanted to know more about this woman, as well as her father. I wonder how her diary got to be hidden in a pair of bibbed overalls in the mountains of Kentucky? Again, I recalled

Abe Farrow and his words about Kentucky. I had intended to think about them, but just hadn't had time. I frowned for this woman's written words said they were moving to North Carolina. A place called 'Beech Mountain.'

I ate a bite of supper, put her diary behind a sack of flour in the bottom of the cabinet and went upstairs to bed. There was no need for me to waste more candle wax on myself.

I awoke to the freezing cold of winter and forced myself to get out of the warm bed where I was laying beneath a feather tick. I could see my breath freeze into a cloud. I was glad for the lovely rug beneath my feet. Not because of its beauty, but because my high top boots were frozen to the wooden floor over near the door where the rug didn't reach. I went to the window and scratched a hole large enough to see through the fern-patterned ice on the glass pane. Snow had fallen throughout the night and continued to fall, no longer like feathers, but as hard knots consisting of snow and ice. It would crust on top of the snow already fallen and make walking difficult.

After my usual building of the fire and cooking breakfast, I went out to do up the work. It seemed such a shame to make tracks in the white snow, but I had no other choice. The snow came to my knees. Again, I was thankful for the man's clothing I was wearing

Rafe was right about the springhouse. Nothing in there had frozen, but I had nailed up quilts over the windows to be safe. I strained the milk and placed it in the trough of water. If I had put it in any other room, except the kitchen, it would have frozen solid. I kept a fire in the cook stove for my own comfort.

The only room in the house warm enough to work in was the kitchen. I cleaned and polished that room until I grew weary of repetition. I remembered the diary and pulled it out from behind the flour sack. I found the place I had stopped reading last night and started again.

I went downtown today. The women crossed the street when they saw me coming or ducked inside stores so they would not have to encounter me. It made me feel as though I had the plague or some other deadly disease they might catch if they breathed the same air I did or looked in my direction. It was even worse when I met women with children in tow. They acted as though the very sight of me would corrupt their innocent children. I longed to grab these women and shake them until their proper hats fell off their heads, and their properly pinned up hair fell about their shoulders. I wanted to yell in their faces that I had done nothing they had not done.

Instead, I held my head high and pretended I was elevated to a position so high above them that their scorn did not matter. But it did. I hurt unbearably as I write. My self-esteem, my very soul is suffering irreparable damage.

I know Father is correct. Neither he nor I can continue to live in this town. We will leave as soon as he gets a fair offer on our home. People are trying to use my shame to their monetary advantage. Strange how people you thought would always be your friends turn on you with vicious intent when you are hurting and in need of their support and understanding.

They sense I am weak. They think they can attack me in my weakened state and tromp me into the earth until their blood-thirst is quenched. I will show them all that Boise Holloway has a backbone they cannot break. I will not run away like a beaten dog with its tail between its legs! I shall tell Father not to be in a rush to accept an offer on our home. I have to face the people of this town and show no shame. I will not allow them to beat me like an unwanted dog!

Today is Sunday and Father could not believe I was dressing for church. This would have been the fifth week I had not attended church. I told Father I refused to lie beneath the feet of the congregation like a doormat. I would rise up and face them eye to eye. Father dressed and attended church with me. We waited until the last minute to enter the church house then took our usual seats. A hush came over the congregation as we walked through the door. People poked each other with their elbows. Shocked eyebrows lifted high. I held my head in what I thought would have benefited the Queen of England. The entire congregation and the minister would not be able to put me down again!

Several days after my church attendance, the minister paid an unexpected visit to me while Father was away. He said I had disregarded the refined sensibilities of the respected ladies of our church. He suggested I not attend again. I asked him if his aim was to mollify the righteous or was he sent by God to save sinners? If he was to save sinners, as the Bible suggested, he should beg me to attend church more often. In fact, he should be holding extra services for me. I suggested we have private sessions on Wednesday and Friday nights. He left in righteous indignity. I will continue going to church. When Father and I leave, I want the people to know they did not run us off. Boise Holloway will not give in to gossip mongers and misguided preachers.

During the past two weeks, I have seen pride and respect for me start to return to Father's eyes. I have not scoured myself with sack and ash. I have not cast my eyes down in shame. I have not locked myself up and hidden away. I walk among the scornful with myself intact. I will not bow down to them, or let them see how badly I ache!

My heart and my soul have left me, but these good people shall witness no more of my tears.

Two more weeks have passed and I have failed writing in my diary until today. I attended church again this morning. The minister and the congregation are becoming unnerved at my presence. They try pretending I am not there, but their eyes take unwilling glances in my direction. The friends and neighbors that always sat in our pew have moved elsewhere. Father and I sit alone.

What I want to write about today is Mrs. Donnelly. She is the self-claimed most righteous of all people in existence. She came knocking at our door with the intent of using her powerful influence to run me out of the church. She said I was an unfit example for the children to see sitting in church each Sunday pretending to be worthy enough to sit in a holy place after my sin of passion. I should realize a woman like me is obligated to keep myself out of sight of the young and impressionable. Needless to say, my temper got the better of me and I said things when I probably should have been silent.

I lied to Mrs. Donnelly. I told her she was absolutely right. I could never receive forgiveness from God unless I confessed my many sins publicly. I told her next Sunday I planned to stand before the congregation and confess. I just hoped the good ladies of the church understood I had to name many of their husbands in my sin of passion. Including Mr. Donnelly.

I have never seen such a righteous woman leave our home in such righteous anger! The words she said to me would have shocked many a sinner.

Another Sunday has come and almost gone. I attended church but did not confess, of course. Being there was nothing for me to confess to, as my crime of passion did not consist of anyone living but me. The pews were almost empty and the minister was as nervous as a dog-chased cat.

Today Father had an offer on our home that was close to reasonable. He may get a decent price yet, seeing how badly the people want us to leave town. The revulsion the good ladies first felt toward me has turned to pure hatred. I, aided by Mrs. Donnelly, have put the fear in them that if I am a bad woman, their husbands might have assisted me. Worse, they may still be able to do so.

I lay her diary down on the table and put more wood in the fire. I had no idea what to think of the woman I was reading about. I wanted to know what her sin of passion was and knew I would find out if I read long enough. She was surely the woman the horrible Zeb had spoken of as Boise. There couldn't be two women with that name. Zeb had said Boise was jealous of her man. Rafe would give Boise and half the farm for me. I remembered those words and wondered about them as I poured myself a glass of milk. I ate a slice of cornbread spread with butter then went out in the cold to do the evening work.

It was a relief to get back into the warm kitchen from the outside cold. The temperature was dropping as night came on, and the sky was looking like more snow was on its way. I filled the wood box behind the stove high with firewood and saw that the coal bucket was still full before I settled down to read the diary while night came on.

I had read only a few lines when I heard a scratching outside the kitchen on the porch. Only an oak limb I thought rubbing against the house. I started to read again and heard a thump. Snow falling off the roof, I thought and lifted my head to listen for the sound of wind blowing that would cause the snow to fall. There was no sound of wind.

The night was dark and silent. A cold shiver crawled over me like an icy wind had entered the room and blew over my naked skin.

My eyes rested on the shotgun Rafe had left leaning against the wall behind the kitchen door. I had forgotten to lock the door as Rafe said for me to do. I didn't know if all of the other doors were locked or not. I had never locked a door in my life before I came here and had never felt the need to do so, but now I was wishing the doors were locked and Rafe was home with me. It just wasn't like me to be this unnerved over nothing.

I lay the book down on the table and eased out of the chair and moved as silently as I could until my hands grabbed the cold metal of the shotgun. I leaned back against the wall and clutched the gun to my chest. I felt my hands tremble and told myself how silly I was acting. A scratch and a thump was nothing to set me panicking like this. It was only a little noise. I had heard similar noise every day of my life, so why was I alarmed this time? I was surely reacting to the incident with Zeb, and expecting every sound to be made by him or someone like him.

There was another thump then scratching followed by what sounded like dragging from the steps across the porch to the kitchen door. The dragging stopped and I heard a wheezing sound coming through the crack beneath the door. An animal, I thought, had crawled across the porch and was sniffing beneath the door. It probably smelled the bread I had baked for my supper and was hungry. I thought of the panther Abe had told me about. How silly. Panthers didn't sniff under doors, but Abe's dogs might. I tried to reassure myself with these thoughts, but the hair on the back of my neck prickled and rose. The door shuddered against weight and I saw the doorknob slowly turning.

I stepped away from the wall, put the gun butt to my shoulder and cocked the gun. I knew Zeb would come through the door and this time I would shoot him dead. I aimed the gun at what I guessed would be the height of a man's chest and waited. Calm! I said to myself. Stay calm and squeeze the trigger, don't jerk it. I knew a shotgun blast at four-foot distance would splatter Zeb all over my kitchen. I felt a little sick.

The door opened slowly, a crack, another crack, and then flew wide open. There was nothing in my line of sight. Then I saw a movement. In slow motion the head and shoulders of a snow-covered child toppled through the door and onto the kitchen floor. For an instant, I almost squeezed the trigger, but stopped myself when I saw long strands of matted hair. There in the floor lay the little Munson girl!

I held my breath and pointed the gun toward the open door expecting to see someone else, but there was nothing through the open door but snow and blackness of a winter night. The glow of my candle threw only a dim light on the little girl lying face down on the floor. I could see no movement or sign of life coming from her.

I held the gun in my right hand, still pointing toward the open door, and kneeled beside the girl, feeling of her to see if she was alive. Her skin was like ice, but I could detect a heartbeat in the pulse of her neck. I grabbed her snow-covered hair with a trembling left hand, and dragged her thin body all the way into the kitchen and slammed the door shut. I listened for further sound outside. There was nothing.

I turned the key in the lock and looked down at the girl lying at my feet. She had on a brown coat that was in tatters and caked in snow. I didn't know if it had been torn into pieces or just worn out. Thin legs stuck out of what appeared to be a hemp sack, and to my horror, she was bare-footed. Her feet and legs were covered in dried blood.

I laid my gun down where I could reach it quickly and rolled her over. My breath stopped in my throat when I saw her face. It had been beaten to a pulp! One eye opened a crack and sounds escaped her lips. I wasn't sure if she said, "hide me," or "help me." One thing was for certain. She was nearly frozen to death.

I got the washtub from the springhouse and sat it in front of the kitchen stove where there was warmth, and then with the bucket in one hand and the shotgun in the other, I filled the washtub. I stuck my bare foot in the tub to check the temperature of the water. It was hot enough to be uncomfortable so I added some cold water. I didn't want to burn her tender, frozen skin.

I dared lay the shotgun down long enough to strip the frozen rags of clothes off her and carry her thin body to the tub. I eased her from my arms into the water. I felt tears running down my cheeks and dripping off my jaw as I rubbed her bruised and cut body that wasn't much bigger around than my arm. She wouldn't weigh much more than a weaned pig, and her ribs stuck up from her skin like a washboard. She must have been starved as well as beaten. Not all of her bruises were recent. Some of them were a shade of yellow-green coming from the passing of time. Who could have done this horrible thing to a child? Whoever it was wasn't fit to be alive! I looked at the gun lying beside me and longed to use it on that bastard! Whoever it was!

I cupped the back of her head in my hand and lowered her hair into the tub of water, making sure all but her face was submerged. I lifted her head out of the water and rubbed the bar of lye soap in her hair. The water ran brown, mostly from dirt but partly from dried blood. I continued to rub soap in her hair and dip her head. I wondered if her hair had ever been washed in her life? I could see lice the size of fat fleas clinging to her hair. I lay her against the tub with her neck resting on the edge and left her while I got a bottle of turpentine out of the springhouse. I came back with all the towels I could find and the small wash pan used to wash hands in. I soaked her hair in turpentine and wrapped it in a towel. I didn't know if the turpentine would kill lice or not, but I would soon find out.

After a long spell in the warm water, her entire body began to jerk and her teeth chattered together. The blue color was fading from her skin and being replaced by sickly white. Her lips moved but no words came out. I thought she was trying to say she was cold, but could not be sure. I poured more hot water in the tub and longed to mutter soothing words that would reassure her of her safety, but was afraid to. I had to remain silent and listen for any sound that might be outside. I expected a window to shatter and someone to come through it at any moment. I found myself wishing Rafe was home. This was the second time I needed him and he was gone.

After five or ten minutes, I took the towel from her head and dipped her hair in the water. I lathered her hair with lye soap but the turpentine didn't want to rinse out. Finally I eased back into the springhouse and got the jug of liquor. The alcohol cut the turpentine and washed the lice from her hair.

I held her in the washtub until the water got cold and the water closet was empty. I needed to put wood in the stove and fill up the water closet, but I didn't want to leave her in the tub while I did it. I dried her with a towel and wrapped her in my over sized sweater then lay her on the floor where the heat from the cook stove would keep her warm. I held the gun in my right hand as I stoked wood in the stove. Thank goodness I had filled the wood box behind the stove full of wood. With luck, it would last until daylight. After I had water in the water closet, I went upstairs and found her some warm clothes from the old woman's supply and brought them and two quilts down to the kitchen. I made her a pallet on the floor and dressed her as best I could.

I heated a cup of milk on the stove, lifted her head and tried to spoon the milk into her mouth. She seemed to swallow a little, but most of it trickled out the corners of her mouth. Finally, I gave up feeding her and allowed her to rest on the pallet, then propped myself against the wall with the gun in my lap. I let the candle burn until it went out.

How, I wondered did she get all the way here? I recalled Abe saying he had never been to Kentucky. Where was I? Why didn't I ask Abe? And just how far away was it to Dad's and the Munson place? The next person I saw, I would be certain to ask.

Several times during the night I filled the firebox with wood and made sure she was wrapped up in the quilt. She was either sleeping deeply or in a coma. I didn't know which. I was just glad she hadn't died on me. I longed for a doctor or at least Granny Mable. Rafe had said a doctor sewed up old Zeb's head and asked him if he had seen Rafe's new wife. I knew there was a doctor somewhere about, but I had no idea how far away he was or what direction to go in to find him.

I closed my eyes and said all the prayers I knew how to say including asking God to tell me what to do to keep her alive and both of us safe. I tried to get milk down her a half dozen times, and hoped a few drops succeeded.

I dozed off to sleep and woke up startled. It was broad daylight and the kitchen was cooling off. I had almost let the fire go out. I got up, stretched, and put shavings on the fire coals to get the fire started blazing, then put the last of the wood from the wood box in the stove.

I kneeled down beside the girl and carefully pulled the quilt from her upper body. Her thin chest was moving in shallow breaths as she breathed through her swollen, deformed nose. Her mouth was split in two places and the inside of her lips were puffed out and discolored. A long cut ran across her left cheekbone and the entire left side of her face was bruised. I lifted her small hand and let it rest limply in mine. There were dozens of scratches crisscrossing each other. Her fingernails had been broken back so far the tissue underneath them looked raw. I pushed up the sleeve of the sweater I had put on her last night. I couldn't put my thumb down on a spot that wasn't cut or bruised on that little bony arm. The tiny body I had washed looked to be in the same condition. I covered her back up as gently as I could. Part of me wanted to cry and the other part was seething with anger. I looked at the shotgun lying beside me on the floor and was glad Rafe had taught me how to shoot it. I wanted to use it now on whoever had done this to her. The thought of certain hell wouldn't stop me from killing that bastard.

I stood up and looked out the window at the deep snow that had fallen during the night covering any tracks left by the little girl. I could not even see tracks she had made when she crawled across the porch to the door because the wind had blown the snow badly during the night. I couldn't backtrack her and find out where she came from, or if anyone had followed her to the house. The good side was no one could track her here. I took another look at the snow and felt an uneasiness grow in my chest. It looked deep and it was still coming down in small flakes that looked like a light fog filling the air.

I left the window trying not to think about how deep the snow was as I went to the stove and put on a pot of water to boil. I would have to make some soup in hopes I could get her to swallow a little of the broth. She would die on me for certain if I didn't get some warm food in her. I tried to feed her again before I dressed warm and went out to do the work.

It took me an hour to tromp a path to the barn through snow above my straddle. Several times I longed to give up and go back to the house and the warm fire. Trying to carry the shotgun with me didn't help my progress. I feared I might shoot myself as I stumbled into drifts and struggled to get back to my feet, but I was afraid to leave the gun behind. Someone could have hid in the barn and be waiting on me. It also worried me to leave the kitchen door unlocked. Someone could slip inside while I was at the barn, but an intruder's footprints in snow could easily be seen.

When the work was done I returned to the house with a feeling of relief. Nothing had gone wrong. Nobody was hiding in wait to attack me. I sat the bucket of milk on the kitchen table and checked on the little girl. She had not moved. At least she was alive and breathing. I left the kitchen and went back outside to get an extra large supply of firewood carried in and a bucket of coal before I took off my wet clothes.

The wind was rising up out of the valleys and blowing the snow into a cloud keeping me from knowing if the snow had stopped falling.

I fixed potato and onion soup and tried to spoon some into the girl's mouth as I held her against me. Finally, I gave up on the soup and put a spoon full of molasses in her mouth and lay her back down. I hoped the sugar in the molasses would give her a little strength. I would try giving her water after the molasses had time to get into her system.

I had nothing to do but feed the fire and wait. I picked up Boise's diary and began to read.

Time is crawling slowly by as I wait to leave. Soon, Father tells me, we will be going to the mountains. Every one in town is watching me and wondering with fear and hatred in their eyes. The women, I expected as much, but the men come as a surprise. Some of the men that sneak out of town to houses of ill repute look at me as though I am a piece of trash they would not touch. Others look me from head to toe with knowing eyes and a crooked grin as though I am a piece of pie and they are considering how I might taste. I even had one man make a disgusting advance toward me. I wasted no time setting him straight. Strange how I once admired and respected these people. Now I detest them and they me.

I long to leave this town and hide myself in some far away mountain where I can cry my heart out for what I have lost. As time passes and the numbness that entered my mind and body wears off, I feel pain greater than I ever realized could exist. I long to close my eyes and never open them again. I long to scream and hurl myself against things. I have allowed deep rivers of water, and horse hooves and buggy wheels to come to my mind. Yet I know I cannot throw myself to either, for I realize I am too much of a coward for that. I will most probably live a long life and suffer mightily. I have a good start.

Chapter 13

*F*ather came into the kitchen with the saddest kind of smile on his face. He tried to make his voice sound happy, but the look in his eyes told a different story. He has finally sold our house after many months. He has given up his and Mother's home where they made and shared their life, love and memories. He did it for me and I am so very unworthy. "Start packing, my daughter." He told me. "We'll be leaving here with nothing less than a full wagon train. The house is sold but every fork and stick of furniture will go with us. Not a towel or curtain will be left behind." I did as Father requested. I began to pack.

It took every minute of three weeks to pack! Father hired seven strong men with wagons and strong draft horses to haul our things. As heavily loaded as each wagon is, I am wondering if he should not have hired eight. Finally we leave. I am both excited and fearful. Father talks and laughs happily, but the sad, haunted look remains in his eyes.

I now have the greatest sympathy and respect for the pioneers that traveled west by wagon train. What they endured was more than I want to imagine. For the first time in my life I discovered what it was like to relieve one's self behind a bush, then have to use the leaves from that same bush to wipe with. Going for days without bathing does no harm, but makes close contact most unpleasant. Father sits beside me on the wagon seat in the heat of a noonday and

174

gives off a rank odor I never knew he possessed. Thank goodness I had the foresight to bring along enough perfume and scents to last me for years. I have been forewarned that the desolate place we are going does not have the luxuries our large town has always bestowed upon me.

Another of my great complaints is food and sleeping facilities. We are not always able to find an inn or even a destitute farmhouse when night falls. I am often forced to sleep in the wagon while father and the men, hired to drive their wagons, sleep on the hard earth underneath the wagons. We should not have many more days until we arrive at this mountain Father has purchased. I longed to leave our town and am glad we did so, but I am beginning to fear what we might find at the end of our journey. It seems we are leaving civilization farther and farther behind us.

I have mentally chastised myself for any complaint I might let enter my mind. From now on I am only stating facts. I am the cause for what Father and I are enduring. I shall never forget that. Poor Father is aging before my eyes. I now see an old man who is tired and worried, where before I only saw my father.

Traveling over rough roads is most painful. I have resorted to sitting on bed pillows as we bump along. My teeth have been jarred together until they are sensitive. My head throbs, and even my toes hurt. A destitute farmhouse or even a log cabin is becoming more appealing the farther we travel. Father refuses a pillow. He is trying to remain manly in front of the other men. I would be willing to get on my knees and beg for comfort, but there is none to be had!

Wagons break down in the most inconvenient places! Time to repair them takes forever. Minutes feel like hours, and hours like years. I shall be shriveled up with age like a prune before we reach our destination.

I shall learn to ride a horse. One might have a shred of dignity sitting in a saddle. A pillow, even a down filled one, does little for bruised egos. It does just a little more for a bruised derriere.

Writing in a journal seems of little importance when one is exhausted. I shall stop writing for now and try to get a little rest before we continue our hell-drive to our new mountain home.

I thought this would be a good spot for me to stop reading in Boise's diary, and I laid it in the cabinet and checked on the little girl. She had not moved the entire time I had been reading. She seemed to be in a deep sleep with no intention of waking up. A growing fear swelled in the pit of my stomach. The little girl was going to die. If she did, I'd have to put her in the parlor where it was cold for there wouldn't be any way I could bury her in the snow. The ground was frozen solid.

Death brought Joey to my mind. An ache of hurt was still there inside me. I hated death.

I raised her body from the floor and tried to slip a spoonful of water between her lips. I watched the water trickle down her chin and drip onto the quilt. I recalled all the medicine and herbs stored in the springhouse and wondered if any of them might help her? If only there was a woman like Granny Mable here, she might be able to help the little girl.

I consoled myself with the thought that at least she did not appear to be in pain. She didn't moan or make jerking movements in her sleep the way people do that are suffering. I sat down on the pallet next to her unmoving body and lifted her carefully in my arms and rocked her gently as I tried to force some of my own strength into her. Surely my will alone would help her live. Finally, I let her slip from my arms and lay back onto the pallet beside the stove. If only I knew what to do for her?

I stood up from the pallet and went to the kitchen window to see if the weather had changed. If Rafe could just make it back home, he could take the little girl to the doctor he had spoken of. I pulled the curtain back and my heart lodged in my throat. There in the yard was a man on horseback with snow touching the belly of the horse. I grabbed the gun off the table and considered shooting him through the window. I didn't want to break the window in the middle of winter, but I didn't want to open the door either. The man removed his hat from his head and wiped his face on the sleeve of his coat as he looked toward the house. I closed my eyes and opened them again. I had to be seeing things! There was no way Jonas Jones would be in Kentucky in a snowstorm. But this man looked like Jonas Jones!

"Hello!" the man called out. "Is anyone home?"

I saw the man look at the tracks I had made from the house to the barn. He knew good and well someone was home. I opened the door a crack and stuck the gun barrel out. At least I wouldn't shoot the window out. He saw the barrel and lifted his hands in the air.

"I intend you no harm!" he called. "Please don't shoot!"

He not only looked like Jonas Jones, he sounded like him.

"Who are you?" I yelled against my better judgment.

"Laine?" he hollered. "That you Laine? It's me, Jonas."

I opened the door wider and found myself wanting to both shoot him for scaring me and run into the snow and throw myself into his arms.

"Thank God you're all right," his voice sounded of great relief. "My horse is lathered and exhausted. Can I put him in your barn then come inside?"

"Yes," I heard myself say, and watched him back his horse up in the same tracks he had just made until he could turn him around and dismount. He opened the barn door with great difficulty and disappeared inside. I closed the kitchen door and wondered if my mind had conjured up Jonas Jones. My mind told me I couldn't have seen him in the middle of the yard in snow like this. I was just over lonely and worried about the Munson girl. Jonas Jones was in North Carolina, not Kentucky! He was riding his fancy horse up and down the road from his dad's house to Eula's store, or somewhere in the woods waiting on me to bring a cow to his dad's bull. There just wasn't a way he would be in Kentucky with me!

I leaned against the door and breathed deep. Maybe I hadn't slept enough last night and it was affecting my mind. I looked at the pallet again just to make sure the little Munson girl was still there, just in case I was suffering from some kind of demented state. She was. I hadn't imagined her. Relief came flooding over me. If Jonas were really here, I would have help with her. I wouldn't be alone with her when she died.

I went to the stove and put a pot of coffee on to perk. If Jonas were real, he would want something to warm him up. I moved the potato and onion soup to the hot part of the stove and picked up the gun just in case. I waited and heard a knock on the door.

"Laine, it's me. Can I come in?"

"Yes," I heard my voice say as though I knew he was real all along and nothing strange was going on. I watched the door open and Jonas came inside and closed the door behind him. He slowly took a few steps toward me, reached out his hand and pushed the gun barrel away from him, then gripped it and took it from my hands. He laid it down carefully on the kitchen table then lifted his hands, cupped my face, and rubbed the tears from my cheeks with his thumbs. The next thing I knew my arms were around him in a desperate grip as I sobbed uncontrollably into the snow covered fabric of his coat.

"It's okay, Laine. I've got you," he whispered softly. "I'm here now, and everything is alright." His voice was soothing although it contained a note of desperation in it.

"She's going to die," I sobbed. "I don't want her to die."

Jonas eased me back a little from his chest and looked down at me with puzzled eyes.

"What?"

I loosened one of my hands from his snow-covered coat and pointed at the girl on the floor. His eyes moved from my face to where I was pointing. I saw his eyes widen and his mouth open then snap closed. His arms tightened on me pulling me hard against him in a protective manner.

"What th' hell?" he mumbled then turned me loose and went to the little girl and kneeled beside her. "What happened?"

"She showed up last night. I reckon somebody beat her," I told him and wished I hadn't pointed her out so soon. I missed the feel of his arms about me. There was comfort and security in his arms and I longed to be back there.

He pushed long strands of hair from her face and lifted her eyelids. He opened her mouth and peered inside. He turned her face from side to side then placed his ear to her chest. He lifted her hand and pushed the sweater back from her arm, then lifted the sweater and looked at her body. I watched his face contort at what he saw.

"God, Laine! Who is she?"

"She's the little Munson girl that lived below Dad's. I don't know how she got to Kentucky, or how you did either," I said and kneeled down beside him on the pallet.

He looked at me as though I was talking out of my head.

"Kentucky?" He shook his head, and then asked, "Who would beat her?"

"I don't know. I was afraid somebody might have followed her here, but I haven't seen anybody but you." I reached up and ran my fingers along his face. "You're real? I'm not dreaming you, am I?"

He turned his lips into the palm of my hand as he spoke. "Have you dreamed about me before?" He grinned, and I saw humor in his blue eyes along with puzzlement on his face. His voice lost its teasing tone as he spoke seriously. "I assure you, you're not dreaming now, Laine." I felt his breath warm on my hand. "I spent the night at the Patrick's place about a mile from here. Junie had her first baby last night. A girl. They're both fine."

What in the world would Jonas be doing at a woman's house in a snow storm while she was having a baby?

"Why were you there?"

"I'm the doctor around here." He looked into my eyes. "You didn't know that did you?"

"You're a doctor?" I couldn't believe what I was hearing. Jonas Jones was a doctor!

"Yeah, I reckon I'm a doctor." He grinned again. "Folks around here insist that I be one, even when I wish I weren't."

"Thank God!" I said with relief. I was thankful for any doctor right now, even if he was Jonas Jones. "She needs you, but why are you here? How did you get here?"

He didn't look at me as he spoke. "I knew Rafford was gone, and I was worried about you in this snow. Since I was close, I decided to see you for myself. Your closest neighbors are the Patricks a mile away. There's not as much snow down in the valley as there is here on the mountain. My horse couldn't have made it if the snow was as deep as it is in your yard. Wind must be drifting it around your house. But then there is always a lot more snow on this mountain top than there is down below."

He lifted his eyes and met mine. I thought his face softened as he looked at me. I realized my hand was still touching his face and moved it away quickly. What he had said registered in my brain. I had neighbors. They were only a mile away and Rafe had never told me about them.

"I have neighbors?" I heard myself say like a child repeating the impossible.

"Of course you have neighbors. Did you think you were living in some isolated part of the world?" he questioned lightly.

"Yes. I thought I might be. I didn't see any houses on our way here." I thought of Rafe. "How did you know Rafe was gone?"

"Half the people in town saw him drive his wagon through. Nobody saw him come back."

"There's a town?"

A frown was on his face as he looked at me. He took his hat off his head and placed it on the floor. He rubbed his hand through his hair and seemed to be debating between words and thoughts. His frown turned into a mighty troubled look.

"Rafe didn't tell you there were neighbors or a town nearby? Did he tell you where he was going when left?"

"Of course he told me where he was going. He is delivering winter supplies to stores like Eula's. And no, he never told me there were neighbors or a town."

Jonas must have heard the sharpness in my voice for he only nodded his head and changed the subject. He looked at the little girl.

"Has her kidneys or bowels moved?"

"No. Can you help her?"

"I hope so. I'll try."

He stood up and opened the kitchen door and picked up a black satchel he had left sitting on the porch in the snow. I wondered why he had left it outside instead of bringing it in with him. I watched him take off his coat then kneel down beside the girl again. I watched his hands touching her, confident, knowing, gentle. Those same hands had touched me only minutes ago. Those hands had given me comfort and I wanted comfort again.

"Nothing is broken. She's been starved and beaten for some time now. It has taken time for her to get in this condition. Some of her injures happened weeks ago. Her fingers look like she's been digging with her hands. How did she show up here, Laine?"

I stared at his hands as I spoke. They didn't look at all like Rafe's hands. Rafe's hands were square and stubby. Jonas' were long and rectangle. Both men's hands appeared to be strong masculine hands, but I had never seen gentleness in Rafe's hands.

"It was dark last night when I heard a noise on the porch. She crawled across the porch, opened the door then fell into the kitchen."

"Did she say anything?"

"I thought she whispered help me or hide me. I couldn't tell which."

Jonas frowned. Flakes of snow had melted on his face and hair. I had an urge to wipe the water away like he had done with my tears.

"Did you see anyone?"

"No, but I waited with the gun near me all night. It felt like somebody was out there." I shivered.

His frown deepened. He took a bottle out of his satchel and poured some in her mouth. Most of it ran out the corners of her lips. When he looked back at me, I wanted to collapse into his arms. I wanted to feel safe. I didn't want to be alone anymore.

"I'm glad you're here," I said and hoped he couldn't read my thoughts. "Can I get you some coffee or a bowl of soup?"

"There aren't many things I would like more right now," he admitted. "There wasn't much food in the Patrick house without Junie able to get up and cook."

I turned from him and busied myself with his food and set it on the table. Finally, he let the little girl lie back down on the pallet, got up and sat down at the table with a disturbed look on his face. I knew he was as worried about the little girl as I was.

"Thank you," he said and began to eat.

"That was good." He finished and pushed the bowl from him. "You're a good cook."

"Coffee and soup hain't much."

"It is when you're cold and hungry." He reached out a finger and lightly touched my arm. "Do you like it here, Laine? In this fancy house on the mountain?"

His eyes were looking into mine as though he was trying to read my soul.

"Oh yes. I love it here. I never dreamed there could be a house like this one in the world."

I thought I saw an emotion flicker over his face. He blinked, raised his brows and looked about the kitchen and made a sound like a sigh. I knew he was feeling the warmth and the comfort of the kitchen. There was nothing like warm food and a wood fire on a snowy winter day.

"Why?" he asked.

"Why? Well it's like a piece of heaven livin here. The land and the house are so beautiful I can't believe they're real. Much less that I'm here."

He did not seem satisfied with my answer. "Why marry Rafford Johnson?" He sounded bewildered and impatient.

I shrugged my shoulders. "He asked Dad if he could marry me. Dad said yes."

"You're young. Couldn't you have waited a few years? Did you love him so much you couldn't wait?"

"Wait? Love him?" My mind was not taking in what he was asking me.

Realization came over his features. "Your father agreed to the marriage. You didn't."

Jonas stood up from the table and gripped me by the shoulder as he raised me from the chair I sat in. He held me against him as he stroked my back. I let my arms slip around his waist and my head rest on his shoulder. It felt good not to be alone that I let my arms tighten around him. I thought I felt Jonas tremble.

"Tell me," Jonas said in my hair after some time had passed and he still held me. "Tell me why your Dad agreed for you to marry Rafford?"

"I figured Dad thought it was time for me to move on with my own life. I reckon he thought Rafe would do as good as anybody."

"But you are still a child. Much too young to marry a man like Rafford Johnson, or any man for that matter."

I didn't like him calling me a child and saying I was too young to marry. I was married and it had been a long time since I had felt like a child.

"I reckon I'm not as much of a child as you think. Besides, Rafe didn't think me too young to marry," I said in my own defense.

"Is he good to you?" Jonas's voice had lowered.

"He never beats on me, if that's what you mean."

Jonas seemed to want to ask me more questions but didn't.

"Ah, Laine!" He let his hand rest on my neck, and his thumb circled my skin.

"You don't approve of me marryin Rafe?"

I didn't need to ask him that question. I was perceptive enough to know Jonas would not like Rafe, and Rafe would surely hate the air Jonas breathed. Jonas would be a little too smooth for Rafe, and Rafe would seem as coarse and rough to Jonas as a partially shelled ear of feed corn. I had an idea it would be best for the two men not to get together often. Nor did I think it would be a good idea for me to be feeling good about Jonas holding me, but I wasn't moving away.

"I'm not approving or disapproving. It's just as I said, I think you are too young to marry, especially to a man as old and experienced as Rafford Johnson."

He suddenly turned me loose and went back to the little girl. A troubled expression had taken over his face as he kneeled beside her.

"Didn't you have a bed to put her in?"

"I thought she would be better off where it's warm. The bedrooms are cold."

"You're right. She does need to be warm." He rubbed his hand over his face then shook his head slowly. "It will take a long time for her to get well if she lives."

"You think she might die?"

"There's a chance she'll live. She has to be a tough little thing to be alive right now. I don't suppose you got any food down her?"

He sounded all doctor and nothing like the man that had just questioned me about marrying Rafe.

"Not much. A few drops of water and soup, maybe a spoonful of molasses."

Jonas moved the quilt back and lifted her legs and examined her feet and toes. I knew seeing the spindly legs that were bruised and cut caused the sadness on his face.

"She's clean," he said under his breath as though he couldn't believe his own words.

"I gave her a bath."

He looked up in surprise. "Why?"

"She was almost frozen. I thought it would warm her up. She was covered in dirt and dried blood, and her hair was filled with lice. I think I got them out. I hope I did."

"Was she wearing these clothes? He asked although his tone said he knew she wasn't.

I pointed to the clothes I had tossed into the corner and hadn't burned yet. He reached over and picked them up.

"Rags," he said. "Dirty stinking rags and a half rotted feed sack. Did she have any kind of shoes on?"

"No. Her feet were bare."

Jonas shook his head then spoke as though he were talking to himself.

"She had to be running or her feet would be frostbit. She could have had rags tied around them in the beginning and lost them in the snow."

"How did she get all the way from Dad's to Kentucky?" I wanted to know. "It took me and Rafe three days travelin to get here."

Jonas gave me a blank look. "Rafford told you he was taking you to Kentucky and you traveled for three days?"

"Wasn't that what I just told you?"

Jonas nodded and looked back at the little girl. "Yes. I think you told me that."

He picked up her feet and examined them again. A troubled look was about him.

"How did she get this far then?" I insisted.

He shook his head slowly. "There are a lot of questions I would like answered. Right now I don't have a clue how she got here."

"Me either," I told him as I picked up the dirty dishes and put them in the dishpan to wash. I filled up the water closet from the bucket of water sitting on the floor and went into the springhouse and refilled the bucket.

"There's all kind of herbs and stuff in there that Boise had," I told him as I entered the kitchen. "There might be something you could use to help the little girl."

Jonas's looked up at me. "You know about Boise?" he asked with a note of disbelief in his tone.

"Rafe said she died not long back. Her husband died not long before her. Did they have some kind of disease, or did they just die of old age?" Being the doctor around here, I thought he might know.

"I never treated either of them," Jonas said slowly as he folded then refolded the quilt over the girl.

"You knew them didn't you?"

"I knew of them," he said the words as he stood up and walked over to the wood stove and stared at the pot of soup as though he had never seen soup before.

"I thought it was mighty decent of Rafe to let them live here after he bought this place from them, but then he probably needed somebody to look after the place since he traveled so much. They must have up and died suddenly bein you never treated them. If they had some kind of long lastin disease, they'd have sent for you."

I felt a need to say something good about Rafe for I was beginning to wonder how he would take the little girl showing up then Jonas Jones coming while he was gone. Something was telling me he wouldn't like it at all.

"Mighty decent," Jonas said absently.

"Do you want some more soup?"

"Not right now, but you might try to give her a little after while." He sounded like his mind was far away.

"You're worried about her, aren't you?"

"I am becoming more worried by the minute." He turned from the stove and his boot hit the edge of the coal bucket. He stared at it just like he did the pot of soup.

"Laine?" his voice was low. "Did Zeb deliver coal to you?"

I remembered Rafe saying the Doc asked Zeb if he had seen Rafe's new wife.

"Yeah," I told him.

"Before or after he had been hit by a limb?"

"Before," I answered and crossed to the window and looked out at the snow. I heard Jonas move across the kitchen and felt his hand on my shoulder.

"Do you want to tell me about it?" he asked as he let his other hand grasp me by the waist and ease me backward until my back rested against his chest.

"No."

Jonas was silent for a few minutes.

"Was he drunk?"

"I think so."

"What did you hit him with?"

"The cast iron skillet."

"Does Rafe know?"

"Yeah."

"How did he take it?"

"Anger. Amusement. He said he would kill Zeb if he ever saw him again. He was pleased that I had hit Zeb. He gave me the shotgun and said if Zeb showed up again to shoot him."

"Did Zeb hurt you in any way?"

I knew what Jonas was trying to ask me in a gentlemanly way.

"No. He made a vulgar attempt but I'm pretty good with a skillet." I took a deep breath determined not to let any emotions about Zeb reenter my mind. "I'm glad I didn't kill him, but I think I'd shoot him if he shows up again," I admitted.

"He won't show up, Laine. I know that and so does Rafford. I would say Zeb is probably still running in the opposite direction from this place. No man alive would want to confront Rafford Johnson when he's mad or drunk."

"Rafe drinks?" I heard myself ask as though I didn't know the man. Which in all reality, I didn't know my husband very well at all.

"He's been known to do so." Jonas was rubbing his hand absently up and down my arm, and I knew he was considering what his next words should be. "Did you know Rafford at all before you married him?"

"I saw him at Eula's store after Joey died, then again at home when he came wantin to buy hogs when I was cannin tomatoes. The next time he came, he and Dad took me to the preacher's and we were married."

"God!" Jonas clenched his teeth. "God! All Mighty!"

"It wasn't that bad. Really it wasn't. I don't regret marryin him. Look what I've got here. I wouldn't give it up and go back to Dad's even if I could." I meant every word I told him, but there was still an uneasy feeling inside me. It wasn't like Rafford Johnson loved me enough to marry me or that I loved him.

"You're willing to marry a man in trade for a fancy house?" Jonas demanded and his hands tightened on me.

"Oh, don't make it sound like that. I didn't know he had a red copper when we were married, but I do like this place. It feels like home to me and I don't want to leave even if it means living with Rafford until I'm ninety years old."

Jonas turned me loose, moved to the kitchen table and sat down. He clutched his hands together and looked at them for several minutes before he spoke to me again.

"I'm not judging you for marrying Rafford, nor am I saying anything bad against your husband. Please forgive me if I sounded as though I were. I truly want you to be happy. I just want you to know I'm near by if you ever need me."

"Why should I need you?" I couldn't help asking.

"Doctors come in handy," he tried to smile. "Sometimes a person can get dragged by a cow, or visited by a beaten up child."

"Doctors can be a great comfort," I said as I left the window and sat down in a chair beside Jonas and looked up at him. "I've got a feeling Rafe is going to be mad when he finds out the little girl is here. Not to mention you showin up."

Jonas touched my cheek with one finger. "Everyone knows Rafe is a jealous man with a mean streak a mile long. He wouldn't want me butting into his business much less being alone with his wife. It is best we let him know up front that I came by as a doctor. You realize I can't leave and take the girl with me yet. She'll die for certain if I put her on my horse and try to carry her to town. She might die even if I stay here with her." He hesitated for a moment before he said; "I'm willing to leave now with or without her if it will make things easier on you."

"You're a doctor, and I don't intend to pack this poor little girl off in the cold for her to die just because I think Rafe won't like her bein here. Nor do I intend for you to leave when you can stay and help her. I don't see any reason Rafe should be jealous of you being here," I added with conviction. "He'll be mad though."

Jonas's eyes met mine. "You and I are alone together for a day and night, maybe longer, and you don't think that's reason enough for Rafford to be jealous?"

"No," I said. "He has no reason to be jealous." I knew I was lying and so did Jonas.

"There is one thing I think we need to keep secret from your husband," Jonas said cautiously, as though he were considering how to phrase his words.

"That is?"

"I think it would be best if Rafford never knew we met before, nor that you know the girl."

"Why?" I had a fear of not telling Rafe the whole truth about anything.

"Please listen to me on this, Laine. Act as though you never saw me or the girl before. It will be simple. A strange girl showed up at your door, and the friendly doctor was at the Patrick place delivering a baby. The friendly doctor knew Rafford was out of town and thought it a neighborly thing to do by stopping to check on his young wife since there was a snowstorm and the doctor didn't know if she could take care of herself in the cold."

"Why should I lie?" I insisted.

"I can't explain why right now. I just beg you to trust me on this one. I hope you never have to tell another lie in you life, but this time I think it is best we both lie to your husband and everyone else. Agreed?"

His eyes bored into mine with pleading and insistence until I decided, whatever his reason, it was important and to both our best interest.

"Agreed," I said hesitantly.

Relief showed clearly on his face. "Nice to meet you, Mrs. Johnson. I shall call you nothing but Mrs. Johnson when someone is around, and I suggest you refer to me as Doctor Jones."

"Doctor Jones. You are an answer to my prayers, you know. I prayed all night for a doctor to show up and you did."

"God answers prayers in mighty strange ways. It might be a good idea for you to appear to dislike me as much as you did our other two encounters." He grinned.

"I didn't dislike you," I told him.

"I know," he said. "I know."

Chapter 14

I watched Jonas work the rest of the evening on the little girl. He continuously put drops of medicine in her mouth, determined she live. His strong arms lifted her against his chest rocking her gently.

"You're safe now, little one. You're safe," he whispered near her ear.

I listened to the sound of his voice, heard its caring and concern. I wanted to feel his nearness, his comfort. I almost envied the little girl. I had to get out of the house. Had to get away from Jonas.

"Jonas, I'll feed and water your horse for you while I'm doing up the work."

"You needn't bother. I'm accustomed to feeding my own horse."

"It's no bother. I have to milk and feed anyway. It won't take five minutes longer."

He looked at what I was wearing. "I'm glad to see you have on sensible clothes for weather like this. I will never understand why women didn't insist on wearing pants for the beginning of time."

"Reckon they want to look like a woman instead of a man."

"You look like a woman." He looked away from me to the little girl.

I went out the door into the cold. When I came back to the house, he had supper cooked and was putting it on the table. He found the cans I had in the springhouse.

"You'll like tomato dumplings," he told me after he noticed my skeptical look into one of the pots.

"And you said I was a good cook for making potato soup."

I strained the milk then dipped warm water to clean up with.

"Hurry up woman before it gets cold."

I liked him calling me a woman. I went to the table and tried to imagine Rafe cooking a meal, or doing much of anything.

"I didn't know doctors could cook."

"They can if they're hungry."

I tried to recall the last time I had eaten a meal I hadn't cooked. I tasted the tomato dumplings and found them delicious.

"Jonas, the woman that gets you will be lucky."

He grinned slightly as he passed me the potatoes. "I was thinking on the same line. Does Rafe appreciate you? Does he know he's got a companion for life instead of getting a good deal on slave labor?"

How could I answer that? I didn't know what Rafe appreciated and I certainly wasn't a slave. Besides, I took pride in the fact that I could work a little. I wasn't like Momma and Susie.

By the time we had finished dinner the wind had started to howl over the mountain. Gusts would occasionally scoop down from the sky and rattle the windows and doors.

"I'm glad this house was built solid," I said with relief. "That wind is blowin up mighty powerful."

"It always blows hard over this mountain. Folks thought old man Holloway was crazy for building a house where he did. At least he had enough sense to nestle the house with the hill in back of it. It blocks the wind a little."

"I didn't know that Mr. Holloway built this house. They must have lived here a long time." Something wasn't adding up in my mind, but I couldn't put a finger on it at the moment.

"Not too long," Jonas said quickly and got up from the table to check on the little girl. "I thought I saw her move. Get me some broth from the pot I cooked the potatoes in. I'll have to get a few drops of food in her every hour or so."

I got up and did as he requested. "She's gettin better," I said with relief as I saw her move.

He fed her a few drops, then laid her down on the pallet and covered her with the quilt. "A child's body can heal from what she's been through, but I don't know about her mind."

"What do you mean by that?"

"If she does live, Laine, the beatings she has received may affect her adversely," he said. "Just as soon as I dare to move her, I'll take her to the Mission Hospital. It's not far from here. They can put her in the Home for Children when she is well enough. That way she'll not have to go back where she came from."

"There's a hospital and a children's home near here?"

He looked me in the eyes as he spoke. "You're living on top of a mountain, Laine, but you're not as isolated as it appears. When you get down this mountain there are hospitals, schools, and towns. There's even a train that runs from Linville to Johnson City, Tennessee."

"Why didn't I see any of that when Rafe bought me here?"

"He brought you up the back side of the mountain. Down the hill a little ways the road will fork. The left fork goes down the back side of the mountain and the right fork will take you to the Patrick place and then on to town." He frowned and his face took on a serious look. "I prefer Rafe didn't know I told you this, but I think it's important to know you can leave this mountain if you want."

Jonas's words made an uneasy feeling grow inside me. "Do you think Rafe intended me to think there weren't people near by?"

"I wouldn't guess at Rafford Johnson's intentions. I want you to know help is available if another emergency arises. Again, I think it best Rafford not know I've told you this. I have an idea he'd think I was interfering in his business."

I didn't ask any more questions as I lit a candle. The room was getting dark and the winds were picking up in their fury.

"We're in for a wind storm right," I said as I sat the candle down in the middle of the table. "It's howlin like a pitiful dog."

"That we are. I'll get my coat on and bring in more firewood and coal before it gets too bad out there. It will be difficult to keep this room warm the way the wind is blowing, and I am afraid for her to get a chill."

"The coal bucket is full," I reminded him. "I'll get the wood. You don't know where it's at."

He stood up from the table and reached for his coat. "You can tell me. It would be a good idea for you to get some extra quilts and a pillow if you have them. I'll sleep in the kitchen tonight and keep a watch on her."

I fixed a pallet for Jonas near the girl and left him with her. I climbed the stairs and got in the cold bed with my clothes on. The winds were up and the room was freezing cold.

It took me a long time to fall asleep.

Sometime during the night I woke up sweating with fear. A nightmare about Rafford being mad brought me wide-awake. I had become the little Munson girl and Rafford had me down under the house in the cellar. His big, square fists were beating the life out of me. I couldn't escape him. He was big and strong, and I was just a little girl.

I jumped out of bed and hurried down stairs to the kitchen. The warmth of the fire would stop my shaking and seeing Jonas might ease my fear.

Jonas was sleeping on the pallet, and the room had grown cold. He hadn't woke up to put wood in the stove. The room was dark for Jonas had blown the candle out, but I didn't need much light to lift the stove lid and rekindle the fire.

Jonas rolled over and sat up. The quilt fell to his lap and I saw he had slept in his clothes also.

"Is it morning?"

"No. I got cold and came downstairs to put wood in the stove."

"I'm sorry. I should have done that already." He got up and came toward the stove.

I saw his bare feet on the cold floor and felt an uneasiness rise inside my chest. "Get back under the cover," I said quickly. "It's mighty cold and the storm has gotten worse."

"Yes. The wind is in a fury, but it's been that way before. This house has withstood worse storms," he said as he reached out and touched my arm.

"You're shivering. You're half frozen."

He put his arm around me and pulled me against him. I wanted to push him away. I knew I should and lifted my hands to do so, but somehow my hands touched his chest then lifted to his face.

"Laine."

I heard him whisper my name as my face rested against his cheek, felt the roughness of his beard, warmth in his flesh. My hands went into his hair, pressing him closer to me.

"Laine," he whispered again. "You don't know what you're doing."

He held me tight a few moments longer then moved me away from the warmth of his body. He took the quilt he had been lying on and wrapped it around me then filled the stove with wood.

"You'll be warm in a minute," he said. "You'll be warm."

"Jonas?" I said his name, but he turned from me and checked on the little girl.

"Try to sleep, Laine. Morning will be here soon."

Light was coming in through the kitchen window when I opened my eyes. I was cradled against a warm body in strong arms. I breathed in deeply the smell of Jonas Jones. He opened his eyes and looked at me. I looked back. We said all that mattered without words or touch.

I got up and cooked breakfast.

"Is she any better?" I asked as I sat down at the table and watched Jonas's hands put food on his plate.

"I think she may be, a little. She opened her eyes a time or two and swallowed more broth."

I looked at the food and didn't think I could force myself to eat a bite. "You're goin to leave?"

I saw pain in his eyes and perhaps regret. "I don't want to, but I haven't a choice. If I stay, I won't be able to keep my hands to myself. I held you wrapped safely in your quilt, but, Laine, I was going out of my mind. I wanted to unwrap the quilt."

I wondered if that would have been so wrong, but didn't say a word.

"Women have been known to leave their husbands," he looked in my eyes as he spoke. "Sometimes a woman marries the wrong man."

I shook my head knowing that I could never leave here. "She might die if you take her off the mountain now," I managed to say, longing to keep him here, with me, one more day.

"The wind storm last night blew the snow into drifts. I can pick my way around the drifts and get to town safely. The sun is coming out and it won't be too cold on her."

The look in his eyes was saying more to me than his words, but I didn't want to listen.

"Please be careful. I don't want anything to happen to you," I told him.

"The worse thing that will ever happen to me, Laine, is going down that road and leaving you behind, but I don't know what else to do." He raked his fingers through his hair in pure bewilderment.

"Don't worry about me. Besides, you're just the neighborhood doctor that was delivering the Patrick baby, remember?"

"Yes," he said. "I remember."

I held the girl while Jonas climbed on his horse then placed her in his lap. She looked like a big bundle of bedclothes, and I hoped she wouldn't tumble from the horse. The trip would be difficult enough for Jonas without any mishaps. He looked down at me and his eyes were dark and troubled.

"Good bye, Mrs. Johnson. Take care of yourself. This mountain can be a harsh place for a girl alone."

"Good bye," I said over the lump in my throat. He looked at me for a moment longer, turned his horse and rode away. I wanted to scream.

For the next few days the sun came out and melted the snow until bare patches of ground could be seen. I knew Rafe would be able to get the wagon home if he wanted to, but I just as soon he didn't come.

The windstorm had blown down trees and tree limbs. I spent my time dragging in deadfall. I knew the nice weather wouldn't last much longer and I was mighty short on firewood. Finally, when I couldn't stand the thought of dragging another limb, I went inside the house and took out Boise's diary. I sat down at the table to rest and began to read in the diary where I had left off before Jonas came.

About mid-day my father stopped the wagon and grinned at me. "Boise, my girl, you have just crossed the line and entered the new county of Avery," he said proudly. "A brand new County for us to start a brand new life in. It's an omen girl, an omen." I tried to give him a big smile and appear happy, but I felt barely alive. There was not a part on my body that didn't hurt. Even my mind ached when I tried to talk. "How much further?" was about all I could get out. A big grin came on Father's face. "You'll be in your new home before the sun sets."

My new home consisted of a poor excuse for a house on a flat spot on the side of a mountain. I wanted to cry from relief of knowing I would not have to ride further in the wagon, and from disappointment in seeing the rusty orange tin roof on the sagging house that was no larger than our living room back home. Father hopped off the wagon like an old man filled with excitement. "This is just temporary, girl. Just temporary. These men have agreed to stay on with me until they have built us the finest house ever seen. It will be even grander than the one we left behind. You will never regret moving here, girl, never!"

Father climbed a mile further up the mountain and chose a spot with acres of land in front with a pastoral view that extended miles in the distance and crested with Tennessee and North Carolina mountains like the points on the crown of a king, and a towering hill in the back to build our house against. He was determined to make it appear like an old country farmhouse and a southern plantation mansion combined. I wish him luck!

We have been here a week and all I have done is rest and heat water to soak my aching body. My tender white flesh looks like I have been rolled over stones and bruised on every inch. The men that came here with us must have been carved from hard pine knots. They act like the trip here was nothing but a summer picnic. They scurry around this mountain and to the tiny town of Elk Park and the larger town of Johnson City buying lumber and other building materials like kids buying Christmas presents. Each man tries to come up with a grander idea than the other men, and Father encourages them. Where and when this will end is beyond me!

Two of the women, living near the foot of this Beech Mountain, came to visit me. Their speech was slow and endearing and their dresses were fashioned as I have never seen before. I am sure they sew their own clothes from cheap cloth. Their dresses were protected by an apron with a bib and large pockets on the bib and skirt of their apron. Their hair was pinned in a tight bun at the nape of their necks. Their shoes were crude and looked like they should belong to a man. The only things feminine about these two women were their build and the delicate features of their faces. They appeared shy around me but their eyes twinkled with welcome and life. I think they were as fascinated by looking at me as I was them. They continued to refer to me as 'you'uns.' One of the women looked at my dress and said. "Hit's a plumb purty dress you'uns air wearin' bein' hit ain't Sunday and all." Their speech had an Elizabethan twang with an Irish-English flavor. They encouraged me to "come down the mount'un this Sunday and listen to the preach'un." I felt tears sting my eyes at their words. It had been many, many months since women had welcomed me to Church. They left behind their gifts of canned sweet and fruit, which was strawberry jam and applesauce.

Needless to say, when Sunday came, Father and I traveled down the mountain and attended their church. Not one person in the entire church failed to shake our hands and welcome us with honest friendship. All the people invited us to go home with them and "eat a bite of dinner. We ain't got much but you'uns air welcome to share hit." I also heard, "I'm much obliged, reckon I better get on."

This 'preach'un' was something I had never heard before. It was packed full of emotion, movement and loudness. The preacher would pound on the pulpit and run back and forth in front of the congregation. Many people yelled, "Aman! Brother!" and others broke out into fits of what I was told was shouting. When the singing began, the preacher came to us and asked if we had been saved? Father said yes before I could ask him what saved meant.

We did not make a habit of going to preach'un often although the people seemed to think we should. Father told them we left the City to be hermits and hide on our mountain. The people accepted Father's statement and left us to ourselves although they continued to be the friendliest people I have ever met. They see no class difference in people, as did the place we left. A person would have to be 'mighty vile' to be looked down on. Mostly, the mountain people leave other 'folks' to live their own lives.

I cannot believe how fast our new house is taking shape. The men Father brought with us are working like demons. They want to get the outer shell completed so they can work inside during the coldest part of winter, which is almost upon us. Father tries to hire additional workers whenever possible. I've heard said Father has more workers on the mountain than are in the entire town of Elk Park. People call him the 'rich man' and 'crazy man'. They say it would take a rich, crazy man to think of building a house on the top of a mountain where the cold winds hit and the snow drifts. An intelligent man builds his house in a protected hollow where he can stay warm in the winter and cool in the summer. They laugh at Father, pat him on the back and shake their head at him, but they treat him as a friend.

I cannot believe last Saturday afternoon. A young man, one that I deemed not too bright because of his actions, came to court me, as mountain people would say. He actually hid in the woods for an hour peeping at our small house before he got up the nerve to knock on our door. I opened the door and he stood there, his hat gripped against his wool coat, and his hair greased slick to his head. A silly grin was on his face as his hand, without the hat, gripped a small, brown paper bag filled with hard candy for me.

"Miz. Holloway," he said. "I've come to call on ye, iffin' you be willin'. I knows I ain't much to look at, but I be hard workin'."

Now, what does one say to a statement like that? I found myself speechless. Father was present and invited him inside to warm up. It took him an hour in the front room talking to Father while I hid in the bedroom before he decided I was not willin'.

That night I cried myself to sleep for the first time in months. I knew I would never find love again, nor did I think I wanted to. No one would ever be able to replace Henry. Certainly not a lanky, greased haired sapling of a mountain man that had no idea how the King's English was spoken.

I reread that part of Boise's diary. Now I was beginning to get close to finding out what her sin of passion might be. I figured it had something to do with this man named Henry and never finding love again. I started to read on when I heard the sound of a wagon outside and knew Rafe was returning home. I quickly hid the diary behind the flour sack and made sure there was enough stuff in front of the flour to make the diary hard to find.

I went outside on the porch in time to see Rafe throw the reins down on the ground and come across the yard toward me. His step faltered for a moment as he looked at me then continued in his swaggering stride.

"I damned near thought you were a man." Were the first words he said. "Fix me some food. I'm so damned hungry I was near eating the ass off the horses." Were his next words.

"Welcome home Rafe." I looked toward the wagon. It was empty. I wouldn't be unloading hogs. "Shouldn't the horses be unharnessed and put in the barn?"

"I've had a hell of a time getting here! You can take care of the horses after you've taken care of me. I walked them the last mile and let them cool down. Won't hurt them to stand a while," he said as he walked past me and into the warm kitchen.

I noticed he had on a new wool coat with fleece lining as I followed him. His cap was of similar material with long ear mitts that hung down and tied with a string beneath his chin. He was also wearing a pair of leather boots I had never seen before. They came almost to his knees and were obviously of fine quality. He had taken well care of himself while he was away. I thought he had put on a little weight.

"If I'd had any sense I'd have stayed down the mountain until the thaw came. Takes a fool to come up this mountain when there's snow on the ground."

He looked in the corner of the room near the stove and saw the pallet I had not removed from the floor. I had slept every night on the pallet Jonas and I had slept on for a few short hours.

"You been sleeping on that?" he asked as he crossed the kitchen.

"I've been for the past few days. I fixed it for the girl."

Rafe stopped in mid-step and looked at me. "Girl?" he said the word slow and looked at the pallet as though it might have an answer.

"I never wanted you home so bad in my life," I told him truthfully. "It was the night the deep snow came, that she showed up."

I told him about the girl coming and how I almost shot her and probably would have if she hadn't been on her knees.

"I told you to lock the damned doors," he said harshly. "Get some food cooking while you talk. I don't want to die of starvation. Where's she at, dead?"

"More'n likely. She didn't have much life left in her when Doctor Jones took her off."

I saw Rafe puff up like a toad frog and color began to flush his ruddy complexion to a deeper red, but he didn't say a word.

"I sat beside the girl and prayed all night that the doctor you said had sewn up Zeb's head might show up. God answered my prayers, Rafe. The doctor had been deliverin a baby at the Patrick place and for some reason he decided to check on me. He said you had been seen leaving town, but not seen coming back. He thought I might not know how to care for things in a snow storm," I told Rafe as I put wood in the fire then peeled potatoes and put them on the stove to cook. "She was too weak to take off the mountain when he first arrived, but he put medicine and broth down her all night until she appeared a little better. You might check on her sometime when you leave the mountain and go to town. Ask the doctor if she lived and let me know. See if he knows who she is," I added for good measure.

"I told you to shoot first and ask questions later," Rafe said harshly. "Yet you let that girl and then the Doctor come right in here."

"You said to shoot first then ask questions later if Zeb showed up." If Rafe heard that I said the doctor put medicine down her all night, he didn't show any interest. I felt my tension ease slightly. I continued my tale.

"Oh Lord, Rafe! Did I ever come close to shooting the doctor. I was so scared whoever beat the girl had showed up here. I almost shot him through the window, but I didn't want to break it in the wintertime so I cracked the door and stuck the gun out. He put his hands up in the air and said not to shoot he was Doctor Jones."

Rafe looked at me long and hard as I stirred up a bowl of corn meal for bread and poured it into a greased pan and stuck it in the oven.

"And it didn't occur to you he might have been lying?"

"I held the gun on him until he came into the house. I knew he was a real doctor when I saw his black satchel. You should have seen that poor little girl. She was starved to the bone and her entire body was bruised and scratched. What do you reckon happened to her? Where do you reckon she came from?"

"Beats the hell outta me."

Rafe sat down at the kitchen table to wait on me to finish cooking him his meal. He seemed to be using more cuss words than I had ever heard him use before, and he didn't seem to be a bit happy to be home.

"Did it even enter your mind the man might have stolen the doctor's bag and you turned that kid over to the one that beat her up?"

I turned from the stove and looked at Rafe in what must have appeared to be total shock. He laughed right out loud.

"No. I'd say that thought never entered your pretty head. What did this Doctor Jones look like?"

"Well, he was a bit taller than you, and thinner. His hair was black and he rode a bay gelding. He looked clean and neat."

"All the markings of a fine country doctor, huh?"

"I hope so," I admitted. "He is a doctor, right? He's the one you said sewed up Zeb's head?"

"Damned woman having a baby in a snow storm ought to die, Junie especially," Rafe said harshly. "I hate a breedin woman. Hate them. Hope to God you're as barren as a hard rock." He looked me over. "Little thing like you, not built to squirt out a litter. Then again, a sow cat has no problem."

Rafe seemed to grow weary of picking at me and his face lost all interest in the doctor and the little girl. His eyes looked at me with that certain look.

"What's my little wife been doin while I've been away?"

The way he said it brought an instant aggravation to me, and I turned and looked him in the eyes.

"You mean besides freezin my ass off on this mountain while you were gone, and havin the livin daylights scared outta me by an almost dead girl and a doctor that stupidly came out to deliver a baby in a snow storm for a damned woman that ought to die?"

"Oh, so my little wife is feelin feisty? Then again you might just be needin a little attention from your husband," his words sounded a little different, kind of slurred together.

I didn't want that kind of attention from Rafe. The thought of him touching me was like smearing something ugly on my skin. Rafe looked at the pallet on the floor.

"Lay down there, then."

"No," I told him firmly. "You can eat then we'll go up stairs to a comfortable bed. A body might lay on that hard floor if you're freezin, but it han't no fit place for bouncin around on."

"You know that for a fact?" Rafe questioned as he looked at me.

"I do indeed. I slept there next to the fire after the doctor took the girl off. I was miserable, but warm. Now that you're home, you can keep me warm, and I can lay where it's not miserable."

Rafe grinned. "Spoken like a real nagging wife."

"I don't nag!"

I saw Rafe lift his brow and look at me questioningly. I realized I no longer had the desire to be the perfect wife. I found that I just wanted to be happy, and if not happy, content.

Rafe filled his belly with food then took me upstairs before I could clean the table off. I went straight to the bed and lay down. Regrettably, I didn't have on a dress where Rafe could lift my skirt and get on with it.

"You don't expect me to take those clothes off you, do you? It'd be like stripping clothes off a man."

I began undoing the britches I had on.

"Get up off that bed and take them off," he told me harshly as he lay down. "Not so fast, little wife. Take it all off slow like. A man needs a show once in a while, and don't give me any sass."

I gritted my teeth to keep harsh words from escaping my mouth. I wanted to give him a lot more than sass. I wanted to knock him up the side of the head with a hoe handle. Instead, I gave him a look that must have shown my disgust for the look on his face became mean and he spoke harshly.

"I suggest you do as I ask. I would hate to teach you to mind me." He lifted his beefy, square hands up in front of his chest and flexed them a few times in a threatening way.

His words and the look on his face sent a shudder through me. Somehow, I knew that he wanted to hit me with those big hands he flexed. I knew not to give him any excuse to ever hit me. I had always told myself if a man ever beat on me I would kill him, and I still felt that way. It might be best just to do as he demanded.

I took each article of clothing off dropping them in a pile on the floor. I hated every moment and every look Rafe gave me. I hated Rafe. I might have shot him if I had the shotgun in my hand. Wished I had it.

A ´smug look came to Rafe's face, and he grinned wickedly at me.

"Is that black fire in your eyes coming from passion? Surely you're not mad at taking your clothes off for your husband. Come here. Take your husband's boots off."

I shivered in the cold as I undid the damp laces of his wet, muddy boots and set them down unable to avoid the pretty rug. He had gotten the bedspread dirty with the boots and didn't care in the least.

"Now, my britches."

The repulsion must have shown in my face for Rafe laughed, but his laughter didn't hold humor. It sounded harsh, even cruel. He came up off the bed, knocking his feet painfully against my bare stomach as he did so, and stood spraddle-legged in front of me. He dropped his pants showing long johns that were dirty and yellow stained in the front. His green eyes were glaring at my face as he dropped them to the floor. I quickly looked away. I had never seen anything so repulsive in my life as Rafe standing there with his private parts thrust toward me. I had only glimpsed him a time or two before or after he was ramming it in me. This time it looked different as it hung out of a clump of bushy black hair, limp and wrinkled as it rested over a dangling sack like a bull had. I wanted to run out of the room and hide from the repugnant sight.

Rafe moved toward me, his jaws set, his eyes hard. He said; "It's time you learned how to get a tired hoss back on its feet."

Chapter 15

The things Rafe made me do were the most disgusting things I had ever done in my life. It made me feel dirty and sick at my stomach. During the entire time I was wishing Rafe would drop dead on the spot, if not Rafe then me. How could any man make a woman do what he made me do? I had never in my life heard of or imagined such things. When he finally rammed it in me, it was with a savageness intended to hurt.

Rafe went right to sleep, and I guessed he would probably sleep like a baby right through the entire night. I would sleep on the pallet in the kitchen. I didn't want him near me. I found his heavy, sweat smelling body repulsive as I looked down on him. The slobbering kisses he forced on me tasted of alcohol, and I realized why he was different than ever before. He had been drinking. I wondered what must have been wrong with me the day I thought he was good looking, for there was nothing good looking about him right now. I turned from his disgusting sight and went outside and put the horses up before I did the work.

I came back into the house feeling tired and dejected. All I wanted to do was curl up in the quilts and cry like a little baby until I was numb. Thinking of Rafford lying upstairs sound asleep after what he did to me was almost more than I could bear. Once, I had wanted to love him. Now, I would have to study on it for a longer period of time. Maybe love was like a boil. Maybe it would hurt you until the pus built up enough to rupture and give relief.

I lay down on the pallet, gripped the pillows and quilt against my throbbing body, and tried to wipe out all thoughts of Rafe. I wanted to make the memory of Jonas fill my mind and sooth me enough to sleep, but nothing soothed me.

I finally fell asleep for what seemed like minutes when I woke up to find morning had already arrived. I dragged my tired body off the floor without feeling any better than I did last night. I stoked the cook stove full of wood and got the kitchen warm. I wondered when Rafe would wake up and what he would be wanting when he did. I put on a pot of coffee to perk and figured I could start cooking his breakfast once I heard him stirring around upstairs.

I went to the kitchen window and looked out at the backyard and woods. It was a fairyland of glistening ice. Sleet had fallen all during the night and I hadn't even known it. There had to be at least an inch covering everything. Trees were bent double with their limbs reaching the ground, and I could tell it was still sleeting a little. Before long the trees wouldn't be able to bear up under the weight, and they would snap. More deadfall I thought. I would be able to drag in more firewood. The thought made me tired, and I felt like crying.

It was almost noon when Rafe finally came clomping down the stairs. I quickly put biscuits in the oven to bake and stirred flour into the sausage drippings to make gravy. I sliced up some potatoes into a pan of hot lard to fry and went into the springhouse for preserves and butter.

Rafe came into the kitchen looking worse than he did last night. I wondered how a red-faced man could have a gray pallor? Hangover, I thought. I had heard men were mean when they had a hangover, and Rafe proved that true.

"What kind of damned mess are you trying to cook up?"

"Breakfast," I said as sweetly as I could manage. "Are you hungry?"

"Not for that stuff. A man could starve to death with a wife like you," he grumbled as he went into the springhouse and clomped around on the floor. I suspected he was looking for the liquor I had found in there and used on the little girl to wash the turpentine and lice away. I had set the jug down in the cellar and was glad that I did. Rafe came back into the kitchen with an aggravated swagger to his walk.

"I thought I saw a jug of liquor in there. What did you do with it?" he demanded.

"There was a little dirty looking stuff in the very bottom of a jug." I found myself trying to think of a way to justify not having any liquor for him to drink. "I washed the girl's hair with it in hopes it would kill the lice," I added softly. "It didn't look like anything I would want to drink."

He grabbed me by the arm and jerked me around to face him.

"You wasted good liquor? Damn you!"

I jerked my arm free of his grasp and looked him in the eyes. The whites of his eyes were bloodshot and the surrounding skin puffy.

"What little was in the jug wouldn't have been fit to pour out to a hog. There was nearly a handful of dead bugs in it," I improvised.

"Couldn't have been as bad as that rot-gut I drunk off the mountain. It's a wonder I'm not a dead man," he growled and seemed to forget about me. "Bad liquor's killed many a good man."

He lifted his hands and pressed his palms to the sides of his head.

"Hell! I might as well go hunting. Fresh air might ease this splittin head."

"It sleeted last night. I could hardly make it to the barn and back. It's not fittin weather out there for huntin."

"Did I ask your opinion on a damned thing?" he asked as he angrily reached for the gun I had leaning in the corner.

I turned my back to him. I had no intention of getting cussed at for giving him good warning. I heard him open the kitchen door and go outside and cross the porch to the steps. I had learned just how slick those steps were when I went to milk. My feet had flown out from under me, and I had a bruise to prove it.

I glanced out the window in time to see Rafe fall and heard the shotgun go off. I went to the window expecting to see Rafe get up. He didn't. I hurried out on the porch and found him lying on the icy ground. I saw blood running from his foot and coloring the ice red. His head was bent sideways against the steps. A tiny trickle of blood ran from under his head. I realized he had hit his head on the steps when he had fallen and knocked himself out.

I carefully eased off the steps and lifted his head trying to determine how bad he was hurt. There was a guinea-egg size knot just above his ear along with about a half-inch gash. The gash was bleeding freely but not enough to concern me. The fact he was out cold did concern me. I slapped his cheeks and called his name repeatedly. Finally, I laid his head down and scooted myself across the ice to check on his foot. The shotgun blast had blown the toe of his boot off and his boot was overflowing with blood. I needed to get him into the warm kitchen, get his boot off and try to stop the bleeding.

I crawled up the icy steps, rushed into the kitchen and ripped a kitchen towel in two, then grabbed a thin stick of stove wood. I went back to Rafe and tied the towel on his leg above his boot and inserted the stick in the towel. I twisted it, slowing the flow of blood. I tried to lift him, but his dead weight was too heavy. When I propped him against a step in order to get a better hold, he slid over again.

I got some rope from the barn and tied a loop around Rafe's chest under his armpits. I wrapped one turn of the rope around the porch post and held the loose end in my hand. I pushed Rafe into a sitting position then tightened the rope. Inch by inch I scooted Rafe until I got him up the steps one body part at a time.

His skin felt icy cold, while sweat poured off my coat less body. Once I got him onto the porch I clamped a calf of his leg under each arm and dragged him into the kitchen. I slumped on the floor beside him and heaved air in and out of my lungs. Finally, I managed to move to his foot and untied the laces of his boot, and then take it off as gentle as I could. I removed his sock and looked at the mangled flesh. One of his toes had been blown off and his big toe was halfway severed. There were several small holes leaking blood where the shot had gone into the top of his foot.

I loosened the towel with the stick. Blood gushed from his toes every time his heart beat. I tightened the towel and tried to think what I should do. He needed a doctor, but if I went to find help, Rafe could bleed to death before I got back. If I left the towel cutting off his blood supply, his foot could die from lack of blood flow. I slapped Rafe in the face a few more time in an effort to bring him around. He was still knocked out cold. I gave him one more good hard slap for not payin attention when I warned him. Now look what he had gone and done to himself.

I grabbed a glass and rushed into the springhouse and pulled out the shelves that opened the door into the can house. I went down the steps and poured the glass full of the liquor I had denied Rafe earlier. I would disinfect his foot with the alcohol before I sewed up his toes to slow the bleeding long enough for me to get help.

I got a needle and thread and started to repair his foot in the same way I would a torn piece of cloth. I wasn't sure just how everything should be connected, but I figured whatever I did would be better than him bleeding to death. I hoped Rafe wouldn't come around before I was finished. I pulled together the skin where his toe had been shot off and sewed the sides together, then started on his big toe by sewing the top layers of his skin together. I thought he should have some stitches connecting the inside meat but I feared the thread would get infected if I tried that. I just took big, deep stitches from the outside and figured Jonas could do what needed to be done once he got here.

It seemed like hours that I worked sewing his wounds for skin was harder to sew through than cloth. When I had finished, I poured liquor on his foot, then bandaged it the best I could. I loosened the towel on his leg and was relieved to see the flow of blood had slowed to a trickle. I lifted his head into my lap and checked on the knot and gash. It was still bleeding some but not enough to deplete his blood supply. I lay his head back down on the floor. He rolled his head from side to side and groaned.

"Rafe?" I said loud. "Rafe, can you hear me?"

He groaned, and I saw his eyes twitch. I slapped his cheeks hard and called his name again.

"Hell," he mumbled. "Quit hittin me." His eyes opened slowly, blinked, then opened again.

"What happened?" he managed to get out in a shaky, breathless voice.

"You fell and shot your foot," I told him.

He frowned. "My head." He tried to lift his head but failed.

"You hit it on the steps when you fell."

"Shot my foot?" he questioned after a few moments of silence.

"You slid off the steps on the ice. The shotgun went off. If you won't try to move, I'll go after help," I told him gently.

"Hell no, you won't! I'm not hurt!"

"Rafe," I said as reassuringly as I could manage. "You are hurt. You've lost one or maybe two toes and you still have lead shot in your foot. The doctor'll have to get the shot out. I'm afraid to try that. I would do more harm than good."

"I won't have that son-of-bitch touching me."

"Somebody will have to do it, Rafe. Otherwise, the shot could set up blood poisoning."

"You're not leaving here and going for that doctor. Do you hear me?"

I wet a towel in warm water and washed Rafe's face then smoothed his hair back with trembling fingers. Rafe managed to sit up in the floor and look at his foot. It was covered with so many bloody bandages he couldn't see the stitches I had put in his flesh. I didn't say a word about them. I didn't know if I had done the right thing, nor how Rafe would take it.

"It's startin to hurt like hell," he said as he looked around him. "The floor is covered in blood. My blood. "

Indeed it was. I hadn't mopped up the blood yet. I got a towel and the wash pan of water and began to soak up the blood.

"I ought to be in bed," Rafe sounded weak and looked pale.

His face was no longer as beet red as it had been last night. This morning's pallor was nothing to what it was now. It was ashen white and contorted with pain. I didn't see any way I could get him up the stairs with his injured foot. Besides I didn't want blood from one end of the house to the other.

"Rafe, I think it might be best for me to fix you a pallet by the stove. I want to keep you warm, and I'm afraid you'll hurt your foot more if you try to walk on it."

Rafe didn't seem to have any argument left in him about a bed, but he bellowed like an angry bull at everything else. He shoved me flat on the floor when I tried to put a pillow under his head, and he kicked the quilt away when I tried to cover him up.

"I want water," he yelled at the top of his lungs.

I carried him a glass and lifted his head as carefully as I could, only to have him knock the glass out of my hands and cuss me because I touched the knot on his head. He yelled for more water until I brought him another glass and spooned it into his mouth without trying to lift him up to drink. After several minutes he knocked the spoon from my hands, lifted his head, grabbed the glass from my hand and drank it by himself.

For the rest of the day Rafe yelled and cussed and hit everything within his reach. He would yell for me to bring him something then strike out at me whenever I got within range. He swore if he could get hold of the shotgun he would shoot me. He said I would take better care of him if I knew what he was suffering. I had no doubts about how badly Rafe was suffering. I just didn't know how to ease him, and he continued to refuse my offer of going for the doctor. I left the shotgun outside in the yard. I would slip it in the house and hide it later when Rafe wouldn't see me. I thought he might shoot me if he got the chance.

By evening, Rafe was running a fever and out of his head. He cussed at Boise as though he was seeing her standing over him.

"You're nothing but a no good piece of Yankee ass," he hissed through his teeth as his eyes gleamed at a spot above him. He turned his head slightly, and his eyes moved as though he was following her movement. "You're a whore.

You'll always be one." A grinning sneer came to his face. "Yes! I'm glad you're dead and rotting in hell. It's where you belong."

His eyes moved until they came to rest on me.

"See her, Boise?" he yelled. "I'll have her sweet virgin ass to replace your diseased cunt with. You can die for all I care. I hope you do. I damned hope you do."

He closed his eyes and seemed to drift into a troubled sleep although he was still mumbling vile words of anger. I tried to ignore the way he talked. He was sick and out of his head with pain and fever, but his talk still made me uneasy.

When I returned from doing the work, he would take spells of being totally silent then raging with anger. I could no longer get him to drink water although I tried several times.

I fixed myself a pallet of the quilts Jonas and I had lain on in the far corner of the room where I could watch over Rafe and maybe get a little sleep.

Once during the night he became so quiet I got up and went to him thinking he had died. I reached out and touched his cheek expecting to find his flesh cold. In a flash he grabbed at my hand but missed. He jumped to his feet as though nothing was wrong with him. "Don't you try coming back alive on me you damned ugly cow," he said viscously. "I'll cut your damned throat."

He chased me around the kitchen until he collapsed on the floor. I hurriedly hid all the kitchen knifes and stayed awake the rest of the night. I dared not go to sleep in case he got to his feet, but I needn't have worried. He didn't get up again. Morning came, and all Rafe could do was moan with his suffering and yell things from his fevered mind.

As soon as it was light enough for me to see, I dressed warmly and headed out over the sleet slick ground. I didn't even do up the work before I left for I had decided Rafe needed a doctor fast. He was burning hot and his clothes were wet with sweat. His teeth were clamped tight, and I couldn't force water in his mouth with a spoon.

It didn't take me long to reach what I thought was the Patrick place. I could see the sagging of the house and the orange rusted roof in the pale morning light. A dog ran out from under the porch barking at me. A man came out the door wearing bibbed overalls and looked at me in amazement. I must have looked at him as hard for I though he was the ugliest man I had ever seen in my life. He was as slender as a ridgepole and so tall he appeared to have an S shape to him. He had sandy colored hair that wasn't brown or red, but a muddy blonde. His eyes were tiny and set close to a nose that was long and hooked.

"Ma'am?" he questioned as though his eyes might be fooling him and he wasn't really seeing me at all.

"I need Dr. Jones," I told him. "Rafe fell yesterday on the ice and shot himself in the foot."

Relief flooded the man's face. "You're Rafford Johnson's wife," he said firmly. "Come on inside and warm up. You look blue in the face."

I followed him inside the house and was grateful for the warmth of the potbellied stove. A young woman pulled a baby from her breast where it was feeding and held it over her shoulder and patted its back as she looked at me.

"Mornin," she greeted me. "Pour her a cup of hot coffee, Nate," she told her husband then turned to me. "Set yourself down in that chair. Did I hear you say Rafford shot his foot?" Concern was strong in her voice.

I nodded at the plain, brown-haired woman and tried to get my breath under control enough to talk normally. I was winded from hurrying on the icy ground.

"I wanted to go for the doctor yesterday, but he wouldn't let me. He's running a fever this mornin and hasn't enough mind or strength to stop me. I just need for somebody to tell me how to go from here. I know there's a road, but I thought I might take a short cut through the woods. He's in a bad way."

The man handed me a cup of coffee then pulled his coat, gloves and cap off a nail on the wall and put them on.

"I'll go after the Doc," he said calmly.

"Oh no, I couldn't let you do that," I wondered if he had animals to take care of for I saw a small barn out behind the house next to the woods. I didn't want to take him away from his work because of me.

He hesitated for a moment and seemed to be in deep thought. "You warm up good then head back in case he needs you. There's no way you could find the road much less a short cut in this weather. You would get lost and freeze to death. There's more ridges and hollers runnin from this mountain than hogs have bristles." He exchanged a glance with his wife then went out the door.

"How bad's he shot?" Junie asked as soon as Nate closed the door.

"He's missin a toe. Mangled his foot some."

I saw the corners of her mouth twitch. "Shouldn't be a killin wound. Man can live without a few toes, won't hold him down long."

"No. It shouldn't be a mortal wound, but he's out of his head."

"You oughta gave him good liquor to drink until he passed out, then soaked his foot in it." She gave me a look that said I didn't know what I had been doing.

"I did."

"Must not have done it right for it didn't help him none. Oughta gone after the Doc when it was first done."

"I know, but Rafe objected. I guess I better get back."

"There hain't a thing you can do for him until the Doc gets here," she told me. "Hit's a long climb up that hill in this slick time. You rest and warm up some. Nate'll have the Doc back in no time."

"I know you're right, but I have to go back anyhow. I've not done up the work yet. I left as soon as it was daylight enough to make my way here."

"There's no need to hurry off, yet. There's nothing you can do for Rafford, now." She gave me a strange look out of her narrow eyes. "Want to hold my baby a while?" she offered as though she was granting me a great honor as she held the baby out for me to look at.

I declined as nicely as I could. "I've got Rafe's blood on me. I wouldn't want it to get on a baby. It's a pretty baby."

"I reckon you'll be havin some of your own soon. How long since you and Rafe were married? September weren't it?"

I stopped myself from being impatient with her. I knew it had probably been a long time since she had talked to another woman. We lived a mile apart and worlds apart from anybody else.

"Yes. It's been since September," I told her.

An odd look came to her face as she looked at my stomach then shook her head. "It took me a long time to get in the family way. I had near given up hope." She tried to grin and failed as she looked beyond me at the closed door as though her mind had wandered. "Givin birth to Rafford Johnson's baby would be a triumph. If a woman had Rafford's baby, she'd have everything. Absolutely everything, almost."

Her voice was soft and soothing as she spoke yet there was a note of longing, and I suspected she was thinking of the fancy house on the hill. I could almost hear her saying you have a big house, but I have a baby. A baby is worth more than all the houses in the world.

"Hain't my little girl perty? Just like a picture book doll. I know she's gonna have green eyes and look just like her daddy.

I thought that an odd thing to say. I wouldn't want one of my younguns to look like Nate Patrick. "Yes," I said as I stole glances about the little house that was not as good as the one I had been raised in. It looked shabby and dirty and the furniture was homemade from planks that were still rough with saw marks. I had an urge to offer to help her clean things up a bit, but knew this would insult her. I took a deep breath and thought Rafe's fancy house was spoiling me some. I didn't want to live in a house like Junie's.

"Where did you come from?" she asked pointedly as though she wanted to determine the life I had before I married Rafe.

I told her and she nodded in a way that said she already knew all about me.

"Oh yeah, I've been to church there a time or two before I married Nate Patrick. Doctor Jones is from there, too. Must have a lot of well-to-do folks livin there."

I looked her in the eyes and thought of Pete Jones and Abraham Miller. After living in this house, they would seem well-to-do. "You traveled all that way to go to church?"

"Oh, hits not really that far. If a body had one of them fancy automobiles, it would take no time a'tall."

Something didn't sound right to me as her words caused a strange feeling to grip my chest. "Were you raised in Kentucky?" I asked.

"Oh goodness no. Can't figure where you'd get an idea like that in your head. I was raised right here in North Carolina on this very mountain. My home place is only a few miles from here toward the Tennessee side."

For a few moments I wondered if she might be mistaken and confused about the location. I wanted to ask her the name of the mountain we were living on, but decided against it. If Rafe had lied to me about being in Kentucky, I didn't want her to know it. Moreover, I didn't want her to realize I didn't know where I lived. It would make me seem foolish.

I stood up then felt like sitting back down in the chair for my legs were as weak as elastic. I wasn't sure my legs would carry me out the door much less get me back up the mountain.

"It's been good talkin to you, but I had better start back in case Rafe needs me. Do you have any idea how long it will be before the doctor gets here?"

"It oughtn't to be too long. Before nightfall, I should think. It's mighty slick. Slow em down a right smart."

"Thank you," I said and slipped out the door into the cold. Nightfall would be eight hours away.

All the way back up the mountain my mind kept saying 'right here in North Carolina on this very mountain' over and over again.

If I wasn't in Kentucky, why would Rafe say I was? Did he want me to think I was far away from Dad's place? Did he think I would get mad at him and run back home? There was little chance of that happening after Dad giving me to Rafe like he did.

Going down the mountain on slick ground had been nothing compared to climbing back up the mountain on it. I had been able to sit down and scoot downhill a time or two, but getting uphill meant I had to find something to get a hand hold on and pull myself up the hill. When I came to a spot where there was no sleet on the ground I felt like a great gift had been given to me.

I was wet with sweat by the time I saw the roof of home through the gray limbs of the bare trees. I clutched a small sapling and stood there and stared at the roof. Home, I though, what a beautiful word.

Rafe was lying against the door that opened into the springhouse, still and unmoving. Sometime while I was gone he had been moving a lot for the chairs were knocked over and the table scooted at an angle. The pallet I had left him lying on was scattered all over the floor with one quilt touching the leg of the stove. I grabbed it quickly away thinking if it had been higher up on the stove it could have caught fire and burned down my home. I would make sure I wasn't careless again and leave bedclothes or anything around that might cause a fire.

I went to him and put my hand on his forehead. He was burning hot to my touch and his clothes were wet with sweat. I went upstairs to find him a dry change of clothes and came back and started to undress him. The smell of sweat and unwashed body odor was powerful. I had to wash him the best I could before Jonas Jones got here. I didn't want Jonas to think Rafe wasn't a man that bathed, or that I would allow my husband to be dirty. I stoked the stove with wood then dipped up hot water in the wash pan and laid a cake of lye soap on the floor beside the pan.

Rafe looked helpless with his eyes closed and his mouth open. His lips were beginning to crack and flake with fever. His face was flame red and his breath sounded strained. I put the damp wash rag over his lips and left it there while I got the butter from the springhouse. Maybe the grease from the butter would ease the cracking of his lips. I washed his face with gentle strokes and brushed his hair from his face with my fingers. I considered washing his sweaty hair but decided against it. I didn't want to give him pneumonia by having wet hair. I removed his shirt and stared at his hairy chest. He was broad across the shoulders and thick in the chest until he looked slightly overweight, but I found no fat on Rafe. The bulk of him was solid muscle. I took my hand from the wash rag and let it lay on his chest above his heart. I could feel the beat steady and strong as I looked down on him--this man that was my husband. I wanted to love him, I truly did. I took my hand away and began the struggle of getting him washed and dressed.

It was after two o'clock in the afternoon when I heard the sound of a horse and rider. I looked out the window and saw it was Jonas Jones on his high stepping sorrel with Nate Patrick riding beside him on a big-footed workhorse. They both dismounted and left their horses ground tied as they walked slowly to the porch where I met them. Nate was looking around the place in a slow assessing way while Jonas looked me in the eyes as each step brought him closer to me.

"Thank you for coming so quickly," I said to Jonas. "I didn't think you'd make it this fast with the ice."

"There's no ice beyond the Patrick place, Mrs. Johnson," Jonas said gently. "Where is your husband?"

"In the kitchen." I turned and went inside with them following behind me. Jonas's voice was cool and polite as he kneeled down and began unwrapping Rafe's foot of the bandages I had put on yesterday.

"Tell me what happened, Mrs. Johnson."

I told how Rafe had slipped on the icy steps and fallen with the loaded gun. Rafe moaned as Jonas pulled the cloth loose that had stuck to his foot.

"It doesn't look good." Jonas first looked at me and then at Nate. "You may have to hold him down, Nate, so I can see the extent of damage that's been done. Mrs. Johnson, get me a pan of hot, clean water if you don't mind. I need to wash away as much of the dried blood as I can."

Rafe moaned but made no attempt to move as Jonas cleaned and examined his foot. He took a thin pair of scissors and sniped the stitches away from his toes, and then shook his head in a bewildered manner.

"You did this?" He indicated the stitches.

I nodded my head. I felt guilty at not knowing how to do a better job. I began to explain as fast as I could.

"He hit his head on the steps when he fell and knocked himself out. His foot was gushing blood so badly I was afraid he would bleed to death. I thought if I sewed his toes to his foot, the bleeding would slow down long enough for me to get help. He came to before I could leave, and he refused to let me go after help. He said he didn't want a doctor. He was out of his head during the night, and this morning he didn't know anything. I knew I had to get help regardless of what he wanted."

Jonas shook his head. "He should have let you get help yesterday when this first happened. His foot looks like sausage and the lead shot has to be taken out. By the looks of it, I'd say the shot buried bits of his dirty boot and sock into the flesh and has set up infection, blood poisoning and possible gangrene

"You can fix him, can't you?" I heard my voice high pitched with worry.

"Was he drunk?" Nate spoke for the first time.

"He said he had drunk some down the mountain before he came home. He said it was bad rot gut." I spoke carefully and looked at Jonas. I didn't know if I should be telling them much of anything other than the accident. "He hadn't drunk anything during the night, and he fell the morning after he arrived home. Does it matter? "

"Nate was just thinking a drunk man will fall easier than a sober man," Jonas told me.

"He didn't fall from being drunk. The steps were covered in ice from all the sleet we had. I fell on the steps earlier that mornin when I went out to milk. I told Rafe to be careful for they were slick, but he paid me no mind."

"Rafford Johnson never paid any man no mind." Nate spoke matter of fact. "No harder headed man ever drawed breath. Has to have his own way about things."

"Nate. Go hitch Rafford's horses to the wagon. I need to get him to the hospital while there is still daylight if I can. The hospital is the only place I know might be able to save his foot."

Nate went out the door without a word. Once he was off the porch and out of hearing, Jonas said to me.

"Mrs. Johnson, were you hurt in any way?"

He looked down at Rafe then back at me as though he was telling me Rafe might be able to understand what we were saying to each other although he seemed to be out cold.

"I wasn't hurt at all." Surely he could tell that by just looking at me. It was Rafe that had me concerned. "Rafe won't want to go to any hospital." I knew that for a fact.

"He hasn't a choice. He could lose his foot or worse if we wait any longer getting him there. You wouldn't want that would you?"

"No. A man needs two good legs and feet. He can manage without a few toes," I said hopefully as I looked at Jonas. I wished he could comfort me with a warm hand or even a warm look, but he gave me neither. He treated me like a total stranger. "I ought to go with him."

"No," Jonas said quickly. "I don't think that's a good idea, Mrs. Johnson. I'll take him to the hospital where expert doctors will make the decision on what to do with him. Neither you nor I will make that decision. Understand?"

I nodded my head, and I thought I understood him. He didn't want Rafe to blame him or me if the doctors took off his foot.

"How will I know what happens if I don't go with him?"

"I'll send word. Get quilts together to wrap him up for the trip. A chill won't do him any good."

I remembered the little girl and wrapping her up for Jonas to take away.

"The little girl?" I asked but Jonas shook his head at me.

"Later," he told me firmly as Nate's feet stomped on the porch.

I wrapped Rafe up as carefully as I could in the wagon and looked down on him with concern. I reached out and touched his beard-roughened jaw with my hand. Rafe really was a good-looking man when he was smiling. It would hurt him bad if he was crippled for the rest of his life. I hoped that didn't happen as I turned away from Rafe and saw Nate watching me with what seemed to be a pleased look on his face.

"Thank you for your help," I said and tried to smile, but a feeling of sadness kept the smile from appearing.

"That's what neighbors are for," he told me. "Anything I can do for you while Rafford's away let me know. Remember Junie and I just live a jump down the road."

"Thanks, but I can manage fine."

I saw a look pass over Nate Patrick's face that I thought might be relief at me not asking him for help. There might have even been a glimmer of respect for me reflected in his eyes.

"You're a mighty little woman to be doin what you do all by yourself," Nate said as he rubbed his hand over the beardy stubble on his chin and seemed to think hard for a minute. "You do know how to use that gun Rafford shot his self with?"

"Rafe taught me how to use it," I told him hesitantly. Surely he didn't think I was the one that shot Rafe's foot.

"Lock your doors and keep it nearby," Nate advised me in a voice lowered enough for Jonas not to hear. "Rafford's crazy to leave you alone like he does."

Nate turned from me and rushed off to mount his horse like he was embarrassed he had spoken.

"Good day, Mrs. Johnson. I assure you your husband will get the finest of care," Jonas said and slapped the reins on the horse's rumps.

I stood on the porch and watched Jonas drive away with his horse tied to the wagon. Nate rode behind the wagon on his way back to Junie, and I was left alone. I went inside the house and sat down at the table. I realized I hadn't eaten anything all day and got back up and put more wood in the stove. I reached in the cabinet for the flour to make bread and saw the edge of Boise's diary. I picked it up and laid it on the table so I could read while my food cooked. I sat down and opened the book where I had left off and read eagerly hoping Boise's diary would take my mind away from Rafe and Jonas. Her writing was precise and neat as a pin with each word clear and well spaced. Boise didn't make mistakes in her writing, like I did, so I read easily and fast.

Days passed without thoughts of Henry ever leaving my mind. Every man I see makes me think of Henry and my losing him. The ache within me is raw and fresh in this new land, and I find myself both wishing the memory of Henry would leave me, and that I could hold onto his memory forever. I can see the blue of his eyes and the blonde of his hair. I hear his voice and see the laughter on his lips. I wish I could kiss those lips one more time and know the feel of my hands touching him. I wish I could speak to him once more. I wish I had told him that day before he left town that I was carrying his child. He might have stayed with me. He might not have been in the accident that killed him if I had only told him about our baby. I shudder as I remember Father coming to me with downcast eyes and tragic face. He told me Henry was dead. I fainted dead away. When I opened my eyes again I didn't know which was worse, the pain in my mind or the pain I was feeling in my lower stomach and back. I remember clutching Father's hands and screaming for Henry with all my mind and strength. My screams brought the doctor along with my closest neighbor. The neighbor learned of Henry's death and my aborted baby at the same time. The entire neighborhood knew within the next hour.

I never received forgiveness or sympathy from a person other than Father. The women thought I got what I deserved for pretending I was a godly woman while doing sinful things. It did not matter that Henry and I were to be married the next week after he returned with his parents. Henry died without knowing he was to become a father. Our baby died without knowing how much its mother still wants it. My arms ache from emptiness even though they never held our baby, but my heart did.

My entire existence aches from the emptiness of not having Henry. I thank God he let me know what it was like to hold Henry in my arms and against my body. I'd rather suffer all that I have suffered and known Henry's love than not to have suffered and not have loved him.

Thinking in this manner has started to put a balm over my life. I consider myself blessed by having known Henry's love. I shall live with this the best I can and let life drift by me in a way similar to each snowflake falling to the ground. I can see the beauty of a snowflake. I just cannot make it mine.

I have heard that time heals all wounds, but I do not believe that to be true. A wound such as mine never heals. The passing of time just makes you grow accustomed to the pain until you are able to ignore it.

Summer has finally come and Father and I have a fancy house to live in. There is water running in the house. Father talks of electricity, both AC and DC. He is wishing there was water further up the hill above the house so he could use the flow as power. Father has the most dreams and ideas I have ever heard. I think he would change the world if he were turned loose. Me. I just want to live a quiet life and dream of what it would be like to hold my child in my arms. I know I could love another child, but I don't think I will ever be able to love another man.

A year has passed since I have written in my diary. I laid it in a drawer and let life drift by me, but it is now time for me to make this entry as it is beyond me to understand. I cannot believe Father has taken up farming. I think he has bought out the town of The Fields of Toe, which was renamed Newland, of all their livestock. We are overrun with cattle, horses, hogs and fowl. They are reproducing with a speed I did not know was possible. Father spends his days plowing and planting and harvesting. He treats animal manure like it was pure gold as he places it on his crops. He brags how he has more corn per acre, and thicker hay to cut, than any man in miles about. He's certain he can show the mountain people a path to a better life by showing them how to grow more food on rocky mountain soil. If only he can convince the mountain men that corn is for cornbread and feeding livestock and not for drinking! Liquor to a mountain man is like manna from heaven. Unfortunately manna from heaven is not showered down for a drunk's family to eat. It always seems to me a man that drinks too much has a family that eats too little.

Again, I have let my diary rest idle for a very long time while I too have rested in this isolated mountain peace. I look in the mirror and see an aging woman where a girl once was. Thirty is an age I shall never see again and I won't write how long it has been since I saw it. My bloom of youth has long gone and a homely woman has emerged. There is no hope of a greasy haired boy coming to my door with a bag of candy.

After years of reproduction, father has decided he must sell some of his livestock. The pastures and barns are overflowing. Not one more chicken can perch on the roost! The cattle have over filled the barn stalls and the barn hall as well. Hogs are as thick as rabbits as little piglets escape through the rails of the fences and run amuck over the farm and in my garden. Soon he will have to move some animals in the house with us if he does not let some go. Father promises he will get the word out he means to sell!

Much to my surprise a young man showed up today driving a team of matched horses and a brand new wagon. Father noticed that I looked at the young man long and hard. Even with Father's gaze upon me, I could not stop staring at the young man. There was something in him that made me think of Henry. It was something about the way he looked at me. His eyes were green where Henry's were blue, but there was that look he gave me just like Henry used to do. He looked me from head to foot then back again, and his eyes began to gleam as though he was seeing something that pleased him very much. I turned my back on him and went into the house.

Father came into the house hours later and said he sold the young man two hogs, a few chickens and a steer. The young man had loaded the hogs and chicken on his wagon in crates, tied the balking steer to the back of the wagon and drove off.

One week later to the day he showed up again. He bought several pigs from Father then claimed he needed a glass of water before he left on his way. With a grin on Father's face, Father brought him to the house by the front door and called for me. He left me alone with the young man to hand him a glass of water. The young man told me his name was Rafford Johnson. He said he was from

Kentucky and he was becoming a great traffic and trader. He said in the past few years he had become more successful than he had ever imagined becoming. He said he hoped to find a wife and settle down soon. I thought two glasses of water were enough for him before I showed him the door. Father whistled a gay tune for the next two days.

Just like clock work, Rafford Johnson showed up the next week for more pigs and a milk cow. He told Father he wanted milk and eggs if Father could think of a way to pack them until they would not spoil or break. It took Father several hours to accomplish this feat while Rafford Johnson drank water and talked to me.

After several months of weekly trips, Rafford Johnson was only allowed to purchase milk, butter and eggs. He had bought Father down to a thin amount of livestock. Father and I both knew Rafford could not afford a trip up the mountain for milk, butter and eggs. Father surprised me when he suggested Rafford find new blood for him. Rafford was now to purchase livestock for Father and deliver them up the mountain to him.

I cornered Father and told him I knew what he was doing. He was trying to keep Rafford around me. Father laughed and said, "Boise my girl. That young man is taken with you. He can't keep his eyes off you when you are around or searching for you when you are not in sight." My heart fluttered in my chest. I suspected what Father had said but I never believed it. Rafford Johnson was interested in me.

Father had purchased a fair amount of animals before the day Rafford delivered a mighty fine bull to be added to Father's stock. "That bull has given me hell for three days," Rafford confessed right before he sat down his glass of water on the kitchen table then proceeded to lock me in a bear hug and kissed me like a man that was starving to death for my kiss. "I best let you know it's you I want before your father kills me trying to bring him a draft horse stallion or something worse. You might as well agree to marry me now while I've still got the strength to do a nights worth of work on our wedding night."

Thank you God for the glory and lightening between a man and a woman. Rafford Johnson and I were married yesterday. Henry's memory is just that, a memory. Rafford is real.

Boise's diary fell from my hands, hit the table then tumbled to the floor. Boise was Rafford's wife. The place I lived in was the fancy house her father had built. Her husband was now my husband. I jumped up from the table and took the bread out of the oven. I felt numb from head to toe. I looked at the bread and didn't know what to do with it. I sat it on the back of the stove and walked outside on the porch and just stared out over the yard. All the things Rafford told me came rushing to my mind. Why had he lied to me? Why had he told me he had bought this place from an old man and woman? He could have admitted he had been married to that woman. There was no sin in that. I would have understood. Realization seemed to hit me like a club as I remembered the garden that had been planted and not completely cared for until harvest time. Rafe's first wife had been alive right before he married me.

I rushed back into the house and grabbed the diary off the floor and sank down in the chair to read further in hopes Boise's written words would tell me what I knew I wouldn't want to know.

I must write that I had an unrealistic idea of what married life would be like. I thought there would be laughter and happiness, sweet words and loving caresses. There are none of those from Rafford Johnson. He treats me like I am a workhorse. He has harsh words for me when we are alone, but never in front of Father. He seems to want Father to think he is devoted to me and I am too embarrassed to admit to Father that he is not. Rafford made love to me on our wedding night then the next night. From that time on he looks at me as though the very thought disgusts him. When I tried to instigate lovemaking he told me I was acting like an old, fat whore. The next day I stood naked in front of the mirror and saw a woman that looked like my mother, but I wasn't exactly fat and I certainly wasn't a whore, but I was hurt and angry at Rafford's words.

One week after our wedding Rafford left and did not return for one month. When he returned, I asked where he had been so long. He told me he was away on business and had no intention of having a wife that cross-examined every move he made. I tried to act normal in front of Father but I sense concern in Father although Father continually tells me that a businessman has to travel and be away from home.

Harsh words rose between Father and Rafford today when Rafford returned from selling some of Father's hogs without Father's permission. Father let Rafford know that the farm and all the animals belonged to Father and would remain that way until the day he died. Father told Rafford he was my husband but nothing more.
The clash between Rafford and Father did some good. Rafford has been nicer to me and has stayed home for two

weeks. He treats Father as though the clash never happened and seems to want to please him.

Rafford left this morning with his team and wagon. He whistled a happy tune before he left. He never said where he was going or why he was so happy. Father watched him leave with a frown on his face. Father said he would have preferred Rafford had not left for he was feeling unsettled in his stomach.

Father was sick for the four days Rafford was gone. He started getting better the day Rafford returned, but Rafford gladly did the work for him without complaint for several days while father recovered from his ailment.

Rafford left again, and again Father is sick. Harvest time is upon us, and I fear Father is overdoing his strength. I do wish Rafford would be home long enough to help. I do all I can to assist Father, but I fear I must be catching what Father has suffered from. There are times when my stomach is upset also. Father finally managed to hire Nate Patrick to come and help with the harvest in return for the rent of the little house he and his wife live in. The house isn't much and the rent even less, but I am thankful they are there to help Father on occasion. For the first time ever, I am noticing how old and feeble Father is. There is no flesh left on his bones and his color is not right. His breathing is labored and I hear him coughing at night when he should be sleeping.

The day after Father and Nate finished storing the hay and corn in the barn Rafford returned home. I saw him put his wagon up and turn his horses loose then go through the barn and observe all the animals Father had in the pasture. He appeared to be counting them for whatever reason.

Father had the strangest man deliver coal today. His skin was the color of coal dust, and I wondered if he slept in a coal bin. I felt so sorry for him I fixed him several sandwiches to take on his way.

That same man has delivered coal three times in the past two weeks. I try to feed him well every time he has come and send food back with him. He told me I was a real lady. He said Rafford should be thankful of his good luck. Any man in his right mind would be willing to trade places with Rafford. He said it as though he knew Rafford holds me in low regard. I often wonder why Rafford married me, but then what man would not want to marry the only child of the richest man in Avery county?

I have canned and stored all the food Father and I grew in the garden. We have hams in the smoke house and meat salted down for the winter now that the weather has gotten colder. Father is getting worse and I have no energy whatsoever. I shiver when I see the snow fly.

Rafford left today and told me he would not be back for several weeks, maybe longer if the snow fell. He seemed unusually happy with himself. He even told Father good-by with a grin on his handsome face that showed all his pretty teeth. His strange actions put chills up my spine for I do not like to think of him being superbly happy to leave me.

I am worried about Father. He is extremely sick. I beg him to see a doctor or better yet go to the hospital. He tells me he only has a stomach complaint and will be better soon, but I see no improvement in him. If anything, he is getting worse. If Rafford were here, I would have him wrap Father in quilts and take him to the hospital in the wagon. He is too weak to ride a horse.

Father was buried last week, with me, the preacher, and what few neighbors that could attend. Rafford is not here when I need him most.

Two weeks after Father's funeral Rafford returned from his trip. He did not seem to care that Father was dead. If anything, he appeared happy as he forced me to the bedroom and did things I would never call making love. He does not respect the fact that I am deep in mourning for the Father that was the mainstay of my life.

Rafford Johnson is a brutal man! He has sold most of Father's livestock and left my arm bruised when I tried to stop him! I wish I knew what to do.

Winter has set in with fury. Beech Mountain is covered in three feet of snow. It is not the first deep snow that has fallen on the mountain, but it is the first time I have been here alone without Father. I do not care that Rafford is not here. I hope he never returns! Imagine him thinking I should take care of Father's livestock that was left on the farm! That is man's work! When he discovered I could not do so, he sold them all and put the money in his own pocket. I have not seen one dollar! Sometimes I wonder if Rafford might have had something to do with Father's death other than being a worry to Father. Then I reconsider after I reassure myself that Rafford was gone every time Father got worse and even the day he died.

When the big snow melted Rafford came home riding a horse without the team and wagon. He demanded money from me and got angry when I told him I did not have any. I explained that Father had money invested in many areas and only a small amount in a bank in Johnson City,

Tennessee. He forced me to write him a check for a large amount and headed for Johnson City leaving me with a bloody mouth from his slap when I told him what I thought of him taking Father's money and leaving me alone all the time.

I do not know what to do now for I know for certain I am going to have a baby. It is due in August. I do not think I will tell Rafford about the baby. I want to think of it as mine alone. How happy my dear, beloved Father would be if he knew.

Spring was in the air when Rafford showed up today with his team and wagon. He has been gone for four months and I wish he would go away again. I despise the sight of him. All I want is to be left alone on the mountain with my baby growing inside me. I feared he would see the thickness of my waist but he did not. I was also afraid he might cause me to lose my precious baby if he dragged me to the bedroom and did to me what he has done before. I was relieved when he told me the amount of money Father had left in the bank account and demanded I write him a check for that exact amount. I did so willingly and Rafford left promptly with his team and empty wagon.

I plan to travel down the mountain and seek a divorce from this evil man as soon as I am able to do so. I have been spotting blood and fear that any activity might cause me to lose this precious baby. I wish Nate, or Junie, or anyone for that matter, would come here so I can send for a doctor. I must take care of this baby for it is more precious than gold and jewels. I shall get rid of Rafford so my baby can live with me on this beautiful mountain Father left me.

I feel wonderful and I even planted a garden this week. I did not need a doctor, and I have no problems whatsoever. My baby is growing and I am sure she is going to be a girl. I walked down the mountain to Nate and Junie's place. Junie promised to check on me every few days and said she would check on me every day the last of July and August. Junie does not have children and I saw in her face how much she longs for a baby. When I told her my wonderful news, I saw the sparkle of tears come to her eyes and sadness on her face before she could hide it. Nate did not seem to notice her sadness as he assured me he could have Doctor Jones with me in a matter of hours. God gave Nate a huge heart and unthinkable kindness to make up for his lack of looks. Nate does indeed look gaunt and hollowed out and far from handsome.

I spend my time making baby clothes and thinking of names. My little girl shall have my mother's name. I know she will be a lovely baby with Rafford as her father. God certainly gave Rafford more looks than any one person deserves

.

July is here and I can no longer work in the garden for the sun is hot and my stomach is huge. My little girl kicks like a mule, and I know she wants to be in her mother's arms instead of her mother's stomach. Rafford has not returned home and I wonder what he will do when he discovers he is going to be a father. I cannot understand why he stays away so much, but I do not care. I wish he would never come back. My baby is all I will ever need. I would go this very minute and seek a divorce but I fear any kind of travel would harm my unborn baby, as I still tend to bleed some.

I cannot stop thinking of my baby. It is the most wonderful thing that has ever happened to me. I just wish Father was alive to hold his grandchild in his arms. I am sure he is in heaven with Mother and the two of them are looking down on me and smiling their joy.

Rafford stomped baby in my stomach - left me on floor to die. There's lots of blood. He thinks I'm dead. I'll live to wrote this. He admitted he married me for house and farm. He poisoned dad and has kilt me and his own boy. I pray somebody will find this diary and know what he did and punish him for it.

Those were the last words written in the diary in shaky huge letters, with a brown smear on the bottom of the page. I wondered if it was put there by Boise's bloody hand. I dropped the diary on the floor as I began to shake violently. I felt like I had been sucker punched in the stomach and robbed of my breath. The room in front of me became hazy and wobbled before my eyes. I closed my eyes and dropped my head on my arms resting on the table. I told myself over, and over to breathe slow and deep, slow and deep, slow and deep. I had to get a perspective on this thing. I couldn't go to pieces. I couldn't beat the table to splinters. I couldn't drop to the floor on my knees and cry my heart out. I had to remain calm and reasonable and think about what I had just read.

Chapter 16

It was noon of the second day when I saw Jonas stop his horse in front of the barn, dismount and lead the horse inside the barn. I thought he took more than enough time to unsaddle it and maybe give it grain and water.

I stood at the window watching until he came out of the barn and hurried across the yard, his steps long and fast, as though he thought someone might see him. I opened the kitchen door as he lifted his hand to knock.

"You saw me?" He seemed surprised as he stepped inside the kitchen and closed the door behind him. "I wasn't sure you were here. Things seemed too quiet."

He seemed jumpy, and I wondered what could be his problem. "I was hoping you would come here today." Or tomorrow, I thought. Or maybe never again. "What's your news on Rafe?"

Jonas took off his hat and placed it in the center of the table. He removed his coat and hung it on the back of a chair, then looked at me closely.

"You look pale and your eyes are sunken. Did you sleep any the past two nights?"

"I've slept," I lied. I had done nothing more than doze as I twisted and turned in the bed, got up and walked the floor from the bedroom, down the stairs, to the kitchen. I couldn't get the thought of Rafe as a killer out of my mind. "What happened with Rafe?" I insisted.

Jonas reached out his hand, caressed my cheek then lifted my face to his. His eyes searched mine as though he might be able to read my thoughts.

"Have you been worried over Rafe?" he asked, and I saw a muscle in his jaw twitch.

Worried did not describe what had been going through my mind since I read Boise's diary. Crazy, desperate, hysterical, out of my mind would be a better description.

I gave Jonas a bewildered look. "Yeah, I've been worried. I don't like not knowin things."

He let go of me, and his eyes skimmed over my body. He frowned. "He'll be all right, Laine. Rafford lost his toes, and had surgery on his foot," his voice sounded strained, hesitant. I waited for what he hadn't said yet.

"And?" I insisted.

"The doctors wanted to remove his foot because of the infection. It was mangled pretty badly, but there was no gangrene in the tissue. Rafford did not know what was going on to give or deny them permission. They asked me what Rafford would want done. I told them, speaking as a man not a doctor, Rafford would not want to lose his foot."

"No man would." I turned from Jonas and sank down in a chair. "You told them right Jonas. Why do you seem worried?"

Jonas pulled a chair next to mine and sat down. "If the foot had been removed, the infection would be gone, and Rafford's body could focus on healing from an amputation. Now, his body has to overcome the infection that is giving him high fever, plus try to heal his mangled foot which is harder to do than a clean cut would be."

He reached out and took my hand from my lap and held it in his. "At worst, he could die from infection. At best, it will take a long time for his body to recover and heal. Once he does heal, he will spend the rest of his life as a cripple. If his body refuses to fight and overcome the infection, he may still lose his foot or even his leg," he explained as he let his thumb rub the calluses on the pads of my palm.

"How much of a cripple?" In my mind, I could see Rafe hobbling around, hating the world because he wasn't perfect.

"They are not sure yet. Without further complications he will have a limp. If he loses a foot...a leg..." Jonas said no more.

"Does he know anything?"

"He's not coherent yet. The fever still has him in delirium. Speaking as a doctor it would have been better to remove his foot, but as I said earlier, Rafford is strong and healthy and will overcome the infection, in my opinion. He is a fighter. Men like Rafford Johnson always come out ahead of the game."

"When will he get well?"

"As I said, the care he is getting is working. It should not take long until improvement occurs."

"Jonas, did I do wrong by sewing on his toes? Did I cause more infection to set in?"

"The infection was caused by the filth from his boot and sock the shot took deep into the tissue. You only put in a few surface stitches trying to stop the flow of blood. What you did didn't cause him any problem."

"You're sure?"

"Of course I'm sure. I am the doctor." He turned my hand over in his, looking at scraped places and broken fingernails.

I hoped he was telling me the truth. I wouldn't want Rafe to know I had caused him harm in any way. I didn't think Rafe was a man to forget a wrong done to him, intentional or not.

"I outta go to him," I said but I did not want to see Rafe yet. I had to think more on what Boise had written in her diary. I could see Rafe as cruel and harsh, but I could not see him killing Boise and his own baby. No matter how hard I tried to imagine Rafe getting drunk and angry with Boise, I didn't see a killer.

"You could do nothing at the hospital for Rafford," Jonas told me in a comforting voice. "You are needed here on the farm. You're not needed at the hospital."

"I see," I thought Jonas might be wanting to keep me away from the hospital in case I realized I was not in Kentucky. I looked long and hard at him and was repaid by him squirming under my gaze. I decided it was time for me to know the truth and shot my first question at him.

"I'm not living in Kentucky am I?"

His hand closed on mine. "No," he said simply, not surprised at my question.

"Why didn't you tell me I'm living on Beech Mountain in Avery County, North Carolina?"

"Did Junie tell you that?"

"Why didn't you tell me, Jonas?" I insisted as I pointedly looked at his hand holding mine. "You're the one to tell me truths. Jonas, you're the only person I have."

Jonas looked me in the eyes then slowly shook his head, but he answered me anyway. "Rafford apparently told you he was taking you to Kentucky for some reason, and I didn't think it was my place to tell you different. Believe me, Laine, I wanted to tell you."

I lifted his hand, that still held mine, and placed it against my cheek. I spoke softly and watched for the effect my words would have on Jonas.

"It's not your place to love his wife, but you do."

I saw Jonas wince and his hand tightened on mine. "Yes," he said, " Yes I do, and it's wrong you're his wife. You know that and so do I."

He was the one that was wrong. It was my place to be Rafe's wife. I wouldn't have this mountain otherwise. "Jonas, I don't want to go into that right now, later maybe, but not now. I want to know why Rafe wanted me to believe I was in Kentucky?"

Jonas shook his head and looked away from me. His mouth moved and I thought he was going to grin, but didn't. "I can't know why Rafford told you such a thing. I suspect he wanted to keep you all to himself. Isolated. He may have feared you would run back home to Daddy if you were close enough."

Jonas was telling me nothing I hadn't thought of myself. "Why didn't you tell me, Jonas?"

"Several reasons. Most of all, as I've been saying, it wasn't my place to tell you."

"That's a poor excuse." I moved his hand from my cheek and rested both our hands, still clutched together, on the table. "Why didn't you tell me he was married to Boise?"

Jonas didn't blink an eye. He answered promptly. "It was up to Rafford to tell you about his former wife. Besides, I knew you had to find out about her soon enough. Years ago, Laine, the king had the bearer of bad news killed."

I didn't see what that had to do with anything.

"Laine," Jonas added. "Rafford Johnson won't like the fact that his wife and I were born and raised within a few miles of each other. Rafford Johnson is the type of man that owns things and that includes his wife."

"But we never met. You were away gettin educated."

"We did meet, and it's best Rafford Johnson never knows about it."

"Why?" I held my breath as I waited on his answer.

"Rafford Johnson is a jealous, possessive man."

"I know that," I felt disappointed and hesitated a moment to study Jonas's face. He seemed like he wanted to say more, but wasn't. "How did she die?" I saw a flicker of sadness come to his face when I asked that.

"From what I understand, Boise started hemorrhaging before her baby was due and bled to death."

I knew his sadness was caused by the thought of Boise losing her baby; after all he was a doctor. "Tell me what you know, what you've heard folks gossip about, and what you suspect," I told him bluntly.

He let out a loud breath of air. "Laine, that is one big order you're demanding."

"I have to know the truth. You know that don't you? You understand? I'm the one that's married to Rafe, now. I'm the one that has to live with what he's done and what he's capable of doing."

He was silent for a long time and seemed to be thinking hard. I suspected he was trying to figure out what to tell me and what to leave out.

"I want the whole truth, Jonas. Anything else will be unfair to me."

"I can only tell you what I know and that's not much."

"It's a start."

"Okay," he said. "Okay. I've heard that Rafford Johnson married Boise Holloway for her father's money. There was talk that Rafford had something to do with the old man's death, and maybe even Boise's death. When I discovered you were his wife, I made it my business to find out as much as I could. From my medical judgment, I think the old man died from pneumonia. There had been something going around that had proven deadly. A lot of people died from it. I know of no poison or herb that Rafford could have given him that would take effect while Rafford was away on one of his long trips. And Rafford was definitely gone during the majority of the old man's sickness, and during the time he actually died."

"Didn't it occur to the old man that Rafe might want to marry his daughter for what he could get out of it?"

"I never personally knew Mr. Holloway, as I told you earlier, but he was nobody's fool. I did some searching and asked a lot of questions after I discovered you married Rafford Johnson. It seemed Mr. Holloway hired a private investigator out of Johnson City, Tennessee to keep an eye on Rafford. I managed to find and talk to the man Mr. Holloway hired. Rafford was what he claimed to be. A young, would be, businessman trying to traffic and trade his way to riches. The only flaw in his business dealings was that he occasionally hauled liquor, which was legal before prohibition. The government made brewing liquor illegal because the government wanted money. It's legal to make and sell liquor if the government is getting money from it. If not, it's against the law. A mountain man would be shot and killed without consequence if it meant putting another dollar in a government pocket. They considered the mountain people like us an irritation. An irritation that distilled mighty good liquor. That hits a raw spot inside me, Laine. It hit a raw spot inside many a mountain man. That's why revenuers became a hated species and a fine target to shoot."

I gave him a get-on-with-it look for I didn't care about the government, and he continued.

"It does seem that Rafford has a small cabin in the hills of Kentucky. I suspect he considered taking you there, and for some reason didn't. Like the reason being Boise died. If Boise hadn't died, I think you would be there as his wife, with him hoping no one would realize he was already married. My guess is he hadn't entirely given up his plan because you were too close your parents."

If Boise lived, I would not be his legal wife, now. That thought repulsed me. I didn't want to think about that, wouldn't think about it. I asked, "Did Rafford get in trouble over the liquor?"

"No. He never got into trouble although the Avery County Sheriff warned him to stop that part of his business dealings. I suspect being married to a Holloway helped him out there. Folks around here took a liking to the old man and his daughter. "

"Jonas, where does Rafe go when he's gone so long? Does he have another woman somewhere?"

"According to the man Mr. Holloway hired, Rafford goes to his cabin in Kentucky and stays there alone for weeks without ever leaving."

"Why?"

"I can't answer that, nor could the private investigator. Speaking as a doctor, and knowing Rafford, I think he has what the medical world is just beginning to recognize. It's called melancholia, or some doctors think of it as a depressed nature. Physicians and people alike want to ignore it."

"What about another woman?"

Jonas searched my face and kind of grinned. I guess he thought I might be jealous, which was the most ridiculous thing that could be thought of.

"Not that the investigator or I know about."

"If there was another woman, would you tell me?"

A twinkle come to Jonas's eyes and a broad smile showed his teeth. "I would tell you with great relish. Nothing like making a wife jealous of another woman to get her to leave her husband."

I knew Jonas was just picking at me, so I ignored him and tried to direct him back to answering my questions. Boise's diary was still burning in my mind.

"Where was Rafe when Boise died?" I asked as calmly as I could manage when I wanted to scream that Boise accused Rafe of killing her.

"That was one of the main questions I asked the investigator. He told me Mr. Holloway had paid him to watch Rafford for one full year, and told him to turn in his report to the sheriff if Mr. Holloway was no longer alive. You see Laine, the old man knew he was seriously ill. He obviously didn't want his daughter or Rafford to know. Anyway, Rafford was in Kentucky at his cabin when Boise died, and on the road when the old man died."

"Are you positive of that?"

"The man Mr. Holloway hired was positive of it."

"Did the investigator turn in his report to the sheriff?"

"He said he did. I have no reason to believe otherwise."

"Did you ask the sheriff about the report?"

"No. I've not done that."

"Could I get that report?"

Jonas looked puzzled. "Why would you want the report?"

"I want to know where he goes and what he does. He doesn't tell me, and I want to know."

"Yes, you would," Jonas said. "I didn't ask for the report because I didn't want to raise any curiosity in the county about Rafford. It might be a good idea for you not to stir up things. Talk can be bad even when it holds no truth. If you run to the sheriff, talk will start buzzing like a swarm of bees. We mountain folks love entertainment, and gossip fits the bill."

Jonas turned loose of my hand, stood up and went into the springhouse and got himself a glass of water. I heard him drink. He came back into the kitchen with the glass full of cold water. He sat it down in front of me and indicated that I drink. I ignored the glass as he sat back down in the chair next to mine.

"This is one of the reasons I never told you anything about Kentucky or Boise. I knew you would want to know all the answers. I can only tell you what I know. Rafford is the man to give you answers."

"Rafe is not here," I said firmly. "You are. Now tell me about Boise."

Jonas looked at me for a minute, sighed, then began to talk. His first words had an edge of irritation.

"My God, Laine. I'm beginning to think Rafford Johnson deserves you, after all. You can be persistent."

"Reasonable," I corrected.

He softened his words with a smile and continued. "Boise was a nice person. Good and helpful to everyone. Folks say she was a true lady, not boastful and struck on herself as rich men's daughters tend to be. She did everything in her power to help people and make them feel good about themselves. She had no enemies."

I remembered Zeb. "Zeb said Rafe would give Boise and half the farm for me. Why would he say that?"

Jonas moved the water glass about the table, looking for an exact place to leave it.

"To be truthful, Boise was noted to resemble a horse in looks and confirmation, while you are very pleasing to the eye." A twinkle came into Jonas's eyes. "When a man looks at you, his heart goes into his throat, and he longs to reach out and touch your cheek just before he kisses your lips."

"Please don't make fun of me, Jonas."

Jonas leaned forward and let his finger brush my cheek, my lips. "I'm not making fun of you Laine. Speaking as a man, I can see how Rafford would want you beyond all reason."

"Jonas—!"

"Okay. I'll continue telling you what little I know about Boise."

"Had she seen a doctor?" I interrupted.

"No. I don't think so. Anyway, Boise said the baby was due in August, according to Junie. It seemed that Junie promised to keep a watch on Boise, and Nate was to go for the doctor as soon as labor began. She paid Junie a little to come by each day and help her out cleaning, gardening and things like that. I had been practicing medicine in town for a while, but folks liked the old doctor better than me. Folks can be slow accepting a young man." He smiled at his own words. "Junie found Boise lying in bed when she came to check on her. She must have started hemorrhaging during the night, for the bed was soaked in her blood, and she was cold and stiff. She had been dead for several hours."

"Junie found her?"

"Yes, she ran back home and sent Nate for me, being I was closer than the old doctor, but I was away on a house call at the time. Nate went after old Doctor Smithy."

"He examined her?"

"Of course he did. He had to fill out her death certificate."

"What did he find?" I insisted impatiently.

"He suspected Boise might have had trouble carrying the baby from the beginning, and wondered if she had spotted a lot during her pregnancy."

I could have told Jonas she had according to her diary, but didn't. I asked, "Why didn't she go for help when she first started bleeding?"

"Laine, there wouldn't have been time. She was dead within minutes after she started hemorrhaging. She evidently woke up, realized she was bleeding, reached for her dress and put it between her legs to catch the flow of blood, became instantly weak from blood loss, lay her head back down on her pillow and died. It wasn't a slow drip, Laine. It was a gush. A hemorrhaging, purging gush."

"There was no sign of violence or bruises on her body? Somebody could have beaten her, left her lying on the floor. She might have crawled around a while then finally got in bed and died?"

Jonas looked at me with bewilderment in his eyes. "Where would you come up with an idea like that? According to Dr. Smithy's report, there were no bruises at all. He even ruled out the possibility of her falling down, causing labor to start early. He didn't think she ever had labor pains. He thought she woke up during the night hemorrhaging."

"The baby?"

"Dr. Smithy took the baby from her. He wanted to determine why she had hemorrhaged, and see if the baby was normal. He said it was a male fetus. It appeared not to be developing correctly. He said the baby was probably due at a later date than Junie reported. As I said, he suspected Boise has something wrong that didn't allow the baby to develop properly. Don't forget that Boise was in her forties. The older the woman the more difficult it can be for her to carry a child."

A feeling of relief touched me for I was young. "Due in August of what year?"

Jonas hesitated, rubbed his hand through his hair. He reached for my hand, took a deep breath, as though he was preparing for his next words.

"Of this past August, Laine."

Of course I had known that already. I just needed to hear Jonas confirm it. Rafe had married me within days of Boise's death.

"When did Rafe come back home?"

"A week after she died." Jonas was watching my reaction. "You knew?" he questioned.

"Someone had planted a garden. There were still vegetables when I arrived here."

"It could have been Rafford," Jonas suggested.

"No. Rafe would never plant a garden. Rafe told me Boise planted the garden when I asked about it, but I

thought Boise was the old man's wife not his daughter.
Rafe never told me he had a wife before me."

"Laine, I can't fault Rafford Johnson for wanting you,
but I can fault him for not telling you about Boise."

Jonas tightened his hold on my hand and pulled me from
the chair and cradled me in his lap like I was a child. I
clung to him like I had a right to.

"You were afraid Rafford might have caused Boise's
death in order to marry you? That is in your mind isn't it?"
he questioned gently. "Well my little Laine, you can just
get that notion out of your head for it did not happen. In my
opinion, if Boise had not died, you would really be living in
Kentucky. When Boise died, Rafford Johnson had what he
wanted. He had the farm, the old man's money, then he got
you, too."

I heard resentment in Jonas's voice although he tried to
keep his tone neutral. I rested my head on his chest and
wondered if he would still be saying the same thing if he
had read Boise's diary.

"How can you be so sure she died from a natural cause
and wasn't helped along a little? What if someone came
here and beat her during the night like someone did the
little Munson girl?"

"That did not happen. I should have told you sooner the
little girl is alive, but I didn't want to go into detail while
Nate was around. I didn't want him to realize I was here
that night, or that I took the girl away. They still have her
on the third floor of the hospital," Jonas said. "The sheriff,
even the doctors at the hospital, took it upon themselves to
find out what really happened to that child. It was her
grandmother that beat her. The grandmother said she was
trying to teach the child wrong from right by locking her in
the root cellar and giving her regular beatings while
starving her to death."

I remembered seeing an old woman jerking that child around by the arm and shaking her then dragging her into the house

"There is talk about sending the grandmother to Morganton. There is an institution there that might be able to help her."

"Is she crazy?"

"Probably."

"Dad said it ran in the Munsons. Is the child crazy, too?"

"Something isn't right with her and specialists are trying to find out what."

"What do you think would make an entire family crazy? Dad said inbreeding."

"It could be inbreeding, nutrition, chemicals, minerals, genetics. There are so many factors that can cause insanity. An exact diagnosis can be hard to corner and the cause even harder to eradicate." Jonas stopped talking and looked down at me with concern in his eyes.

"Laine have you been staying here alone with the fear there is some monster running wild on this mountain that beats little girls and pregnant women to death?"

"I've been staying here alone with a lot of unanswered questions running through my head. I have wondered why both Rafe and Nate insisted I keep the doors locked and a loaded gun handy?"

"It's good advice for a woman alone."

His hand reached out and rubbed my face gently, carefully, as his eyes bored into mine with a mixture of fire and tenderness showing in them. He lifted me off his lap, his hand touching my stomach as he sat me on my feet.

"Forgive me Laine, for thinking you were too young." Jonas put on his coat in preparation to leave me.

"Too young for what?" I asked.

Jonas put his hat on his head. "Marriage."

I ignored that. "Jonas, bring a horse back tomorrow and take me to the hospital, unless you'll let me ride pillion off the mountain with you now."

He turned to me with a look of surprise on his face. "I don't think it would be a good idea for you to go to the hospital."

"Why not?"

"It's a long hard ride you don't need to be making, especially in your condition. Besides, there's nothing you can do there."

I felt my chest tighten. He knew I was carrying a baby. His hand had touched my stomach and he knew. I wasn't going to admit it though, not just yet.

"You want me to hide out on this mountain? Don't you think folks will wonder why a man's wife won't go to the hospital to see him?"

Jonas shook his head at me as though I was a stubborn child. "Be patient and let's see how things go," he said as he went out the kitchen door.

I stood at the window watching him go into the barn, get his horse and ride away, down the far side of the mountain, not the road that led by the Patrick's place. I went to the stove and started baking a cake.

What Jonas had told me about Boise bleeding to death in a matter of minutes stuck in my mind. I tried to figure how much time it would take for an injured woman to find her diary, a pencil, write several lines in it, hide it in a dresser drawer inside a pair of overalls, drag her bleeding self from that room to her bedroom, lie down in bed, cram her dress between her legs to stop the flow of blood, and then die without leaving a trail of blood through the house. She had to be bleeding if what Jonas said was true. She even had blood on the bottom of the page in the diary. I took the diary out from behind the flour and opened it to the page with the bloodstain. I found a sewing needle and pricked my finger and squeezed several drops of blood onto the page, smearing it in a circle then placed the diary on the table for the blood to dry.

That evening, just before dark, I took the diary to the window where the light was good and compared the two stains. My bloodstain was entirely different from the stain on the page.

🕊

I slept that night for the first time since Jonas took Rafe away. I awoke feeling alert and determined. I hurried to get the work done and put on the old man's clothes I wore on cold days. This time I made a special effort not to hide my increasing girth. I took the cake in my hands and headed down the road.

The dog came out from under the porch of the Patrick house and barked at me just as it had done before. This time Junie instead of Nate came to the door and called the dog down. She looked surprised to see me as she glanced at the cake then smiled showing teeth that were dark with cavities.

"Why, I hadn't expected to see you, but do come in out of the cold air." She looked at the overalls I was wearing then glanced away without a word, but she couldn't hide her expression. The look on her face made me realize that my stomach must be bigger than I thought.

I went inside and found nothing different from when I was here before except that the baby was lying on the bed asleep instead of sucking at its mother's breast.

"I just wanted to bring you this cake and say thanks for helping me when Rafe was hurt."

"That's what neighbors are for, helpin each other," Junie said as she indicated a chair for me to sit in. Her little birdlike eyes studied my face closely.

I sat down and watched Junie look at her sleeping baby with triumphant pride on her face. There was pleasure shining in her eyes. I had a feeling she was telling me she had something that I didn't have, yet. After all, Boise and her baby had both died before giving birth. The same could happen to me. She reached out and took the cake from my hands.

"I'll perk us some coffee, and we can eat a piece of this cake. It looks mighty fine. I reckon it'll taste just as good as it looks."

"That I wouldn't count on. I'm not the best cake baker that ever was. Sometimes Rafe fusses at my cookin," I told her lightly.

"How is Rafford?" she asked as her brow furrowed and her expression showed concern.

"I was hoping you or Nate might have heard word of him. I reckon if he was in a bad way someone would have come and told me." I didn't exactly lie to Junie, but I didn't want her to know Jonas had been to my house. I also wanted to find out if Jonas kept himself hidden from sight as he came to me.

"Yeah," Junie said. "I reckon that's true enough. No word's good word. If he died, they would've been knockin on your door long before now."

She put wood in the stove and carefully spooned out coffee into the basket. Then she dipped water from the bucket sitting on the wooden top table with a long handled dipper and poured the water into the coffee pot. Junie set the pot on the stove to perk. I watched her move deftly and silently at her task. I noticed her hands were white and delicate. I saw no traces of calluses and hard work. Most mountain women, except Momma and Susie, had hands like mine, roughened by work. I concluded Momma longed to make herself appear the kind of woman folks thought

Boise had been. Rich and well cared for. Junie fell a few more notches in my estimation.

"Where's Nate?"

She lifted her head and looked at me. I saw a flash of irritation pass over her eyes. "He left the mountain early this morning to help at the church house. Were you wantin him for somethin now that you've not got Rafford?"

I heard a note of anger in her voice. Was she afraid I was after her man in some way? Surely not. There was nothing Nate Patrick could do for me that I couldn't do for myself.

"I only wanted to ask him if he'd heard from Rafe?"

"He hain't heard a single word about Rafford. I reckon he would've come told you if he had. I can't be runnin up that hill to deliver messages now that I have my own baby. I can't be lookin after you like I did Boise."

"Yes," I said, watching her every move and expression without seeming to do so. "Rafford said you looked after Boise when she was expecting."

Her eyes widened and her hand paused in mid air. "I did all I could for her. Nobody coulda done better." She crossed the floor and sat down in a chair near me. There was something about Junie I should be acknowledging, but my mind would not tell me what it was.

"Rafe told me Boise never went to see a doctor that he knew of. I just wondered why. The doctor might have saved her life, and the baby, if she had gone," I said.

"If that had happened, you wouldn't be his wife now, would you?" she said. "So, you've come here to find out about Rafford's first wife." Her tone was harsh and her small eyes flashed. "I wondered how long it'd take you to come to me with questions." She looked at the overalls I was wearing, and then lifted her eyes to my face.

"What do you want to know besides why she didn't go to a doctor? I reckon she had her own reason for not seeing the doctor. Of course, most mountain women don't go runnin to a doctor just because they're in a family way. I thought you was country enough to know that. You hain't seen a doctor yet either, have you? You was probably raised rich like Boise. Rafford has a likin for them kind." Her words sounded like an insult.

"I didn't come to talk about myself or Boise. Rafford told me all about her and her father. Rafe even gave me her dad's overalls to wear in the snow. I didn't want to wear men's clothes, but Rafe insisted. He packed all Mr. Holloway's things in a box to take off and trade on except for a couple of pairs of overalls, a pair of long johns and some wool socks. He brought them downstairs for me to put on. He said it got mighty cold on this mountain, and he didn't want me to freeze." I lied to her effortlessly as I lifted the leg of the overalls and showed her what I was wearing.

"I thought it would be all right to dress this way. Don't you think it's all right?" I wanted to sound young and not too bright in an effort to make her feel more confident in herself. That way she might tell me more about Boise. It didn't work for she gripped her hands together and looked flustered.

"I don't reckon most folks care what you wear."

"That's a good thing for they're warm. I'd hate to give them up for Rafe to trade on at some store like he did the rest of the old man's things. You know it was right after he came back from selling the old man's things that he went flyin out of the house with his shotgun and fell down them steps. Something seemed to have upset him." I lied to Junie again and watched her reactions.

She jumped up from the chair and took two cups from a shelf on the wall. Her hands shook enough for her to spill a few drops of coffee as she poured, but she seemed to have calmed herself as she cut the cake, put thin slices on saucers and set the saucers on the rough planks of the tiny kitchen table.

"Here eat a bite before the baby wakes up. Nate said Rafford was in a mighty bad way when Doc hauled him away. Said he was out of his head and didn't know a thing."

"That's true," I sighed and sipped the hot coffee while I watched Junie.

"I reckon there's a chance he might never get his right mind back. High fevers can do that to folks you know. Makes them talk out of their head something crazy. Say things that make no sense."

"Not Rafe," I told her with conviction. "Rafe is young and strong. He'll be back home in a day or two, and in his right mind."

"A body never knows how folks will do after they've been shot and put in the hospital. He might come outta that place as crazy as a bed bug. I've heard of that, and I'd say you have, too. You'd better eat that slice of cake afore my baby wakes up."

Junie ate her cake in silence and didn't have much more to say to me. She was entirely different than the last time I was here. She didn't object to me leaving when I said it was time for me to go. Instead, she seemed glad.

I walked the mile up the mountain with something niggling at my brain, and for the life of me I couldn't put my finger on what it was. But given enough time, it would come to me.

When I got back home, I took Boise's diary from the cabinet and looked at the last page. I inspected the shaky writing then turned back a few pages to the beautiful writing. I could almost hear a voice whisper, "they're different, too different." I had thought the difference was due to Bosie's being near death. What if it wasn't? I turned back to the last page and sniffed at the brown print on the bottom of the page. Perfume lingered in the paper. It smelled like Boise's perfume, and like Junie's. That was what had been niggling at my mind. Junie was wearing Boise's perfume.

☙

I went upstairs to Boise's room and took out what I thought was her prettiest wool dress and found a needle and some thread. I had to make over something for me to wear in case I went to the hospital to see Rafe. I knew I had to look respectful when I went to the hospital. Jonas was right. Eyes would be watching me, and tongues would be wagging. I didn't need to look like a simpleton in front of the people Jonas worked with. I wanted everyone to think that Rafford Johnson married a real lady his second time around as well as his first.

I remade a dark green dress until it fit me well enough. I found a black wool coat folded in the bottom of the wardrobe along with a little black hat that fit fairly well and matched the coat. I got a pair of Boise's' boots that were several sizes too large, but they would be all right with thick socks, and they looked dressy enough to wear to church.

When I had finished with the clothes I bathed and washed my hair until it squeaked then brushed it almost dry. I took a pair of scissors and found a Prince Albert tobacco can and cut out strips of tin then wrapped the tin strips with pieces of a brown paper bag. I carefully rolled my hair over the center of the strips and folded each end of the strip toward the center and over my hair. I would leave my hair rolled up until morning then I would have curls and waves in it just in case I went to the hospital.

But I did all that for nothing. Jonas didn't show up to take me to see Rafe. Instead, a cold snow started to fall at daybreak, flakes the size of Robin's eggs came drifting down. I realized how much I hated winter. Really hated it. It's like putting a white blanket of death over everything. Challenging the strong to survive. Killing the weak with no compassion.

I felt myself closing in, wrapping up, wanting to be warm while dreaming of the hot kiss of summer sun on bare skin. Wanting new life, growing life, lush with promise. Plants living, birds singing as the cold creeks warmed just a little while bullfrogs croaked. Yes, I realized how much I hated winter as I listened to the silent, lonely sound of falling snow. The noise of silence penetrated me to the bone.

Chapter 17

ꗭ

Time passes with each slow tick of the clock, and still time flies. I lost track of the number of weeks Rafe had been in the hospital. I lost track of my thoughts about Junie and Boise as a calm came over me. Words whispered in my head telling me that Junie didn't matter. Boise didn't matter any more either. The only thing that mattered was me, the animals and the land we were living on. For all I knew, Rafe could be dead. Jonas could be dead. The world could be dead. All that was living was what I came in contact with. Like cold, wet feet as the snow melted into puddles in the barnyard. Like the sound of a rooster crowing me awake before dawn lightened the sky. Like today when the sun came out warm and took all the snow away. The sky above my head was spotless blue while the gentle wind was a caress on my face.

I first heard the robins call, then turned my head to see them come lighting on the ground. Spring was coming; oh thank God, spring was coming. I felt tears slide down my cheeks, lifted my hand in surprise at my tears and wiped them away. I stayed outside all day long. And was still outside watching life return.

My breath caught in my chest with pleasure as I saw the distant mountains turn dark against the flame of a dying sun. Shades of gold hugged the skyline as though it did not want to give way to the gloaming of night. Beauty beyond imagination hung there for me to see. It filled me, lifted me, and then it was gone. Night slipped around me with its warning of a freezing night to come. I said a prayer of thanks. I knew I was standing smack dab in heaven. Rafford Johnson had given me this, a mountain to call home. A house beyond any structure I knew could exist. A mansion true and simple. This was the answer to a dream I never knew I possessed until now. Tolerating Rafe was a small price to pay, especially since he was gone almost all the time.

"Thank you, Dad," I whispered as I pulled Dad's coat closer to my body. If only Dad knew what I had. If he hadn't given me to Rafe, I wouldn't be standing here looking at the setting sun. I recalled what Dad always told me. Red clouds in the morning shepherds take warning; red clouds at night shepherds delight. The clouds were moving out, and the sky would be clear tomorrow after the red sunset.

The gentle wind lifted upward and brought to my ears the barking of dogs in the hollow below the barn. I left the rail fence I was leaning against and walked to the back of the barn near the creek, listening. Sounded to me like the dogs were barking on a cold trail. Their voices were slow and drawn out instead of the excited singing of a dog on a hot trail.

I wondered if the dogs belonged to Abe Farrow. I smiled to myself as I recalled the gangly, redheaded boy with his pups. He reminded me of a blackberry briar in the spring of the year before its leaves sprouted out, long, and thin, and tough. He had almost grown into a man, almost but not yet.

The dogs were getting closer and headed straight toward my barn. I stood there and waited on them. I would like to see Abe again along with his rare Rhodesian Ridgebacks. All the dogs I had ever seen were hunting hounds and rabbit beagles, or just a plain scraggly mix.

Abe was only a few feet away when he saw me. "Ma'am," he said. "You pert near made my heart stop beatin. You oughta called out to me. I coulda shot you or something." His breath came rapid. He had been running behind his dogs holding them by their leads. He carried a gun in the crook of his arm. His cap was tied beneath his chin with a coarse string to keep his ears warm in the cool air. I wasn't sure if it was winter or spring. I would have to ask Abe if it was the last of February or the first of March just as soon as I got over the joy of seeing somebody I liked.

"Hello to you too," I said lightly. "I heard your dogs and waited for you." I looked at his four dogs pulling and whining as they tried to continue on the trail. Only two of them were Ridgebacks.

"Halt!" He yanked on the leads with a sharp jerk. "Halt!"

The dogs hesitated unwillingly, their bodies trembling with eagerness to continue.

"Ma'am. It's mighty fine seein you again. But, if you don't mind my sayin, you ought not to be out here at dark, at least not without a gun."

"Oh, I knew it was you. Who else would be huntin?" I laughed a little at his concern for me.

"There's a lot of hunters beside me. Coon hunters and fox hunters are all over these hills. But they're not what I'm talkin about. I've been trackin that pant'er since supper was over. It got a baby lamb from the Smith farm right there in Banners Elk. Dogs picked up a hot track for a ways, and then got onto this cold one. I let them run on it to see where the cat traveled. It's been around your place sometime not long ago."

"I've not had anything killed."

"You better shut the animals up at night just to be safe. Although, it's not been killin grown stock. It seems to be after newborns. Attracted by the birthin smell, I reckon." He looked down at his dogs. "Just like I thought. Cat's holdin up in them rocks at the pinnacle. If I was you, I wouldn't go walkin up there, Ma'am. Least ways not until I get that thing killed. Cat's usually afraid of people, but you never know. This un's kinda odd, or something. I think this un's been hurt or else he's old as Adam's dog. He's not killin right. Mauls too much. Never makes a clean kill, but he's smart. He shore knows how to fool some mighty fine trackin dogs. I'll have to study on him a while uh fore I can figure out how to kill him."

Abe shook his head, expressing his bewilderment at the cat out-smarting his dogs and him both. Like it was a thing a cat couldn't do to him and his dogs together.

"Aren't you afraid to be huntin alone?"

"Law, no, Ma'am. If I turned these here four dogs loose, they'd tear a pant'er to pieces. It might whip one dog, but not four, Ma'am." He screwed up his mouth and spat off to his side into the darkness. I noticed his mouth was empty of any tobacco. He was surely mimicking a much older man, one that chewed. "I'd like to talk a spell longer, but these here dogs are itchin to go on. You best get yourself inside the house come darkness, and keep a watch out during the day. Probably never give you a problem, but you're a lot closer to the rocks than any of the other farmers. That Pinnacle is the perfect den for big cats. Don't take a chance, keep a gun handy cause he's a strange cat. Bye now."

"Bye, Abe," I said, and he and his dogs were gone, leaving me standing alone. So much for finding somebody to talk to.

I stood there listening until the dogs along with their sound buried into the deep woods. The cat's trail was leading away from the rocky Pinnacle. No cat with half its wits would ever leave a clear track straight to its den. Abe said this was a smart panther. Old cat had to be smart to live. A young, dumb cat can survive on physical ability, but living old required some brainpower.

That night I slept fitful. Dreams tumbled through my head most all night long. I kept hearing the pitiful wheezing of an old panther, not the screaming call of a young cat, just the wheezing growl of an aged, dying one.

ℑ

The brief interlude of spring was short-lived as wind hit the mountain with raging fury, bringing freezing rain then pure sleet that coated everything in its path. Trees bent double with ice that glittered like rainbows in the light. Many trees couldn't bear up under the tremendous weight and split or uprooted with trembling force. I heard the crash and the shake of the earth as the big trees hit ground. Smaller trees snapped off clean and quick.

I stepped out onto the kitchen porch and thought about Rafe and his shot foot. He would have no difficulty knowing it was slick this morning. My mountain home was one giant diamond of glittering colors. I longed to capture this beauty in some kind of room where I could open the door and view this sight whenever I wanted. How could God create something this lovely knowing it would last only a few hours? "Simple, Laine," a voice in my head said, "he can create it anytime he wants. He doesn't need a room and neither do you. Lock it in a memory." I went back inside the house smiling. I sure to heck wouldn't be carrying any gun with me today.

The ice didn't last for hours. It lasted for days. Finally, it began to melt, but I was still carrying water to Pet. I didn't want her slippery feet sliding on the ice as she tried to drink water from the creek. Although the ground was mostly clear, there was ice on the edge of the creek. I was lifting my second bucket of water from the creek behind the barn when I looked up and saw Nate coming out of the woods. I sat the heavy bucket down on the ground and waited for him. Maybe he had heard word of Rafe.

"Day to ye," Nate said as he came close to me.

He looked a bit uncertain as his eyes darted about the place as though he just might catch sight of somebody if he looked about quick enough. My heartbeat quickened. He was surely bringing me bad news from Rafe. Disappointment seeped inside me because it wasn't Jonas that had come to me.

"Rafe...?" I questioned.

"Oh no, Ma'am. Didn't tend to upset you. Hain't heard nary a word about him. Least ways, not in a good while. Last I heard he's all right."

"Then why hasn't Rafe come home? Why hasn't anybody showed up to tell me how he is? Where's Doctor Jones been all this time?" I knew my voice snapped, but I couldn't help myself. There was something about the way Nate was looking at me that made me feel uncomfortable.

"Guess you'll have to ask the doc that."

"Guess I could if he would come by to tell me about Rafe. If I knew which way to go, I'd walk to that blamed hospital."

Nate shuffled his sled-runner feet, and looked me over. I shivered. He was a shy man, respectful in his way, but the look he gave me this time made me squirm.

"This mountain's a tricky place. It's best not to walk about much unless you know your directions right good. You can walk off into a hollar and end up God knows where."

"I'll just have to learn directions, won't I?"

Nate lifted his brow and grinned at me. He took a step, then another step closer to me. His shyness seemed to fade in order to make room for determination. He lifted his head and said as bold as you please. "Ma'am, Lainey, you've been left alone so long I thought you might be hankering for company. A pretty little thing like you with a laid up husband has got to get mighty lonesome."

I reached down and picked up the bucket of water, sloshing some out. "Don't want company, and I'm not lonesome." I said as I marched to the barn, ignoring patches of ice. Something told me not to go into the barn with Pet's water for Nate was following right on my heels. Instead, I set the bucket inside the hog lot. The boar hog made a beeline from the stall when he saw me set the bucket down. The sow was right behind him. He gave a snort of disgust when he found the bucket didn't contain slop. He knocked it sideways with his tusk, turned toward the fence and rammed the fence with a force that shook the locust planks.

"Damned," said Nate as he backed up a few steps while I stayed close the fence. "Damned if that hain't the biggest, meanest lookin boar I've ever laid my eyes on."

As though angered by the sound of a man's voice, the boar hog let out a snort, shook slobber from his mouth, and charged the fence next to Nate. Nate jumped backward, blushed, and then took several slower steps even farther away from the fence.

"He's mean," Nate said as though I might not have noticed. "That thing ought to be killed before he hurts you."

"Naw, he hain't mean." I shrugged my shoulders. "Rafe says he just needs someone that knows how to handle him."

"You handle that thing?"

I thought of Dad and Abraham Miller's bull. "Rafe says he's gentle as a kitten. Want to step through the gate and pet him a little?"

"Rafford Johnson's outta his friggin mind. That's a quarter ton of a killing machine hog. You outta butcher that thing now, before he hurts you bad."

"Can't. Rafe says that boar hog has to breed my sows so he can get his money's worth." I needlessly pointed to the sow, now rooting the bucket across the pasture lot as though she wanted to crush it into the ground. "She'll be dropping pigs before long. I'll have to take her away from the boar in a few weeks. She might need a little help farrowing."

"How in tha hell would abody help a sow as mean as that one appears to be?"

"Carefully," I said to Nate. "She's a bit difficult. I had to hold her head while the boar bred her. Didn't want her to hurt him none." I lied just for the fun of it. It would take a bigger fool than me to get into a lot with those two, or just one of them.

Nate's face scrunched into a frown. Belief was barely tapping him on the head. Just the looks of that boar, and the vicious movements of the sow, told Nate I was stretching the truth a long ways. But, he wasn't quite sure I was poking fun at him.

"They're ruinin your bucket."

"Yeah, they are. How about steppin in there and gettin it for me?"

Nate was silent for a few seconds as he thought it over. Finally, he shook his head. "Can't. Need all my legs."

I could have laughed at Nate's honesty.

"How's Junie and your baby girl?"

"Good, I reckon."

He looked me over again. His eyes lingered on my belly, and I knew I could no longer hide my protruding belly. My baby had grown tremendous in the past few weeks.

His face colored up again, and he seemed aggravated. "Damned Rafford Johnson. That bastard's got all the luck."

"Yeah, it's a lucky man that shoots his own foot off."

Nate hung his shaggy head. "Stupidity that was. Won't matter much if he's crippled. He's got you. A woman like you's worth a million dollars to a man. Hain't right he's got you all to his self. Not when he shucks other men's corn like he does."

I didn't know what to say, so I was silent as Nate looked me over again from the top of my hair to the boots I wore on my feet. He licked his lips like he tasted something good.

"Don't reckon you ever consider foolin around?" he asked as bold as you please.

My first reaction was anger, then insult. I thought about knocking him clean into the hog lot. Then, I heard Dad's soft voice saying, *"Handle this gently, girl. Don't make an enemy when you don't have to"* After all, Nate was only asking me. It wasn't like he had knocked me down and straddled me. Still, I was insulted.

"No, I've not," I said sharper than intended.

"Don't make enemies."

I softened my words by adding, "Do you?"

His head lifted. His eyes brightened. "Every time I get a chance," he said proudly.

I stepped against the fence and leaned against the planks, ignoring the angry grunts of the hogs. I rested my hand on the gate. The boar stuck his snout between the planks and smelled of my pants leg. He behaved without ripping out a chunk of material. Probably associated my smell with feeding time and didn't try to rip me to pieces.

Nate looked at the hog, then at my hand on the latch. All I had to do was flip the latch and the boar would be loose. He shook his head. "Well, Ma'am, if you decide you want to fool around, would you let me know?"

I almost laughed.

"You can count on being the first man I'll let know."

A pleased look came to his face. "Since you don't need nothin, I'll mosey on back home." He frowned. "Hope you don't mind me sayin again, if I was you, I'd butcher that boar right away. I wouldn't wait on him to service the sows. Looks to me like he's a loaded gun ready to explode. Why, he'd kill a body if he got loose. See the way he's lookin at me?"

"He don't like men none too good," I warned.

"Yeah," he said mostly to himself. "I'd say he don't like women much either. Reckon I might as well leave as you don't want nothing right now."

"Good idea," I said as my fingers rattled the gate latch.

Memories of Nate Patrick's disgusting attempt at seduction lingered in my mind. Did a man actually think a woman being left alone for a while would make her want to have sex with a man? Any man? That was plain crazy thinking. It was bad enough for a woman to have to do it with her husband. Why would she want to do it for somebody else when she didn't have to? The mind of a man was beyond me.

Winds brought a breeze up the mountain that contained warmth. Daffodils broke through cold ground and bloomed up against the house. I got down on my knees and scooped up a handful of the rich mountain dirt and breathed in its sweetness, then I kissed the yellow blossoms of the tender daffodils. I broke one off and pinned it in my hair with a bobby pin. I would put it in a glass of water when I went back inside the house.

Life was returning to my mountain. Life was growing in me.

I walked across the yard eagerly looking for the green of grass sparingly starting to grow. I went beyond the pasture and stopped; letting the warm air surround me, caress me. I could actually smell spring in the air, but I knew it wouldn't last long. There would be more cold, with touches of warm air coming to tease and entice me for a few weeks more. Then, finally, spring would be on my mountain to stay. I laughed and lifted my face to the wind and breathed in deeply as I had seen Dad do many times. *"Get a whiff of that."* I heard the words Dad always said to me when the warm air came. *"Won't be long now, girl. Spring's around the corner."*

I heard Dad's words as clear as if he was standing beside me. I turned but I was alone. Still, I felt the lightest touch on my hair, just as Dad would sometimes touch me.

It was nearing three o'clock that evening when the air turned cold again. I knew spring was through teasing me. I felt a sadness come over me. I felt myself longing for Dad so badly I would have run all the way back home if home had been close enough. But it wasn't. I would just have to get rid of this feeling the best I could. Strange, how badly a married woman could want her daddy. I could see his bent shoulders and his tired eyes as clearly as if he were standing in front of me. I saw his sad smile as he pushed his cap back on his head, revealing hair sticking out as white as the winter's snow.

There was one thing for certain; I didn't want Momma and Susie. The thought of them put a cold knot in my stomach, so I put them from my mind. I'm too happy here on my mountain to let thoughts of them ruin the contentment I found.

I went back to the barn and stood watching the sky turn gray, then glow blood red just before the sun dropped out of sight. An ache began to throb in me. I heard Dad's voice again. He said, *"It's all right, girl. You'll be all right without me. Remember, love the land, girl. It's life, your life."*

I hurried inside the house and filled the cook stove plumb full of wood until it glowed with heat. I didn't care if the excess heat did shorten the life of the wood-grate. I had to get rid of the coldness that clutched me.

Days passed, and the sadness I felt hadn't left me. I wanted to hit something and yell, but what good would it do? No one would hear me, and the mountain wouldn't care. I could run start naked screaming to high heaven and all I would accomplish might be to make a crow fly. Tears stung the back of my eyes as I strained the evening's dab of milk. Soon, I would have to turn Pet dry. She would be calving in May, and she needed a dry spell so she could freshen.

I guess it was the sadness I was feeling that made me jumpy and angry with the world. It really wasn't fear I felt when I heard a knock on the front door. It was more an accumulation of aggravation. I sat my unwashed bucket down and grabbed the gun leaning in its place behind the kitchen door. Only a stranger would knock on the front door, a stranger that had no business being on my land. That left the possibility of it being anyone in the world but Jonas or Nate Patrick.

I peeped around the rose curtain to see a man, wearing a shabby suit of clothes and carrying a Bible, standing there.

A preacher!

He rubbed his hand through his slicked-back hair and adjusted his faded necktie. He pulled at his suit coat and looked down at his feet. Tied to the round porch column was a sway-backed horse. He knocked on the door again, louder, determined to enter my house.

Just like a preacher.

Somehow I was unbelievably angry as memory of the preacher during Joey's death filled my mind. I yanked the door open and shoved the barrel of the gun in his face.

"What th' hell you want?" I demanded.

His eyes widened. He took several steps backward. His chin jerked as he tried to talk.

"Elaine?" he managed. "Elaine Elder Johnson?"

"You best have a fine excuse for being on my land," I told him none-to-friendly. I didn't know what came over me, but I feared this preacher man almost as much as I did the man Zeb. I longed to pull the trigger of the shotgun and splatter the preacher all over the yard.

"I'm a traveling preacher," he said quickly as he looked at the gun and my shaking hand. He acted like he wanted to do something fast, but he didn't know exactly what. "I've come with news of your father."

"I've got a direct line to God, thank you. I don't need input from a travelin preacher. You best be movin off my land in a hurry or you'll be meetin your father in heaven or hell, one."

I hated this traveling preacher. Hated him with a passion deep within my soul. I didn't want him to open his mouth and speak, or breathe my mountain air. I wanted him gone, out of my sight forever.

He slowly lifted his hands up in the air and moved backward, all the way to the half-circle steps.

His words tumbled over each other as he said, "He's dead. Presley Elder was killed ball hootin timber."

My knees buckled and I swayed as the gun drooped in my hands, pointing to the porch floor. I squeezed the trigger and heard the blast as the gun kicked me backward through the open door. The haze I was looking through began to clear. I saw the traveling preacher man, in the suit, clutching his Bible, rapidly crawling on his hands and knees down the porch steps toward his horse. He was moving too fast to have been hit by the gun blast. Somehow my mind was telling me if this traveling preacher were dead, my Dad could still be alive. My hands patted over the floor searching for the shotgun.

I had one more shell left in the gun. One more chance to keep Dad alive.

I felt my fingers touch the cold of gun metal. Dang. It was heavy. I was having trouble getting it lifted up and aimed at the lying bugger. He was on his horse. I saw his polished shoe heel kick into the horse's side. He was getting away. I lifted the gun and pulled the second trigger. I saw a spot on the porch post darken where my shot hit. The horse speeded up. The lying bugger was still hanging on.

Chapter 18

I felt hands touch me and lift me up from the floor. I didn't try to find the shotgun. It wouldn't do any good until I got more shells. I strained my eyes open and saw Jonas's face close above mine.

"It's all right, Laine," he soothed.

"Did he fall off?" I asked as I felt Jonas move me in his arms; heard him kick the front door closed.

"Who?" He asked softly against my hair.

"That damned lying bugger."

"What?"

He laid me down on the red couch in the living room. I sat right back up. "It's cold in here," I objected. "I'm freezing."

"Did you fall down? Have you hurt yourself?" He lifted me again and took me into the kitchen where I had the cook stove warm. He sat me down in a chair at the table, and I heard him go into the springhouse.

"Here drink this." He held a glass of water to my lips.

I turned my head without drinking. "I missed, didn't I?"

"Missed what? What happened to you?"

"I didn't hit that lying bugger?"

Jonas rubbed his hand over my hair, and knelt down on the floor until he was eye level with me. "Can you tell me what happened?"

"That damned preacher. Did I get him?"

"Well, I'll be damned," Jonas said. Surely he didn't beat me here. I came as soon as I heard."

I grabbed Jonas by the hair, knocking his hat off, and pulled him within an inch of my face. "He was lyin. Tell me he was lyin."

Jonas took hold of my hands and worked my finger loose from his hair. He moved back, still holding my hands.

"Laine, dear girl, I don't know any other way to tell you this but straight out. Your dad was in an accident five days ago."

Somebody was screaming and I thought they really should shut up at a time like this.

"Stop it, Laine. Stop it," I heard Jonas's voice saying over and over.

I felt him shake me. A cold glass of water hit me full in the face. My right hand hit something. Jonas' face. My hand was stinging.

"I think I broke my hand," my voice said.

"Your hand's not broken. Damn, you hit hard." Jonas was silent for a moment. I saw his chin move about. He spoke. "Laine, you're got to get yourself under control. I can't give you any medicine or it might hurt the baby you're carrying. If you keep this up, you can abort on your own.

Jonas lifted me in his arms again and sat down in the chair with me in his lap. I felt his hand rub over my stomach. It felt like his hand was touching my skin even through the material of the overall.

"Is it true. Is Dad...?"

"Let me hold you for a little while. We'll talk later."

I felt tears roll down my face. If I had shot that traveling preacher first thing, I wouldn't know this yet.

Jonas held me against his body and rocked me back and forth, slow and deliberate until shadows formed in the kitchen.

Silence!

The entire world was silent.

I had to speak. Break that bone aching silence.

"How's Rafe?" I finally asked.

A sound came from Jonas, and then he spoke. "He's okay. His fever has gone down. He's in a rage to come home."

I could see Rafe red in the face, yelling and cussing.

"Why isn't he here?" I asked.

"They won't let him leave yet. His foot is healing slowly. He isn't healing fast for some reason. They won't let him come home until the infection is totally gone, and his tissue has started to heal itself adequately."

"It's been a long time. Is it March yet?"

"Yes, Laine. It's the last week of March."

Time, how fast it moved on.

"I don't have a calendar. I've been trying to guess by the weather."

"It's colder on this mountain than anywhere else. About ten degrees colder."

"Would you bring me a calendar?"

I felt his arms tighten around me. His mouth was close to my hair and his warm breath touched my cheek.

"When are you due, Laine?"

"June, July. It's hardly noticeable." I felt a sob jerk me. "Tell me what happened to Dad."

"Later. Let's talk about your baby right now. Do you want a boy or girl?"

I knew what Jonas was doing. He wanted to calm me down. Keep me quiet.

I would let him.

"Girl," I said. "I want a little girl." Somehow I had in my mind that a boy baby would be like Rafe. I didn't want another Rafe, even if he was a baby.

"Yes. I want that, too. A sweet, little girl, just like its mother." His voice was soothing, and I knew the effort he was going through to calm me down. He was right. I had to stop my violent reaction.

I just didn't know why I let myself get so completely out of control.

"Jonas."

"What?"

"Don't call me sweet. I'm not sweet."

I saw Jonas grin. His arms enclosed me a little firmer, and his lips touched my hair.

"I know that," he said.

"Rafe said he hoped I was barren as a rock."

Jonas didn't say a word.

"A man that doesn't want children..." I said as a tremble went through me.

"I can see that in Rafford Johnson. He has difficulty caring for himself, much less somebody else."

"Why?"

Jonas moved his legs beneath my weight. I knew I was getting heavy and wondered if his legs were going to sleep, but I didn't want him to put me away from him just yet.

I took a deep breath. "You don't have to hold me, Jonas. I know I'm heavy."

"Like an armful of roses."

"What do you see in Rafe?" I asked, knowing Jonas and I both were talking around the subject of my Dad. Yes, we'd talk soon, but not right now.

"I believe Rafford Johnson has what some doctors call melancholia. I have concluded he'll never be completely happy with anybody or anything, including himself."

Jonas took a handkerchief from the front pocket of his coat and handed it to me.

"What's a melancholia?" I wiped my eyes and nose then clutched the handkerchief in my hand.

"I'm seeing things in Rafford that most doctors swear don't exist. I've been reading arguments and debates on the matter, especially by Dr. Kroepelin, and I have come to a firm conclusion. Speaking as a doctor, I think Rafford has some sort of mental disorder that comes from factors inside the person. He shows strong symptoms of having psychosis characterized by alternating periods of high elation, and periods of severe depression. He comes home to you when he is in the elation phase. He hides out in his cabin in Kentucky when he is in the depressed phase."

"What causes such a thing?"

"Many psychiatrists believe that melancholia, or I find depression a simpler term, may have its roots in the experiences of a person's childhood. It could also run in families, from heredity. Of course, there are other doctors that say such things don't exist. They say it is an illness doctors have coined to excuse people of bad behavior. Some refer to it simply as a difficult person."

"What can be done for it?"

"Well, there's not an extensive remedy. He could have electroconvulsive therapy, or shock therapy. That's the passage of an electric current through the brain to induce alterations in the brain's electrical activity."

I listened to Jonas, puzzled, and clutched the handkerchief tighter. "That sounds awful. Would it cure him?"

"I don't know. I just don't know."

"Would it hurt him to try?"

"He'd have to acknowledge he has a problem first, and then be willing to be institutionalized and treated."

"He won't do that. Couldn't you do it for him while he's in the hospital with his foot?"

"Sorry. It doesn't work that way."

"Then what can be done?"

"Not one thing until Rafford agrees to it, or he gets worse."

"Can he get well on his own?"

"Probably not, but we can hope. Just realize that I don't know this for a fact. I only suspect it."

"Jonas," I dreaded to ask my question, but I had to know. "If it's heredity, will my baby have it, too?"

Jonas let his cheek rest against my hair. "I hope not, Laine. I honestly hope the baby takes one hundred percent after its mother. You could actually carry strong enough genes to counter Rafford."

I felt his body tense slightly and wondered if he knew anything about the way Momma was.

Rafford and Momma.

I was suddenly afraid for my baby. I took a deep, steadying breath. Yes. I could actually be strong enough to counter Rafe and Momma...and Dad's death.

"What happen to Dad?" I wanted to know. Now, that I was determined to be strong for my baby.

Jonas seemed to understand my resolve. "He had an accident at the sawmill, so I heard."

"What kind?"

"Ball hooting the logs out. The team of horses started to pull while your Dad was working on the chain behind the horses and in front of the logs."

In my mind I saw Dad standing behind the horses' hind legs as he fastened the grab-chain to massive logs. I saw the horses spook and start to run. I saw the logs move, gouging up groves in the dirt. I saw the cut ends of the logs hit Dad, knock him down, gouge him into the earth and continue on.

I wasn't as strong as I thought I was.

Jonas held me against him and let me cry tears of anguish, not the hysteria I had before, just quiet tears of loss.

"Jonas," I finally managed to say. "Can I borrow your saddle horse? I don't know if Rafe's are broke to ride." Besides they were still at Jonas' place somewhere off the mountain.

"What are you talking about?"

"I need a horse to ride to Dad's funeral. How far are we from Dad's place?"

"It's almost a day's slow ride, but you won't need a horse."

"Why?"

"I wouldn't let you ride that far when you are pregnant. Besides it's too late, unless you want to be with your mother and sister."

"Too late?"

"Your dad's funeral was several days ago."

I thought of Dad lying in a grave next to Joey's. I wondered if Momma was trying to dig him up. No. I decided. No way did I want to be anywhere near Momma and Susie ever again.

Thank God for this mountain. Thank God for Dad's wisdom.

"Let me carry you upstairs and lay you in bed," Jonas suggested as he stood up from the chair. He had been holding me in his lap for what seemed like forever.

"I'm fine, now. You can put me down."

"No," he said gently. "I'll not put you down. As your doctor, I'm going to put you to bed, and then fix you some hot soup. I'll do your work up tonight and in the morning. I'm not going to leave you alone."

Jonas carried me up the stairs with no effort at all.

"You don't have to do this. I'm perfectly capable of caring for myself."

"I know, but allow me to do this. I want to do something for you Laine, and this is all I can do at this moment." He carried me into the bedroom opposite Rafe's, and laid me down on top of the cover.

"Jonas."

"What?"

"Joey's dead and now Dad. Death comes in threes you know." I put my hand on my stomach as Jonas spread a quilt over me. "I'm not going to lose my baby. I'll never let anything happen to my baby."

"I know," Jonas said. "And I won't let anything ever happen to you."

Chapter 19

Each day seemed long and cold and never-ending while the nights were almost unbearable for me. Loneliness set in, and I longed for Jonas to come back, but he didn't. The only thing I had to be thankful for was the traveling preacher didn't come back either.

Sometimes I would be outside when the wind blew up the mountain with its sweet warmth. I thought I could feel the presence of Dad on the breeze. All I had to do was chase the wind around the corner, behind the next tree and Dad would be there. But he never was. He was gone for good. Gone like the melted snow. Gone like yesterday. I felt a sadness grow and settle deep in my bones. It filled my marrow, my tissues, my aching heart. I longed to find a quiet spot and cry and cry until my soul was empty of pain, of loneliness. But I couldn't do that! I was Elaine Elder Johnson! I was tough and strong. Nothing would ever get me down.

I leaned against the rail fence and watched the hogs root under the trough in hopes of finding a missed potato peel that I had just tossed out for them. I had to shut up that old sow in a barn stall, and then move the boar hog to a smaller area. I dreaded that. I found my growing baby made my reactions a little slower than normal, but I could manage.

I assured myself the moisture in my eyes was caused by the cold wind that hit me in the face and not from this feeling of doom that had a hold on me. I gazed in the distance at the darkening sky and felt the closing in of twilight engulfing me like it was a fog. The wind lifted my hair and brought to my ears the sound of a wagon coming up the rutted road that had not been used since February, since Rafe had shot himself. I knew Rafe was coming home. Instead of feeling joy, a fear hit me that made me want to climb into the barn loft and bury myself in the hay. Instead, I turned to face the road and waited.

It seemed to take forever, a noisy, rattling forever, as I listened to the wagon coming closer and closer. I didn't remember Rafe's wagon being so noisy. It sounded as bad as Dad's old wagon. My fear multiplied until I looked around in earnest to find a place to hide, but before I could move I saw Dad's old mule stick its head around the bend in the road. Then came the rest of him pulling the broken down remains of the wagon filled to its busted boards with assorted sacks and junk. Susie was sitting on a sack driving the mule. I knew Momma was in there somewhere.

"What tha' hell?" I managed to say as the wagon pulled up beside me. I jumped backward as the mule stretched his neck toward me with the intention of taking a bite. He was wet with sweat and skinny as a plucked chicken. I could count every bone in his rib cage and his backbone stuck up like a wooden rail. He probably hadn't been fed a bite of grain since Dad died. He had to be weak as a baby duck for Susie to be able to drive him all the long distance from Dad's to here. Suddenly his head drooped and all the fire went out of him. I feared he was going to die right there still hitched to the wagon. I would have a heck of a time getting him buried.

Momma raised herself from a feather tick lying in the back of the wagon and looked at the house, the barn, the out buildings, the yard, then at me.

"Thank God! I finally found my sweet baby girl," she said before moans escaped her open mouth and tears ran down her cheeks like a trickle of thawing ice.

I looked from her to Susie. Susie's face was paler than the feather tick Momma was sitting on. Susie was about as skinny as the mule and looked more worn out. She was trembling from head to toe as she dropped the reins as though they were fouled, and looked at her hands. Raw blisters popped open and oozed bloody liquid. I heard Dad's voice say, *"The leaches have arrived!"* A terrible anger filled my entire being. I trembled with it. It was all I could do not to start crying with rage and hatred for the two women that were my next of kin.

"Elaine, my baby, help your Momma off this thing. I'm nearly dead of exhaustion and sorrow."

I didn't move.

"Susie, don't just sit there like a stump. Jump down and give your sister a hand with me."

Susie started to move.

"Sit right where you are Suzanne Elder." My voice was deep and authoritative. The sound of it surprised even me. Susie froze on the sack she sat on.

"You two leaches aren't coming in on me. Turn around and get yourself back where you belong!" My whole body was shaking like I had a freezing chill, but my words were strong and harsh.

Momma's breath sunk into her chest making a shocked sound. Both of her soft hands clamped over her heart.

"You talk like that to your mother! The one person that sacrificed for you all these years! How dare you! Your poor departed dad has just turned over in his grave!"

"My poor departed dad is getting the only rest he's gotten since the day he married you!" I heard myself saying yet I couldn't hush. "You never sacrificed a broken fingernail for me. You thought only of yourself just like you're doing now. Susie, turn that mule around and go back where you belong, the both of you!"

Tears dripped off Susie's jawbones as she curved her hands into claws.

"I can't," she sobbed. "I can't hold the leather straps any longer."

Her knees came up and her arms locked around her legs. Her face dropped onto the dirty fabric of her skirt and she cried like a wounded baby.

"Look what you've done to your sister! Help me off this wagon."

If Momma thought I was going to help her off that wagon, she was even crazier than I thought. I knew if she ever set foot in my house, it would take hell and high water to get her out. I just wasn't up to that today.

"Trade places with Susie. Your hands aren't blistered. You can drive back off this mountain and go back where you came from. It's time the two of you took care of yourselves, for I won't and Dad's in his grave."

I wanted to walk away from them. Have no more words with them. But I knew if I left, they would be off the wagon and in my home like a swarm of hungry locusts. They would eat up my life and what contentment I now had. There would be nothing left of me but an empty shell waiting hand and foot on Momma and Susie. I had to fight for my life, for my baby, and by dickens I was going to.

"It's nearly dark and the mule is dead tired," Momma wheedled. "Surely you've got enough decency in you to let your poor old mother and sister spend the night." She was whimpering like I had heard her do many times before. I felt bile rise in my throat, and I fought not to throw up right there in front of them.

"Please..." Susie sobbed. "Just let us stay tonight. I can't ride in this wagon any longer."

I had ridden in a wagon with Rafe for three days, three long hard days and nights with a husband I didn't even know, a man Dad had given me to because Momma and

Susie didn't want me around any more, and they thought I would feel sorry for them?

"Why have you come here? Why did you leave home?" I demanded, but didn't need to. They had come for me to take care of them. Somebody had told them what a fancy place I lived in.

"Momma made me," Susie sobbed. "She made me drive this thing!"

I turned to face Susie and hoped the look I was giving her conveyed at least half of what I was feeling toward her.

"Susie, do you remember telling me I couldn't be in Momma's house except to clean and cook your meals? Guess what big sister? You and Momma can't be in my house for any reason."

Momma came off the wagon without help. I could tell by the look on her face she was fighting mad. I recalled her hitting Dad with the shovel when he tried to stop her from digging up Joey's body. She came at me like a fighting rooster, determined to put me in my place and take over.

"I'll learn you a lesson!" she snapped at me as she tried to slap me in the face. My hand caught her right wrist, and she swung with her left hand. I caught her left hand too and twisted both wrists with all my strength. She kicked me on the shin before she dropped to her knees in pain. I wanted to break both her wrists but came up just a little short of enough strength to do it. Momma screamed to the top of her lungs before she crumpled to the ground. I heard the chickens cackle at the horrible sound she made. I turned her loose and stepped back.

Susie was looking from Momma to me in horror.

"You hurt her," Susie accused in disbelief.

"Not much, but if she ever tries that again I'll break both her arms. Do you hear me Momma?" My leg hurt, but I wouldn't show it. I looked at Susie. "Get her in the barn loft where you'll spend the night. That mule will die if he don't get some food and water in him. No need for a mule to die because of two women's confounded laziness."

I unhitched the mule and lead him into the barn and put him in a stall, and then carried him a small amount of water and gave him a handful of hay. A starved animal had to be fed and watered carefully. He'd founder if he had too much, but then a mule wasn't like a horse. A mule had enough sense not to founder himself, but I wasn't going to take a chance. I didn't have a horse to drag that wagon back to Dad's place, and I was determined Momma and Susie weren't going to destroy the life I had now. I would drag them off this mountain all the way back to their home by the hair of their head if I had to.

I saw that Susie had taken the feather tick off the wagon and was carrying it into the barn loft while Momma followed behind her carrying a quilt in her arms. They gave me a look that said they wished I would drop dead on the very spot where I stood. At least I didn't wish them dead, but I wished I would never have to look at them again.

I went into the house and made sure every door and window was locked. I expected to hear a window shatter and them to take over the house. I huddled in the kitchen corner with the gun beside me. It gave me comfort even though I knew I wouldn't shoot them. A gun could make a good bluff though, and I thought I was good at bluffing. Unwanted tears ran down my cheeks as I waited for morning.

I opened my eyes and discovered the kitchen was light enough for me to see the cook stove. I got up off the floor unable to believe I had slept the night away. I looked out the window and saw the wagon in front of the barn. It wasn't just a nightmare that Momma and Susie had come to torment me. They were here! Now what was I going to do? Did I feed them breakfast or should I pretend they didn't exist? I feared if I appeared to give in one inch they would think I was weak and take over. I wanted to crumple back into the corner again, but I wouldn't allow myself that weakness.

I dipped water from the water closet and washed my hands and face. I ate a cold biscuit and drank a glass of milk. I thought about doing the work, but dreaded angry eyes watching me.

I sat down at the table and tried to make my mind think clearly. Dad had been dead less than three weeks. How would his death be a hardship on Momma and Susie? Their land and house was paid for. They had milk cows, chickens and hogs. They had all the cans I had put up during the summer and fall. The root cellar was full of potatoes, apples, and walnuts. There was hog meat in the smoke house and gallons of molasses. There was corn and hay in the barn for the animals. Momma had stashed nearly every penny Dad had earned from the sawmill plus the money Dad and I brought in from selling milk, eggs, hams, live hogs and molasses. The two of them should be able to live just as good as I was living if not a whole lot better.

It was clear to me the traveling preacher had wasted no time running back and telling Momma about the fancy house I was living in. I would also guess he had found out at the hospital that Rafe was flat on his back in one of the hospital beds with a gunshot wound and high fever.

I reluctantly left the house and went to the barn. What was I going to do about this problem? What I wanted to do was show them the road and tell them to hit it. I went to the barn stall where the mule was. His head was hung down, and I could see his shallow breath beneath bony ribs. He made me think of Dad the night he married me off to Rafe. Like life had left him, and he just didn't care. There was no way that mule could pull the wagon for a day. I got him grain, hay and a bucket of water.

I went up the stairs into the barn loft. Momma and Susie were sleeping in the hay. They had placed a feather tick mattress on the floor, and another feather tick comforter over the top of them, and a quilt on top of that. Soft pillows were beneath their heads. They looked comfortable and content lying there sound asleep.

The anger that hit me!

How could I hate two people so much?

Too bad I hadn't shot that traveling preacher dead. He'd never been able to tell Momma where I was. I could have buried him in the garden and had me a horse besides. Even that thought didn't ease the anger in me.

I reached down and jerked the comforter and quilt off them. They lay there, curled up against each other.

"Get up," I demanded. "Get outta that bed right now."

They opened their eyes and looked at me as though they were trying to figure out where they were.

"You're at my home now, and while you're here, you're going to work like hell."

Susie's face screwed up like she was going to cry. She rubbed her puffy eyes with the back of her hand, avoiding her blistered palms. Momma looked at me with hatred, and then changed to a look I had seen her give Dad. Cunning.

"Laine, honey, what in this world has come over you? My sweet little girl's not acting like herself."

I actually laughed. Did she think I was foolish?

"Regrettable, you're not leaving here today," I told them firmly and not at all friendly. "The only reason you're not leaving is the mule isn't in condition to pull the wagon. If I had my way, the mule would hitch the two of you to the wagon and he would ride the wagon back. Since that's not possible, and you have done your best to starve the mule to death, you'll have to stay here and work until he has more strength."

The look on Momma's face changed to one of authority. She was going to pull the mother-daughter thing.

"You watch how you talk to your Mother, young lady. You're not too high and mighty for me to give you a good whippin."

"It'll be a cold day in hell when a sickly old woman without the strength to walk to the toilet gives me a whippin. You done it when I was little, but you'll never do it again," I told her sassily and waited for the feeling of guilt to hit me. After all, a child was supposed to honor her mother.

No guilt came.

I saw some of the bluff go out of her face. Fear flickered through her eyes. I knew she was trying to decide what to do next. She wasn't used to having somebody stand up to her.

"Ohhhh!" she screeched, and went limp with her eyes rolling back in her head.

"Momma?" Susie whimpered and grabbed Momma by the arm and began shaking her.

"For the love of Pete," I said. "Stop that disgusting behavior."

"Momma's dyin," Susie moaned. "Help her."

"I'll help her all right. I'll help dig the hole to bury her in."

I looked at the two of them and shook my head. I grabbed Susie by the arm and jerked her off the feather tick. She scratched my hand with her long fingernails, and I turned her loose letting her fall into the hay. I turned my back on her without a word and went down the barn stairs.

I heard her whimpering over Momma again.

"It's all right old fellow," I said to the mule as I got the water bucket out of his stall. He had only drunk half the water.

When I got back up to the loft, Momma was still lying there limp and suffering. I lifted the bucket. Cold water covered Momma and part of Susie.

"You damned bitch!" Momma yelled as she came to her feet and took a step toward me.

I gave the bucket a little swing, showing her I could easily smash it into her head. She stopped. Water dripped from her wet hair. She snarled, her little pointy teeth exposed.

"I suggest you both put on dry clothes before you come to the kitchen. I'll feed you before you start to work," I told them.

As I left the barn, I saw Jonas riding his sorrel horse out of the woods. He looked at Dad's old wagon then saw me. He rode up to me and dismounted.

"Are you always going to show up when I'm going out of my mind?" I asked him. "You knew they were here, didn't you?"

Jonas kind of grinned as he looked from the wagon toward the house. "There's only one road up this side of the mountain, Laine. Folks watch and know when somebody enters or leaves."

"Unless they sneak through the woods," I couldn't resist saying.

"It's hard to get a wagon through the woods. Riding a horse isn't."

"Tell me about it." I remembered my wagon trip with Rafe.

"They also stopped down in Banners Elk to ask directions to where you lived."

"And somebody told you?"

"Gossip travels fast."

"Then why weren't you here last night?" I asked but he didn't respond. "Come on inside. I'll build a fire and get breakfast."

"What are you going to do, Laine?"

I stopped at the kitchen porch, turned to look at Jonas and said, "I'm going to work the livin hell outta them until the mule is able to pull them back home. I can't send them back knowing it'll kill Dad's old mule. You have a different suggestion?"

Jonas sighed and shook his head as we walked across the porch. "You're not going to let them stay?"

"Do I look that crazy?"

"No, hardly crazy. Exhausted." Jonas answered and followed me into the kitchen. "Are you doing all right with the baby?"

"Of course. How's Rafe?" I couldn't help feeling hurt because Jonas had been away so long. He left the day after I found out about Dad, and he hadn't been back.

Jonas pulled out a kitchen chair and sat down while I built a fire in the cook stove. "They are going to discharge him tomorrow, Laine." His voice dropped as he said my name. "I had the hospital keep him as long as possible."

"Why?" I wanted to know as I put lard in a bowl and cut flour into it for biscuits.

"He's difficult, extremely difficult. I tried to protect you from that part of Rafford as long as I could."

"You don't have to protect me. I know how my own husband is."

Jonas made a face and didn't say anything for a minute. "Where are they?" He looked at the closed door that led from the kitchen to the stairs.

"In the barn."

"What are they doing in the barn? The work?"

I laughed. "Not yet, but that's my plan. I made em sleep there last night." I added milk to the bowl.

I saw surprise come to Jonas's face.

"Why?"

"Jonas, I didn't know what else to do. When I was home, Dad waited on them hand and foot, and I did too. They wouldn't do a thing for themselves. That's why they're here. They want to live in this fancy house and have me take care of them again, now they don't have Dad. They treated me like I was dirt before, told me I could only be in the house to cook and clean. They made life so miserable on Dad, until he finally gave me away to Rafe. They're like vultures ready to swoop down when they think their victim can't fight. They're dead wrong. I can and will fight. I'll fight until they're destroyed if I have to."

I looked at Jonas for his reaction as I dumped the biscuit dough out onto the counter top I had just floured. "I'm having a baby, and I won't let them hurt my baby in any way. They won't take one thing from it. Not my time and certainly not this home and farm. I owe that to this baby. I owe them nothing."

"Laine, they are your mother and sister."

"Yeah, they are." I admitted. " but we wouldn't be akin if either of us had a choice in the matter."

Jonas took his hat off his head and laid it in the center of the table. "I have heard talk about their helplessness, but I never knew for sure."'

"Whatever you heard, you can probably believe it. But it's not helplessness. They're smart, Jonas. Smart and lazy."

Jonas frowned as though he were in deep thought. Finally, he looked up at me and said, "I'm sorry, Laine. I'll hitch my horse to the wagon and drive them home if you want."

I stuck more kindling in the firebox and shook my head. If I sent them off, I feared they would be more determined than ever to come back, to show me they were top hogs in the wallow, that they could control me.

"You say Rafe is coming home tomorrow?" I rinsed off my hands in the wash pan, dried them on a towel then cut the biscuits out of the dough with a glass.

"Afraid so."

The grin that played at my lips felt good as I thought of them and Rafe meeting each other. Momma and Rafe were obsessed only with themselves and their own comfort. I grinned again.

I really didn't want to fix them breakfast, but I couldn't stand the thought of them being hungry, as I recalled the Munson girl stealing food from the garden.

"How's the little Munson girl?"

"She's still in the hospital. She's got a long way to go before she's healthy."

"Bless her little heart," I said and thought of Momma and Susie with bewilderment. There was one thing I knew for certain. If I let them in my home, they'd be like a bad stain. I'd never get them out.

Chapter 20

From the kitchen window, I saw Momma and Susie come out of the barn. Susie had her arm around Momma as though she was supporting part of Momma's weight. Momma hobbled and limped a slow step at a time. They followed the path I had worn from the barn to the kitchen.

"Jonas," I asked as I watched them. "Could you examine Momma and Susie and tell me if there is anything wrong with them?"

Jonas turned and looked out the window. He watched them in silence for a few moments.

"I'll be glad to examine them." He said. "Why?"

"I want to know if there's anything really wrong with em."

Jonas started to speak then stopped.

"Physically," I added.

"Some things require tests. Laine, they may not want examined."

I scooted the pan full of biscuits into the oven, closed the door. Then I got potatoes out of a sack from under the counter and started peeling them to fry.

"Dad left them well off. They'll be able to manage better'n me."

Jonas turned and looked at me, again. I saw pity in his eyes and wondered if it was for them or me. "I'll take them back home, Laine. Just tell me when."

I smiled. Thank God I had one friend in this world. His eyes met mine, and our gaze held for a moment. I looked away for I knew what interest Jonas had in me would fade soon. There were just too many girls in this world for a man like Jonas to look at an old married woman that was expecting a baby.

The thought made me sad.

Momma actually knocked on the kitchen door. I opened it knowing I was making a big mistake. Momma stood there with her head hung, dejected. Strands of hair stuck out all over her damp head, along with hay. I didn't recall hay in her hair earlier. Her mouth was turned down, and she looked like she was about to cry. Another look I had seen her give too often.

She knew Jonas was here.

Susie hadn't changed clothes like Momma had. Her dress was still damp in places, and I could see chill bumps on her arms below her sleeves. Her face was pale, and she held her hands so she wouldn't touch anything with her palms. A speck of genuine sympathy crept into me.

"Momma needs to get warm." Susie turned on me. "The devil will burn you in hell for the way you treat Momma."

The speck disappeared.

I saw Momma's elbow shoot out and poke Susie in the ribs. Susie didn't say another word.

"Laine, baby, I do need to come inside and get warmed up a bit. That water you poured on me was mighty cold."

Jonas' expression remained blank, as though he hadn't heard her words.

Momma let her feeble glance take in Jonas then scan the stove for what was cooking. I wondered what they had eaten on their trip yesterday. I stepped back from the door and let them enter without a word.

"Good morning, ladies," Jonas said as he stood up and pulled out a chair for Momma to sit in.

Momma sank down in it like her legs had just given out. Jonas pulled out a second chair for Susie. She sat in it, her behavior defiant, eyes angry. Her hands lay in her lap, palms up. Jonas looked at her hands, noted the blisters and said nothing about them as he introduced himself.

"I'm Doctor Jones, I stopped by to let Laine know how Rafford is doing."

Momma managed to gain enough strength to give him an exhausted look. Her eyes narrowed, observing Jonas closely. I knew she was seeing his handsome face, his tall strong body, his age. Her eyes shot to his left hand. No wedding band, but not all folks could afford a ring. I wasn't wearing one.

"Your wife don't mind you paying house calls this early in the morning?" She asked.

"Morning calls come with the job," Jonas said easily.

I opened a can of sausage and spooned it into a frying pan. I took what little milk I had left and added water to it. I had to have enough gravy for four people. I could have made red-eye gravy, but the fried hog meat and cold coffee mixture was too strong for my stomach.

Momma wasn't satisfied. "You got children?"

"No," Jonas said calmly. "Not yet."

"Momma," I said. "Do you and Susie need to wash your hands before I take this food up?"

"Law, honey, I don't have strength left to get out of this chair."

"Are you sick, Mrs. Elder?"

Momma seemed to realize that Jonas was actually a doctor. She smiled faintly. "I've got a weak constitution. It was a long trip yesterday, a horrible ordeal just getting here to check on my baby girl. Thank goodness she's all right, and I'll be able to rest my weary bones," she sighed. "All this addin to my dear departed husband's accident's just too much for me. Thank the dear Lord there was a place for me to come to and rest."

Jonas looked her over. "I'll be glad to examine you." Jonas reach out and took her hand, his fingers on her pulse. "Being I'm already here."

She jerked her hand away. "I wouldn't dream of imposin on a body."

"No imposition." Jonas took her hand again.

I noticed that Susie was watching his hand holding Momma's. She looked at his face, his dark hair. She looked down at her owns hands lying in her lap. Color came to her pale cheeks. I knew she liked the looks of Jonas Jones. I took up the food and sat it on the table in front of them. I set three plates, spoons and forks on the table.

Jonas noticed I hadn't set a plate for myself. "Aren't you going to eat?" he questioned.

"I ate a long time ago." I didn't think I could have forced one bite of food down my throat.

🕊

I left Momma and Susie sitting at the table as I walked with Jonas to his horse.

"Well, what do you think? Are they sickly in any way?"

Jonas shook his head. "I didn't notice anything evident. Your mother had a strong heart beat, and her breathing is good. She had great strength in her arm and hand when she pulled away from me. Your sister looks physically stronger than you. She's certainly bigger boned and weighs considerably more." Jonas was silent for a minute. "Laine, what if Rafford were to come home this afternoon, instead of tomorrow?"

"Yeah." I grinned at Jonas, knowing what Rafe would think of Momma.

He nodded his head and looked thoughtful. He finally frowned and turned to me. "Laine, I'm warning you again, be cautious with Rafford. He's angry and resentful, and it's not all because he's in physical pain."

"I understand."

Jonas gave me a bewildered look, like I didn't understand at all. "Do you understand that you can walk off this mountain and come to me if you need to?"

"Thanks, Jonas, but I won't need to."

Jonas let his finger briefly touch the back of my hand. "Ask any place off the mountain where Dr. Jones is located. And Laine, be sure to take the road. You can get lost easily on the mountain. If you need to, get Nate's help. He's a good enough man."

I watched Jonas mount his horse and ride away. I could have cried. I was alone with Momma and Susie. I stiffened my spine, put one foot before the other and went back to the house.

They weren't in the kitchen where I had left them eating. Momma was in the fancy living room lying on the red couch. Susie was standing in front of the mirror watching her reflection.

Time to take a stand, Laine ole gal, I told myself with dread. Put em out of your home now or you never will.

"Momma, get up off that couch. You won't be lying on my couch and you won't be lying in my bed either. The only place you're allow in my house is the kitchen, and then only to eat."

Momma looked at me like I was an irritating fly buzzing about her. "Girl, it's high time you learned respect for your Momma. The likes of you don't talk to me in that tone of voice."

She got up off the couch with deliberate slowness and stood tall and threatening in front of me. Susie edged against the mirror. So, Momma thought she was stronger than me. I recalled how difficult it was for Dad to control her in the graveyard. I recalled how she picked up Susie and carried her. I recalled her demented state when she stripped naked and held Susie against her.

I shivered as I thought of my unborn baby. I turned my back on her and walked into the kitchen. I heard Susie giggle.

She didn't giggle when I pointed the double barrel shotgun at Momma who had taken her former place lying on the couch.

"Would you kindly get yourself off the couch," I said in a voice dripping sweetness. "It's gonna be a lot easier getting your blood off the rug than outta the couch."

Momma looked me in the eyes and didn't move. She thought I was bluffing and she was calling my bluff.

It was now or never. I took dead aim between Momma's eyes.

I let the gun barrel slip, and shot the pretty end table full of holes. Blew it clean away from the couch.

Momma sucked in breath like a rooster getting ready to crow. A thin squeak escaped her lips as I turned the gun back on her.

"There's one more shot before I reload." I squinted and took aim dead between her eyes again. " I missed that time on purpose, but I don't miss twice" I smiled. "You think I won't shoot you? Rafe didn't think I would shoot him either." I cocked the gun hammer, slow, deliberate.

I saw color fade from Momma's face as she slowly sat up. She was not willing to call my bluff any longer. Even I wasn't sure I wouldn't squeeze the trigger. "Susie honey, come here and help your Momma to th' barn. You need to change outta them damp clothes."

I didn't say another word as Momma kept Susie between her and me as she went out the front door. I heard her mumbling something about me losing my mind as she ambled down the circular steps. When the door closed I locked it, and went to the wounded table to determine what could be done to put it back to normal.

I reloaded the gun and hid it. Rafe and Nate were right. I needed to keep a loaded gun handy. But holy hell, what was I going to do now?

Chapter 21

The sun was hanging low when I heard it. At first, I thought it might be that panther hollering, the one Abe Farrow told me about. Then I thought it was Momma pitching one of her fits from the barn loft where she and Susie were hiding to get out of work.

It was a pitiful, high-pitched sound rising in volume as the wind carried it up the mountain. I walked away from the barn, to the edge of the yard, where I could hear better. It sounded almost human, like someone in severe pain. Then came the thump and rattle carried on the wind, and I knew Rafe was coming home.

Horses, wagon and Rafe rounded the bend in the road. Rafe was singing to the top of his lungs, if it could be called that. The horses were just short of being out of control, trying to outrun the horrible sound, I reckon. They were headed straight for Dad's old wagon, and Rafe wasn't holding the reins.

"Gee. Gee. Gee!" I yelled to the top of my lungs in hope the horses would turn and pull out of the road before they collided with Dad's wagon.

I took out running after the wagon still yelling "gee". At the last moment the horses swerved missing the wagon with their bodies but knocking Rafe's wagon against Dad's. A few more boards in Dad's wagon broke.

The horses came to a stop in front of the barn allowing me to catch up. I didn't see Rafe. I climbed on the wagon and found him lying on the floorboard flat of his back.

"Rafe? Rafe?" I shook him by the arm and his eyes opened.

"God damned horses; God damned women," he said.

He reeked of liquor.

"You're drunk," was all in the world I could think of saying.

"A man's gotta screw with a bunch of damned women," he mumbled as he wiggled on the boards. He sat up and tried to make his eyes focus. They wobbled like he was trying to focus them on a moving object.

Oh great! I told Jonas to send Rafe home in hopes he would help me get rid of Momma and all I got was another problem in the form of a drunken man.

"Get off that wagon. Let's see if I can get you to the house." I turned him loose and he toppled over.

"*She'll be comin' round da' mountain,*" he squawked to the top of his lungs, as he lay there looking up at the sky. "*When she comes*" he hollered, frowned, "Damned whores," he yelled. "They cum," he started laughing. "Little Lainie never will." His was a cynical, sneering laugh. "Hell, no. My wife will never cum."

I had no idea what he was ranting about as I looked at his beet-red face and noticed how thin it appeared. His clothes were hanging about his body, like a boy in his daddy's shirt and pants. His injured foot was a big oval blob of bandages. The bandages were starting to come unwrapped and were as dirty as if he had dragged his foot through plowed ground. I wanted to slap him up the side of the head until my hand wore out. Still, at the same time, I felt sorry for him.

"Get up, Rafe," I said tiredly. "Lets see if I can get you inside."

"Hell if I'm going inside. I've been inside that hospital for a lifetime. I'm out now. I'm free." He finally worked himself into a sitting position and gave me that cynical grin. "Whore, Laine, old gal. You know what that is?"

I got another smell of his breath as I kneeled beside him. "Rafe where did you get the liquor?"

"Accommodating," he slurred. "Accommodating Junie the whore." He tried to spit, but the spittle dribbled on his chin. "She cums. The lying bitch. She hain't got no bastard of mine."

I had heard enough from him. "Do you want help inside?"

"Hell, no."

I took him at his word and climbed over the top of Rafe and found the reins lying on the ground. The horses were quivering with sweat and heaving in breaths of air, but they knew they were home and weren't offering to run again. I climbed back onto the wagon, sat on the seat, and drove the horses and wagon around the barn. Rafe was bouncing about, but I didn't care.

I shut the horses in a barn stall to keep them from drinking water until they cooled down a little. When I went back to the wagon, Rafe was lying in the same spot sound asleep. I went to the house, got a quilt, came back and covered Rafe up. He could sleep off a little of the liquor, but I didn't want him to get a chill.

During all this, I hadn't heard a peep from Momma or Susie, but I knew they would be looking out a crack somewhere watching what was going on.

For one red copper, I would leave the three of them here together, and I would go back to Dad's. But I knew I wouldn't do that. I loved this place, and nobody would run me off. Not Rafe, and certainly not Momma and Susie.

I heard the sound of a horse and left Rafe in the wagon as I went around the front of the barn. There was Abe Farrow straddle of a nice saddle horse.

Months of cold on this mountain without seeing a soul, and now with warm weather, it was a major road.

"Day Miz Johnson." He looked about. "Did Rafford get home all right?"

He dismounted and tugged at the galluses of his bibbed overalls, getting them straight over his bony shoulder.

"He got here."

"That's good. I'm mighty sorry, Ma'am. I shoulda been here hours ago. This confound horse of Jonas's throwed me when I was ridin him to the hospital. Like to never caught up with him on foot. Don't pay to get careless like." He shrugged his shoulders and shook his red head. "When I finally got to the hospital, Rafe had already slipped off with the wagon." He spat real tobacco juice off to the side. "Don't mind tellin you, Jonas chawed my ears a bit. He thought I had already left with Rafford in the wagon, but Rafford snuck off all by his self. Didn't even take his jars of medicine with him. Jonas had me bring em on up. He said to tell you to give him one each, twice a day."

"Hours ago?" Reckon that figured. He had to go somewhere and get liquored up. "He just got here. He's in the wagon behind the barn, passed out drunk."

"Drunk? Why, he's still on medicine. Don't reckon that would mix good with liquor."

"Where would he get liquor?" I asked Abe.

Abe downed his head and shuffled one foot. "Most any place, Ma'am. Let's have a look at him. Don't know what liquor and pills done to him, but I heard Jonas say he's not to drink any liquor."

Abe followed me around the barn to the wagon and climbed on to check Rafe. "Well now, I reckon he's out cold."

"No kiddin," I said. "Should we try draggin him into the house?"

"It's best not to leave him out here to get cold. That foot of his hain't well yet. How'd he get it so dirty?" He looked at me for an answer, and his eyes lowered to my stomach then looked away quick. "Don't reckon you ought to be totin his weight. Wish we had somebody to help carry him."

I smiled.

Momma flat out refused. "My back is painin me something awful ever since you shot at me. Made me jerk my insides loose. I couldn't lift a pone of cornbread," she whined.

I looked her straight in the eyes as she lay there on the feather tick trying to look helpless. Susie was sitting beside her, leaning her weight against Momma like a frightened child.

"If the two of you don't get up from there and help carry Rafe, you won't get a pone of cornbread or any other bite of food."

"Don't matter. You hain't fed us much like it is." She tried to look pitiful. "A child of mine, lettin her poor old momma go hungry and cold. Her so high and mighty she makes her own momma sleep in the barn. House's too good for her own momma to be in." She sniffed and wiped at her nose with the back of her hand. "My own baby girl, threatening to shoot and kill her momma. What's this world comin to?"

I had heard such talk too often for it to do anything other than aggravate me.

"Momma, while you've got one foot on my land you'll help out. Dad let you get away with that puny crap, but I won't. Now, both of you get down to that wagon and help Abe with Rafe."

Momma didn't move. Her face was set with determination. I took a few steps across the loft and grabbed the pitchfork out of the hay.

Why in the devil couldn't I just have that confounded red bull instead of Momma? It wasn't nearly as aggravating.

I turned to face Momma and held the pitchfork out in front of me. "Get your lazy ass up from there, or so help me, I'll poke it as full of holes as a sieve."

To my surprise Momma got up, followed by Susie. I carried the pitchfork with me as I followed them down the stairs. I knew I would have to keep it inside the house with me for as long as Momma and Susie remained, or I would never find my pitchfork again.

Abe looked them over in a glance. His glance lingered on Susie.

"Sorry to put you ladies out, but I can't manage a man as big as Rafford Johnson by myself without bumping his injured foot about," Abe said as he scooted Rafe to the edge of the wagon. "If the two of you will get him by the feet, I'll carry his upper body. That's the heaviest part."

Susie gave me an ill look. "Why hain't she helpin carry him?"

"She don't need too," Abe told her firmly.

I led the way, still holding the pitchfork, and opened the kitchen, hall and bedroom doors. Momma didn't miss looking at one thing inside the house as she passed it. I could almost see her licking her lips at what she saw. Things she had dreamed of owning, but I wasn't going to feel sorry for her. Momma watched as Abe lay Rafe down and tossed a quilt over him. Her eyes were sparkling and I knew what she was thinking. I would be too busy taking care of Rafe to fight her. She would be able to take over inch by inch until she had it all.

"Momma," I said firmly. "You go back to the barn now. Susie will stay here and wash Rafe then change the bandage on his foot. I might as well get some use outta her."

"No," Momma said firmly. "I need her helpin me."

"You don't need nobody." I opened the bedroom door and couldn't believe Momma walked out and left Susie without puttin up a fight.

"Abe, would you mind walkin Momma back to the barn? I have to show Susie what all she's goin to do for Rafe."

"I'm goin with Momma," Susie said as she made for the door.

I stepped in front of her, still holding the pitchfork. "Get his boot and dirty clothes off him. I'll be back with water to wash him and bandages for his foot." I bounced the handle of the pitchfork on the floor a couple of times when I saw the defiance in her eyes. "Your hind end is almost as big a target as Momma's."

Susie turned from me and started pulling at Rafe's boot strings. Danged if hateful people didn't respond to the same treatment as a hateful red bull did. Wished Dad had known that.

Abe came in the kitchen while I was dipping up a wash pan of water. I felt his eyes watching me and turned to face him.

"What's wrong?" I asked.

"Do you think it's right to be mean to your momma and sister?"

"No. I don't think it's right. I think it's necessary."

"How's that?"

"They have a life of their own. They can't have mine."

Abe nodded. "Jonas mentioned somethin toward that. But makin em stay in the barn loft?"

I tried to remain calm at his words of criticism when he didn't know how things were. "What would you suggest?"

"Surely they could sleep in a bed. There's so many beds in this place it wouldn't hurt nothin."

"Humph. I'd say it would hurt. I'd never get em outta here. They'd suck the life outta me like suckin marrow from a bone."

"Hain't right." He looked at me, shaking his head and started to say more.

I heard a scream and Susie came running down the stairs into the kitchen. She held the torn bodice of her dress as she passed me up and went out the door. Abe and I stood there watching her go.

"Reckon he's come around some," Abe grinned just a little. "Liquor and pills can give a man a buzz for a while." He stopped his grin and added quickly. "It can make a man do things he ought not do. Things he don't know about and don't intend to do."

I knew Abe was trying to remedy a situation he thought I wouldn't approve of.

"Follow her out to the barn and see that she's all right. I'll go up to Rafe."

There was no use for Abe to try and defend Rafe's actions with Susie. I wasn't holding Susie's torn dress against Rafe, especially if it made Momma willing to leave faster.

Rafe sat on the edge of the bed with his hands gripping his skull. He slowly lifted his head and peered at me over his fingertips.

"Who tha hell was that?" he mumbled, his words sounding slurred. "Crazy girl. Stripping my clothes off me like she couldn't wait on nothing. Straight outta the hospital, too weak to get it up and two women jump my bones. Just don't make good sense now does it." His bloodshot eyes looked into mine. His voice cleared as he whispered, "I've gotta wife that could knock a man's eyeballs out and she don't give a damn about me." He buried his head back into his hands and moaned lightly. "Who was she, Laine?"

"Susie, my sister. Her and Momma showed up yesterday."

"God!" The word sounded torn from him. "I knew that would happen. Once they found out where you lived, they'd squatter in. They can't survive without you to feed on. Everybody told me that. I knew to take you further away than they could travel." He ran his fingers through his hair like he was desperate to get something untangled from the long strands. "Laine, they have to go back. You're mine."

"I know."

"Where's your dad?"

"Dad was killed."

"Oh hell! Shoulda taken you to Kentucky." He shook his head still resting in his hands. "I'll not put up with the likes of them. I'll put their lazy asses off this mountain."

I wondered if Rafe realized he just admitted we weren't in Kentucky. If he did, he didn't seem to care.

"Rafe, why did you tell me you were taking me to Kentucky?"

"I intended to go there but it was just too far to go when we didn't have to."

I knew that wasn't all his reasons, but I didn't want to go into it right now. There would be plenty time for explanations later.

"You won't have to get rid of them. It's up to me to do that." A faint feeling of compassion flickered in me for Rafe as he sat there haggard and dejected. I crossed the room to his side.

"Rafe, why don't you lay back down? I'll bring up water and change the bandage on your foot."

I put my hands on his shoulders and pushed gently. He lay back on the bed and said no more as I left the room and went back to the kitchen.

Momma burst though the kitchen door like the dogs of hell were biting her heels. The door slammed against the wall so hard I looked to see if the glass had broken.

"You'll not get away with it!" she yelled as she grabbed me by the arm and slung me against the stove. "You'll not hurt my baby girl no more!" her right hand struck me across the face.

I saw her hand lift again as I felt the coarseness of her hair in my hands. I yanked her head sideways as my foot flew out and kicked her feet out from under her. She hit the floor hard. She came to her knees, eyes wild and glaring.

Calmness took possession of me as I looked down on her. The woman before me was my mother, but I didn't want her to be. I came from her by a freak of nature, one I had nothing to do with.

"Mert Elder!" I said her name strong and deep. "You better never touch me again. Furthermore, don't you be pullin your fits on me. I know you're puttin on an act. You best remember that you'll become what you pretend to be."

She didn't move from her kneeling position as she looked up at me. "I gave you life," she hissed like an angry goose.

I laughed, short and harsh as I watched the fury drain from her face. "Mert Elder, you get out of my house."

She did.

I crossed the room and gently closed the door behind her. I didn't even want to hear the click of it closing. I silently pulled out a chair from under the table and sat down.

I felt my baby move.

Ɏ

Abe carried their supper to the barn as he left for home. I didn't think I was tough enough to see them sitting at my table, eating the food I cooked. My hands shook as I dished up a plate of food. My legs felt tired, almost rubbery, as I carried the food up the stairs for Rafe. I looked at the closed bedroom door across from Rafe's room. Why couldn't I open that door, walk inside, lay down on the bed and sleep? But I knew I couldn't go to bed just yet.

I went into the bedroom, sat on the bed beside Rafe and fed him every bit of food on the plate. He ate without complaint and lay back down and closed his eyes.

"I'm sorry," I whispered, and I was. Sorry that Rafe had shot himself, sorry that Dad was dead, sorry that Momma and Susie was here, sorry they were in the barn loft, sorry to my eyeballs.

"What?" he mumbled.

"Sleep if you can," I told him as I left the room.

I made sure the outside doors were locked before I went to bed in the room across from Rafe. I had a vision in my head of Momma coming in and running me out. It made me feel sick to my stomach.

I admitted to myself that Abe had been right. Nobody should have their relatives sleeping in a barn. It was disgusting and degrading. But what was I to do?

It took a long time for me to calm my feelings of guilt enough to fall asleep.

I couldn't have been asleep long when I sat straight up in bed. I felt goose bumps all over my body. The sound that woke me scared the living daylights out of me. I heard it again and knew it was Momma having one of her fits. She screamed to the top of her lungs.

My feet swung out of bed even though I didn't want them to. I wanted nothing more than to lie back down in bed and let Momma cut whatever shine she wanted. It might do her good if nobody paid any attention to her. Instead, I put the bibbed overalls back on and found shoes. I mumbled angry words all the way down the dark stairs

into the kitchen and put Dad's old coat on. I heard the
whining scream again, this time fainter. I lit a candle and
headed out the door wondering what would have to be done
to get Momma to shut up. I got the pitchfork from behind
the door where I usually kept the shotgun, but I had hidden
the shotgun away. For a moment I considered getting it, but
what use would it be? Besides, this time of night I just
might shoot her.

The moon was round and bright in the clear sky. I didn't
need the candle to see with but I carried it anyway. It would
be dark in the barn. I heard the sound of dogs barking not
too far off and thought Abe was probably out hunting again
tonight. I had begun to think his panther was an excuse for
him to run the hills. If there had been a dangerous panther
about, surely Jonas or Nate would have warned me about it.

I noticed the silence of the animals inside the barn as I
walked through the yard. I would have thought Momma's
screams would have them disturbed. But they were quiet
and so was Momma. I stopped and listened. I heard strange
sounds coming from the barn loft. It was a grunting,
wheezing sound.

I opened the barn door even though something in my
head was telling me to go back. I ignored it and climbed the
stairs making as much noise as I could by hitting the handle
of the pitchfork on each step. I wanted to let them know
how mad I was.

"Now what?" I demanded as I stepped from the stairs
into the hay.

I held up the candle until it cast a faint light on the
feather tick bed. I saw two humps that were Momma and
Susie covered from head to toe. Their sounds mingled
together into a frightened whine.

It was then I heard the deep warning growl mixed with
angry hissing. I saw a shadow climb up from the hay chute
in the corner of the barn not ten feet from me.

I knew I had made a bad mistake by not having the gun.

I lifted the candle and saw them. Two burning yellow eyes staring at me, angry eyes burning with hate. I was paralyzed with fear as I looked back into the unblinking eyes. I made out the bulk of the large animal crouching low in the hay. Sensed the vibration of its long, lithe body as it tensed its muscles and dipped lower to the floor.

What was I to do?

Divert its attention until I could get down the stairs, shut the barn door and get the gun.

"Susie. Fan the feather tick," I said. But the feather tick didn't move.

The cat did.

It sprang high into the air like a black shadow floating above me. I flung my body against the wall at the top of the stairs, bracing the handle end of the pitchfork against the wall, letting the tines stick out in front of me, above my head.

I felt the overwhelming weight of the cat hit. There was searing pain along my neck, my left arm and down my side as my knees buckled under the weight. I felt each stair step as I rolled downward. I tried to double myself into a ball with my arms protecting my stomach and let myself roll away from the devil cat.

I landed in the packed dirt of the hallway and tried to maneuver my body underneath the stairs for what little protection that would give me. The cat was screaming and snarling as it thumped and knocked at the top of the stairs. I knew the cat would be down the stairs on me any second for it wailed a constant scream of anger.

I had moments to live.

Barking dogs came through the open barn door. I felt their feet and toe nails on my skin as they ran over me and pounded up the stairs.

I hoped Abe's hunting dogs were as tough as he claimed them to be. I knew the powerful steel-bound muscles; the piston-like jerk of the deadly hind claws of the cat could rip out the guts of a dog. How could the teeth of four hound dogs match the razor-sharp claws and the long fangs of the devil cat?

It let out a squall as the sound of vicious, fighting fury filled the barn.

I tried to sit up only to be knocked over by Abe as his foot hit me in his rush to get up the stairs. My eyes followed him and I saw a glow in the dark barn. I knew what had happened. The candle had been knocked from my hand into the hay.

"Use your coat!" I heard Abe yelling above the sound of fighting. "Beat the fire out! Stomp it with your feet. Hurry! Hurry! Don't stop! Don't slow down! We can't quit. We can't."

I pulled my legs underneath me and reached for the stairs with my right hand. I gripped and pulled myself up.

I'm okay. I thought. Bruised and scraped but okay.

My left arm clutched my stomach. I felt something warm, something dripping. Still, I couldn't stop. I needed to get to the top of the stairs and help Abe put out the fire. I knew Momma and Susie would be useless.

One, two, three steps. I sank to the fourth step and lay my head on my knees. The sounds of the cat and dogs fighting, and Abe's yelling blended into a distant noise. Different shades of darkness swirled in my head. I closed my eyes tight and breathed deep and slow. Everything became strange, unreal. I thought I could hear Dad's voice saying, *You're all right girl. You're tough.* I tried to tell Dad I was tired. I wanted to rest, but he wouldn't listen. *"Stop now and you've lost your barn. You'll lose everything."*

I held onto the walls as I went down the three steps to the horse stalls. I heard their nervous whinny. The smell of smoke was spooking them. I opened their doors. They shot by me for the open door. They were safe in the pasture. I let Pet out.

Almost full buckets of water were in the horse's stalls. I lifted a bucket in my right hand, my left still clutching my stomach. The bucket seemed much heavier carrying it up the stairs than when I had carried it from the creek.

Abe took the bucket from my hand and poured the water on the hay. The barn loft was dark again, but I could see Abe's movement and thought I could see the faint outline of Momma and Susie in the far corner.

"The fire's out?" I wasn't sure if I had spoken the words or thought them. Things just weren't real.

"Yeah, thank God. A minute later getting in this barn and she'd have gone up," he said as he turned from me and moved through the scorched hay toward his dogs. Half-hearted growls came from them. No sound came from the panther.

"Back off!" Abe demanded. "Back. Back."

"Dear God." A feeble moan came from Momma. "My dear God."

Not a sound came from Susie.

I felt the heat from scorched wood and hay beneath my body.

I opened my eyes to the bright shine of candles and kerosene lamps. A kerosene lantern hung from the ceiling. A piece of twine was tied to the handle and fastened around a bent nail in the ceiling. I wanted to fuss at somebody for putting a nail in the nice bead wood plank.

"That nail?" I said.

I heard a movement and saw Jonas's face above mine. His face looked strange in all that artificial light. It was red and scrunched up looking.

"You're back with me?" His hand touched my hair. His other hand my face.

"A hole," I said. "That nail."

Black colors danced with yellow light. I didn't want everything to close out on me. I wanted to know what was going on.

I opened my eyes again and there was sunshine on the quilt of my bed. Somebody had done a good job of sewing small, neat quilting stitches around the star pattern. It had to take a long time. I lifted my right hand and touched the pattern. I wanted my left hand to join my right, but it didn't move. I tried again. A shaft of pain went up my arm into my collarbone. This time the sunshine danced with darkness.

I felt a throbbing ache. It went from my toes out the top of my head. I wanted to cry with the hurt of it. I wasn't sure I hadn't cried out for I could hear a voice.

"She's lost too much blood," an authoritative voice said. "It's her life or the baby's. The mother's life comes first, you know that. We must take the baby from her. There is a small chance of it living."

"No." Jonas said firmly. "Her injuries have her weak now. Taking the baby will cause more blood loss. You won't touch her."

"Doctor Jones. Do I need to remind you I'm the specialist you sent for? You make a grave error if you do not choose to take my advice."

I came wide-awake with knowing fear. They were discussing my baby. I saw Jonas with his back toward me, and a wizened, white looking doctor facing me. Even his beard was white. My right hand felt under the cover for my stomach. It was there. My bulging belly was there. My baby was alive.

"Like hell!" I heard my own voice and saw Jonas whirl around to face me.

"Laine. Thank God."

He came to my bed and went down on his knees. His face level with mine. I saw moisture sparkling in his eyes. I wanted to lift my hand, touch his face, but I was still feeling the mound of my baby.

"It's okay," I managed to say. "My baby's still okay?"

He smiled faintly. "Yes, your baby is okay."

The old, white looking doctor moved until he stood above Jonas. He looked down at me with a critical frown on his face. His white goatee of a beard seemed to vibrate before my eyes.

"Young lady, do you realize how sick you are?" His voice was short, curt, authoritative.

If I had a little more strength, I would have really been aggravated by the way he spoke. He reminded me of a Baptist preacher "No," I said. "I'm not sick. Just a little tired."

"A little tired. You've been unconscious for two days! You better say your thanks to God that panther had a broken leg sometime in the past."

I looked at Jonas for his denial of this. Jonas stood up and faced the other doctor.

"Why don't you go downstairs and have a cup of coffee. I'll come down shortly, after I've talked with Laine."

A "humph," came out of the doctor as he turned sharp on his heels and walked out of the room. The door shut firmly. Jonas came back to me, bent and kissed me on the forehead.

"You have been out for two days. When I couldn't get you to wake up, I called him in for a second opinion."

"I lost blood?"

"That panther put some pretty nasty gashes in you. You've got more stitches than a patchwork quilt. You do remember killing that cat with the pitchfork don't you?"

"The dogs killed it."

"They just chewed on him a little. You put the pitchfork through his rib cage, part of his stomach, nicked the heart."

"It had a broken leg?"

"Abe thought somebody might have shot it in the leg a year or so ago, and it healed twisted. That's why it killed newborn animals."

I remembered Abe saying something about the way the cat mauled. "The barn didn't burn?"

"Abe put it out in time. He said you were carrying water before you fainted."

"I fainted?"

He smiled, nodded his head. "Um hum."

"I've never done that in my life."

"You lost a lot of blood. You left a blood trail through the barn and up the steps. Abe said he didn't know you were hurt until you hit the floor. He carried you to the house and bandaged up your scratches before he rode after me. He thought you were dying. Said you would be dead by the time I got to you." He stopped talking suddenly, bent over me and moved the quilt away from my left side. He looked at my arm, touching it lightly. His eyes blinked as he turned his face from me to check the bandages down my side.

"Jonas?"

He didn't say anything.

"Will my loss of blood hurt my baby?"

"No," his voice sounded deeper than normal. I felt his hands touch my feet as he adjusted the cover. He walked over to the dresser and dipped a cloth in the wash pan. He wrung it out and placed it on my forehead.

"Personally I think you will be all right now that you've regained consciousness, but it'll be a week or two before I'll let you out of bed." He sat down on the edge of my bed, careful not to bump my arm or side.

"But I've got to do the work."

Jonas grinned, and he didn't look as sad. "I have Mrs. Elder and your sister doing that."

I tried to shake my head but it made my neck hurt.

"Not very well," Jonas added. "I also told Mrs. Elder she had to take care of Rafford. Last I heard, Rafford threw a plate of food at her along with inventing names to call her. It would appear those two don't get along."

"Let Susie take care of him. He'd like her better."

Jonas lifted my hair from the bandage on my neck. "You were lucky Laine. That cat missed your jugular less than a fourth inch. If it had gotten that vein, I might not have able to stop the bleeding even if I had been standing beside you. Laine..." He started to say something else then stopped. Finally, he asked, "Do you think you could keep a little soup down?"

"I'm not hungry."

"The baby needs the nutrition."

Those were the magic words. I'd eat the dead panther if it would help my baby.

"Okay." I agreed and tried to get out of bed.

"Whoa there girl." He put out his hand and gently eased me back. "There's no way you can get up yet. We don't want to take chances on you aborting."

"The soup? I need to make it."

"I'm an excellent cook, remember?" He touched my cheek with his fingertips. "Promise you'll lie still and not move while I'm gone."

"I promise."

I watched Jonas leave. I really was tired.

Chapter 22

"Laine, Laine."

I heard my name being called and opened my eyes. Jonas set food down on the dresser, and then picked up my hand and checked my pulse.

"You were just sleeping." Relief sounded in his voice. "Sorry to wake you, but I believe you need food greater than sleep."

He put his hand behind my back, eased me to a sitting position and packed pillows behind me. Pain shot from my neck down my side. I must have winced for I saw a look of concern come to Jonas' face.

"I'm not hurt much. The tape and stuff makes it hard to move."

"Yes," Jonas agreed. "Yes, it does."

He looked at me closely as he pushed hair back from my face.

"I feel my baby move." I told him, relieved.

Jonas placed his hand under the cover on my bare stomach. I seemed to be wearing a man's shirt with most of the left side cut out. That was all I had on and I was embarrassed, but Jonas didn't seem to notice.

"Yes. I feel it, too." Relief showed in his eyes. "You're both going to be fine. Now, let's see if you can eat a little."

He got the soup from the dresser and came back to the bed. He sat on the edge and fed me spoons full of potato soup like I was helpless. He held a glass of warm tea to my lips and insisted I drink.

"I don't like tea," I objected.

"Doesn't matter. This will help build your blood and aid in getting your strength back. Your baby needs it."

I drank the foul stuff.

The door flew open while Jonas was wiping soup from my chin with his handkerchief. Rafe looked at us. His face reddened as he stomped into the room with his bandaged foot thumping on the floor.

"What the hell's goin on here?" he demanded as he came to my bed.

Jonas sat the soup bowl and glass on the floor, stood up and moved between the bed and Rafe, blocking my view of Rafe.

"Your wife is finally awake. She's been in serious condition. I'm trying to get some soup down her. Two days without food intake hasn't been good for her."

"She looks all right to me." Rafe tried to move past Jonas to my bed, but Jonas managed to block his way.

"You can speak with her for a moment. I know how concerned you must be about her and your baby."

"Baby?" Rafe's sounded confused. "What baby?"

"She is pregnant with your baby, and she needs to rest. She doesn't need you to disturb her."

I heard Rafe's breath rumble in his throat. "You don't give orders here."

"You're correct, Rafford. Still, she is my patient and it is my job to see to her care. She can't handle more trauma or visitors. She has to rest." I saw Jonas reach out and place his hand on Rafe's shoulder. Rafe knocked his hand away.

"Don't you be telling me what to do with my own wife. She don't need to be lying there in bed with you coddling her."

"I'm a doctor. It's my job," Jonas said firmly.

"Let that old she-devil that claims to be her mother take care of her. She ought to be good for something. Besides, Laine promised she'd get rid of her. I won't have that woman in my house."

"I thought Mrs. Elder was taking care of you. What would you do without her? You certainly can't give your wife the care she needs. I'm not sure you are capable of caring for yourself."

"The hell I'm not. I've never needed a damned woman. Don't need one now."

"That's good to hear considering it will be two or three weeks before your wife is able to look after you."

"Told you I don't need no damned woman."

"Guess not, but you do look tired. I probably should check on your foot. Maybe Susie could bring food to your bedroom unless you feel like going down to the kitchen." Jonas's voice sounded conspiring, man-to-man. "It's got to be hard on a man with his wife down and out. Susie can look after you."

I saw Jonas put his hand on Rafe's shoulder again. This time Rafe left it as Jonas walked toward the door, guiding Rafe out. At the door, Rafe turned and glared back at me.

"You best be outta that bed by tomorrow or you'll be going back home with those other two no-accounts."

Jonas took him into the hall and closed the door. I shut my eyes and rested my head against the headboard. I wanted to scoot down into a more comfortable position. I'd do it, in just a minute.

In no time Jonas was back easing me into the softness of the bed. His hands gentle, his words softly spoken.

"There now. Let your weight rest against my hands. Don't try to move yourself. Let me do it for you."

"Rafe...?"

"Don't concern yourself about him."

"He can't take care of himself."

"He'll get by. You take a little nap. I'll be right here beside you."

"You shouldn't be here. You're a doctor. People need you."

"I should." He interrupted my objection. "And I am here."

I must have slept for a while, but my sleep was interrupted by my need to pee. Jonas was beside me when I tried to sit up.

"What is it?"

"I have to go to the toilet."

"I'll get the bedpan."

"No." I was repulsed at the idea of Jonas getting me the pot. "I want to go outside to the toilet."

Jonas shook his head. "You're not strong enough to use a pot, yet. We can't take a chance on you getting up too quick, so I had Abe bring a bed pan from the hospital." He pulled a flat, four-inch deep, tapered contraption from under the bed.

"I'll just put this under your hips. When you're finished, I'll take it away."

"No." I knew I was all right. A few scratches and bruises weren't going to kill me.

Jonas smiled down at me like he knew what I was thinking. Finally, he said gently, "I'm your doctor, Laine. You don't have to be modest with me. I've already examined every inch of your body."

The thought of him touching every inch of me while I was out was almost as bad as the thought of him doing it while I was awake. Besides, this was different. Peeing was a private matter and he might as well not argue with me.

"Just a moment," Jonas said. I thought I saw a sparkle in his eyes as he turned and walked out of the room.

He came back with Momma. She looked anything but happy. Her hair was uncombed. Her face was creased with deep frown lines. Her eyes looked at me like she wished the panther had finished me off.

"Mrs. Elder, please put this under your daughter's hips and help her relieve herself. You need to learn how to do it for you may be doing this for her until after the baby is born."

She took a step backward as she looked at the bedpan Jonas held in front of her.

"The wide end goes under her hips. I'll be just outside the door."

She took the pan in her hand like it was a pile of manure and made her way toward me. "How can you expect me to do such a disgusting thing? He's your doctor. Let him do it if you can't do for yourself."

I would have preferred Jonas, but something inside me wouldn't let me say so. I wanted her to handle someone else's refuse.

"Oh my God!" she said as moved the quilt aside and saw the bloody bandage from my neck to my leg. "You'll never be good for nothin again. Not the way you're all tore up. I shoulda believed him right off." Her glance took in my stomach. "You broodin as big as a horse. It's a wonder that pant'er hadn't tore it outta you like rippin a paper sack. Might'a been best. If it lives, you'll never be able to take care of it. You're a cripple for life. More'n likely it's deformed. Marked by that pant'er"

I looked at my arm and side as best as I could. The skin beyond the bandages looked bruised blue and yellowish. My left arm was taped against me in a position where I couldn't lift it. Even my leg had an odd color to it.

Momma none too gently shoved the pan under me.

"There," she announced. "You can hollar at him to come get it when you're done. I'll not touch it after it's been used. He can't make me."

She turned on her heel and marched out of the room, past Jonas without closing the door. Jonas stared after her, and then came inside the room. He gently adjusted the pan underneath me to a more comfortable position, covered my exposed body with the quilt. He bent over me and wiped away the tears on both my cheeks before he spoke.

"You are neither a cripple or helpless. You will be normal in about three weeks, except for taking it easy and a few scars that will fade with time. Your baby is not deformed."

"Are you sure? She said..."

"I heard what she said. I'm not lying to you, Laine. I never will."

"It looks bad."

"Other than the scratches, you only have a little bruising in your tissue which is to be expected. All the yellowing is stuff I put on you to kill germs. Believe me, it looks worse than it is." Jonas grinned. "I'll tell her she'll have to stay here and take care of Rafford, you and the baby when it is born. I'll tell her it will be a full time job for her and your sister. I might even suggest she sell her place and use the money to help pay off this house and farm being that Rafford nor you will be able to work again and her house will be too small for all of you." He chuckled lightly. "What would you think of that?"

"Does Rafe owe for this place?"

"No. I don't think he owes a dime."

"Good." I still wasn't convinced all was right. "I was out for two days. That doesn't mean anything bad?"

"That was from loss of blood. Your body wanted you to sleep while it repaired itself. Believe me, you will be fine."

"Truthfully?"

"Yes. What will it take to convince you?"

I smiled at him. "Tell her I'm having twins, and step outside the door so you can't hear me go."

He did.

Morning came with the rattle of Dad's old wagon. Jonas got up from the chair he was sitting in, and went to the window and looked out into the dawn's light.

"They're gone," he said.

"Who's driving?" I asked.

"Your sister." He came over to my bed and lifted my wrist to check my pulse.

I hoped Dad's danged old mule had rested up enough.

I heard a tap on the bedroom door and knew it wasn't Jonas or Rafe. Rafe wouldn't knock, and Jonas had left that morning after assuring me he would be back to spend the night.

"Come in," I said.

The door opened a crack, and then opened further in jerky movements. Abe was using his foot to push it open as he carried a plate in one hand and a glass in the other. I had to grin at the sight of that freckled-face boy with unruly red hair, skinny as a post in bibbed overalls, carrying food to me. I wanted to get out of bed and do for myself. Five days in bed was about all I could stand, all I was going to stand. I ought to be the judge of what I was able to do and what I wasn't.

"Ma'am, I hain't no cook, so as my own Momma sent this stuff up to you. She said I'd dang pizen you if you ate my cookin." He grinned down at me like a kid that had eaten an entire pie. I knew he was pleased his Momma had sent me food.

I eased myself to a sitting position. I was sorer now than I had ever been, but it was only surface sore. It would have been gone by now if Jonas had allowed me to be up and about.

"Abe, thank your Momma for me, but I should get up and do for myself."

"Oh no, Ma'am. If you was to get up while I'm here and Jonas is gone, he'd flat out have my hide. He'd sure enough skin me like you would a gray squirrel. He said you wasn't to get outta that bed for nothing."

He set the plate of food in my lap. It contained green beans, potatoes, hog meat and a big chunk of corn bread. There was enough for three people on that one plate.

"I don't think I can eat all this."

"That's all right. Didn't think you could. What you leave I'll take across the hall to Rafford." Abe stood beside my bed looking about the room like he didn't know what to do next.

"Why don't you go downstairs and bring up another plate and fork. We can give most of this to Rafe." Rafe hadn't been back in my room since Jonas put him out. I wondered why. "Abe, what has Rafe been doing the past few days?"

"Sleepin mostly."

"Has his foot been botherin him?"

"Nope. His foot's lookin fine and dandy. He's healin faster'n you. Pan'ter puts a lota dirt in a scratch. Course, Jonas went to all kinds of effort to clean you good before he sewed you up."

Jonas still went to all kinds of effort every time he changed my bandages. He painted me up nice and yellow before he left this morning. I didn't bother telling Abe Rafe had been shot nearly two months ago. He should be healed.

"Why's he been sleepin so much?"

Abe scratched his head. "Well now, I reckon I can answer that. Jonas has me givin him sleepin potion along with his other medicine."

"Why?"

"To keep him quiet until you get better. If he weren't sleepin, he'd be pesterin you. Don't wanta take a chance on losin that baby of yourn cause Rafford Johnson is being his normal self."

It didn't seem exactly right to drug Rafe, but how could I argue against it? My baby came first.

"Abe, I want to thank you for puttin out the fire and killin the pant'er, then helping me. Jonas said you saved my life."

"I didn't do nothin much Ma'am. I mean, I reckon I did save the barn, but you was the one that killed that pant'er, and you wasn't about to die. You was just banged and scratched. Heck, most everybody all over the county is talkin about you." He smiled a toothy smile. "I took that pant'er off the mountain with the pitchfork still stuck in it. Near everybody had to eyeball that sight. Yep, reckon they'll talk about that for a time to come."

I ate hearty of the food, although I had no appetite for it. Jonas kept telling me I had to eat for my baby. Abe came and carried my plate away. Sympathy touched me as I watched him trying to do a woman's job when he wasn't even a man yet.

The urge to pee hit me. I looked at the bedpan lying on the foot of my bed where Jonas had left it within easy reach along with orders to use it while he was gone. Just taking precautions, he had said.

The thing looked especially hateful today, beyond what my dignity would allow. I slowly eased my legs from under the cover and let them dangle over the side of the bed. I lay there wiggling about for a minute. I felt fine as I braced my right hand on the bed and slowly eased myself into a sitting position ignoring the prickling pain of pulled stitches in sore flesh. After a good five minutes, I moved my feet to the floor and carefully tested the strength of my legs. They felt a bit wobbly at first, but nothing to what I expected. I stepped to the end of the bed, holding onto the bedpost as I eased the chamber pot from under the bed with my foot. I smiled, pleased with myself. I was fine but I moved slow and easy just to please Jonas.

Squatting down on the pot was an entirely different matter. Pinching pain in my side turned to stabbing pain, but I had felt it before when I made Jonas let me use the pot. It wasn't deep down inside where my baby was. It was just the hurt of skin pulled tight by stitches. I sat on the pot with my head leaning against the bed. The trouble with being in this position was that I had to get out of it and back in bed. Jonas kept saying I had to stay in bed for my baby's sake. He knew I'd do any thing for the sake of my baby.

I had never seen an animal laid up in bed until it got stiff and stove up from not moving about like I was being forced to do. But I reckon doctors know more than animals. I hoped they did.

Chapter 23

I woke up to the sound of a woman's voice. At first, I though it might be Momma and Susie, but it didn't sound like either of them. I hadn't heard a thing from them since they slipped off. They must have made it home before the mule died. I realized the voice was coming from Rafe's room. I eased myself out of bed for the second time that day and crept carefully to the bedroom and opened my door. It was definitely a woman's voice. I crossed the hall and leaned against Rafe's door where I could hear clearly.

"You're outta your friggin mind." Rafe said in a voice that sounded irritated and sleepy.

"Rafford, honey, you know you want your Junie here when you're ailin. I'll take care of you real proper like."

"By hell, I don't want you here."

"Now, don't you be talkin such nonsense. You know you do."

I heard Junie move across the room. If she came to the door, there was no way I could get back to my room before she caught me listening. Then it dawned on me. This was my house. She was trespassing in my home. But she didn't come toward the door. Her footsteps sounded like she went to the dresser, then back to the bed.

"Get your damned hands off me."

"Stop being so loud. Abe said *she's* in the other room asleep. You wouldn't want your little wife to come in here while you're having a nice bath would you?"

"Bath?"

"Oh yeah, you know how much you like a bath. Junie knows all those places you like washed."

"I gotta wife, now. Don't need you."

"You had a wife before, and you needed me most all the time. Besides you know *she* hain't able to do you any good lying in that bed all tore up. Besides, that doctor's been takin care of her. Reckon you ought to know he came about mighty often while you were away. A man like you needs him a woman. A real woman."

I heard Rafe grunt and Junie giggle.

"Gettin them britches off wasn't so hard, was it?" Junie said, still giggling.

"No damned man better ever lay a finger on my wife."

Junie laughed. "Why, that doctor's laid his hands and fingers all over your precious wife. How's this?"

"Whore," I heard Rafe say, but his voice no longer had the angry tone. I listened a little longer feeling sicker by the moment as they grunted and groaned.

"Fuckin whore, ahaa."

I made my way back to my bedroom and lay back down in bed. I was trembling all over. I didn't know if it was from weakness or the disgust I was feeling. I closed my eyes and tried to ignore what was going on. So, Junie and Rafe had been fooling around when he was married to Boise. Things started to make sense. The movement at the window when I was at the barn, the open door, the perfume, the writing in the diary. Junie had written in the diary knowing I would read it. She wanted me to be afraid of Rafe. She wanted me to leave him so she could have him for herself. Now, Junie was in my house, in my bedroom with my husband. What was I going to do?

The disgust I felt started being replaced by anger. How dare she come into my house! How dare Rafe! Me. My baby. Them! I was on my feet, but I didn't feel any weakness or pain. I grabbed the chamber pot by the handle.

Rafe's bedroom door slammed open and banged against the wall with the force of my growing anger.

Junie was stark naked astraddle of Rafe. Their heads turned, their eyes widened. A satisfied grin came to Junie's face. She wanted me to see this. She wanted me to know.

"You filthy bitch!" I yelled.

The chamber pot I was carrying in my hand swung in an arch as I crossed the room. It clanged with a thud as I hit Junie up the side of the head with it. It knocked her off Rafe, splashing piss all over Rafe. I hit her again as she jumped off the bed, grabbing her clothes.

Rafe lay there on sheets I had washed, naked from his waist down, except for his bandaged foot. I hated the sight of him as I swung that enamel chamber pot. Rafe sat straight up with a roar of pain as I bashed the pot into his injured foot. Blood squirted from his nose with my second strike of the pot. I hoped his nose was broke in to a dozen pieces.

My attention went back to Junie. "I'll kill you," I told her, and she knew I meant it. She ran from the room with her clothes clutched against her tits. I left Rafe behind holding his nose and cussing as he tried to get out of bed.

I was going down the kitchen porch steps as Junie streaked across the yard. In the road, beside the barn stood Nate talking to Abe, with the baby in his arms.

Junie whirled and headed toward the barn away from the road.

The sun reflected off her naked body like it was a white cloth. Nate's mouth dropped open. No words came out. Abe took several steps backward, eyes glued to the sight.

There was too much anger in me to stop. She wasn't going to hide in my barn while she got her clothes back on, but she didn't go toward the barn doors where Nate could see her. She went toward the opposite side, away from

Nate, where the hog lot was. She flipped the gate open as she ran toward an open stall.

She didn't bother to close the gate.

"God damn it, Laine!" I heard Rafe right behind me. "You've broke my damned nose. Stop. You hear me. Stop!" he was roaring like an angry bull, his voice filling the air with his rage.

I had no intention of stopping. I was going to put Junie off my land, out of my sight. Then I would take care of Rafe. I saw Abe start to run toward me in a long-legged stride. I dropped the pot as he scooped me up in his arms and continued to run. I glanced back at the sound of a clang as I clutched at his bibbed overalls to keep from falling from his grasp. The boar hog had stopped in his run from the open gate to seek food from the pot I had been carrying. Finding none, he attacked it viciously with his long tusks.

Abe dived behind a clump of trees dragging me with him, and then covering my body with his.

"Don't move," he demanded in a whisper. "Don't you move an inch. Don't make one sound." He clutched me around the waist and pressed his body over mine.

I heard a squealing grunt similar to the sound Rafe was making and saw the boar hog run past Abe and me, straight toward Rafe. I wanted to tell Rafe to stop yelling, opened my mouth to do so, but Abe clamped his hand over my mouth.

"Hurry." Abe whispered. "Hurry." He yanked me to my feet half pulling and half dragging me back toward the house.

I was trying to run and look over my shoulder at the same time. I saw the boar hog ram into Rafe with enough force to take both his legs out from under him. Rafe fell face forward into the dirt. The boar whirled around swinging his powerful head sideways causing Rafe's shirt tail to flip up like a puff of air had blown it as the hog's tusk gored into Rafe's side.

Rafe screamed.

The hog continued his attack, hitting Rafe in the face with his tusk.

"Hurry!" Abe insisted as I stopped running.

"No!" I yelled at Abe. "It's killin him." I tried to pull away from Abe. I had to stop the hog, but Abe held me tight. I saw Rafe raise his upper body off the ground in an effort to escape, but the hog hit him in the chest knocking him back down in the dirt. The hog seemed to gather himself low to the ground as it centered its attack on Rafe. It was on top of him, grunting and twisting and slashing. His tail was straight up in the air like a stick while his bristles were standing out from his body. His moves were smooth, effortless fury as he repeatedly slashed with his tusks. Blood was all over Rafe. I smelled its hot metallic scent. I tried again to free myself from Abe, but he held on.

"The gun," he yelled. "Get me the gun."

I didn't know I was moving, but I felt the porch, the kitchen floor, the cool of the springhouse on my bare feet. I took the gun from the top step of the cellar stairs. Abe jerked it from my hands.

"Loaded?"

"Yes."

I followed Abe outside. He rested the gun on the porch rail as he took aim at the hog.

"Get closer," I demanded. "You'll hit Rafe."

"Won't matter. He's done for."

The gun exploded and the rear end of the hog dipped down. He stopped tearing at Rafe as he whirled sideways and tried to attack his own hip where the shotgun blast had hit. The second barrel fired. The hog's head jerked as he went down on his knees with ear-splitting squeals. He came back up on shaky legs as his vicious eyes searched, seeking the cause of his pain.

"Don't get off this porch for nothing!" Abe demanded as he dropped the shotgun, jumped off the porch and ran behind the house.

I hadn't made it all the way to Rafe when Abe ran by me with the double-bitted axe in his hands.

Bloody froth dripped from the hog's mouth as he shook his head and staggered about as though wanting to fight something--anything. Abe swung the axe in an arch burying the blade in the back of the hog's neck. The hog went down on his front knees. Abe jerked on the axe until it freed. He swung again, this time at its throat. A gurgling sound mixed with pathetic grunts. All four legs splayed out, and the hog went down in the dirt. Abe struck a third time. The hog gave one last attempt to gather strength, then kicked his legs in a death struggle. Abe backed up, wiped his arm across his forehead. His body trembled.

I made my way to Rafe.

Abe put his arm around me. "You best not see this."

He tried to turn me around, but I pulled free. Rafe lay there in the dirt. His blood was pooling around him staining the ground dark. One sleeve of his shirt remained on his arm, the rest torn away. The pants he had taken time to put on were torn down one leg. His stomach was ripped open. Coils of pale maroon intestines hung over his pants. The side of his face was missing, showing bloody flesh, gums and teeth. The smell hit me, repugnant with the scent of death. Dear God, I know he is dying, but I couldn't let it happen. I had to stop it. Keep him alive until Jonas got there. Jonas could save him. I knew he could. Rafe made a sound and I dropped to my knees beside him.

"Laine," he whispered making the torn flesh of his lips moved slightly.

I lifted his head and placed it in my lap. "No, no, no." I repeated as I saw all the places on him that were bleeding. I had to stop the blood somehow. "Abe, get me a needle and thread."

Abe frowned down at me.

A shudder went through Rafe's body. He tried to speak through a mouth with half his lips gone.

"You---I---loved." he said as a gurgling sound came up out of his throat. Blood ran from his mouth.

I sat there in the dirt saying nothing, doing nothing.

Abe kneeled beside me with tears running down his cheeks. He had Junie's baby in his arms. She was sleeping like nothing had happened. I turned my head and saw Nate with one of Rafe's legs under each arm, dragging him toward the barn. I tried to speak.

"Close your eyes," Abe said. "For God's sake, close your eyes."

I couldn't close my eyes. I watched the slow, bumping progress and wondered if Junie was still in the barn.

I heard Nate mumble to the air. "My God Junie, my God, look what you've gone and done now!"

Chapter 24

"**I**'m cold," I told Jonas as he looked down on me lying in bed. I wanted to get up but it seemed I was going to spend the rest of my lifetime lying in a blasted bed.

"I know. Abe's bringing hot water bottles. He had to start a fire in the cook stove. For goodness sake, Laine, lie still. I don't want shock to cause you to abort."

He reached out his hand and stroked my hair and face like I was a baby. His adam's apple moved up and down. "How much is one girl supposed to take?"

An unwanted tear slid down my cheek and lodged in my ear. "He's dead isn't he?" I didn't have to ask. I just needed to hear it said.

"Yes."

"Junie let the hog out."

"Don't think about it anymore."

"How do I stop thinking about it?"

"I don't know, but try if you can."

"Will this mark my baby?"

Jonas sat down on the bed beside me as though he knew I would get up if he didn't. He took my hand in his. "That's an old wives tale. Miraculously, you're still carrying that baby. Shock and trauma aren't old wives tales. The fact you need to lie still right now isn't a tale either."

"I told you I would protect my baby."

"And I want to protect you." He sounded tired.

"Did it do much damage to Rafe?" I didn't know why I was asking such a question. I had seen with my own eyes what damage the hog had done. Still, I wanted to know.

"Yeah," Jonas said. "You saw it happen."

"She wanted the hog to get me. It would have too, if it hadn't been for Abe."

"Abe told me what happened. Junie didn't know the hog was in the lot."

"Don't defend her. Don't you dare." I gritted my teeth. "I saw em in bed. She was on top of him, naked. It wasn't the first time, you know. They done it when Boise was alive. She was here in the house when I first arrived. I saw her at the window. I know it was her. She wrote in Bosie's diary too. She tried to make me think Rafe killed Boise so I would get scared and run away. Then she could get Rafe and all this. But she spilled perfume on the page and I knew."

Jonas lowered his head into his hands. "Can you forgive me?"

"What?"

He lifted his head and looked toward the window. "I went by her house when I left this morning. I asked her to drop by here if she had a chance. I thought she could help Abe until I got back. I'm sorry, so very sorry."

"It wasn't your fault. It was her, only her." Why wasn't he listening to me?

"If fault were water, it would fill an ocean," he said

More tears slid down my cheeks. Strange, because I didn't know I was crying. "I won't go back to Dad's." The words escaped me, and I didn't even know I was thinking them.

"You won't have to. This place is yours now."

"Mine?"

"Yes." Jonas stood up. "Let me check on those water bottles before you go into shock. You're shaking all over."

I reached out and grabbed him by the hand. "How do you mean it's mine now?"

"This place went to Rafford Johnson when Boise died. You're his sole heir. The place belongs to you."

He left the room with his shoulders stooped and his head hung. It took me several minutes for my mind to grasp what he told me.

This place was mine.

🕊

"I don't want the coroner touching him."

"What?" Jonas looked at me like I had lost my mind.

"You heard me. I won't have the coroner messing with him, and he won't be hauled back to Kentucky. I don't care where his parents are buried." I got up from the chair I was sitting in and faced Jonas and Abe. "Get somebody to make a plain pine box and dig a grave beside Boise and her baby. That's where he belongs."

I opened the kitchen door and walked out onto the porch.

"Where are you going?" Jonas demanded.

"Toilet."

"You know you should be in bed."

"I don't intend to lie in bed ever again."

"Laine…"

"Jonas, will you stop trying to tell me what to do. I'm tired of being told what to do."

"The baby…"

"It's my baby and it's safe. So leave me be a while." I walked away from him, around behind the house like I was going toward the toilet. I circled the house and went to the barn. I opened the door and went into the dark hall and stood there wondering where Nate had left Rafe's body.

"He's in the cuttin room," Jonas said. He and Abe were standing at the open door. "You shouldn't look at him. It's not a sight you should see."

I looked Jonas in the eyes. "Maybe not, but I'm going to."

"Wait until the coroner..."

"No," I told him firmly. "I told you earlier I won't have a coroner touch him." I opened the cuttin room door. I could see shadows and outlines but nothing in distinct details while my eyes adjusted to the dim light. What got my attention was the smell. It wasn't the smell of rotting flesh. It was the smell of meat, and blood, and ruptured intestines. It was like being in an air less room at hog killing time with too much flesh and offal. I wanted to gag, but I couldn't allow myself, not with Jonas and Abe watching me.

There on the bare planks near my feet lay the body of Rafe. What clothes remained on him were dirty strips. His entire side, from his belly to his back had been ripped open. What appeared to be his stomach, or it could have been his bladder, was protruding out like a blown up balloon. His intestines were still hanging out, but they seemed to have dried up and shrunk in size. The hair on his head was a caked mat of blood and dirt. His mouth was open as though frozen in a scream with his tongue sticking out the gaping hole in a dark, swollen blob.

It wasn't real.

Only life is real.

What lay at my feet wasn't Rafe.

There was no life, no man left. It was the horrible remains after the person was gone. I turned away from the corpse and walked out the door, down the hall and out into the fresh air.

Birds were singing, the cow bawled, the chickens were cackling. Life was all around me. Jonas's hand touched the small of my back as he walked me toward the house.

Jonas was life.

As we reached the porch I turned to Jonas. "I'll bury him just as soon as possible. Just as he is."

"Why? You know he deserves to be made presentable, even in a closed casket."

I saw all the women washing Joey's naked body. Fixing curls in his hair. Putting a blue suit of clothes on him. Laying him in a tiny coffin.

"He's been through enough. He wouldn't want anybody to see what he looks like now, not even a coroner. Leave his remains alone. He deserves that much dignity left to him."

Jonas started to say something else but didn't. It wouldn't do any good. I knew I wouldn't want someone messing with my dead body. Rafe wouldn't either.

Chapter 25

I was on the rise in the graveyard thinking time moved on like the continuous tick of a clock. Spring had finally come to Beech Mountain. The heat of the sun warmed my skin and encouraged the blue violets, I called Johnny jump ups, to bloom in profusion over the little graveyard.

I felt big as a cow when I bent over and raked the damp earth around the fern I was planting at the head of Rafe's grave. I lifted a handful of the dirt and smelled the sweet spring aroma. It was good dirt. Ready to give life and sustain what was already there. I raised my bulky body up from the ground and looked out over the farm.

I could see Abe's head of red hair bobbing above his skinny body. His bare shoulders were almost as red as his hair where the sun had burned him. He didn't seem to mind for he hadn't put his shirt on underneath his bibbed overalls. I smiled. He looked like a plucked chicken plowing behind one of the horses. I had hired him to help me out a little on the farm until my baby was born. Jonas insisted on it since doctors tend to be over cautious, but I knew it wasn't necessary. I was as tough as poison ivy growing up a fence post.

I closed my eyes and breathed in deep of the clean air as it blew over me. I heard Dad's voice saying, *'It's your land girl, all yours. It belongs to you heaven high and hell deep.'* And so it was. It was going to stay that way, too.

A flick of emotion touched me as I thought of Jonas. He tried to wait on me hand and foot. His eyes watched me like he was afraid for me to get out of his sight, like I might fall and break. He always wanted to touch me or tried to kiss me, but I wouldn't allow that. I knew time had to pass before that would be proper. He kept saying my unborn baby needed a father. What he didn't seem to understand was that my baby had a father. A good father, now that he was six feet under the ground.

I didn't care how many times Jonas asked me to marry him. I wasn't going to do it. Once a woman got married all she owned reverted to her husband. Jonas would get the land and all I would get was bossed around.

I walked to the edge of the graveyard and looked back. There in the shade of the big oak trees were the graves of Mr. Holloway, Boise and her baby. Next to them was the fresh grave of a few weeks. I thought about Joey, Dad and Rafe. Yes, death came in threes, and I hoped it would be many years before another grave was added to the patch of mountain wild flowers.

I touched a violet with my toe, and turned away from Rafe's grave. Life was waiting for me and I could hardly wait to live it. I hurried down the hill thinking no one could share another person's death.

Death is such a lonesome thing.

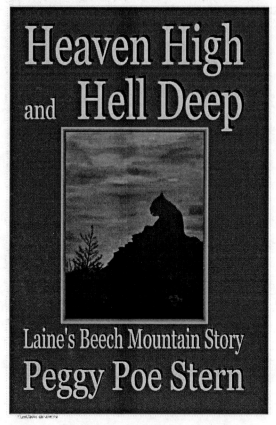

Heaven High and Hell Deep

Laine's Beech Mountain Story

Peggy Poe Stern

Book 1, ISBN # 1-59513-055-1 $16.95

A mountain girl in the early 1900's copes with a marriage arranged by her dad. Her story is titled from an old saying "I own my land, heaven-high and hell-deep."

"Your pa gave his consent for us to marry," he said the words as though it was a simple matter. It wasn't a romantic proposal of love and devotion. It wasn't a proposal at all. I opened my mouth but nothing came out. I tried again.

"I don't know your name," I managed to say ... .

Tamarack

The Beekeeper's Daughter
Peggy Poe Stern

ISBN # 1-59513-054-3 $14.95

A gripping story about the dark side of a mountain family: a legacy of abuse that leads to murder. Told from an authentic mountain perspective, the reader experiences the family's desperation as well as their strength and determination to keep on going. The author's simple unabashed voice completely absorbs the reader. So many emotions are evoked that the story echoes long after the last page is read.

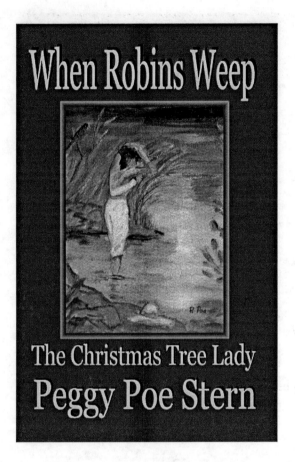

When Robins Weep

The Christmas Tree Lady
Peggy Poe Stern

ISBN # 1-59513-053-5 $17.95

A happenstance encounter between an Appalachian mountain girl and a Florida developer embarks them on a romantic relationship. Existing family ties coupled with completely diverse lifestyles complicate their love.

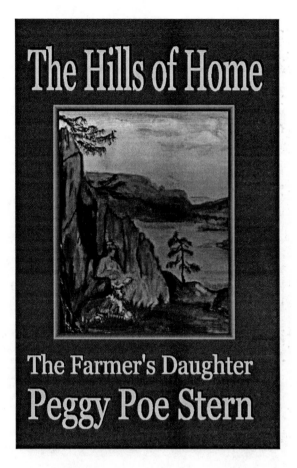

The Hills of Home

The Farmer's Daughter
Peggy Poe Stern

ISBN # 1-59513-052-7 $16.95

Theo Walden learns of love and understanding in her hills of home, plus a whole lot more. Granny teaches her that life isn't always fair or good. Greta fills her young head with ghost stories scary enough to keep her awake at night. Popaw and Daddy show her what its like to be mountain men: fair, tough, and yet gentle. Most important, Theo learns that wealth doesn't make a person happy. Love does.

Stud from Horney Hollow

The Collier Mistress
Peggy Poe Stern

ISBN # 1-59513-051-9 $16.95

Willi Smith, a hard-nosed Florida real estate broker, had determined to get above her roots by obtaining wealth for the security it should bring. Having set her career before relationships, she realizes that her biological clock is ticking. She wants a child, but doesn't have a man.

Burl Horney, a widowed mountain Christmas tree grower, travels to Florida to sell his trees. Little does he know how he is being caught up in her quest.

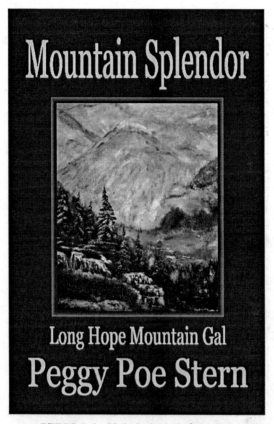

Mountain Splendor

Long Hope Mountain Gal
Peggy Poe Stern

ISBN # 1-59513-050-0 $16.95

Needing to make the farm payment, Ramona pretends to be a man and takes on her recently departed husband's next job assignment; guiding a group of Yankees through the mountains.

"You Barlow?" I had a naturally deep voice for a woman. Husky some called it, but I tried to make it sound manly. He nodded, looked at my horse and then at my clothes, all a trademark of Jake Triplet.
"Where's Jake?"
"Dead," I answered, and saw a faint flicker of surprise ....

Blood Moon Rising

Restless Revenge
Peggy Poe Stern

EAN # 978-1-59513-049-5 $16.95

The fires of hell would burn me in time for what I was about to do, but right now, that didn't matter. I was on my way to kill him. Someone should have killed Buck Walsh a long time ago for the things he did, but people were scared of him. I'm scared of him, but that no longer mattered either. He had raped me.

Wild Thing

Aggie's Legacy

Peggy Poe Stern

EAN #978-1-59513-048-8 $17.95

Cadence Williams settled beneath the quilt willing to go into a deep sleep. He hadn't slept much for the past two nights. Fear mixed with self-anger kept him awake. He hated fear. It was a sign of weakness, especially when it was his own. It angered him to fear when he wasn't sure if the cause of it was real or imagined. Yet, his gut told him *that thing* was near his house, moving in the woods like a dark shadow, stalking him when he went outside to do up the work, and even coming to his window during the night to watch him.

Above-all
a sequel to
Heaven-high and Hell-deep

Laine's Beech Mountain Story, Book 2
Peggy Poe Stern

EAN #978-1-59513-047-1 $17.00

His hat was pulled low over his black hair and his shirt sleeves were rolled up almost to his elbows. His hands appeared strong and in control as he held the reins of his high stepping horse. He looked a little thinner than he used to be and a lot more tired.

"What's wrong?" he asked me fast.

"You've got to go back to Banners Elk," I told him, forgetting about supper.

His eyes widened with concern. "Should you ride? I can deliver the baby here."

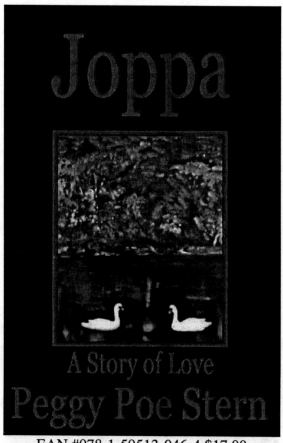

Joppa

A Story of Love

Peggy Poe Stern

EAN #978-1-59513-046-4 $17.00

"Leona," he sipped his hot coffee. "I know I'm going to regret asking this, but tell me the story of Joppa and Harry Barnard from the beginning to the end.

"It's a seventeen year stretch of time," I warned.

"This place isn't overrun with customers."

"If I tell you, will you use it against me. Claim I'm crazy; refuse to help me?"

"Attorney-client information is privileged. I don't tell anything you say not to tell."

"You'll think I'm a fruitcake."

"You're not?"

Thunder Hole

The Blackberry Summer
Peggy Poe Stern

EAN #978-1-59513-045-7 $17.00

He started to say more then hesitated before he added, "Do you know what I want, Billie, really want?"

"Besides me being five years older?"

Her ignored that. "I want you to go to college."

She laughed.

"I'm serious."

Her laughter stopped too sudden and she looked at Malone with eyes beyond those of childhood. "It won't happen."

"Why not?"

An Honorable Man

Surviving Daniel
Peggy Poe Stern

EAN #978-1-59513-045-7 $17.00

After twenty-four years of marriage to Daniel, Carrie Jane can take it no longer. Leaving everything behind, she slips off one evening to start anew.

"Tell me, Dad, why does this woman interest you?"
He scratched at his gray hair again before he spoke.
"Something wasn't exactly right about her. A teenage girl might run away for any number of reasons, but a woman her age doesn't. She was . . . well, I kinda pitied her. There has to be a mighty powerful reason when a woman hides in a moving van."

Mountain Talk

A Guide to Mountain Speech
Peggy Poe Stern

ISBN #1-59513-024-1 $9.95

The isolation of the Appalachian Mountains preserved some of the old sayings and speech of the earliest American settlers. This guide is a dictionary of commonly used mountain words and phrases.

To Everything
There is a Season

A Guide to Growing Things in
Harmony with the Moon Signs
Peggy Poe Stern

ISBN #1-59513-025-X

The pull of the moon affects all living things just as it influences the ebb and flow of the tides. Old timers have learned and past down the wisdom of gardening and living in tune with the signs, phases, cycles, and seasons effected on the earth by the moon, sun, stars, and planets. This guide assists in determining the best times and methods to take advantage of these time honored traditions. In addition to Peggy's own comments and excerpts on country life, this guide contains generous useful information for living close with the earth.